THE FINAL PROPOSITION

TREVOR DOUGLAS

BOOKS

Vinci Books

vinci-books.com

Published by Vinci Books Ltd in 2026

1

Copyright © Trevor Douglas 2015

The author has asserted their moral right to be identified as the author of this work in accordance with the Copyright, Designs and Patents Act 1988. This work is a work of fiction. Names, characters, places and incidents are the product of the author's imagination or are used fictitiously. Any resemblance to actual persons, living or dead, places and incidents is entirely coincidental.

All rights reserved. No part of this publication may be copied, reproduced, distributed, stored in any retrieval system, or transmitted in any form or by any means, including photocopying, recording, or other electronic or mechanical methods, nor used as a source for any form of machine learning including AI datasets, without the prior written permission of the publisher.

The publisher and the author have made every effort to obtain permissions for any third party material used in this book and to comply with copyright law. Any queries in this respect should be brought to the attention of the publisher and any omissions will be corrected in future editions.

A CIP catalogue record for this book is available from the British Library.

Paperback ISBN: 9781036704025

The EU GPSR authorised representative is Logos Europe, 9 rue Nicolas Poussion, 17000 La Rochelle, France contact@logoseurope.eu

By Trevor Douglas

Standalone Novel

The Final Proposition

The Bridgette Cash Mystery Thriller Series

Cold Comfort

Cold Trail

Cold Hard Cash

The Cold Light of Day

Out in the Cold

Hot and Cold

The Catalin Series

The Catalin Connection

The Catalin Code

The Catalin Crossing

Rowan Whitecross Murder Mystery Series

Murder on Stark Street

This book is dedicated to the people I call family. Your love and support is appreciated in more ways than I can describe.

Prologue

Seven Years Ago

Joseph Penmen followed the man through the crosshairs of his Remington rifle as he walked across the empty concrete parking lot at the back of the warehouse. The man stopped, leaned against the front of his van, and lit another cigarette—his fourth in less than twenty minutes. Wearing a light gray sports coat over the top of designer jeans, he looked out of place and was becoming increasingly agitated as he waited for the truck to appear.

From his hidden position, high up on the remote rocky hillside, Joseph had a perfect view of the complex below. He stole a quick look at his watch and then cursed under his breath. He had been in position for over an hour and was now becoming worried.

As if verbalizing his thoughts would magically make his brother appear, he whispered, "Come on, Tony, where are you?"

The man he was watching shifted restlessly before

throwing his cigarette to the ground in disgust. He pushed impatiently off the van and called out to his partner who had remained in the vehicle.

Joseph had not been able to get a good look at the other man until now. The man had been waiting patiently in the van, largely hidden in the shadows of the two-story steel and concrete building. He shifted the rifle position slowly to the right until the crosshairs rested on the second man as he opened the van door to get out. He was slim, had short blond hair, and looked considerably younger than his partner. As Joseph observed the two men in conversation, it was clear from the younger man's hand gestures and controlled demeanor that he was the one in charge. Joseph knew this was the man who was the bigger threat to Tony's safety. If things turned ugly, it would be the blond man who gave the orders.

Joseph used the collar of his sleeve to wipe sweat from his forehead while he waited. His brother had, until recently, run a successful pharmaceutical supplies business. He ate in the finest restaurants, lived in a gated estate with water views, and holidayed in Europe every year. Joseph never imagined Tony having money problems until he arrived at a family function driving a secondhand Toyota several months ago. When Joseph asked him about his Porsche, Tony confided he had some cash flow issues and the car "*had to go.*"

Joseph had not realized how serious his brother's predicament was until he called three days ago requesting a meeting. Over coffee, Tony confessed he had business debts in excess of two million dollars and that he was on the verge of bankruptcy. "Within days, I'm going to lose everything I've worked for, Joe. I need a favor, can you help me?"

Joseph assumed the favor would be for money, or a place to live, or both and was completely taken aback when Tony revealed what he wanted.

"I have an opportunity to sell some of my stock for three million dollars. I can pay out the loans and make a new start somewhere else."

Joseph recalled thinking this sounded like a great deal until Tony gave him the details.

"There's one catch, Joe. The sale's not strictly legal. In fact…"

Tony went on to explain that his stock would be on-sold to suppliers who would use it to produce a range of illegal narcotics. The remainder of the conversation had been little more than an argument. As Joseph replayed the conversation over in his mind, he remembered pleading with Tony to take bankruptcy over doing business with drug dealers, fearing his brother would wind up in prison —or dead.

Tony had promised to think it over before he did anything. The phone call Joseph received barely twenty-four hours later confirmed his worst fears. "I'm going ahead with the deal, Joe. It's too good to pass up. I really need that favor?"

Joseph couldn't refuse his brother's request and knew it was going to be complicated when Tony insisted on driving over to Joseph's house to talk in person. Sitting in Tony's car, their relationship had changed forever when Tony reached into the backseat and lifted a blanket to reveal a Remington rifle fitted with a silencer.

"I need you to be my lookout tomorrow, Joe. Just in case things get complicated with the exchange."

As Joseph sat, staring in disbelief at the rifle, Tony played down the risks.

"I'm not anticipating any problems, Joe. We've agreed on the time and place for the exchange—it's at the back of a warehouse complex, and it's closed on Sundays. I just want a little insurance. You won't be close, and hopefully no one will ever know you were even there."

Sitting hidden in the thick brush cover with the crosshairs of the rifle trained on the chest of the blond man, Joseph now thought the whole situation seemed surreal. Two days ago, he had been a law-abiding citizen, happily married with a young son, working a job he loved, and carrying no criminal record. Now he was prepared to protect his brother, with lethal force if necessary, while Tony engaged in an illegal drug sale that could land them both with lengthy prison sentences if they were caught.

As he shifted his position slightly to keep comfortable, he noticed the two men had stopped talking. Joseph looked up from the rifle and saw a small truck driving slowly down the driveway at the left-hand side of the complex. As the truck drove into the loading area at the back, Joseph's stomach tightened. With Tony's arrival, he knew there was no backing out now for either of them.

He watched as Tony performed a neat U-turn in front of the two men and parked his truck so that it faced back toward the driveway. As Tony got out and walked around the back of his truck toward the two men, Joseph bent down and switched on a small receiver that was connected to an earphone he would use to hopefully monitor the conversation.

Tony didn't think he would be checked for a wire but had decided it wasn't worth the risk. Instead, he had attached a microphone and transmitter under the rear bumper of the truck and arranged a monitoring receiver for Joseph. The audio quality was far from ideal, but he hoped it would be sufficient for Joseph to be able to hear what was happening and intervene if necessary.

After placing the earphone in his left ear and spending several seconds adjusting the volume, Joseph was able to faintly hear Tony's footfalls as he walked across the concrete surface toward the men. Satisfied that he had the sound level about right, Joseph shouldered the rifle and resumed his watch of the two drug dealers through the scope.

Tony stopped a few paces short of where the two men stood waiting. As expected, it was the blond man who spoke first. "You're twenty minutes late. I don't like people who make me wait."

"Sorry, there was roadwork, and I had to make a detour."

The younger man pointed to Tony's truck. "You got my merchandise?"

"It's locked in the back. Have you got the three million?"

"I'll decide what the merchandise is worth."

"We had a deal."

Becoming increasingly anxious about his brother's safety, Joseph whispered, "Be careful, Tony."

The blond man took a step toward Tony and pointed a finger at him. "We have a deal when I say we have a deal and not before. Now open the truck."

"I open it *after* I've seen the money."

Joseph struggled to keep the young drug dealer in the crosshairs of his rifle scope as the man quickly advanced on Tony. By the time he had him back in focus, the man had stopped directly in front of his brother and had the barrel of a gun pressed against his forehead.

As the young drug dealer began screaming threats and

obscenities at his brother, Joseph clicked off the safety and rested his index finger on the trigger. Doing his best to control his breathing, Joseph gambled on it being a bluff. He knew Tony had the cargo area fitted with a heavy combination lock to make it difficult for anyone else to access the drugs. As he watched the drug dealer continue to threaten Tony, Joseph had to admire his brother's nerve.

The seconds seemed like minutes for Joseph until he could see a wry smile beginning to spread across the young drug dealer's face. Joseph breathed a sigh of relief as the man removed the gun from Tony's head. As the drug dealer took a step backward, he said, "You've got balls, I'll give you that much."

The drug dealer turned and spoke with his associate, but his voice was too low to be picked up by the microphone. Joseph lifted his head from the scope and watched as the associate turned and walked back to the van. The associate opened the rear door and removed a black attache case. He found it difficult to breathe as he watched the man move back to his boss and prayed it contained the money and that the transaction would be over quickly.

The drug dealer, who had not taken his eyes off Tony, placed the case at Tony's feet.

"I want this over and done with. The longer we stay here, the more likely we are to be discovered—now unlock the truck. You can count while we do the transfer. None of us should be out here any longer than absolutely necessary."

Joseph watched his brother closely. Tony had told him the truck would remain locked until he was sure he was getting his money. Without responding to the drug dealer,

The Final Proposition

Tony bent down and opened the attache case. He pulled out several bundles of cash and quickly thumbed through them.

Straightening up, he said, "Three million, right?"

"Right."

Joseph watched as Tony debated what to do. Finally, he said, "Okay. You check the load, and I'll check the money. I packed this in under fifteen minutes, so it won't take long. Deal?"

The drug dealer looked at his associate and then responded, "Deal."

Tony nodded in agreement and then turned his back on the two men and began to unlock the rear compartment of his truck. Joseph's stomach tightened for a second time in as many minutes as a third man emerged from the rear of the drug dealers' van. As the man walked determinedly toward his two associates, Joseph didn't need his telescopic sight to see the man was carrying a gun. With his back to the men, Tony continued unlocking the van, oblivious to what was happening behind him. As the third man began to raise his gun to the firing position, Joseph knew the deal was a setup and that his brother was about to be executed.

There was no time to contemplate the morals of what he was about to do or how this would change his life. As the man walked the last few steps toward Tony and his two associates parted to let him through, Joseph had seen enough. He sighted on the man through the crosshairs and pulled the trigger.

Time seemed to slow down for Joseph as his rifle exploded and the man with the gun lurched sideways before collapsing to the concrete. The two other drug dealers immediately pulled guns from their jackets, and both began firing blindly in Joseph's general direction. As Joseph ducked for cover, he caught a glimpse of Tony collapsing to the ground at the back of the truck.

Amid the cacophony of gunfire, Joseph tried to lift his head for a second look at Tony, but a bullet ricocheting off a boulder behind his left shoulder convinced him to keep his head down.

While he waited for the gunfire to die down, Joseph heard the unmistakable sound of police sirens in the background. Risking another look, Joseph was shocked to see everything below turning to chaos as police cars pulled up and blocked both exits from the complex. Six police officers wearing helmets and bulletproof vests emerged from their vehicles and began firing at the two drug dealers who returned fire as they were driven back toward their van.

Joseph focused on Tony. Amid the gunfire and the arrival of the police officers, Tony had lain perfectly still. Joseph's concern for his brother heightened as one of the officers bent down and checked Tony's pulse before quickly moving forward to join his fellow officers who had now cornered the drug dealers behind their van. Joseph feared the worst until he saw Tony's head move slightly.

As the gunfight raged, Joseph was stunned to see his brother rise slowly and unsteadily to his feet. All of the officers had moved past Tony toward the drug van, and nobody noticed as he limped toward the body of the drug dealer Joseph had just shot.

Joseph's hopes rose as he saw Tony pick up the attache case and slowly limp toward his truck. Tony was a long way from free, but at least he had a chance. As Joseph contemplated what to do next, he felt something cold and hard being firmly pressed into the back of his neck.

The Final Proposition

A measured and controlled voice from behind him said, "Drop the rifle and place your hands in the air."

Joseph froze, contemplating if he should turn around and face whoever it was behind him.

In a louder voice, the command was reissued, "This is the police, drop the weapon now!"

Joseph realized that trying to flee would likely get him killed and dropped the rifle.

As he began to raise his hands, the voice behind him said, "Hands behind your back. You're under arrest for aiding and abetting an illegal sale of narcotics and I would presume murder as well, since the man you shot hasn't moved."

A thousand different thoughts rushed through Joseph's mind as he felt the handcuffs being tightened around his wrists. He thought of his wife Hannah and his baby son. He wondered what they were doing right now and how they would cope with the news of what had just happened. His thoughts about how his life had changed forever in just a few moments were interrupted by the sight of Tony struggling into his truck with the attache case and the crackling sound of a two-way radio coming to life behind him.

The voice behind him spoke again, this time with urgency in his voice. "Penmen's getting away. He's in the truck."

Joseph watched as several of the police officers turned and fired on Tony's truck as it drove erratically toward the exit on the left side of the complex. The truck crashed into one of the two police cars that currently blocked his way out, but the truck's momentum kept it moving. The police officers gave chase and continued firing at Tony's truck as it swerved wildly out of the complex and disappeared onto the street.

The voice behind him swore softly and then pushed Joseph forward and down onto the ground. As he began to pat Joseph down, searching for other weapons, he continued, "You better hope we find your brother before they do. If they get to him first, stealing three million from the cartel will be the least of his worries."

Chapter One

Hartbourne Correctional Facility, Present Day

Joseph woke to the sound of heavy footsteps outside his cell. He blinked sleep from his eyes and realized he had dozed off again. As his eyes began to bring his small, drab gray cell back into focus, he stared at the cell's heavy steel door and watched it open and his cellmate walk in. In spite of his incarceration, Adam Wells was usually positive, and Joseph had enjoyed the last eleven months they had spent together as cellmates.

After the guards had closed and locked the door, Joseph asked, "How did it go?"

Adam sat down on the concrete floor opposite the lower bunk bed which Joseph lay on and leaned back against the wall.

In an almost disbelieving voice, he replied, "I'm getting out, Joe… There's still a formal court appeal process to go through, but the DNA evidence now proves conclusively it wasn't me. My lawyer comes in tomorrow to explain it in more detail, but barring any red tape, I'll be a free man within six weeks."

Joseph swung his legs out from the bunk and slowly pulled himself up into a sitting position. "I'm really happy for you, Adam. When you first moved in here, I knew almost straight away you were no murderer."

Reaching out to shake Adam's hand, Joseph continued, "Congratulations, my friend, you deserve it."

Adam thanked Joseph for his good wishes, but his smile turned to a frown as he let the handshake linger. Joseph's grip was feeble, and his hand felt like a block of ice. In recent weeks, Adam had noticed that his cellmate spent a lot of time resting or sitting quietly on his own.

Joseph continued, "So, are you making plans yet for what you'll do when you're released?"

Adam barely heard the question. "Joe, I don't mean to pry, but is everything okay? If you don't mind me saying, you look rundown, and if I didn't know better, I'd say you're losing weight?"

Trying to keep the smile on his face, Joseph thought for a moment about how best he should answer the question. He had planned to tell Adam about his condition in the next few days before it became too obvious—but not today. Today was not the day to burden Adam with his problems. As Joseph contemplated what to say, Adam pressed on.

"Joe, I'm not an idiot. What's happening here?"

Throughout Joseph's seven-year detention, almost all of his cellmates had been violent criminals who rightfully belonged behind bars. Joseph had never liked any of them, and most of them he secretly despised. Adam was different. When Adam had been transferred to the facility and allocated to his cell, he had initially been quiet and withdrawn. Joseph was usually good at reading people, and something about this six-foot-three man with dark, wavy hair and a quiet and gentle disposition stood out. Adam Wells was unlike any other inmate he had ever met, and for the first time in his long stay in prison, Joseph believed a fellow inmate's story of innocence.

He soon realized Adam was not only an innocent man but also highly intelligent. Joseph contemplated the question and knew he would need to answer truthfully. Anything less and Adam would know it was a lie.

Holding his cellmate's gaze, Joseph let out a long sigh and then answered in his softly spoken voice.

"I have pancreatic cancer, Adam. It's incurable. I've got two months at best if I'm lucky."

There was more Joseph wanted to say, but Adam looked completely stunned. As his words hung in the air, Joseph decided to wait until Adam had processed what he had said before he continued. Joseph felt slightly guilty as he watched Adam struggling to make sense of what he had just said. The days that you could celebrate something inside the Hartbourne Correctional Facility were rare. This should have been one of them.

"I'm sorry, Adam. Today should be about you, not me."

"Surely the doctors can do something, Joe. Just two months?"

Shaking his head slowly, Joseph responded in a tired and resigned voice. "The survival rate from pancreatic cancer is low...very low. It's insidious. It kills you in just months according to the doctors. Wouldn't matter how much money I had to throw at treatments even if I was a free man. The bottom line is they don't buy you much time."

Adam got to his feet and started slowly pacing up and down in the confined space of the cell. Joseph let him be. It had taken him weeks to finally accept what was happening. He knew Adam would need time as well.

Finally, Adam stopped, sat down on the floor again, and leaned back against the wall. As they sat in silence, Adam studied Joseph, trying to think of something positive or encouraging that he could say. Joseph suddenly looked far older than his forty-seven years and only a sliver of the robust man Adam had first met eleven months earlier.

In a quiet voice, Adam responded, "Joe, I'm really sorry. How long have you known?"

"About three months."

Adam nodded, and they were silent again.

"Does Hannah know?"

Joseph looked away from Adam. Telling his wife, who had remained loyal and faithful throughout his seven years in prison, had been the hardest thing he had ever done in his life. Joseph remembered her initial shock and the silence that followed when he had broken the news to her on her last visit. His eyes started to glisten as he recalled the sad resignation on her face as she realized there was no hope.

"I told her two weeks ago. She's taking it pretty hard. I don't think Michael knows yet."

Adam nodded but said nothing. He knew Michael was Joseph's only son and his pride and joy. Michael had only been two when Joseph was convicted of murder and sent to prison. Adam knew that having to watch his son grow up from behind bars had been the hardest thing of all for Joseph, even harder than his separation from Hannah.

At only nine years of age, Michael was, by all

accounts, an intelligent and well-adjusted young boy. Joseph would often talk fondly about the son he loved and was obviously very proud of. Adam could only begin to imagine how hard it would be to tell Michael his father was dying. Both men were quiet again.

After almost ten minutes, Adam broke the silence. "Joe, is there anything I can do for you?"

Joseph held Adam's gaze for a moment before lowering his head to stare at the floor. This was not the time to be asking favors of Adam, but Joseph knew he needed help. As Adam had grown excited in the past week about the real prospect of freedom, Joseph had spent a lot of his time thinking through his problem. He decided it was now or never. With a slight tremble in his voice, he answered.

"There's something else, Adam. Michael is also very sick… He started having small convulsions every now and then about twelve months ago. They didn't last long, but Hannah was concerned. She took Michael to a number of doctors, but they couldn't find anything. Six months ago, the convulsions started getting worse and then turned into full-blown seizures. They can last up to several minutes and leave Michael very weak and frightened."

Joseph paused for a moment. Adam could clearly see this was hard for Joseph and waited patiently.

"The doctors finally diagnosed a brain tumor. It's got some long name which I don't recall, but it's growing and will eventually…"

Joseph paused again and looked at Adam before he continued. "It's only a matter of time before it…"

Seeing the distress on Joseph's face, Adam interrupted. He didn't need to be a doctor to know that a brain tumor would eventually kill Michael.

"Joe, you don't need to explain. Is there anything they can do?"

Joseph stared at the floor again. Adam waited while he composed himself.

"The brain tumor's very deep in his brain, but there's a new treatment that the doctor he's seeing thinks will work. Even though it's still very new, results so far show it's very successful."

Adam replied cautiously, "It sounds positive."

"It's complicated. Hannah flew Michael to see a specialist in Bolton. He's the best in the business by all reports. The surgery is risky for a boy Michael's age."

"But it can be done."

Joseph's voice trailed off as he replied, "Yes, it can be done."

As both men went quiet again, Adam began to think through the dilemma that Joseph was facing. Clearly, Joseph was not going to be around to support his wife and son through this trial. Adam sensed Joseph wanted to say more and quietly sat and waited.

"The other complication is the money… There's no insurance for this sort of surgery. We have to pay the bill ourselves…"

"How much?"

Joseph looked up at Adam. "Close to half a million dollars with all the specialist care he needs in the first six months."

Adam let out a low whistle and grimaced. He knew most of Joseph's money had been paid to lawyers for his unsuccessful defense seven years ago and that Hannah was now working four days a week to make ends meet. They barely had enough money to cover food and rent.

Half a million dollars for an operation was way out of the question.

Joseph let out a sigh, lay back down on his bunk, and closed his eyes. Adam knew the conversation must have been very hard for Joseph and very draining in his condition. As Adam went to rise from the floor, Joseph started speaking again.

"I've never told you the full story about what happened seven years ago. It's time I told you... You need to know."

Adam resumed his position on the floor and made himself comfortable again.

"The truth is, Adam, I did kill someone to protect my brother. That you already know. If I could take back the decision to help Tony, I wouldn't be here and maybe not even dying of cancer."

Joseph paused again as if gathering his thoughts. Adam waited patiently for Joseph to resume. He thought he already knew everything he needed to know about the incident. Joseph had been candid in what he had told Adam not long after he had arrived. He had readily confessed to being a murderer, albeit of a drug dealer to save his brother's life. Joseph had then gone into great detail describing what happened that day, how Tony had been seriously wounded in his escape, and how Joseph and the leader and only surviving member of the drug gang had been arrested.

Adam waited for Joseph to resume telling his story. He recalled how accepting Joseph had seemed of his situation, particularly as Tony had died from gunshot wounds two days after the incident. It had made everything seem totally pointless, and yet Joseph was not bitter.

"When I first told Hannah about the cancer, she was

very upset. We talked for a long time about it. The guards were nice and gave us an extra half hour. As she left, she said she had something to tell me. Something she had been keeping from me ever since Tony's death. I asked her what it was, and she said she would explain it all on her next visit."

Adam watched as Joseph lifted his head off his pillow and twisted his body toward the cell wall to retrieve something from underneath his mattress. As Joseph lay back down on his pillow, he held up a crumpled white envelope.

"Tony wrote me a letter. It was written after he got away. I don't think he realized how badly wounded he was. When you read it, you'll understand more why Hannah kept it from me."

Joseph closed his eyes and held the white envelope out for Adam. Leaning forward, Adam took the envelope from Joseph's outstretched hand and then settled back against the wall. Adam looked at Joseph, who still had his eyes closed and looked to be sleeping. Joseph remained silent, and Adam took this as his cue. After reading the address on the front, Adam turned the envelope over and lifted the flap. With a thumb and forefinger, he gently pried out and unfolded a single sheet of crumpled paper. The letter was written in the same handwriting as the address on the envelope, although slightly more legible.

Joe

I'm hoping you got away OK, and I'm sorry I got you in this. I took a bullet high in my left leg. It's stopped bleeding, but it looks infected. I've driven back to the old farm to see Doctor Farnworth (can't risk seeing a doctor in Hartbourne). He's away until tomorrow night, so I'm hiding out until he gets back. I've taken 5K of the money and hidden the rest in the rafters of the old pump shed. If for some reason I don't get back to it, you know where it is.

Again, I'm sorry I got you into this mess. I will call you when I get patched up and figure out what I'm going to do...

Adam could not read the last two lines of the letter because the writing had become illegible. He looked back at Joseph who was now propped up on one elbow and looking directly at Adam.

As he held Adam's gaze, Joseph said, "Doctor Farnworth is a veterinary surgeon and an old family friend. He had a small farm next to ours and was best friends with our father. He came home from his trip the day after the letter was posted and found Tony's car parked in his driveway with Tony slumped behind the wheel. They estimate Tony had already been dead for about eight hours when he was discovered."

"The gunshot wound?"

Joseph nodded, and Adam let out a breath. The last thirty minutes had been a rollercoaster of emotions like none he could ever recall in his life. Half an hour ago, he had been on top of the world and looking forward to his release. Feeling tired and down, Adam felt uneasy as he put the letter back in the envelope and handed it back to Joseph.

Both men looked at each other in silence. Finally, Adam said, "Joe, you've told me this for a reason."

Joseph nodded and sat up again. "Hannah never told anyone about the letter or the money. As far as we know, it's still there. She never wanted any part of it on account of it being drug money."

Joseph paused for a moment before continuing in a voice barely above a whisper. "Your principles and priorities change when your child's life is at stake. What was important yesterday is no longer important today."

"Where are we going with this, Joe?"

Joseph's voice trailed off as he looked away. "I know where the pump shed is that Tony wrote about in his letter. It's in a remote location not far from the farm and is no longer used. Nobody goes there. There's a good chance the money is still there…"

Joseph looked back at Adam and paused as if he was undecided about what to say next. Finally, he continued, "I need someone I can trust to go and get the money for Michael and Hannah. It might be dangerous, I don't know… Apart from Hannah and Michael, I have no friends on the outside anymore, Adam. Seven years inside has seen to that."

He looked away again as he continued, "You're the only one I trust, Adam. You will be free soon. If you recover the money, you can have half. Michael will get his operation and a chance to lead a normal life, and Hannah will still have enough to set herself up for life. And God knows, after what's happened to you, the money would be a just reward for what you've been through too."

Adam stared back at Joseph, shocked and not sure what to say. He didn't need to do the calculations. Joseph was offering him one and a half million dollars if the money was still there. He would be able to go back to his old life as a craftsman furniture maker. He could buy a small rural acreage somewhere and live in peace. He figured he would become at least partially responsible for Hannah and Michael until the money was collected. As tempting as the offer was, Joseph was right when he had said it was "not without risk." Drug dealers rarely walk away from that kind of money and would kill in a heartbeat to get it back. Adam also knew there was no way this was legal, and he did not want to wind up back in jail.

He did not need long to come up with his answer. Michael and Hannah could certainly do with the money, and he knew it would give Joseph enormous peace of mind in his last days if he said yes. Focusing on Joseph's pleading eyes, Adam breathed in deeply before answering. He knew Joseph would be crushed when he told him no.

Chapter Two

Adam watched the green line on the small monitor as it continued to pulse at regular intervals in line with Joseph's heartbeat. The pulses were not as strong as they had been two hours ago when he had arrived at the infirmary, and he knew the end for Joseph was not far. Adam looked up from the monitor and around the room that was to become Joseph's last home on earth. It was not much bigger than the hospital bed in which Joseph lay, and with its flaking gray paint, steel bed frame, and hospital fittings, it was even more depressing than his cell.

The sound of the monitor beeping in time with Joseph's heartbeat and growing softer was a constant reminder that Joseph was getting weaker. Adam could no longer stand it and reached up and turned the volume on the monitor down to zero. No longer distracted by the sound, Adam relaxed a little and returned his focus to his dying friend.

The quietness that descended on the room was barely broken by Joseph's shallow breathing through the

The Final Proposition

oxygen tube. With sunken eyes and his gray skin hanging loosely over his skeletal frame, Joseph was almost unrecognizable as the man who had informed him of his terminal condition just four weeks ago. It had happened so quickly that Adam still found it hard to believe his friend would soon be gone. Adam turned toward the door as a gentle knock interrupted his thoughts.

"You mind if I have a couple of minutes with him?"

Doctor Hugh Knight was one of the few people within the Hartbourne Correctional Facility with any compassion or humanity, a far cry from the warden or the cold and heartless guards. Adam was glad the physician managing Joseph's transition from this world to the next was giving him the care and attention he deserved.

Adam got up from his chair for the gentle gray-haired doctor and replied, "Not at all, Doctor." As Adam passed the doctor in the doorway, the doctor nodded his thanks and said in a soft, reassuring tone, "I won't need long."

After Adam waited several minutes in the corridor, the doctor emerged from Joseph's room to speak with him. After taking off his glasses, he massaged the bridge of his nose for several seconds while he composed his thoughts. After putting his glasses back on, he looked up at Adam and said, "Even though he's in a coma, I have increased his morphine—just to make sure he's not in any pain. It won't be long now... You should go back in and say goodbye."

Adam nodded and said nothing for a few seconds while he processed what the doctor had told him. He knew it was coming, but being told by Doctor Knight made it final, like a judge rapping his gavel as he passed sentence. Finally, he said, "Thanks, Doctor. I appreciate what you're doing. This might seem a strange thing to say inside a prison, but he's a good man."

The doctor smiled gently. "I've been treating Joseph since the onset of his disease and know his background well. Sadly, one mistake in an otherwise good life is sometimes all it takes to wind up here."

Adam nodded but did not respond and made no move to go back into Joseph's room.

"So, Adam, I hear you will be a free man soon? That's wonderful news."

"Day after tomorrow, Doctor. Although, I don't want to leave Joseph until…"

The elderly doctor placed a hand on Adam's shoulder. "Joseph's time is very short, Adam. He won't see the day out, I'm afraid."

Shaking his head, Adam responded, "I feel for Hannah and Michael, they should get to say a final goodbye."

"I pushed hard, Adam, but it fell on deaf ears. The warden was most emphatic that his decision allowing them to visit Joseph every second day was more than fair. 'He's a convicted murderer and lucky to be getting any extra privileges at all' were his final words to me as I left his office."

Walking to a barred window, Adam gazed out at the high steel perimeter fence topped with razor wire. "No offense, Doctor, but how a daily visit from your wife and son while you're lying in a coma dying could be seen as a privilege is beyond me."

"Frankly, Adam, we were lucky to get that. Ordinarily, terminal prisoners will only get one or two extra visits at most. I think we have you to thank for getting more."

Adam looked back at the doctor, slightly confused. "Me?"

With a knowing smile, the doctor responded, "Adam, you are going to have your fair share of media attention when you're first released, and the warden isn't stupid. He knows it's a bad look to have an innocent man in jail. He's hoping you'll blame the justice system and not him. He certainly isn't about to give you any extra ammunition by being able to complain about the treatment a dying inmate received."

Adam returned to looking out the window. "The warden needn't worry about the media. I have been advised by my lawyer to keep away from them—for the time being at least."

Doctor Knight looked perplexed. "A lawyer not wanting media attention? Now that is something new."

Still gazing out the window, Adam replied, "I was framed and convicted of murder on DNA evidence which we now know was flawed. The police are blaming the company that supplied the DNA processing equipment, and the company is claiming police incompetence in its use. I'm caught in the middle, and until the court can determine who's at fault, I don't get any compensation."

Adam turned, looked back at the doctor, and then continued, "I've been advised not to say anything to anyone until it's sorted out. Both sides are blaming each other, and if I'm not careful, it will be me who loses out."

"It hardly seems fair that you should be made to wait, Adam. Surely you can sue the government, and they can countersue the company?"

"You would think so. My lawyer says taking on government lawyers isn't easy and the whole process could drag on for years if it all goes public. I don't have the money or the will to fight, Doctor. My best hope is the two parties will reach an out-of-court settlement."

Doctor Knight looked dismayed. "I'm sorry, Adam, you deserve far better than this."

Adam shrugged as he turned back to the window. "I just want my old life back."

Adam waited until the doctor had walked off before he went back into the tiny room. As he sat down, he could no longer hear Joseph's shallow raspy breathing. Quickly turning his head, Adam focused on the green line of Joseph's heart monitor. Holding his breath, Adam watched the green line as it faintly registered Joseph's heartbeat at regular intervals. It was noticeably weaker than when he had left the room just minutes earlier. Doctor Knight had been right—Joseph's remaining time was short.

As Adam stared at the flickering green line on the monitor, his thoughts turned to Hannah and Michael. Joseph had been gracious when Adam had politely but firmly said no to his proposition. Adam doubted the money would still be there and did not want to risk going back to jail to find out. Trying to hide his disappointment, Joseph had said he understood, but the look on his face clearly showed he was disappointed and worried for his family. Although they had never talked about it again, Adam still felt guilty that he had let Joseph down. He wondered how Hannah would cope with Michael's illness and whether Joseph had arranged some other way to try and get her the money.

Feeling a presence behind him, Adam turned and looked back toward the door. A guard he knew only by his name badge of Hegarty was staring at him. Satisfied that everything was in order, Hegarty broke eye contact and

The Final Proposition

silently continued on his rounds. Technically, Adam had overstayed his allotted time for the visit, but the guards no longer seemed interested in him. They knew where he was and that his release was only two days away. Adam was thankful that they had relaxed the regulations for his last few days in prison.

Returning his focus to his friend who now hovered between life and death, Adam smiled to himself as he recalled some of the great discussions he had enjoyed with Joseph in their cell. Whether it was politics, news, sports, or religion, Joseph had an opinion about everything and had never been afraid to express it. Joseph's passion had made him all the more interesting and likable. Adam wiped a small tear from his eye and whispered, "I'm not going to miss this place, Joe, but I sure am going to miss you."

Taking and softly holding Joseph's left hand, Adam whispered a promise to his friend that he would be the one who would call Hannah and let her know when the time came. Although not overly religious, Adam felt a need to pray. He closed his eyes and bent forward. He continued to hold Joseph's hand and gave thanks for Joseph's life and then prayed for Hannah and Michael.

At the end of his prayer, Adam opened his eyes and looked across at the small monitor. The green line was now lifeless and no longer registered the faint flickering of a heartbeat.

Chapter Three

After seven years of wearing prison-issue clothing, dressing in normal civilian clothes felt strange to Adam. When he had finished doing up the final button of his shirt, Adam paused and looked over his outfit. He didn't think many prisoners would care what they wore when being released from prison, but for Adam, today was important in more ways than one. Satisfied that he would look presentable in a button-down white shirt and gray chinos, Adam took one last look around the cell that had been his home for more than a year. The cell was little more than two bunk beds and a steel toilet, and yet he had heard of prisoners quickly reoffending so they could return to an environment they felt comfortable in.

Adam knew he would not be one of them. He was thankful the warden had respected his lawyer's request and not allocated another prisoner to his cell when Joseph had been transferred to the infirmary. Not having to share his cell with a new inmate in the last few days of his sentence had given him the solitude he needed to plan

The Final Proposition

what he would do when he was released. He knew closure for his wrongful incarceration would be a long time coming, but he had managed to resolve some of his bitterness and resentment already, which he took to be a good sign.

Hearing the sound of footsteps approaching his cell door, Adam picked up his small travel bag from the lower bunk. He watched as the door was unlocked and opened by one of two prison guards that would escort him to the front office.

Neither guard made a move to enter the cell, and the older of the two guards said aggressively, "You got everything? Let's go."

Adam followed the guards in silence as they made their way through the high-security prison wing and across a secure elevated and reinforced glass walkway to the main administration block. He was surprised by the level of hostility the guards still showed toward him, even though they all knew he was innocent. He kept walking and said nothing—after today, he would never see them again, and that was all right with him.

After identifying themselves to a security guard who sat in a tiny bulletproof glass enclosure, Adam followed the two guards into the main administration block through a large reinforced glass security door the guard unlocked for them. Adam had only been in this part of the prison once before. The bland decor was slightly more in keeping with a normal office environment, but Adam still found it oppressive and could not wait to finally taste freedom.

The guards motioned Adam to follow them down a flight of stairs to the ground floor. Adam followed them along a long wide hallway until they abruptly stopped outside a door at the far end of the corridor.

The lead guard opened the door and motioned Adam inside. "We wait out here. Don't take too long, we've got real prisoners to manage."

Adam walked past the guard and into a small conference room. Sitting at the far end of a battered oval wooden table and surrounded by a sea of documents was his lawyer, Aaron Winter. Although only in his late thirties, a full head of prematurely gray hair made Winter looked older. The lawyer had a propensity to cut people off mid-sentence and a condescending attitude. Adam didn't overly like the diminutive man. He was abrupt and overly confident but had come highly recommended. Winter's "no win, no fee policy" had also been very attractive to Adam, who no longer had any assets apart from seven thousand dollars in one savings account. It was an association born and sustained by need alone.

Winter looked up from his pile of work and motioned for Adam to sit down. "You needn't worry, this is not all for you. I have two other client meetings here after this."

"Okay."

Winter removed his reading glasses and began to clean them with a small cloth. Smiling briefly, he looked up and said, "Today's the day, Adam. How does it feel?"

"I'm glad to be getting out, but…"

Winter finished the sentence for him as Adam sat down. "—disappointed you don't have your money yet."

"I'm an innocent man, Aaron. I've spent seven years in jail for a crime I didn't commit, and no one wants to say sorry. Right now, all I'm seeing is a lot of people pointing their fingers at one another and saying it's not their fault. You'll forgive me for feeling a little bitter and twisted."

Winter put his glasses back on. "Adam, we're going to win this. When I've finished with them, you'll never have to worry about money again. You can start a new life and do whatever you want. You just have to be patient and trust me."

Adam rose and started pacing. "How long is it going to take?"

Winter looked down at the table and shook his head. "Adam, we've been through this before. It's going to take time. Months, maybe longer. You need to be patient. If I push for a settlement now, we'll only get a fraction of what this is worth. I've put a lot of my own time and money into this, and I know what I'm doing. We work the system right, and we'll get the settlement."

Winter paused for a moment to study Adam before he added, "Trust me, that's all the government officials and company executives really understand. You want sorry, you won't get it. Whoever ends up owning this will qualify their apology with so much spin, no one will really know who's right and who's wrong. It's the money that counts. We get the money, then you get your right of reply."

Winter closed the folder he had open in front of him. In a quieter voice, he continued, "Adam, I know this is hard. Your day in front of the cameras is coming, but it's going to have to wait—for now at least. We sign your release and get you out of jail today, and you let me handle the media. When we get the settlement agreed, I'll organize you a press conference and you can blow off all the steam you want. Sound fair?"

To Adam, none of it sounded fair, but he did not think he had much of a choice at present.

"Where do I sign?"

Winter motioned for Adam to sit down again. "There are three documents to sign today. The first one is from the Hartbourne Correctional Facility, acknowledging you were examined yesterday by their physicians and pronounced of sound mind and body. Basically, its butt-covering for the prison. You can't sue them for any mistreatment while incarcerated."

"And if I choose not to sign?"

"They take you back to your cell, and I go and fight it out with a judge. You still have recourse if you sign it, but it takes longer. This isn't a big deal, Adam, you should sign it."

As Adam went to pick up a pen to sign the document, Winter quickly moved the second document in front of Adam. "Now we don't sign this until we have the official meeting. I'm just walking you through the documents now so you're fully briefed. This second document has been through several drafts at my insistence. It basically acknowledges that you're an innocent man and were convicted of a crime you didn't commit. Your criminal record is to be expunged and you are to be freed from prison today. It also acknowledges that your incarceration is a mistake and that you should be compensated."

Adam thumbed through the document, scanning a number of pages as he went.

"It's a thick document."

"Lawyers are not known for their compact writing style, Adam. My summary accurately described what five lawyers have spent twelve pages trying to document. It mostly describes what happens from here on. They acknowledge that either the state or the company that manufactured the DNA processing equipment is liable for damages and the legal process to follow that will determine who pays compensation. That's the part I redrafted. There was too much ambiguity in the first two drafts. This is now watertight. One of them is ultimately responsible."

Adam spent several more minutes reading the document and was interrupted by a knock on the door. Winter said to Adam, "Keep reading," as he got up and opened the door.

The lead guard went to step in the door. "Hey, can we hurry this along? We've got real work to do."

Winter blocked his way. "This is a private meeting, and unless you want me to register a formal complaint with both the warden and his superiors, you'll back off. We're almost done, and this isn't helping."

Before the guard had a chance to protest, Winter closed the door in his face and returned to the table. As he sat down, he said, "Take your time, Adam, they can't bully you anymore."

Adam continued to study the document for several more minutes. Winter began to get edgy.

"Problem?"

Adam didn't trust the lawyer but wasn't about to say so. "This is all extremely legalistic. It reads like something written in the eighteenth century."

"You have our law schools and legal precedents to thank for that."

Adam sighed and pushed the document across the table to Winter.

"I have one further document for you to review. This one you get to sign here and now. You'll be a free man today and no longer a convicted murderer. That changes our legal relationship. This enables me to continue to legally represent you."

Adam spent several minutes reading the document to make sure Winter wasn't taking advantage of him. Satisfied that the contract was in order, Adam signed the document and pushed back from the table.

Winter quickly gathered all three documents and said, "Let's get you out of here," as he stowed them in his leather satchel.

Adam followed Winter to the door. After opening the door, Winter demanded the guards take them to the front of the building immediately.

While they followed the guards, Adam said to Winter, "We're heading toward the front of the prison. Prisoners aren't normally released through the administration block."

Winter smiled. "You're not normal, Adam. When they discovered they had an innocent man locked up, everything changed. We go from here to another processing room where we see a prison bureaucrat for the formalities. We'll be in and out in under five minutes."

The group rounded another corner of the corridor and came into the main foyer and reception area. Adam had only taken two steps into the area before he stopped. The view through the wide glass windows at the front of the building mesmerized him. Beyond the short driveway, he could see an uninterrupted view of a road lined with cars and trucks going about their daily business. With no security fences or razor wire, Adam could finally taste freedom.

His thoughts were interrupted by a young woman in a business suit who came and stood in front of them.

The Final Proposition

"The warden will see you now."

Adam started walking again, and he fell in beside Winter as they followed the young woman across the foyer toward the warden's office. Adam murmured under his breath to Winter, "The warden is now a prison bureaucrat?"

Winter replied, "It's not entirely surprising he would want to see you."

Adam and Winter followed the young woman into the warden's office. The warden's office was larger than Adam had expected and was paneled in a wood veneer finish that went out of style twenty years ago. They were led to a small conference table where the warden and two other men dressed in business suits were already seated. Adam could not recall ever seeing the two stony-faced men before and pegged them as either the warden's superiors or lawyers.

The young woman motioned for Adam and his lawyer to be seated. The warden and his two associates watched Adam and his lawyer sit down but made no move to acknowledge their presence or introduce themselves. As soon as they were settled, Winter withdrew the documents from his satchel and placed them on the table. "My client has reviewed these documents and is happy to sign them as an acknowledgment of recognition of his innocence and release from prison today. Further, in signing these documents, all parties agree to an expungement of his record and that compensation will be paid for his incarceration once liability has been finally determined by the court. Any questions, gentlemen?"

The older of the warden's two associates took the lead and picked up a copy of each document. He began quickly scanning each page in silence. After finishing the scan, the lead associate looked across at Winter.

"They appear to be in order. Let's get them signed and all be on our way."

In a deft move, the lead associate produced a fountain pen from his jacket pocket and handed it to the warden.

"We'll get you to sign the documents first, Warden."

Adam watched as the lead associate got the warden to sign the documents before sliding them across the table to Winter and handing him his fountain pen. Winter turned to Adam and said in a low voice, "You sign them where marked, and I'll countersign them as your witness, and we're done."

Adam nodded and quickly scribbled his signature on the documents as the other men watched in silence. After Winter countersigned, he slid one copy of each document back across the table with the fountain pen and put the other copy in his satchel.

Winter closed his satchel and said, "I think we're done here, gentlemen. My client just needs his belongings you confiscated when he was incarcerated, and the rest we'll leave to the court."

The lead associate turned and nodded at the young woman who stood waiting patiently beside the door. As she handed the man a bag that appeared to contain Adam's belongings, he responded to Winter, "All taken care of. Please have your client check and sign for the contents."

Winter handed Adam the bag and a receipt. "Please check the contents, Adam, and if you're satisfied, sign the receipt."

Adam had no intention of checking the bag in front

of the assembled audience. While staring down the warden who had started drumming his fingers impatiently on the table, he signed the receipt and slid it back across the table in front of him. The warden continued to hold Adam's stare, which prompted the lead associate to quickly rise from his chair before either man did something stupid. "This meeting is now concluded. Mr. Wells, you are free to leave."

Winter quickly led Adam out of the warden's office and to a corner of the reception area. Before Adam had a chance to say anything, Winter grabbed Adam by the shoulders and said in a hushed tone, "Adam, before we go any further, look outside."

Adam turned and looked through the front doors of the administration block. He knew there would be some media but was surprised at how many were in attendance. Clearly, this was going to be the lead story on the six o'clock news.

Winter pointed at the media. "I've organized a cab to take you wherever you want to go. I'll walk you through them and put you in the cab. It's very important you don't make any comment right now. They will eat you alive if you let them. Once you're in the cab and on your way, I'll hold a quick media conference so that they leave you in peace and don't follow you. We'll use the media to help us with the settlement when the time is right. You need to trust me on this, Adam. I know what I'm doing, and I'll get you a great settlement."

Adam continued to stare out the window. The photographers were already taking pictures, and he knew it would be madness the moment he walked through the front doors. He suddenly felt very tired and longed for this day to be over. Sighing, he replied, "Okay, we do it your way. I just want out of here."

"I know this isn't easy for you, Adam, but you're playing it smart."

Before Adam had a chance to respond, Winter opened his satchel. "I have some things to give you before we go outside."

Winter produced a brown envelope and handed it to Adam. "Here's your bank account access card. I also withdrew two hundred dollars for you. That should be enough to keep you going for a couple of days until the media attention dies down. The balance is just under seven thousand."

Adam said, "Thanks," and pocketed the money.

Winter asked, "You don't have a cell phone, do you?"

"Of course not, they're illegal in prison."

Winter reached into his satchel again and withdrew a cell phone. "You're going to need a phone. This one's not new, but it works fine and has a new battery. I need you to keep it charged and on so that I can reach you. When we get a settlement offer, I need to be able to contact you straight away."

Handing Adam the phone, Winter looked out the window again. "I think that's enough for now. You ready?"

Adam nodded. "Thanks, Aaron, I appreciate this."

"No problem. You and I are both going to be handsomely compensated for all this."

Winter gripped Aaron by the shoulder again. "This is going to be a bit like running the gauntlet. You follow close behind me, and I'll lead you to the cab. They know I'm going to hold a press conference as soon as you're on your way, so keep your head down and don't say anything, okay?"

Adam looked out at the crowd. This was not how he pictured himself leaving prison. Taking a breath, he replied, "Okay."

Adam followed closely behind Winter as he strode to the front glass doors. Pausing before he opened the glass doors, Winter murmured, "Ready?"

"Ready."

The sound of reporters screaming questions was deafening as Winter opened the front doors and they began their descent of the stairs to the driveway. Winter did not need to worry about Adam keeping his head down. The flash photography was blinding and quickly convinced Adam to look down and straight ahead. Winter veered left at the bottom of the stairs and kept walking at a brisk pace as the media throng quickly regrouped around them.

The pair walked quickly across the lawn to a waiting yellow cab. Winter roughly pushed a cameraman and female reporter away from the cab's rear door, screaming to Adam, "Get in," as he opened the door.

Adam quickly moved forward, seeking sanctuary inside the cab. As he clambered inside, Winter slammed the door behind him, shouting, "I'll call you."

The quietness of the cab was a welcome relief for Adam. As the cab pulled away from the curb, Adam turned and looked through the rear window at the media crowd. Several photographers gave chase, trying to get a final shot of him which made the whole scene very surreal to Adam. This was not the way he imagined he would leave prison. Finally a free man, he was not sure how he felt, but it didn't feel like being free. Turning to face the front, Adam noticed the cab driver had been watching him through the rearview mirror.

"Where to?"

After seven years of being told where to go and when, it was going to take Adam a while to get used to being able to decide for himself.

"Redwood Cemetery, please."

Chapter Four

Leyland Darcy poured the last of his coffee from a battered steel thermos into a well-used plastic cup and set it on the dashboard of his aging Toyota four-wheel-drive to cool. He checked the time on his watch again before reaching out and gripping his sideview mirror. Turning the mirror slowly from left to right, he surveyed the media throng that had gathered on the front lawn of the Hartbourne Correctional Facility. Since arriving two hours ago, they had done little more than unpack and set up. He smiled to himself as he watched some of them pace with cell phones glued to their ears while the rest conversed earnestly in small huddles. They reminded him of vultures—not overly intelligent and impatient for their victim to appear and the feast to begin.

Unlike the media, he was content to wait. Waiting was one of the things he was very good at. As a former police detective with thirty years of service, he was used to long stretches in a car. Sometimes it would pay off, and sometimes it wouldn't. While he watched the media through the mirror, he was confident his seven-year investment was about to pay off.

Normally wary of being anywhere near a TV camera or reporter, he was glad of the media presence today and had used it to his advantage. Arriving at three a.m. that morning, he had patiently experimented with various parking lots on the deserted street before settling on one which was a short distance from the entrance to the prison facility and on the opposite side of the road. The spot provided him with a clear view of the entrance to the building through his side mirror, and with a slight adjustment, he was also able to see vehicles exiting the driveway. By six thirty, every legal parking spot had been taken, and with media trucks now parked in front and behind him, he was largely hidden and satisfied he could operate unobserved.

Darcy let go of the side mirror, reached across to the passenger seat, and pulled a bottle of Yellow Jackets from his calico knapsack. After removing two capsules, he placed them in his mouth and washed them down with two sips of coffee. He wasn't sure how many he was going to need this time and hoped he would be able to finish what he needed to do inside two days. His record for going without sleep had been just over four days, but he knew from past experience that his ability to function became impaired from day three onward.

He sat sipping his coffee and thought back to the event seven years ago that had started this. Drug busts almost always never went to plan, and the takedown of Tony Penmen had been no exception. They had recovered the drugs but not the money. He knew the deal was worth around three million, and when Penmen turned up dead two days later, he and many others had asked the obvious question—where was the money?

He hated loose ends and worked hard in the days following the bust to find the money. He and his partner had searched Penmen's house first and then his office and warehouse. After turning each location upside down and finding nothing, they had been given permission by their superiors to continue searching, but after a further two weeks without uncovering any concrete leads, they were reassigned to other cases. By this time, both he and his partner were almost obsessed with finding the money and vowed to continue the search in their own time and split the money fifty-fifty if they ever found it.

They had spent every day off in the months following in close observation of a number of key suspects they thought might have a connection to the money; Hannah Penmen, the elderly veterinarian who had found Tony Penmen dead in his driveway, and a number of senior members of the drug cartel had all been closely watched. After almost twelve months of fruitless searching and on the brink of a divorce, his partner, Leo Gibson, had declared they were wasting their time and promptly asked for a transfer.

Darcy had survived and prospered as a police detective by never trusting anyone. Everyone had an angle regardless of which side of the law they stood on. He wasn't buying what his partner said for a moment and began following him. Within two days, he learned that Finn Prosser, the surviving drug dealer from the Penmen raid, had been recently released from prison after his lawyer got him off all charges on a technicality.

He had made some further discreet inquiries and found out that Gibson had teamed up with Prosser for a healthy monthly bonus. Gibson was now on the cartel's payroll, providing inside information on surveillance being conducted by the police on the cartel's operation. He had briefly contemplated reporting Gibson to internal affairs but quickly dismissed the idea. His former partner knew too much about his own criminal activities as a police officer and would certainly rat him out for a lighter sentence. He only needed another day before deciding Gibson was now too much of a risk. Being associated with Finn Prosser would eventually backfire, and Gibson would wind up either dead or arrested.

Prior to that point in his life, Darcy had only killed two people, both criminals and both in the line of duty. He was initially surprised at how easy it had been to make the decision to kill his former partner and even more surprised at how little remorse he felt as he shot and killed his former partner three days later.

He recalled how easy it had been. Gibson had established a pattern of meeting Prosser in a quiet suburban bar every few nights to pass on information. He was easy to follow and always parked in the same spot in a parking lot behind the bar. Darcy had waited patiently in the shadows of the rear parking lot one night until a half-drunk Gibson emerged from the rear entrance of the bar. He visualized the moment he walked up behind his former partner and shot him in the back of the head with a silenced pistol as Leo unlocked his car. He had felt no remorse as he watched Leo Gibson lying on the ground in an expanding pool of his own blood.

His thoughts were interrupted as the chatter of the media throng increased. Reaching out, he grabbed the side mirror again and moved it left and right to scan the group. He noticed a distinct change in their behavior—

cigarettes were being extinguished and cell phone calls were rapidly concluding. He watched the camera operators start shouldering their equipment and knew it wouldn't be long before Wells was released. While he watched the media get ready, he wondered how the next forty-eight hours would unfold and who would be alive at the end of it.

The media surged forward in unison toward the front of the building. He knew the wait was over. Darcy swallowed the remainder of his coffee and started the engine of his four-wheel drive. He had gambled on Wells heading back into the city upon his release and had picked this side of the road to avoid having to make a conspicuous U-turn. As he adjusted the mirror, he saw Wells and his lawyer emerge from the building and quickly head through the media crowd toward a waiting cab. Darcy watched Wells get into the cab and smiled to himself as the cab pulled out of the driveway and turned right in the direction of the city.

Shifting the Toyota into gear, he waited for several cars to pass before he pulled out to follow. He wasn't too worried about losing his quarry today. Using the information he had been able to bribe from one of the guards, he was fairly confident he knew where Adam Wells was heading.

Chapter Five

Adam watched as the black hearse emerged from the shadows of the tree-lined road and drove slowly through the cemetery toward the small crowd of mourners that had begun to assemble. As the hearse came to a stop, the priest invited the mourners to gather at the graveside so that the service could commence.

Still not feeling like a free man, Adam was reluctant to move forward and stand with everyone else. He hung back and watched as Joseph's plain wooden coffin was removed from the hearse and carried toward the grave by four men he didn't recognize. Although he had been with Joseph when he died, he was still finding his friend's death hard to accept.

When the coffin was placed in position, the priest thanked everyone for their attendance and then opened the service with a prayer. Adam found it difficult to concentrate. Hannah, the one person he felt sure would be here today, was missing. While he tried his best to listen, he kept scanning the group for signs of Hannah's

The Final Proposition

arrival. They had talked on the phone twice since Joseph's death. The first conversation had been shortly after Joseph's passing. The prison doctor had agreed to Adam's request and allowed him to phone Hannah and break the news. The second conversation had been more lengthy. Hannah had contacted him while he was still in prison to discuss the details of the funeral service. She had even insisted on delaying the service by one day so that Adam could attend.

Something was wrong. Hannah had every intention of being here today. While he tried to listen to the priest's words, he noticed several other mourners were also looking around. At the conclusion of the prayer, the priest said a few comforting words and then started reading a psalm. Adam barely heard a word. Hannah had stuck by Joseph through seven years of prison; surely she would be here for the final farewell?

Adam's thoughts were interrupted by the sight of a small aging red Mazda making its way slowly along a raked gravel road through the cemetery. The car did not stop in the parking lot as he expected but continued across a grassy area at the side of the cemetery before coming to a halt under the shade of a large elm tree. Adam watched as a diminutive young woman who was wearing dark sunglasses emerged from the car. She was in her early thirties and had long auburn hair, and even though he had never met her in person, he knew by Joseph's description of his wife that it was Hannah who was making her way between the gravestones toward the gathering.

Adam breathed a sigh of relief and returned his focus to the service as the priest finished reading the psalm and then began making a few general remarks about how difficult the death of a loved one could be. While addressing the gathering, the priest subtly scanned the crowd for signs of Hannah's arrival. After spotting her making her way quickly to the gathering, he gave her a subtle nod of welcome and began his eulogy for Joseph.

"As you all know, Joseph has spent the past seven years in prison. Far from being an innocent man, Joseph admitted to his crime and accepted the judgment and punishment that followed. As a chaplain at the Hartbourne Correctional Facility, I first met Joseph five years ago and was struck by how gentle and humble a man he was. I was intrigued. Most of the men I deal with as a prison chaplain have a hard edge and protest their innocence. Joseph was quite the opposite. He readily admitted to his crime and was racked by guilt and regret every day because he could no longer care and provide for the thing he loved the most: his family."

As the priest continued his eulogy, the words were lost on Adam as he watched Hannah break down and sob uncontrollably. A middle-aged woman he did not recognize put an arm around Hannah to comfort her. Adam found it difficult to concentrate. Hannah began to regain her composure, but tears continued to stream down her face as she stared at the coffin and tried to absorb the priest's words.

The priest closed his eulogy by focusing on Joseph as a devoted husband and father who had made one life-changing mistake that he could never rectify. Adam was thankful Hannah had chosen the man who had been Joseph's chaplain to lead the service. It was clear the priest had genuinely liked Joseph and was doing his best to make the service dignified and personal. After completing the eulogy and leading the small group in a prayer of commitment, the priest stepped forward and in silence pressed a small foot lever that began to lower the coffin into the grave.

"Friends, at this point in a funeral service, I normally close with a final reading. Today, I leave you with a final thought instead. Joseph died a condemned man in the eyes of the world, but in the eyes of God, he received forgiveness and acceptance. As we leave here today, may we remember Joseph with the heart of God rather than the heart of man."

The priest walked across and grasped both of Hannah's hands in his own and shared a few quiet moments with her. When he stepped back from her, Adam was surprised to see Hannah quickly turn and head back toward her car. The small group of mourners watched her leave, but no one attempted to follow her. Adam was not sure what to do. He did not want to intrude upon her privacy and grief, but he did want to thank her personally for delaying the funeral service so he could attend.

Being unsure that he would ever see her again made his decision easy. Adam left the group and started following Hannah back toward her car. As he closed the gap between them, he called out softly, "Hannah."

Hannah stopped and quickly turned to see who had called her name. Her face softened as she said, "Thank you for coming today, Adam."

Without waiting for a reply, Hannah turned and started walking again. "I need to get back to my car. Will you walk with me?"

Adam walked quickly and within a few strides caught up with Hannah. "Hannah, I just wanted…"

Before Adam had a chance to continue, Hannah

interrupted, "Sorry, Adam, but I need to check on Michael first."

Without further explanation, Hannah left Adam and walked the few remaining steps to her car. He watched as Hannah gently opened the rear door and leaned in. Although his view was obstructed, he could see a child curled up on the back seat—Michael.

Walking several steps closer, Adam watched as Hannah placed the open palm of her hand close to her son's nose and mouth. He was covered in sweat and looked to be in a restless sleep. Adam felt helpless as he watched as Hannah kept her hand in position for more than thirty seconds before gently withdrawing it and softly closing the car door. As she turned and walked back to Adam, she said, "He had a seizure on the way here. The stress of his father's funeral, I guess."

"Is he…?"

"He's okay for now. His breathing is back to normal. He'll probably sleep for another hour or more before he wakes up."

Hannah wrapped her arms around herself as if she were cold. In a quieter voice, almost as if she was thinking out aloud, she continued, "That's why I was late. When Michael has a seizure, I have a list of things the doctors need me to do straight away. If I don't, he can easily choke, and then there's always the risk of brain damage…"

Feeling awkward, Adam replied, "Hannah, I don't know what to say, other than I'm sorry."

"You don't have to say sorry, Adam. Like it or not, this is my life now, even if it means I'm late for my husband's funeral."

The Final Proposition

Looking across at the car, Adam gently asked, "How's Michael coping with his father's death?"

Hannah thought for a moment before responding. "He took it harder than I thought he would. He has no memory of his father before he went to jail, and I only took him to see Joseph once a month. His bond with Joseph was stronger than I thought. He cried a lot at first, but now he's beginning to accept it. Even though he's only nine, he's a very smart and determined boy. I know in time he will adjust and grow to accept it."

Adam was not sure how to respond. After seven years in jail, expressing himself did not come easy. "Hannah, I just wanted to thank you for delaying Joseph's funeral so I could attend. It means a lot to me."

"I wanted you to be here, Adam. You were Joseph's only real friend in prison. I know he would have appreciated you coming."

"He was a good man. I'm sorry it ended this way."

"Me too."

After a short, awkward silence, Hannah continued, "What are you going to do now that you're free?"

"I'm not sure yet. My compensation settlement has stalled, so I'm thinking I'll head back to my hometown of Stanwyck for a few days. There are a few things I need to sort out, and my car is in storage there. And you?"

"There's nothing more for me here. Michael and I are leaving tomorrow."

"A fresh start is probably for the best."

"The fresh start is on hold for now. We've got a seven-hour road trip tomorrow to Bolton. I need to get Michael his operation."

"Bolton, as in the city four hours north?"

"Yes. My sister lives there, and Michael and I are

going to stay with her. The surgeon who we hope will operate on Michael works out of a private hospital there."

The slight vagueness in Hannah's answer was not lost on Adam. "Forgive me, Hannah, but where do the seven hours come in?"

Hannah looked slightly flushed and turned her head to avoid Adam's gaze. As she stared back toward her car, she replied, "I know Joseph told you about the money."

Adam recalled the one and only conversation he ever had with Joseph about the money. After he had gently but firmly said no, Joseph never mentioned the money or the proposition again. Until now, he wasn't even sure Joseph had told Hannah. As he answered, he realized that there was very little she didn't know.

"Yes."

"I'm going to make a detour through Windmere. I need to get the money."

Turning back to look directly at Adam, Hannah continued, "Michael won't survive without the operation, Adam. The money is his only chance."

As Hannah stared back, almost defiantly, Adam felt uncomfortable. It had been extremely hard telling Joseph he thought the idea was foolish and that the money wasn't likely to still be there this long after it had been hidden. As he looked into Hannah's eyes, he realized it was impossible to give the same message to a mother who was alone and desperate.

Instead, he simply said, "I wish you well, Hannah."

Hannah's features softened. "Thank you, Adam."

The two were quiet for a moment. Adam looked back at the small group of mourners who were now starting to disperse. He found the silence awkward and did not want to detain Hannah any further.

The Final Proposition

"I'm going to say my own goodbyes to Joseph, and then I'll be on my way. Good luck, Hannah. I hope Michael gets his operation and everything works out."

Hannah gave a faint smile and thanked Adam for his good wishes. Although she was small in stature and clearly sad and upset, she had a resolve and determination he admired. He was concerned what the coming days might bring for her and Michael. Her determination and resolve would not guarantee their safety, particularly if three million dollars somehow became part of the equation.

Her situation was close to impossible to comprehend, and Adam knew it was not his place to provide advice. In a quiet voice, he said, "Please be careful, Hannah."

Without waiting for a reply, Adam turned and walked back toward the grave to say his own final goodbye to Joseph. He was no longer in the mood to celebrate, and the cold beer he had been looking forward to for months would need to wait. He was not sure what he would do after leaving the cemetery, but a long walk and a motel room started to look like his best option.

Chapter Six

Adam checked the time on his watch as he sat on the concrete steps at the front of the four-story apartment building. He had been there for almost an hour, and in that time, only two people had emerged from the rundown gray residential building. He gazed at the small, aging red Mazda parked on the street in front of the building and was confident Hannah had not left yet.

Feeling down after the funeral, he had gone for a long walk before checking into a cheap inner-city hotel for his first night's accommodation as a free man. After dining on a steak and two light beers, Adam had retired to his hotel room to relax and plan his next move. After flicking through the channels, he discovered hotel TV was no different to prison TV, quickly grew bored, and turned it off.

He lay on the bed and spent the next hour examining the phone that Aaron Winter had given him. He marveled at how much phone technology had changed in the seven years he had been in prison. The last phone he had owned barely did anything more than make phone calls. Even though his new phone was secondhand, it seemed capable of a lot more than that. After discovering the phone had a map application, he managed to locate the town that Hannah was heading for in search of the money. He learned that Windmere had a population of nine hundred and eighty people and was on an isolated road far from any main highway.

Adam had no idea when Hannah was going to leave and had risen at daybreak to make sure he didn't miss her. After checking out of the hotel, he caught a cab to her apartment but decided not to interrupt her. Still getting used to being a free man, he was happy to sit and wait out front. He did his best to watch the neighborhood wake up and head off to work, but his focus kept returning to Hannah's Mazda. He guessed the car was at least fifteen years old, and if its multiple dented panels, rust, and balding tires were anything to go by, he had serious doubts the car would make it out of the city, let alone survive the trip to Bolton.

He was still not sure why he had come or what had changed his mind. His conversation with Hannah after the funeral still weighed heavily on his mind. Even though she was on her own with a son in desperate need of serious medical care, he didn't pity her. In spite of her unrealistic expectations about recovering a large sum of money, her determined, almost defiant attitude was something he admired. He wasn't after a share of the money even though it had been Joseph's wish. While he contemplated his own question, he was oblivious to the footsteps behind him as the door to the apartment building opened for the third time within the hour.

"Adam?"

Adam looked back to see Hannah standing in the entranceway of the apartment building, holding a cardboard box. She was dressed in blue jeans and a black jacket, and the puzzled look on her face showed she was clearly surprised to see him.

Suddenly feeling awkward, Adam quickly rose to his feet and replied, "Hi, Hannah."

He was not sure what to say next. He realized his unannounced presence could be interpreted the wrong way. Although Hannah didn't look intimidated, she made no move to respond to his greeting. He realized she was waiting for him to explain himself and said, "I was hoping I could talk with you for a moment before you leave?"

With no attempt to hide her surprise, Hannah replied cautiously, "Okay, but let me put this box in the car first."

Without waiting for a reply, Hannah walked past Adam and down the steps to her car. Adam watched as she unlocked the car and placed the box on the back seat. He waited until she returned before he continued.

"I didn't sleep much last night. I kept coming back to the conversation I had with Joe when I found out I was going to be released…"

Hannah nodded slightly but didn't say anything. Adam took this as his cue to continue.

"That was when he told me about his illness and Michael's as well. He also showed me the letter from his brother. Joe asked if I would help you get the money when I was released… I said no. Truth is, I thought it was a long shot at best, and even if the money was there, recovering it wouldn't be legal."

Adam paused for a moment to collect his thoughts. He had never been overly good at expressing himself, and

The Final Proposition

seven years with just prisoners, guards, and the odd lawyer to talk to hadn't helped.

"When I saw you checking on Michael after the funeral, it made it personal. I think I began to understand why Joe asked me. What you're planning to do could be very risky. People have been killed for a lot less than three million dollars, and Michael needs you now more than ever. I don't want any of the money, Hannah, but I don't think you should be going alone. I would like to help if you'll let me?"

Adam waited for Hannah to respond. Her face showed no reaction as she processed what he had said. Instead of responding, she walked several paces toward the street and stood looking away from him.

"I knew Joseph was going to ask you. He said he would trust you with his life. When he told me you said no, I wasn't sure how I felt. I don't trust people as easily as Joseph did, and I have Michael to think of…"

The silence that followed was answer enough for Adam. Rather than push it, Adam walked past Hannah and down onto the street. Slowly walking around Hannah's car, his fears about the car's reliability grew.

He looked back at Hannah, who had been watching his every move.

"Hannah, you know as well as I do that this car isn't safe. One of your front tires is so bald I can see the steel mesh reinforcing. If you hit any rain, you won't be able to keep it on the road."

Adam could see the determined, almost defiant look that he had first seen after the funeral returning to Hannah's face.

"I barely have enough money for fuel, Adam. Tires will have to wait."

Adam walked around the car once more. He paused at the back, which was more black than red from exhaust smoke and wanted to say, *The car must burn almost as much oil as it does fuel.*

Instead, he settled for, "There are two ways to get to Windmere from Hartbourne. One of them is through Stanwyck, which is where I'm headed. I have a close friend who owns a garage there. You give me a lift, I'll get him to fit a new set of tires for free. You can pay me for the tires when you get back on your feet."

Hannah replied, "I don't accept charity."

"It's not charity, it's a loan."

Adam could see Hannah thinking through the offer. She was clearly a very independent woman, which didn't surprise him after what she had been through. With just a little more encouragement, he thought he could get her to accept.

"It's a win for both of us, Hannah. You get tires, and I get a ride home."

"You make it sound like I have no choice."

"You always have choices, Hannah."

Hannah folded her arms across her chest and shook her head. "I haven't had choices for seven years."

"Well, if you put it that way, you don't have choices. Right now, your car is dangerous, and you have an offer of help you shouldn't refuse."

Adam was about to add something about being a responsible parent as well but decided that wasn't fair. Instead, he waited for Hannah's response.

"I wasn't planning on going through Stanwyck, but it won't slow us down any going that way. Thanks for the offer, Adam. I will pay you back as soon as I can."

The Final Proposition

Adam smiled. He was relieved Hannah was showing good common sense.

"When you're on your feet, Hannah."

A slightly awkward silence followed before Hannah replied, "Michael should be finished with his breakfast by now. I'll go and get him and our bags."

"Do you want a hand?"

"We're not taking much, just a couple of bags and another box of Michael's books and toys. I'll be locked up and ready to go in five minutes."

Even though he had spent seven years in prison and was still learning how to communicate again, he took the hint from Hannah's polite response.

"I'll just wait here until you're ready. Take your time."

Adam went back to sitting on the concrete steps as he waited for Hannah to return. He was hopeful he could change her mind about making the trip to Windmere alone while they were on their way to Stanwyck. With Michael being as sick as he was, Hannah needed a backup plan. If she ran into any kind of trouble, even just a car breakdown on the remote roads, they were both very vulnerable. He needed to convince her that he was no threat and had their best interests at heart.

He was formulating a plan for how he would convince her when his phone rang. He had not given the number out yet, so it had to be either Aaron Winter or a wrong number.

"Hello."

"Adam, it's Aaron. Sorry to call you so early, but there's been a development."

The way Winter had delivered the word "development" put Adam on edge. He immediately got the feeling the lawyer was not ringing with good news.

"Okay."

"I got a call from the lawyer representing Kennox Industries, the company that makes the DNA lab equipment."

"Yes."

"The company is in financial trouble, Adam. Apparently, this is not the first lawsuit of this kind against them. They're currently looking for a buyer, but no one wants to touch them while this is going on. I'm really sorry, Adam."

"So what does this mean for me?"

"Right now, it's hard to predict. Kennox is in a weakened position and can't afford a proper legal defense against the government in a court of law. There's a chance they'll fold. We can still seek a secondary settlement from the government, but it's likely to be a much lower figure."

"How much lower?"

Adam knew from the silence that followed before Winter responded that the figure was going to be much lower.

"As it stands, anything over one hundred thousand is probably optimistic. We can always employ a media consultant to create some headlines and promote public support. If we can get the public on board, we can pressure the government to increase their offer."

Feeling the anger within him begin to rise, Adam let out a long, slow breath as he tried to regain control of his emotions. Yelling at his lawyer right now was not going to help, and he didn't want to make a scene in front of Hannah's apartment. He did the calculations in his head before he responded. After giving one-third of the settlement to his lawyer, he would walk away with a little over sixty thousand dollars in compensation for seven years in jail for a crime he did not commit. It was a far cry from the original seven-figure sum Winter had promised.

"And who pays for this media consultant?"

"You would, Adam."

"And what's the likelihood of success?"

There was another pause before Winter replied, "It's a roll of the dice, Adam."

Adam began pacing back and forth in front of the building. Apart from when he had been originally charged with murder, he could not remember a time in his life when he had been more angry or frustrated. He was glad Winter was on the other end of the phone and not there in person.

Winter knew better than to try and sugarcoat the bad news and waited for Adam to respond.

"So, an innocent man is locked up for seven years, and this is the best you can do? This is totally unbelievable. The whole legal system is…"

Adam was interrupted as the door to the front of the apartment building was opened by a boy about nine years of age who was being closely followed by his mother. The boy looked very alert, and with his tousled sandy red hair and freckled complexion, he reminded Adam of the Will Robinson character from the original *Lost in Space* TV series. As the boy held the door open for his mother who emerged from the building carrying two large bags, Adam found it hard to imagine he was sick and not likely to live much longer without a risky operation.

In a low voice, Adam said, "I'm going to need some time to think about this, which may include getting a second opinion. I'll call you later, Aaron."

Without waiting for a reply, Adam hung up, walked

over to the boy, and extended his hand. With a smile, he said, "Hi, Michael, my name's Adam. I was a friend of your dad's."

Chapter Seven

Adam's concern about the reliability of Hannah's Mazda only grew worse on the trip from Hartbourne to Stanwyck. The car behaved reasonably well on the way out of the city but struggled to maintain highway speed on the forty-minute trip. When they reached the halfway point of their journey, Adam noticed the Mazda was being regularly passed by other cars, even though the terrain of the countryside was relatively flat.

Pretending not to notice, he tried to concentrate on the peaceful scenery provided by the undulating green fields of the farmlands beyond the freeway. Almost in spite of the car's reliability, the further they moved away from the city, the more relaxed he felt. After seven years living in a depressingly confined space dominated by gray brick walls, bars, convicts, and violence, his first real taste of freedom was close to overwhelming.

He contemplated how long it might take to adjust to life as a free man and figured he would need to be in a place of his own with a steady job before he would start to feel normal again. His thoughts were interrupted by the sound of the Mazda's engine, which was sounding increasingly labored. The engine was starting to develop a noticeable and persistent knock.

Michael, who had been sitting in the back seat engrossed in a book, looked up at his mother and asked, "Is the car okay, Mom?"

Hannah pretended not to notice and replied, "We'll be in Stanwyck soon, Michael, and the mechanic who's going to change our tires can take a look at it. Okay?"

Michael didn't sound convinced.

"It doesn't sound good, Mom. Do you think it's going to be hard to fix?"

"We'll let the mechanic decide, sweetie. He's the expert."

"Mom!"

Hannah smiled and looked in the rearview mirror. "Sorry, Michael, I forgot."

Briefly turning to Adam, she explained, "I promised Michael I wouldn't call him 'sweetie' in public. Sometimes I forget."

It was the first time Adam had seen Hannah smile. Her whole face changed, and for an instant, she became a different person. He thought about his reply. He wanted to encourage her by saying something along the lines of "you have a nice smile" but settled for "okay" to avoid giving her the wrong impression.

More silence followed before Michael asked, "Adam, is Stanwyck where you used to live?"

Adam was pleased that Michael felt comfortable enough with him to ask questions. "Sort of. I had a house and workshop at a little place out of Stanwyck called Tangmere Falls. I used to make furniture."

"So you're a carpenter?"

"Sort of. I designed furniture pieces and then made them."

"So what kind of stuff did you make?"

"All kinds of furniture—tables, chairs, sideboards, bookcases, you name it."

"Sounds like stuff for rich people."

Adam had to smile. For nine years of age, Michael was very perceptive. He looked at Hannah who was also smiling again as he answered.

"You got it, Michael, mainly rich people."

Hannah asked, "Joseph told me you were an engineer?"

"A long time ago. I did a degree in civil engineering, but I was never passionate about it. The furniture making was something I did as a sideline to make money while I completed the degree. In the end, I was able to turn it into a full-time living. I loved every minute of it. Life was pretty good back then."

Hannah glanced in the rearview mirror. Confident Michael had gone back to reading his book, she replied, "Joseph filled me in a little bit on what happened to you. It must have been hard to lose everything you worked for?"

Adam thought for a moment as he looked out the car window at the rolling green farmland they were passing.

"Yes, it was very hard. For a long time, I was very angry about being charged with a murder I didn't commit. The anger then gave way to frustration when I realized my life was being taken away from me. Not being able to create and do the thing I loved was almost like living without oxygen."

"You used the word 'create' where most people would say 'make'?"

"Everything I made was unique. No two pieces were ever the same. Each client gets something different, and many of them are intimately involved in the design process."

Hannah was silent for a moment while she thought about Adam's answer. She was starting to understand why Joseph had liked Adam so much. Her thoughts were interrupted by another loud noise coming from the engine. No longer able to hide her concern for the Mazda, she turned to Adam and asked, "Do you think we'll make it?"

Adam wasn't a mechanic but knew enough about engines to know the sound coming from the motor was terminal. Not wanting to alarm Michael too much, he tried to downplay his response.

"We're about ten minutes away. We shouldn't stop, just in case the motor seizes. Just keep a steady pace, and we should be okay."

Before Hannah had a chance to respond, Michael asked, "Mom, what are we going to do? I don't think the car's going to make it to Bolton."

"We'll think of something, Michael, we always do."

Hannah, Adam, and Michael were silent for the remainder of the trip into Stanwyck as if any further talking might cause the car to stop altogether. Adam breathed a sigh of relief as they turned off the freeway and headed toward the main part of the town.

In an attempt to take his mind off the sound coming from the car's engine, Adam surveyed the outskirts of the town as they drove through the new residential areas that had sprung up during his time in prison.

The new housing complexes were all dominated by

modest one- and two-story houses built to a budget for working families. The town's population had crept up to almost forty thousand as some of Hartbourne's three million residents were being drawn to Stanwyck's quieter, less expensive lifestyle in the still largely rural community. The closer they got to the main part of town, the more everything looked the same. He was happy Stanwyck had not changed too much during his seven years in prison.

As they entered the main town center and drove past the one- and two-story shops and offices that flanked both sides of the street, Adam became increasingly confident the Mazda would get them to their destination.

"Only about two minutes now, Hannah. My friend's garage is at the end of the main street."

Hannah nodded in response. The noise the car was now making was attracting the attention of locals, who were stopping to watch as the car inched down the road, blowing large plumes of black smoke from the exhaust.

Michael, who had been looking out the rear window, turned back to face the front. "Hey, Mom, there's so much smoke you can hardly see out the back anymore!"

Hannah replied under her breath, "This is so embarrassing, everyone is looking."

Pointing to the concrete driveway of an aging single-story steel and concrete building signposted simply as "Max's Garage," Adam replied, "We turn in here."

Hannah turned into the driveway and parked in front of the garage between a large commercial icebox and two fuel pumps that would have been modern in the mid-fifties. Adam smiled to himself as he watched Hannah breathe an audible sigh of relief as she switched the engine off.

"You did a great job, Hannah. I'll go and find Max and get him to take a look and see how bad it is."

Hannah shook her head. "It's bad. You don't need to be Einstein to figure that one out."

Adam opened the car door and then paused. "I need to fill you in on a couple of things before I see Max..."

Hannah watched as Adam's face turned grim and he struggled to express his thoughts.

"Max and I are more like family than friends. I was engaged to his daughter at the time of my arrest."

Hannah nodded. "Joseph never mentioned you were engaged. Prison can be very tough on relationships."

Adam looked out the front window of the Mazda to see a slightly overweight man in his early fifties with bushy gray hair emerge from a tiny shop front next to the workshop. As he stood there dressed in oil-stained overalls, wiping grease off his hands, he recognized Adam and began walking toward the car.

Adam replied, "No, we never broke up. Justine was murdered shortly after I was convicted."

Before Hannah had a chance to respond, Adam was out of the car and walking over to Max.

Hannah recalled Joseph telling her that both Adam's parents were dead. She began to wonder if Max was now the closest thing to family he had left, when Michael asked, "Mom, did Adam say his girlfriend was murdered?"

In a distracted voice, Hannah replied, "Yes," as she watched the two men embrace. She saw Max begin to weep openly and was glad they had stayed in the car. The two men began what looked like an emotional conversation after their embrace. She decided they needed their privacy and said to Michael, "Michael, we're just going

The Final Proposition

to sit in the car a minute and give them some alone time."

They both watched as Max and Adam remained in deep conversation for some time. As an afterthought, Hannah softly added, "This must be very hard for both of them."

After several minutes, both men turned and looked at Hannah's car. Hannah took this as her cue and said to Michael, "We can get out now."

Hannah and Michael emerged from the car and walked over to meet the two men. Turning to Max as they approached, Adam said, "Max, I would like you to meet Hannah and Michael."

Max nodded at both of them in turn and smiled as he said, "Pleased to meet you both."

They all watched as Max stepped forward to look at the car. He turned to Michael and in a gravelly voice said, "Adam tells me you're pretty smart?"

Doing his best to suppress a smile, Michael replied, "I guess…"

Smiling at Michael, Max replied, "I bet you know how to pop the hood on your Mom's car?"

Michael raced around to the driver's side of his mother's car, opened the door, reached in, and unlatched the hood.

Max gave Michael a thumbs-up as he lifted the hood to start his check.

Michael went and stood between Adam and Hannah as they waited in silence for Max to conclude his inspection. Everyone was expecting the worst as Max attempted to restart the car and failed to even get the motor to turn over.

Scratching his chin, Max delivered the verdict.

"I'm sorry, Hannah, but if this car was a person, I'd be calling a priest to administer the last rites…"

Max let his words hang in the air as Adam looked at Hannah for a response. Hannah frowned and nodded but said no more as she silently began to realize her predicament.

Max walked back to them and said to Hannah, "Your engine's seized. Most likely due to faulty piston rings. That's common for a car this age. It'll cost about twice what the car is worth to fix it."

Adam looked at Hannah as he watched her process the news. In a way, he was glad the verdict on the Mazda was as bleak as it was. *Better to break down here than out in the middle of nowhere.*

Max broke the silence. "Adam, I have something to show you out back that may solve your problems. I think Hannah and Michael should come as well."

Without waiting for a reply, Max turned and walked back into the workshop. Adam, Hannah, and Michael followed Max through the main workshop area and past three mechanics who were all busy working on cars and paid them no attention.

They stopped at the rear of the workshop in front of a large roller door that had the words "Spray Room" painted on it. After lifting the roller door, Max gestured for everyone to follow him inside. The smaller workshop was spotlessly clean and contained only two cars. Pointing to a rusting antique red MG sports car, Max said, "This is my next project."

Max looked at Adam and grinned as he pointed to the second car which was covered with a white dust cover. "And this was my last project…"

Max stepped forward and pulled the sheet away to

The Final Proposition

reveal a fully restored two-door 1969 Chevrolet Camaro. The car looked to be in showroom condition with a highly polished white and chrome finish. Unable to hide the huge grin that was spreading across his face, Adam stepped forward to inspect the car in detail.

After circling the car, Adam stopped and said, "You've done a great job, Max, this is really something."

Max waved him off. "I can't take all the credit, you did most of the work before you went to jail. All I had to do was finish the top coat, the chrome, and fit the wheels you ordered."

Adam opened the driver's side door and asked Max, "Okay if I get in?"

Max flashed a smile as he pulled a set of keys from his pocket and tossed them to Adam. "It's your car."

Adam seated himself in the driver's seat and placed his hands lightly on the steering wheel. Hannah moved to stand beside Max and said, "He looks like an eight-year-old boy on Christmas morning."

Max replied, "The car was a three-year labor of love. It was left behind in one of the two barns on the property he bought for his furniture-making business. It was in bad shape, no motor and full of rust, but Adam could see the potential and couldn't part with it. He had planned to give it to my daughter Justine as a wedding present when they got married but…"

Hannah looked at Max as he paused mid-sentence. Tears started to well in the big man's eyes, and she realized she had inadvertently struck a nerve.

"Max, you don't have to…"

"It's all right, Hannah, you weren't to know."

Adam, who had not heard any of their conversation,

got out of the car and walked back to them. "The new wheels look even better than I imagined, Max."

Max replied, "I remember you ordered five alloys. If memory serves, the spare is in the trunk, but we need to check. I've taken the car for regular drives to keep the battery charged, but I can't remember exactly what I did with the spare."

Adam nodded, walked to the back of the car, and opened the trunk. "It's here along with the original spare. It looks to be still inflated but…"

Adam stopped mid-sentence and lifted a brown cardboard archive box from the trunk. "You know anything about this, Max?"

Max raised his eyebrows. "I thought it was yours? It's been there as long as I can remember, but I never opened it."

Adam lifted the lid from the box to reveal its contents. The box was about half full and contained a number of photographs and handwritten notes.

Adam carefully withdrew the first photograph from the box. It was a grainy black-and-white image of two men sitting in a car and looked to have been taken some distance from the car and then blown up. The two men appeared to have been photographed without their knowledge, almost as if they were under surveillance.

Puzzled, Adam turned the photo over to see if there were any notes or clues on the back that would help. Written on the back in a neat cursive script was a brief note capturing the date and time where the photograph had been taken. His mood turned instantly somber as he recognized the handwriting. As they stood in silence, Max reached across and took the photo from Adam's hand.

Max stared, almost in disbelief, as he recognized the handwriting of his daughter.

Their thoughts were interrupted by a soft thud coming from behind the Camaro. They all turned to see Michael lying on the concrete floor convulsing.

Hannah ran to her son, dropped to her knees, and rolled Michael onto his side with a practiced motion to check and clear his airway. Feeling totally helpless, Adam and Max stood back to allow Hannah space to care for her son as he continued to shake uncontrollably on the floor.

Chapter Eight

Adam and Max watched as Hannah nursed Michael through his seizure. The young boy was a lather of sweat by the time his convulsing stopped. Both men remained on edge and felt totally helpless as they watched Hannah monitor Michael's breathing for several more minutes. When she was satisfied the danger had passed, she looked up at Adam and Max and said, "He usually sleeps for between fifteen minutes and an hour after a seizure. Is there anywhere I can lay him down to make him more comfortable?"

Looking slightly dazed and still in shock from what he had just witnessed, Max nodded and softly replied, "I have a loft office in the main workshop area. It's got an old couch, if that will do?"

"That will be fine, Max, thank you."

As she began to cradle Michael in her arms, Adam came forward.

"Hannah, let me carry him. I'm used to Max's stairs —it will be easier for me."

The Final Proposition

With the same determined and almost defiant look that Adam was quickly becoming accustomed to, Hannah opened her mouth to reply. He could see her starting to form the word "no" before her features softened. Instead of replying, she nodded once to Adam who then gently bent down and lifted Michael off the floor.

"Thank you, Adam. I'm sorry, I'm so used to doing things on my own I—"

Adam didn't let her finish. "No need to apologize, Hannah. I can't even begin to imagine how hard this must be for you."

Adam was surprised that the young boy stayed totally oblivious to what was happening as Adam carefully lifted and cradled him.

"Is he asleep or unconscious?"

"The doctor calls it a fugue state. He can hear and sometimes respond, but mostly he's just in a form of shutdown while he recovers from the shock."

Max came forward to stand briefly beside Adam and said, "I'll go and unlock the office."

Hannah and Adam followed Max into the back of the main workshop to a set of steel steps that led up to a balcony and a small prefabricated office.

Cradling Michael, Adam carefully walked up the steps and followed Max into his office. The room was small and contained little more than an old wooden desk, an aging computer, and a slightly torn brown leather three-seat couch. The air smelled musty and of grease without being overpowering. After moving several piles of papers off the couch, Max gestured to Adam. "You can lay him here. Hopefully, he'll be comfortable."

Adam gently laid Michael on the couch and did a quick scan of Max's collection of wall calendars. Max had a habit of putting up a new calendar each year without taking down the old one. Satisfied the calendar pictures of bikini-clad girls draped over cars contained nothing a nine-year-old boy shouldn't see, he turned to Hannah and said, "Is there anything else we can do?"

"No. I'll be fine. Michael just needs his recovery time. It will give me a chance to think about what I do from here now that I don't have a car."

"I have the Camaro. I'd be happy to drive you?"

"I'll think about it, Adam."

Adam watched Hannah as she retrieved a cell phone from her coat pocket.

"I'm going to call my sister before I do anything. It's highly unlikely Michael and I will get to Bolton tonight, and she'll worry if I don't tell her."

"Okay."

Deciding not to push the offer any further, Adam turned to Max and said, "We should go and look at what's in that box."

Max nodded. "And also figure out how it wound up in the back of your car. I'm positive I didn't put it there."

Adam and Max left Hannah and the still sleeping Michael in the office and walked back down the stairs and out back to the other workshop. Adam explained Michael's condition to Max as they walked through the workshop and then told him part of Hannah and Michael's story. He left out the part about the money and was relieved when Max didn't ask any questions.

When they were alone in the other workshop, Max picked up the Camaro's dust cover and spread it over the bonnet of the MG. "Let's stay out here to look at the photos, I don't want anyone else seeing this just yet."

After briefly examining the box's contents, Max began

laying out the photographs. Adam looked from one photo to another and quickly spotted a common theme.

"They've all been taken at a long distance and then blown up."

"Surveillance?"

Adam picked up one of the photos for a closer look and replied, "Can't be anything else."

Unlike the first photo, this photo was taken with a building as a backdrop. The photo again showed two men in conversation, but the images were still too grainy for identification.

Adam held his breath as he turned the photo over to check for handwritten notes. He looked down, saw Justine's neat handwritten script again, and closed his eyes for a moment to compose himself. Her handwriting reminded him again of how much he had loved her. Justine had been his rock and had never given up fighting for his release. He remembered the day Max had visited him in person to tell him they were now treating Justine's disappearance as a murder and the emptiness that followed.

Adam opened his eyes and passed the photo to Max.

"I think we can safely assume all these photos were taken by Justine. This one has her handwritten notes as well."

Max studied the handwriting for a moment and then put the photo down and pulled the two notebooks out of the archive box. Quickly scanning the pages of both books, he responded to Adam, "You're right, Adam. It looks like it's all Justine."

Max got down on the floor and positioned himself with his back up against the MG to read more. After opening the first notebook and silently reading the first two pages, he turned to Adam and said, "This is what got her killed. All these years I've wondered why, and the answer has been under my nose the whole time."

Max became quiet again and kept reading. Even though there were a thousand questions Adam wanted to ask, he decided to let his friend read in peace. He used the time to continue studying the photographs. He started by taking a count—twenty-three in total and all of them appeared to be surveillance of the same two men. Adam scanned the collection of grainy images, looking for any that had a slightly better resolution.

Picking up the photo that appeared to be the best of the group, Adam studied the image in detail. It was another photograph of two men in front of a building, this time taken at night without the aid of flash photography. Adam held the picture at various angles, but it was still impossible to see the faces of the men in any detail. The thinner of the two men appeared to have dark hair, while the other man appeared to be older and had lighter hair, possibly even gray hair, although it was hard to tell from the poor image quality.

He turned the photo over and saw Justine's neat cursive script again. He paused to study her date and time notation and then whispered, "Who were you following, Justine?"

From his sitting position on the floor, Max held out one of the two notebooks for Adam and said quietly, "You need to read this, Adam."

Adam took the notebook and opened it to the first page.

"She was tracking two guys that she was positive had you framed. It makes sense now. I thought it was just a big mistake—cops eager for an arrest and prosecution and they went after the wrong man. Justine insisted you had been deliberately set up to take the fall… It looks like she was right."

In a quiet and reflective voice, Adam replied, "When you rang to tell me she was missing, I fooled myself into thinking she just needed to get away and clear her head. The following day, I realized how out of character that was. She was a fighter, not a quitter. I had a sinking feeling something bad had happened, but I went on hoping for a long time."

Both men sat in silence, each trying to come to terms with what they had just learned.

Finally, Max said, "From my quick scan of the notebooks, she didn't write down any names. I wonder why that was?"

Adam thought for a moment before he responded, "Maybe the notes were just for herself and only needed to be cryptic? Or maybe she knew how dangerous this was and didn't want to leave a trail. That might explain why the archive box was in the Camaro?"

Max thought for a moment before replying, "I had already finished the restoration when she disappeared. I remember her standing here in this workshop admiring the car. She was so excited with the way it had turned out. She couldn't wait to tell you."

"If she was worried about someone discovering what she was working on, the Camaro would be as good a place as any to hide the evidence."

Max got to his feet and replied, "I agree, Adam. I would like to take all this to the police straight away and get them to reopen her case."

Max thought for a moment before he continued. In a softer voice, almost as if he were thinking out loud, he said, "I just don't know who to trust. I thought your case was botched, and don't get me started on the way Justine's case was handled…"

Max began to pack the photographs back into the archive box and said, "I don't think it's wise to talk about this here anymore. I'm going to take all this home and study it in more detail tonight. When you get back, we can decide what to do then."

Pausing for a moment, he looked Adam directly in the eye before he continued.

"Adam, it goes without saying you're family and I want you to come and stay at my place until you get on your feet. I…"

Max didn't finish the sentence but let it hang in the air and waited for Adam to respond.

"Thanks, Max, I really appreciate it."

Adam thought for a moment about how much more he should say.

"It's a long story, Max, but I shared a cell with Hannah's husband for over a year. He was a good man and my only friend inside. He got sick and died just a couple of days ago in the prison hospital. He knew he was dying and asked me if I would help Hannah get Michael safely to Bolton for his operation. Hannah hasn't accepted my offer yet, but I hope she does. This is Michael's second seizure in less than twenty-four hours."

"Michael seems like a real nice kid. For what it's worth, I think you're doing the right thing. After seven years, a day or two isn't going to make much difference."

Adam went to reply but paused as Hannah appeared at the entrance to the workshop.

She looked drained as she said, "Michael is awake."

Adam replied, "Is he okay?"

"Yes, I've left him up on the balcony watching the mechanics work."

Sensing Hannah wanted to talk with Adam alone, Max said to Hannah, "I can show him around the workshop if you like?"

"Thank you, Max, I'm sure he would like that."

Max quickly packed the photographs back in the archive box along with Justine's two notebooks. After he had left the workshop, Hannah turned to Adam and said, "Right now, I have very few choices. I need to get to Bolton, and I need to get the money if it's there. It's my only hope for Michael."

Hannah paused as if she were thinking about what to say next. Adam decided not to say anything. His offer was on the table, and he wasn't going to push it any further.

"I spoke to Michael about your offer. If it's still available, then we accept. But I have one condition—if we do find the money, you get half as Joseph wished."

Not wanting to go over old ground again, Adam replied, "And I too have one condition."

Slightly taken aback, Hannah replied, "Okay…"

Adam smiled. "I need to get to a bank and get some money before we leave."

With a faint hint of a smile, Hannah replied, "Deal."

Her face turned serious again as she asked, "It's not my place to pry, but is everything okay with the box you discovered?"

Adam let out his breath and replied, "It's complicated, Hannah, but we think it may hold a clue to Justine's murder."

Looking stunned, Hannah replied, "Should you be staying here with Max?"

"Max and I have already discussed it. He thought it was right for me to make the trip first if you asked."

"I don't know what to say, Adam, except thank you."

"I'm glad you asked. You can concentrate on Michael, and I'll do the driving."

An awkward moment of silence followed. Hannah was a very attractive woman, and Adam had to remind himself that she had very recently become a widow. He quickly shook off any thoughts beyond helping them get to Bolton and said, "I'll meet you back here in half an hour."

Adam went to walk away but noticed tears beginning to well in Hannah's eyes. Still struggling with how to communicate outside a prison, he pretended not to notice and simply said, "I'm glad Michael's feeling better."

He turned and walked back through the garage and out onto the main street. Checking the time on his phone as he headed back toward the main business area of Stanwyck, he was glad for the opportunity to think. It was only midday, and so much had already happened on his first full day of freedom. He wondered how many more curveballs he would have to deal with before the day was over.

Chapter Nine

It was almost one thirty before Adam headed back to Max's garage. He smiled as he spotted Max, Hannah, and Michael standing in the tiny shop front laughing and eating ice creams as he walked back up the concrete driveway.

After opening the front door, Max was the first to greet him. "You want an ice cream?"

Adam smiled. "That's the best offer I've had all day."

Max pulled an ice cream out of a small commercial chest freezer and handed it to Adam. After thanking Max, he studied Michael for a moment as he peeled off the wrapper.

"How are you feeling, Champ?"

Michael smiled and blushed at the same time. Adam sensed he liked being called "Champ" and made a mental note to keep using the nickname if his mother didn't object.

"Much better. Are you really going to drive me and Mom to Bolton in the Camaro?"

"That's the plan."

A huge grin spread across the boy's face as he said, "Cool."

Adam looked at Hannah. "I'm ready to go whenever you are?"

"We don't want to mess up your car, Adam, so we'll finish our ice creams first."

Max swallowed the remainder of his ice cream in one gulp and made his way to the front door.

"I'll bring the Camaro around front so you can move your bags from the Mazda."

Hannah's face turned serious as she looked out through the window at her car. "Max, I…"

Max waved her off as he opened the door. "Relax, Hannah, you've got enough to worry about. I'll get one of my mechanics to tow it around back out of the way. If you like, I can get a junkyard to come and put a price on it. It's worth a few bucks for scrap metal if nothing else."

"Max, I don't want to put you out."

"No problem, I do it all the time."

Without waiting for a reply, Max slipped out the front door and headed down the side driveway to his second workshop.

Turning to Adam, Hannah said, "He really is very generous."

"He knows no other way, Hannah." After savoring another mouthful of his ice cream, he said, "Let's get those bags out of the car."

They walked out to unpack Mazda, and before they had all the bags and boxes removed, Adam heard the familiar deep, throaty sound of his Camaro as Max drove it around to the front of the garage and carefully parked it next to the Mazda.

The Final Proposition

After getting out of the car, Max looked back admiringly at the vehicle and said, "I'm going to miss my Sunday drives in this baby."

Adam smiled. "I'll be back tomorrow or the day after, Max, and I don't plan on going far. We'll have plenty of time for Sunday drives."

Michael started dragging suitcases and boxes to the Camaro. "Help me, Mom, I want to get going."

With Max and Hannah helping, it only took Adam a couple of minutes to get the car fully packed and ready for the trip. After buckling Michael into the back seat, Hannah turned and walked over to Max. Putting her arms around the burly man, Hannah said, "Thank you, Max, for all your help today. I might have lost a car, but I gained a friend."

Max brushed off the praise and said, "Hannah, it was nice to meet you. I hope next time I see you, Michael is all better—you deserve no less."

Max watched Hannah get into the car and then walked over to Adam. While the two men embraced, he said, "Take care, Adam, I'll see you soon."

After Adam said goodbye, he got into the driver's seat, closed the door, and started the engine. He found it hard to contain his smile as he waved to Max and drove out of the driveway and onto the main street.

Adam stole a quick look in the rearview mirror at Michael as they drove back down the main street. The boy still had an ear-to-ear grin.

"How do you like the car so far, Champ?"

"It's way better than the Mazda."

Adam and Hannah both laughed before Hannah asked, "Do you know how to get to Windmere, Adam?"

"I can get us to the town, but you'll have to take it from there."

"I can do that."

After driving through the main town center, they turned left onto a dirt road that led them up through the state's pine forest. The road quickly became steep and hilly, prompting Hannah to say, "Your car is going to get dirty, Adam, I'm sorry."

"It's okay, Hannah. Every day I was inside, I dreamed about driving this car. I'm having fun, and the dirt will wash off, so don't worry about it."

They passed a signpost which showed the distance to Windmere and several other small townships along the same stretch of road.

Adam said, "I figure it will be almost three hours driving to get to Windmere from here. We won't have much daylight to search for the money today."

"One more day won't matter, so don't feel you have to push it too hard."

Adam wasn't sure whether he should ask his next question or not but felt he should prepare Hannah for the possible letdown.

In a quieter voice, he said, "Have you thought about what you'll do if the money isn't there?"

Hannah was silent for a moment before she responded, "It's my only hope, Adam. It's all that keeps me going."

Adam could not think of a response that would give Hannah either the comfort or hope she desperately needed. He decided to concentrate on the driving for a while as the Camaro wound its way up the picturesque tree-covered mountain. He had no regrets about making the trip but wasn't optimistic it would have the happy ending Hannah was hoping for.

After almost twenty minutes of silence, which was broken only by the occasional excited burst of chatter between Michael and his mother, Hannah turned to Adam and said, "You're very quiet, Adam?"

Adam glanced across at Hannah momentarily before returning his gaze to the narrow, winding road, which required most of his concentration. He was going to use this as an excuse for his silence but found himself being honest instead.

"If you exclude visits from Max, I've only had guards, other cons, and the odd lawyer to talk to for the past seven years. I guess I'm a bit out of practice."

Hannah nodded as she responded, "I noticed a change in Joseph over the years that he was in prison. We gradually found it harder to communicate. At first, I thought it was me. I remember one day when I visited, he broke down because he knew prison was changing him and there wasn't a thing we could do about it."

"It's an incredibly tough place—we all go into survival mode. I'm a big guy and was never raped or physically assaulted, but the mental battles you go through can't be described. I…"

Adam paused. He didn't feel it was right to share any more details; Hannah had enough worries of her own.

Sensing what he was thinking, Hannah urged him to continue. "Adam, it will do you good to share. After listening to Joseph's horror stories, I doubt there is anything you can say that will shock me."

"I'm just looking forward to being normal again. I think going back to work and a simple everyday routine is going to be my best therapy. If I can get back to that, hopefully everything else will fall into place."

"Let's hope that happens sooner rather than later for you."

"Thanks, although it might have to wait. The box we found in my car was a curveball I wasn't expecting."

Hannah hesitated for a moment and then asked, "I don't mean to pry, Adam, but it sounds like your fiancée was on to something?"

"It looks that way. The photographs Justine took were clearly some type of surveillance and looked to be the same two men. When I get back, Max and I will go over everything with a fine-toothed comb. I don't know exactly what she was doing, but I'm sure that's what got her killed."

"It's all connected to your case, isn't it?"

"It's the only thing that makes sense. I want whoever killed her brought to justice."

Adam looked in the rearview mirror at Michael, who was now engrossed in another book. Confident he was distracted, he continued, "Three days before I was officially charged, I delivered a dining room table to a holiday house on the lake near Tangmere Falls. It was a custom order for one of Stanwyck's most prominent businessmen. I had been given a set of keys by the owner to let myself in, but when I got there, a young woman answered the door.

"She was the girlfriend of the owner's son, and they were planning to stay there together for a couple of nights. The son was driving up there later in the day to meet up with her, and I thought nothing more of it. I delivered the table, said goodbye, and headed home. Early the following morning, I was awoken by a knock at my door. I opened the door and had two detectives in my face. They explained that the girl had been raped and murdered early the previous evening, and I was their number one suspect."

"Simply because you delivered a table?"

"The house was in a remote spot on the lake. There were no other houses close by and no witnesses. I was one of only two suspects."

"The other being the boyfriend?"

"Yes. He claims he arrived about eight o'clock that night and found her lying on a bed in a loft bedroom above the main living room. She had been raped and stabbed. The cops believed him and focused their investigation on me because I had access and opportunity. They took DNA swabs and held me in custody for forty-eight hours while they used a new DNA matching technology to check whether any of my DNA matched samples taken from the loft."

"Were you ever in the loft?"

"No. I was in the house for less than ten minutes and only went into the main living area. After I assembled the table, I said goodbye and left. That knock on the door changed my life forever."

"Joseph told me they made a mistake with your sample?"

"Yes. I was charged with murder and refused bail on the basis of a DNA match, which we now know was faulty. When the cops drove me away from my house that morning for questioning, I had no idea my life was changing forever and I would never see the place again."

"I've had two days like that in my life. The first when I

got the call that Joseph had been arrested and charged. Michael was not much more than a baby. My world changed forever with that phone call. It took me years to really forgive Joseph for being so reckless and stupid."

"For what it's worth, Joe never forgave himself. He battled with it every day."

Hannah nodded. "In the end, that's why I forgave him. He was mad enough for both of us, and I knew that as Michael grew and became more aware of what was happening, I needed to be positive and not bitter."

"He's a great kid. You should be very proud, I know Joe was."

Hannah smiled. "Yes, I am proud".

Adam looked briefly in the rearview mirror as he asked, "You mentioned two days that changed your life, I think I can guess the second one?"

Hannah briefly turned in her seat to look at Michael, who was still reading.

"One day, almost two years ago, he was playing in his bedroom. He was a normal little boy—cheeky, full of energy, and singing his way through life. I'll never forget the moment everything went quiet. I walked into his room and found him lying on the floor…"

Tears began to well in Hannah's eyes. Adam felt terrible for steering the conversation in the direction of Michael's health and said, "Hannah, I'm sorry, we don't have to—"

"It's all right, Adam. I wouldn't have said anything if I didn't want to. The seizure only lasted about twenty seconds, but I knew in my heart something was seriously wrong."

The Camaro rounded another corner that marked the summit of the mountain they had just driven up. Adam

The Final Proposition

pointed to a lookout area ahead, which provided a panoramic view across the long, fir tree-covered valley below. Eager to savor the moment and lighten the mood, he said, "Let's stop and have a break for a minute?"

Adam was greeted by a chorus of agreement from Hannah and Michael as he pulled off the road and parked in the small parking lot. After getting out of the car, Michael rushed toward the platform, excited to see the view from the top of the mountain.

After calling out to Michael to be careful, Hannah looked at Adam and said, "You know, Adam, for a guy who has only had prisoners and lawyers for company for the past seven years, you communicate fine."

Adam did his best to wave off the compliment as they walked across to join Michael on the platform. After bending down to pick up two small rocks, he turned to Michael who was engrossed in the view of the trees and the valley below. "Hey, Champ, how about a rock-dropping contest?"

With a slightly puzzled look, Michael asked, "What's a rock-dropping contest?"

After handing one rock to Michael, Adam took the other rock and held it over the side of the viewing platform.

"We drop the rocks at the same time and see whose rock hits the ground first. You ready?"

Michael grinned as he held his rock out past the edge of the platform next to Adam's. "I think my rock's going to win, Adam."

Adam smiled. "On the count of three: one, two…"

Chapter Ten

Max watched the Camaro as it drove away from his garage until it disappeared out of sight. Walking back into the garage, he spoke briefly with his chief mechanic to get a work update. It was a slow Friday, and his mechanics did not overly need his assistance.

He walked back up to his office and sat down at his desk to think about everything that had happened so far that day. It had been good to see Adam again. In spite of his seven years in prison, he looked remarkably well. Scratching the stubble on his chin, Max looked across at Justine's archive box that now sat on his old leather couch. He decided he would not investigate its contents any further until Adam returned. Adam had loved Justine as much as he had, and it was right to wait.

Max closed his eyes and leaned back in his chair. Images of happier times when Justine was still a child and her mother was still alive flashed before his eyes. Max knew he shouldn't be thinking about the past and breathed in and out deeply to avoid another anxiety attack. Justine had been gone almost seven years, yet he still only coped by keeping himself busy to block out the pain. He knew he wouldn't have proper closure until they found her, brought her home, and gave her a proper funeral and farewell.

Pushing back from the desk, Max decided he needed a walk to clear his head. When he reached the door, he paused and looked at the box again. He found it hard to comprehend that for seven years this connection with his daughter had gone unnoticed in his garage. He thought about the notes she had written and how similar her handwriting had been to her mother's. Finding himself drawn to the box, Max walked back into his office and sat down on the couch. After gently removing the box's lid, Max lifted the larger of the two notebooks out and began slowly turning the pages.

The pages only seemed to contain short, cryptic notes, but he found comfort in the connection to his daughter as he looked at Justine's handwriting. He blinked the tears away that began to well in his eyes and whispered, "I'm going to need you here to get through this, Adam."

He continued to scan each page of notes until he reached the halfway point of the notebook, where Justine's last entry had been recorded. It was dated just two days before Justine had been officially listed as a missing person—a date he would never forget. Closing the notebook, Max decided he needed the walk more than ever. As he went to put the notebook back in the box, something bothered him about the last page.

Reopening the notebook, Max flipped to the last entry and began reading the cryptic notes again. Nothing jumped out at Max until he reread the last entry in the notebook:

"It all fits—Starch."

Max repeated the word "Starch" softly to himself several times. This was definitely the word that bothered him. Putting the notebook down, he leaned back on the couch and scratched his chin again. He knew Justine had not used the word in its traditional sense, but he couldn't remember where or when he'd heard it. After several frustrating minutes, Max got up and retrieved his jacket from behind the door. After descending the stairs, he called out to his chief mechanic, "Rusty, I'll be out for a while. Anything comes up, I've got my phone."

His senior mechanic lifted his head from the engine bay of a car and gave Max a thumbs-up signal before returning to his work. Max walked out of the driveway and decided to head up a side road and around to a small park and picnic area. After his wife's death, Max would sometimes take his still very young daughter to the park to play on the swings. The walk took him twenty minutes, and the fresh air and a chance to stretch his legs improved his mood.

After arriving at the park, he sat on what had been Justine's favorite swing as a young girl. While lost in some happy memories, he suddenly made the connection to the notebook. Standing up, he said the words, "Stacey Archer."

The swing had been the trigger. Justine had many friends, but one of her closest had been Stacey Archer, a friend since childhood. He remembered he had occasionally brought them both to the park and the squeals of delight as he pushed both of them on the swings.

He hurried back down to his garage and became increasingly confident he had made a breakthrough the more he thought about what Justine had written. Since

The Final Proposition

their mid-teens, Justine had always called Stacey "Starch," an abbreviation of her first and last name. Max had not seen Stacey in some time, but he was fairly sure she still lived in Stanwyck. His senior mechanic knew almost everyone in the town. *If anyone knows it will be Rusty.*

After completing the walk back to his garage in half the time it normally took, Max walked back into the workshop and found Rusty still working on the same car. Slightly out of breath, he said, "Hey, Rusty?"

Lifting his head up from deep in the car's engine bay, the red-headed mechanic looked at his boss. "I wasn't sure we'd see you again today. Are you all right?"

Max waved him off. "Long story, I'll fill you in later. Do you know Stacey Archer? Is she still in town?"

The confused mechanic replied, "She still works as a fitness instructor at GymFit, as far as I know?"

Without waiting to hear any more, Max thanked Rusty for the information and headed back upstairs to his office. After closing the door behind him, Max sat down behind his desk and looked up a local business directory. After locating and dialing the number for GymFit, Max held his breath as he waited for his call to be answered.

"GymFit, Anna speaking, can I help you?"

After introducing himself, Max asked if Stacey Archer still worked there.

"She does, would you like to speak with her?"

"I'm not a client, but yes, I would if she's available?"

The phone was silent for almost a minute. Max thought he might have been disconnected and was just about to hang up when a relaxed voice he recognized responded, "This is Stacey."

Max could hardly believe he had tracked Stacey down so quickly. "Stacey, it's Max—Justine's dad."

There was silence on the phone for several seconds before Stacey responded in a more guarded manner. "Hi, Max, what can I do for you?"

Max thought for a moment before he responded. He had not seen Stacey in a long time, and the change in the tone in her voice suggested he needed to be careful about what he said. "Stacey, I've discovered some information that might help find Justine."

"Okay."

"I'm hoping I might be able to talk to you about it when you have a moment?"

"Max, I really don't think I have anything that would help, it's been—"

"I found a diary of sorts that Justine kept right up until when she disappeared. In the last entry, she mentions you."

"Max, I want to help, but this has been very hard for me as well. She was my best friend…"

Sensing her reluctance, Max decided to lay it all on the line. "Stacey, we all want whoever killed her brought to justice. The diary might really help. I just want to ask you a couple of questions. I know you want the same thing as I do."

More silence followed. Finally, Stacey said, "Max, I have to go, I've got a class in five minutes that I need to prepare for."

Max persisted, "I understand, Stacey. Can I meet you after work perhaps? Just tell me what time you get off, and I'll drop by."

"No, not here… Do you have some place quiet at your garage?"

"I have an upstairs office. You can park around the back. No one even needs to know you're here."

The Final Proposition

"My classes finishes at four. I'll come see you then."

Before Max could respond, the line went dead. He wasn't sure what to make of the call. Stacey was reluctant at best, which surprised him. He hoped she would keep her promise and show up for the meeting. He had a feeling she knew a lot more than she was letting on.

Chapter Eleven

The Camaro came over a crest in the road and emerged from the forest into a vista of rolling green farmland. Michael shielded his eyes from the late afternoon sun as he looked up from his book and said, "Hey, Mom, we're out of the forest."

"Yes, Michael, we are."

Adam looked across the sprawling farmland to the hills in the distance. The sun was already low in the sky. He figured they had about half an hour of daylight left. Looking across at Hannah, he asked, "How much further?"

"Not far. Windmere is still twenty minutes, but the farm that Joseph and Tony grew up on is only about fifteen minutes from here."

"Good. Hopefully, we will still have daylight."

Adam had enjoyed the trip so far. Hannah and Michael had proven to be very good company and were helping him to feel normal again. As they had engaged in small talk, he began to realize Hannah was very intelligent. He found her dry sense of humor remarkable considering the issues she was currently dealing with.

The conversation in the car had almost stopped in the last ten minutes, and Adam sensed it had nothing to do with him. Glancing over, Adam could see the tension in Hannah's face. He could only begin to imagine her situation and how difficult it must be to have your future pinned to the faint hope that a large sum of money had gone undiscovered for seven years.

"We'll know soon enough, Hannah, one way or another…"

Hannah nodded and then turned to look out the window. Realizing there was nothing more he could say, Adam returned his gaze to the roadway in front of him. He was enjoying the change of scenery as they drove through the farming district. It prompted him to try and change the subject to take Hannah's mind off what was coming.

"Do you prefer the city or the country?"

"The country. I never lived in the city before I met Joseph."

"So how did you two meet?"

"I used to compete professionally in equestrian events. When I was in my early twenties, one of my favorite horses became lame after an event. My vet suggested Joseph's equine center in North Hartbourne for treatment and rehabilitation. He was really good with horses—very patient and gentle. Our relationship started there, and after we got married, I moved there and helped Joseph manage the center."

"After you and Michael, that was the thing he talked about the most."

"We had a great life. Even though he was twelve years

older than me, it never mattered. Sadly, we had to sell the business after Joseph was arrested to pay all the legal bills…"

They were quiet for a moment until Hannah pointed to a road sign ahead. "We turn off up here to the left."

Adam turned the Camaro onto the narrow lane. They had only gone a short distance before they passed a sign that read "No Through Road."

Hannah could see Adam's puzzled look and said, "This road leads down to a river. The farm Joseph grew up on is the last one on the left."

Adam nodded and drove slowly down the road for a short distance with his eyes fixed on the rearview mirror before pulling off to the side of the road to park.

With a look of confusion, Hannah asked, "Problem?"

Adam managed a smile. "Not really. Just want to make sure we have room to turn around."

Before Hannah had a chance to respond, Adam was out of the car and walking back toward the main road.

Turning to Michael, Hannah said, "Sit tight, sweetie, I'll be back in a minute."

Hannah got out of the car and walked back up to the main road where Adam now stood with his gaze fixed on the section of road they had just traveled.

"Adam?"

Without taking his eyes off the road, Adam replied, "Sorry to be so cryptic, but I didn't want to scare Michael. The no-through road bothers me. If by some chance the money is there, and someone has followed us…"

Adam shifted his gaze momentarily from the road to Hannah. "I'm just being cautious. I don't like the idea of not having an escape route."

The Final Proposition

Hannah looked alarmed, "Do you think we'll need one?"

"I hope not. But this is a huge sum of money, Hannah. If it's still there, who knows? The drug dealers may still be watching you—waiting for you to do something like this."

"Do you think we've been followed?"

With his gaze firmly fixed on the road again, Adam replied, "I don't think so. I haven't seen any cars close behind us, but it was hard to tell when we were in the forest with all the twists and turns in the road. I'm just cautious. Joe wanted me here because he was worried. People don't forget about sums of money like this."

They were silent for another minute before Adam spoke again. "I don't see any cars coming, and the light is fading, so we should get moving."

"Okay."

Adam started to walk back but stopped and looked at Hannah. "When we get back to the car, I'll drive down as far as we need to go and then turn the car around and face it back this way. I'll leave it running, and you can take the driver's seat. Any sign of trouble, hit the horn to warn me and drive off—don't stop. Michael's safety has to be your priority."

Hannah nodded but looked uncertain.

Adam started walking again and said, "We keep it low key in front of Michael—there's no need to alarm him."

"Thank you, Adam. For what it's worth, I'm glad you're here."

Hannah put on a brave face as they approached the car. She could see by the look on Michael's face as he wound down the passenger side window that he was worried.

"Is everything all right, Mom?"

"Yes, Michael. Adam and I were just talking about what we do when we leave here."

Michael didn't look convinced. Hannah had explained about the money and what they had planned before they had started the trip but had not mentioned anything about it being dangerous.

Sensing Michael's anxiety as he got in the car, Adam asked, "You getting hungry, Champ? I know I am. How about we get a burger when we finish here and get to the next town?"

Michael instantly brightened. "Cool. I'm starving."

They all laughed as Adam put the car into gear and drove slowly down the road. Pointing to an old white house further down the lane, Hannah said, "That's the house Joseph grew up in."

It was set back from the road in an overgrown garden, making it hard for Adam to see much of the house's detail in the rapidly fading light. With broken front windows and sections of the roof gutter missing, the house was clearly no longer occupied.

After they had passed the house, he asked, "Are there any other houses?"

"No. There were only ever two houses on this lane, Joseph's old house and the one nearer the main road that the vet used to own."

Adam nodded but said nothing. He was glad he wouldn't have to worry too much about being spotted by neighbors on private property.

As they approached the end of the lane, Hannah said, "We need to stop here. Any further and we won't be able to turn the car around."

Adam slowed the car to a stop and then did a neat

The Final Proposition

three-point maneuver to turn the car around so that it faced back to the main road. Keeping the engine running, he turned to Hannah and said, "Okay, where to from here?"

Hannah pointed to a small, rusted gate in a dilapidated fence that separated the lane from the surrounding farmland.

"Through that gate. According to Joseph, it's about a two-minute walk through those trees. There should be a path that leads up over the ridge and then down to the river. The pump shed is supposed to be close to the river."

Hannah looked increasingly anxious. Adam wasn't sure whether it was the tension of the situation or an issue of trust. As if she had been reading his mind, Hannah said, "I trust you, Adam. Please be careful."

Promising he would, Adam retrieved a flashlight from the Camaro's glove compartment, got out of the car, and walked across to the gate. He turned and looked back briefly at the Camaro. The daylight was fading rapidly, and he could just make out the faces of Hannah and Michael as they sat in the car, watching.

With darkness closing in, he stood still for a moment and listened for any sounds that appeared out of the ordinary. Above the faint sound of running water from the river and the low rumble of the Camaro's engine, he could hear nothing else. As satisfied as he could be, Adam switched on the flashlight and opened the gate. Leaving it ajar, Adam started his walk along the path up through the trees.

Like everything else he had seen so far on the lane, the path was overgrown with weeds and had not been used recently. He followed Hannah's directions and started walking up through the trees but found the path becoming more and more difficult to make out with every step he took. After having to backtrack several times, he began to wonder if it might be better to wait until daylight as he reached the top of the small ridge.

Adam stopped for a moment and noticed the sound of running water was now distinctly louder. He directed the beam of the flashlight up from the path in the direction of the sound. He couldn't see anything beyond the trees and vegetation in front of him and began slowly scanning the terrain ahead in a wide arc. He did a second sweep and noticed one small, almost indiscernible reflection of light. Adam took a few steps forward and held the flashlight steady on the reflection again. He expected to finally see a small glimpse of the river and was relieved to be staring at the metal siding of a small shed instead.

Adam half jogged the remaining distance to the shed and stopped a few paces short to survey the structure in more detail with his flashlight. The shed was made from corrugated iron, and although it was starting to rust in spots, it still looked sturdy. He was relieved to see that none of the knee-high weeds that surrounded the shed or the irrigation pipe that led down to the river had been recently disturbed.

Stepping up to the shed's sturdy wooden door, Adam began working the rusty latch back and forward with one hand while continuing to hold the flashlight in the other. After a minute of patiently working the mechanism, the bolt in the latch finally slid back. Adam paused and looked around into the darkness again before opening the door. He realized he wasn't being overly rational, but knowing that criminals don't normally walk away from such a large sum of money played on his mind.

The Final Proposition

Taking another deep breath, Adam gently pushed on the door and was surprised that it swung easily. Before stepping inside, Adam shone the flashlight into the shed's interior. Apart from the large diesel engine and two drums of oil, he could see nothing else beneath the layers of dust and spiderwebs. Like everything else in the shed, the engine was covered in dust and had clearly not been used recently.

After taking one step inside the shed and sweeping away cobwebs in his path, Adam pointed the flashlight up to the roof. His attention was immediately drawn to four wide wooden planks that straddled the support beams to form a makeshift roof space. He didn't think a man who had been shot and badly wounded would be capable of digging up the floor and burying the money, but he might be capable of throwing a case full of money up onto the rafters out of sight.

The rafters were well above head height, and anything stored there would be hidden, even from a tall man like Adam. Grabbing hold of one of the oil drums, he moved it into the middle of the shed to stand on.

Steadying himself as he climbed onto the drum, Adam stood up and pointed the flashlight into the roof space. In the semi-darkness, he carefully ran the beam back and forth across the top of the planks, hoping to see a bag or case used to store the money in. The first scan showed nothing. As his gut muscles tightened, he repeated his scan, this time more slowly. With the beam of the flashlight reflecting off the cobwebs, it was difficult to see clearly.

Reaching forward, he brushed away the cobwebs that were within arm's reach and scanned a third time. The search yielded nothing, and even though he had never really expected to find the money, Adam felt let down and was surprised by his level of disappointment.

As he stepped down off the drum, he knew his disappointment was mostly for Hannah. He started thinking about what he would say to her as he looked around the shed again for any other possible hiding place he had missed. So far, happiness as a free man was proving elusive—his first day taken up attending a funeral and his second day dashing the hopes of a woman desperate to save her son's life.

With a heavy sigh, Adam stepped to the doorway. He would use the walk back to figure out what to say to Hannah. As he scanned the interior of the shed again, he knew he was now stalling for time. As he played the beam over the rafters again, he paused and then swept the beam back. Intrigued by a subtle, almost indiscernible change in the way the beam reflected its shadow across two of the planks in the far corner of the shed, Adam walked around the diesel motor and stood directly below the beams.

He pointed the flashlight beam up between the two planks again and began moving the beam slightly, backward and forward, over the spot. The scan revealed nothing. Puzzled, Adam returned to the doorway and played the beam back over the same spot again. He was again rewarded with the smallest hint of a deviation in the shadow.

Adam returned to standing in the same position and looked up again. This was the furthest point away from where he had checked the roof space when he had stood on the oil drum. Had he missed something in the dust and cobwebs? He debated using the oil drum to take a closer look, but it was still half full of oil and too heavy to lift over the diesel engine without draining it first. Searching the shed for something else that might be able to help him, he found an oil-stained wooden measuring stick next to the other oil drum.

Adam grabbed the stick and used it to push upward against the bottom of the first plank. To his surprise, the plank wasn't nailed down and moved easily. Continuing to gently lift and move the plank forward, he quickly separated the plank from the other three until he had made a sizeable gap.

Moving his flashlight across the opening, Adam could see the outline of something square resting across the top of the rafters. Encouraged, he pushed the stick up gently at the object and was rewarded as it moved slightly. Adam quickly went back to work on the first plank and, using the stick, moved the plank further forward until the object was clearly visible. He carefully moved the stick back underneath the object and began to inch it forward off the plank.

Without warning, the object slid off the plank amid a cloud of dust and brushed the side of Adam's face as it crashed to the ground below him. Holding his breath, he swung the beam of the flashlight to the ground next to his feet. Even though the object was covered in a thick layer of cobwebs and dust, it was instantly recognizable as a slimline attache case.

Adam picked up the case and gently shook it to confirm it wasn't empty before laying it on top of the drum. After retrieving an oil-stained cloth from the top of the diesel motor, he carefully began wiping away the cobwebs, dust, and grime. As he cleaned the case down, he hoped the contents of the expensive leather case would change Michael's and Hannah's lives forever. Satisfied with his cleaning work, he opened the two locks one by one. As he went to open the case, he paused. It didn't seem right for Hannah not to know what was in the case first and whether her life was about to change or not. He decided that, money or no money, she should be the first one to see inside.

With his decision made, he closed the locks and put the case under his arm. After stepping outside, he gently pulled the door closed and slid the bolt back into place. He could still faintly hear the sound of the Camaro's engine idling in the distance as he turned and started his walk back up the path.

Chapter Twelve

After briefly venturing back out into the workshop, Max returned to his office to wait for Stacey. He had no idea what to expect from the conversation or even if she would show.

Max checked his watch regularly. Waiting was something he was never good at, and today it was torture. After an hour, he began to doubt Stacey would come. Deciding he needed to get out of the office for a while, Max got up from his chair. He went to move out from behind his desk but paused as he heard the sound of footsteps on the stairway leading up to his office. He had three mechanics working for him, and over the years, he had become familiar with their individual footfalls. He knew which mechanic was coming to see him long before they ever got to his office. The footsteps he heard today were unfamiliar —much lighter and measured.

He sat back down and watched as a slim woman in her late twenties with shoulder-length brown hair tied off in a ponytail appeared in the doorway to his office.

"Hi, Max."

"Hi, Stacey, thanks for coming."

Still dressed in her aerobic workout gear, Stacey Archer made her way into the office and sat on Max's old couch.

"You look well, Stacey."

Stacey managed half a smile as she replied, "Thanks, Max, the job keeps me trim, so I can't complain."

"I've got something to show you."

Without waiting for a reply, Max came around from behind his desk and handed Stacey the notebook as he sat down beside her.

"This is the diary I mentioned on the phone."

Stacey's face turned grim as she opened the notebook and began scanning the pages.

In a softly spoken voice, she said, "It's definitely Justine. She had the neatest writing of all of us during school."

Max gently encouraged her to go to the last entry. "The reference to you is about halfway through the notebook on the last page she wrote on."

Stacey slowly turned the pages, almost as if she was trying to delay what was coming. Max watched as she came to the middle of the notebook and started reading. As tears began to form in her eyes, she closed the notebook and handed it back to Max.

Max put an arm around Stacey, and they sat in silence for several minutes. He sensed she would open up when she was ready and decided to hold off on any questions.

Finally, Stacey wiped her eyes and said, "Just after Adam was arrested, she rang me to talk about it. We both knew he was innocent—he was just in the wrong place at the wrong time. At first, we thought it was the boyfriend.

The Final Proposition

She started following him but quickly dismissed him as a suspect. He was a mess, drunk most of the time, and, according to Justine, clearly distraught and in mourning."

Stacey shifted slightly on the couch and continued in a voice barely above a whisper, "We met for coffee several times after that. She told me she had started tracking someone else. She wouldn't say who, only that she was gathering evidence to take to the police. I told her to be careful…"

More silence followed before Max replied, "I knew about the boyfriend but no one else. Who do you think she was following?"

"The night that she made that last entry, she rang me and told me she had enough information to take to the police. She said she had proof of a payoff that was keeping Adam in jail."

"I asked her who it was, and when she told me, I said, 'it all fits.'"

Biting her bottom lip as tears began to stream down her face again, she said, "Justine had been following Jerry Lennox, the boyfriend's father."

"So Jerry Lennox was paying somebody off to keep his son out of jail?"

Stacey shook her head as she closed her eyes. "When I was in my last year of high school, I worked part-time at the Aquatic Centre. One night, the night manager became violently ill and went home early. He asked me to close up, and I said okay. Jerry Lennox came by just as I was closing up to pick up the cash drawer. He was the owner and didn't want any money left there overnight… I said good night and went to leave, and he asked me to come into the manager's office for a minute… He locked the door and…raped me."

Max sat in stunned silence. He had no idea what to expect from the meeting, but this was the last thing he expected.

"I'm so sorry, Stacey, I had no idea."

"You weren't to know, Max. I never told anyone... When he finished, he told me my dad was a good employee and he hoped he wouldn't have to fire him over any 'misunderstanding' as he called it."

Shaking his head, Max said, "He threatened to fire your father if you reported what happened?"

Wiping the tears from her eyes, Stacey nodded. "Dad was a recovering alcoholic and had struggled to find work. He got a job as a forklift driver at Lennox Timber and Hardware a few months before it happened. He was happy there and getting his life back together..."

"The bastard knew you wouldn't say anything and took advantage of you."

"I left Stanwyck as soon as I finished high school and moved to Hartbourne. I completed my studies and was happy enough working there. I only came back two years ago, after I heard Lennox had almost died from a stroke and wasn't expected to recover. I figured he couldn't hurt me anymore and I was safe."

"You never told the police?"

"Justine was the only one that ever knew. When she called that night and told me she thought it was Jerry Lennox who raped and murdered the girl, that's when I told her. Jerry Lennox owned half of Stanwyck, so I'm sure I wasn't the only one he raped."

"Stacey, I don't know what to say. I'm so sorry."

"Thank you, Max. I was really worried about Justine. I told her to be really careful. When you rang after she disappeared to ask if I'd seen her, I feared the worst. I hoped for months that she would turn up one day, that she had just been in hiding."

"You never told anyone else?"

Stacey stood and placed a business card with her contact details on his desk before walking to the door. She looked back, held Max's gaze, and said, "I was afraid Max. I didn't want Lennox to hurt me again. Justine mentioned two men but never let on who the other man was. I didn't know who I could trust, so I said nothing. I'm sorry."

Max barely heard Stacey's footfalls on the stairs as she left his office. He sat alone in his office for a long time, thinking through everything Stacey had told him and contemplating what he should do next.

After an hour of sitting on the couch and staring at nothing, Max decided he would call Stacey the following day to see if there was anything he could do to help. He thought again about what Jerry Lennox had done to her. In spite of Stanwyck only having a population of forty thousand, he could only remember a handful of occasions where he had actually spoken to Lennox. He remembered Lennox as a short, lean man with wavy dark hair and an arrogant and dismissive attitude. Although he didn't like him, Max had never considered him capable of rape and murder.

His thoughts returned to his daughter. If Jerry Lennox had raped and murdered his own son's girlfriend, had he done the same to Justine as well? Shaking his head, Max tried to dismiss the thought. He picked up Justine's notebook to return it to the box and stared down at the photographs again. Selecting several from the top of the pile, he studied the photographs in more detail. It was clear one man had dark hair and the other had lighter, perhaps even gray, hair. The man with the dark hair was possibly Lennox, but the image quality was too poor to be sure.

He placed all but one of the photographs back in the box. The photograph he held on to had been taken at night and showed the two men in front of a building. Max racked his brain to think of a building in Stanwyck that had distinctive columns like those in the photo. He knew every building on the main street and the surrounding commercial district, and none of them were remotely close. There were a number of wineries in the area that he had not visited, perhaps it was one of them?

Frustrated and feeling no more could be accomplished now, Max decided to take off early and leave Rusty to close up. He had half a bottle of malt whiskey at home left over from his last birthday and a steak in the fridge. After the day he'd had, he couldn't think of two better companions to share the evening with. After putting on his coat and picking up the box, he headed back down to the workshop area.

"Hey, Rusty, you mind closing up for me? I've got a lot on my mind and want to get out of here early."

His lead mechanic replied, "No problem, boss—see you Monday?" Rusty prepared to lower a car on a hoist.

Max had almost forgotten it was Friday. They usually didn't work on Saturday unless they had a backlog of work.

"Yeah, see you Monday."

Chapter Thirteen

The drive out of town to his small farm normally took Max ten minutes. Today's trip would take almost double that time—Max had a habit of driving slow when he was thinking. He found it hard to think about anything other than the image of Stacey Archer as she sat in his office and shared the nightmare she endured as a seventeen-year-old girl.

Max shook his head and did his best to shut the image out of his mind and focus his thoughts on Jerry Lennox. After what he had learned today, he was almost certain Lennox was one of the two men in each of Justine's photos. He wondered again who the other man in the photos might be. *It had to be a senior cop.* Someone who could influence the arrest and prosecution. He decided he would call Adam tonight and tell him what he had learned.

After rounding a sweeping bend that marked the halfway point of his trip home, Max suddenly applied the brakes and pulled his truck to a halt on the graveled edge of the road. Twisting in his seat, he looked back across the road at a large southern colonial-style house on acreage that he just passed. The imposing two-story white house was set well back from the road amidst a large, manicured mature garden. The tree-lined driveway that led down to the house obscured much of Max's view. After checking his rearview mirror, he put his truck in reverse and backed up along the road until he was adjacent to the house's commanding sandstone entrance.

While Max still could not see the entire house through the trees, he could see the one area that intrigued him most —the front entrance. The house had a wide slate roof that extended well over the front of the building to provide a large covered entranceway and verandah. Max stared at the entry area and focused on the support columns. Although the columns were not unusual, he was almost positive he had seen them recently. Reaching into the pocket on the front of his overalls, he withdrew the photograph Justine had taken of the two men in front of a building at night. He held the photograph up at eye level and compared the columns in the photo to those on the house in front of him.

"I'll be damned."

From his current roadside position, he was still not certain the support columns on this house were the ones in the photo, but they looked very close. He thought about the possibility of there being another house with this kind of column somewhere else in Stanwyck. It seemed unlikely, and as he sat there with the engine running, he debated what to do. He knew the house belonged to the retired judge Simpson Hanley. In his early seventies, Hanley apparently only lived there part of the year and spent much of each year holidaying in Europe.

The Final Proposition

Max recalled speaking to Jonas Small, the judge's part-time gardener and handyman, just a few days ago. According to Jonas, Hanley was currently in Europe on another holiday. Max felt sorry for Jonas. Unlike his name, Jonas was a huge man with a below average IQ due to complications at birth. Jonas had been in Max's garage looking for work and in despair because the judge wasn't paying him regularly as agreed. He was not surprised. Since Hanley's retirement, he had built a reputation as a heavy-drinking womanizer who was not to be trusted.

Max was fairly sure he knew no one else worked here while the judge was away. After slipping the photo back into his top pocket, he put the truck into gear and drove in slowly through the front gate. From the perspective in the photo, he was fairly sure the photo had been taken from the cover of a large fruit orchard that ran down the right-hand side of the property.

Max slowly cruised down the driveway, keeping a watchful eye on the house for any sign of its occupants. He pulled the truck to a halt halfway down the driveway and decided he didn't need to drive any further. After parking the truck, he walked across the wide manicured lawn and scaled a waist-high fence to enter the orchard.

He removed the photo from his pocket again and held it up to compare the perspective of the columns in the photo with where he stood. Although his position wasn't quite right, he was certain he had the right location. He moved down through the fruit trees another twenty steps and held up the photo again for another comparison. The position he now stood in was a very close match to the photo but still not quite right. Max walked another five steps toward the center of the orchard and stood beside a large peach tree.

He held up the photo for the third time and gasped as the visual perspective of the columns on the house were now an almost perfect match with the photo. Rather than feeling elated with his discovery, Max felt sick in the stomach as he realized this was one of the last places his daughter had stood before her disappearance.

Max shook his head as a thousand thoughts began to race through his mind—now was not the time to speculate. His truck was still visible from the road, and he realized he needed to keep moving if he was to avoid being spotted. After making his way back to the truck, Max debated whether to do a three-point turn or drive down to the front of the house and turn around in the large circular driveway.

After mumbling "screw it," Max put the truck in gear and made his way down the driveway to the front of the house. Max was amazed at the size of the house. It looked imposing from the road but even more so up close. He had no idea what it was worth, but well over a million was his conservative estimate. No one emerged from the house when he pulled up in his truck, and after checking that all the curtains across the front of the house were drawn, he was reasonably confident no one was home.

He relaxed a little and pulled the photo out of his top pocket again to better understand where Lennox and the other man, who he now felt sure was the judge, stood on the night they were photographed.

He decided it was safe to take a quick look around, got out of the truck, and walked up onto the marble-covered entryway. He stood between the austere marble columns where the two men were photographed and

The Final Proposition

wondered what they were discussing on the night Justine had taken the photograph. He was certain it was connected to Adam's arrest and looked to him increasingly like a payoff.

He was startled by the sudden sound of the front door opening and turned to see a very agitated and overweight man standing in the doorway, glaring at him.

In a cultured and measured voice, the man said, "You're on private property. You better have a good explanation, or I'm calling the police."

Surprised by Simpson Hanley's sudden appearance, Max thought for a moment before he responded.

"I'd be happy if you called the police, Judge. I have a photo taken by my daughter of you and Jerry Lennox right here on this very porch—two days before her disappearance. I also have her diary. Seems like you and Lennox had a lot of meetings around that time. Why is that?"

Max watched as the glare on the retired judge's face momentarily turned to surprise. The judge recovered quickly, and as the glare returned, he said, "I've no idea what you're talking about, now get off my property."

Max turned to leave but decided to push a little further. Holding the photo up, he said, "This isn't the only one, Judge. I've got more cozy snaps of you and Jerry."

Max paused for a second and looked up to admire the house. "Did Jerry pay for this, Judge? Keeping him out of jail and Adam Wells in jail, was that…"

Hanley exploded in rage, "Get off my land now! I'm going to sue you for every cent you own and shut down that worthless garage of yours in the process."

Max turned and walked back to the truck. After

opening the truck's door, he looked back at the judge who continued to stare him down.

"It's not over, Judge. I intend to get justice for my daughter's murder. I promise you, if you're involved, you'll pay."

After retreating back inside his house, Hanley quickly waddled into his office and pulled back the curtains just in time to see Max's truck disappear out his front gates and back onto the road. Satisfied the mechanic had gone, he walked over to his desk and picked up a telephone. After dialing a number from memory, he waited for the connection. He listened to the voice mail greeting and then uttered three words, "Call me immediately," before disconnecting.

Chapter Fourteen

The walk back to the Camaro seemed to take Adam no time at all. He was both excited and anxious as he thought about what was in the case and used the time to rehearse what he would say to Hannah if the case didn't contain the money. After walking through the gate and back onto the lane, he was relieved to see the faint outline of Hannah and Michael still sitting in the car, watching him through the darkness. Before he was halfway across the lane, Hannah was out of the car.

"You have it?"

"I have a filthy attache case that's been hidden in the shed for a long time. I don't know what's in it."

"You haven't checked?"

"It didn't feel right. I wanted to wait for you."

As they walked to the Camaro, Hannah replied, "Thank you, Adam. Let's open it in front of Michael. We've been talking about it while you were gone. When we saw you carrying something back, we both got excited."

Adam paused before opening the door and said, "There are no guarantees, Hannah. The case contains something, but it may not be money."

Hannah replied, "I know. I've already told Michael not to get his hopes up too much."

Adam opened his door and said, "Hey, Champ, sorry I took so long."

Michael replied, "Was it scary? It's way dark out there now."

"Not too scary, I'm used to the dark."

After settling into the car, Adam handed the case to Hannah, who rested it on her lap. Michael leaned forward between the two front seats and said excitedly, "Open it, Mom."

Adam held the flashlight steady on the case for Hannah and watched as she rested her fingers on the locks.

She said, "I'm a little scared," and popped the locks. Letting out a deep breath, Hannah slowly opened the case. As she began to sob, Michael exclaimed, "Wow."

Letting out a deep breath as he looked at the neat, tightly packed bundles of hundred-dollar bills, Adam thought of Joseph and his wish to see Michael well again. The money was no guarantee of a cure, but hope was still alive.

The short trip into Windmere bordered on surreal for Adam. Michael's excitement about finding the money was short-lived as his focus quickly turned to hamburgers and the fact that he was hungry. Hannah seemed lost for words and a million miles away, which didn't surprise Adam.

He had politely listened to Michael's chatter and engaged in conversation about their favorite hamburgers, while he watched Hannah. He had tried to put himself in her shoes and began to realize she was probably in shock or overwhelmed or both.

Living day by day with the knowledge that the next seizure your son had could kill him must be almost impossible. He tried to understand the emotions she must be feeling now as she realized there was real hope for Michael.

After stopping in the small township of Windmere for hamburgers at the only diner still open after seven p.m., Adam and Hannah quietly decided to press on with the three-hour drive to Bolton. Neither of them liked the idea of spending any more time on the road than was needed with so much money in their possession.

While they had not counted the money yet, Adam had done some quick estimates in his head based on the number of bundles of cash he had seen in the case. He had concluded that the original figure of three million dollars Joseph had mentioned was probably right. Hannah had phoned her sister and told her they would be arriving around midnight with an extra visitor who would need a bed for the night.

After they got back in the Camaro for the three-hour drive, Adam said to Michael, "Hey, Champ, how good was that burger?"

"It was awesome, Adam. Did you enjoy yours?"

They all laughed as Adam replied, "Best burger I've had in seven years."

Michael was in good spirits, and now that it was dark and he could no longer read, he kept Hannah and Adam busy with conversation as they headed out of town and past a sign that pointed them to Bolton. Adam felt relieved that they were finally on the road again. He wouldn't relax until Michael and Hannah were safely in a city again and the money had been deposited in a bank.

They were barely five minutes into their journey when the conversation from Michael suddenly stopped. Hannah turned around to look at her son in the back and said in an urgent voice, "Michael?"

When he did not respond, Hannah grabbed Adam's arm and said, "Pull over, Adam, he's having another seizure."

Chapter Fifteen

Concealed amidst a clump of fir trees in a secluded position above the mechanic's house, the man checked his watch again. It was now almost two hours since the mechanic had switched off the last light in his house. If he followed normal sleep patterns and had taken fifteen to twenty minutes to drift off, he figured he should be in the REM or deep sleep cycle by now. If he found sleep difficult, there was always a chance he could still be awake. The man checked the safety on his gun again before sliding it into the inner top pocket of his jacket. He was hopeful he wouldn't need to use it tonight, but he had done this often enough to know that you planned for every possible outcome.

He felt as confident as he could about the task ahead of him as he sat in his dark gray SUV. The mechanic's house was set well back from the road with no close neighbors. He did one last sweep of the area with his night scope and was confident no one else would see him come or go. He reached across to the passenger seat and checked the contents of the bag again—more out of habit than necessity. Satisfied that everything was in order, he switched the interior light setting of his vehicle to the off position and opened the door. He stood in the darkness, looked up at the half moon, and debated whether to use the night scope or not. The scope would give him additional visibility on the trail down to the house but would be useless after that and just another thing he would need to worry about.

As a professional, his golden rule was to never take more than was absolutely necessary. After reviewing the plan in his head one last time, he left the scope on the seat and gently closed the vehicle door. If all went well, he would be back here and on his way well inside ten minutes and fifty thousand dollars richer.

The man moved steadily down through the sparse trees and undergrowth toward the back of the mechanic's house. Years of practice had made his footfalls careful and almost silent. The precision of his movement brought him to the back fence of the man's property without breaking the stillness of the night. He silently climbed over the back fence, thankful the mechanic didn't keep dogs. While his finely honed skills would allow him to avoid detection from all but the most alert humans, dogs were an entirely different proposition. The man had no problem killing humans, but dogs were another matter entirely.

He had driven around the service road earlier in the day to plan the job. The two-story timber house had a semi-enclosed wooden front porch that was ideal for his purposes. He crept silently around the side of the house, pausing regularly to listen for any sounds that would signal the occupant was awake. He heard no sound that would signal caution, and after several patient minutes, he reached his destination.

He stood in the darkness on the front porch and carefully withdrew a pair of stained work overalls from his bag. They were about the size that the mechanic wore and contained enough oil and grease to make them reasonably flammable. Balling the overalls up loosely, he wedged them against the front timber fascia of the house behind a large ornamental pot. He carefully adjusted the overalls so they were slightly above ground level to allow enough room for oxygen to circulate. After withdrawing a cigarette lighter from his bag, he spun the lighter's flint wheel with a practiced movement of his thumb. After the lighter came to life, he moved the small blue flame over the base of the overalls for just a few seconds and smiled as the fabric ignited and began to burn.

The man quickly retreated from the porch back into the darkness of the yard and watched for another thirty seconds. Even though his list of credits included professional arsonist, the man still marveled at how little time it took for a fire to take hold in the right conditions. He continued to watch as the flames spread across the front timber fascia until they reached the porch ceiling. The house was almost beyond saving already as large, dark plumes of smoke started to spread out beyond the porch.

Satisfied that his work was complete, he retraced his steps to the rear of the property. He paused after climbing over the back fence and looked back briefly at the house which was now silhouetted by an orange and yellow hue. As the flames became visible above the roof line, he knew nothing short of a miracle would save its occupant now. He would have given anything to stay and watch, but as the fire started to light up the night sky, he knew that was too risky and quickly made his way back up the trail and out of sight.

After going to bed shortly after eleven p.m., Max tossed and turned as sleep eluded him. It was neither the steak nor the malt whiskey that kept him awake but everything he had learned that day about Justine's photographs. He had tried calling Adam to discuss what he now knew, but Adam hadn't answered his phone call. He thought about his encounter with Hanley again as he lay staring at the ceiling.

Even though he had been angry and taken by surprise, he realized now it had been foolish to let the judge know about the photographs. He would need to keep his emotions in check and be far more careful about what he said in the future. He was determined to see those responsible for his Justine's murder brought to justice and was now convinced Judge Hanley was involved.

He checked his bedside clock—it was shortly after one a.m., and he needed to urinate. Without bothering to turn on a light, he got out of bed and trudged across the upstairs landing and into the bathroom. While he stood relieving himself, he made a mental note to go downstairs and turn off the porch light which he had left switched on. After finishing up in the bathroom, he paused and inhaled deeply. He could almost swear he smelled smoke. He would need to check he had switched off all the cooking appliances as well.

He walked out of the bathroom and stopped when he reached the landing. In an instant, it all made sense. The light from the porch was much brighter now and increasing in magnitude with every passing second. Realizing his house was on fire, Max quickly descended the stairs. He barely made it to the bottom landing before the flames took hold on the inside of his house.

Momentarily transfixed, he watched as the curtains in the front room erupted in flames and the front entrance transformed into a wall of fire. He looked around through the rapidly descending smoke haze as best he could but could see no safe way out. Shielding his face from the now searing heat, he quickly retreated back upstairs to the top landing.

Max knew very little about fires but figured he had less than a minute before the top floor would be engulfed as well. The upper floor started to quickly heat, and the bottom of the staircase had already caught on fire. He knew he needed to get out now before he succumbed to the smoke which was now becoming thick on the upper floor as well.

He walked quickly back through his bedroom and out onto a small balcony at the back of the house. He coughed and gulped in fresh air and then looked left and right. He was surprised to see the entire back of the house was already on fire as well. In the moment it had taken him to scan left and right, the wooden floorboards on the small porch on which he stood caught fire. Feeling slightly disorientated by the smoke and oppressive heat, Max knew he would be dead within a minute if he didn't move now. As he felt his skin begin to burn, he clambered over the burning balcony rail and jumped without a second thought.

Landing heavily on a garden bed below the balcony, he groaned as a sharp pain shot up his left leg. He realized he was still in a vulnerable position below the burning balcony and rolled out of the garden bed and onto the lawn area.

The pain began to ease in his left leg as he looked up with despair at the house that he had built almost twenty-five years ago. As the fire roared and the flames rose high into the night sky, Max stared in disbelief. The house that he had spent two years building for his family would be gone within minutes. The heat from the fire continued to build as the fire fed on the wooden structure and its contents. Forced further away by the searing heat, Max turned to shield his face from the furnace. He hobbled toward the back fence but stopped and looked up when he heard the sound of a large vehicle starting.

Max's despair turned to rage as he located the source of the sound. Staring up into the small forest area above his property, he watched as a vehicle, illuminated by the glow of the fire, sped away on a narrow fire trail.

Chapter Sixteen

Adam shifted his position on the narrow couch again but couldn't get comfortable. While he never wanted to return to prison, he would have gladly traded the lumpy motel couch for his old prison bunk bed. He checked his watch and was surprised that he had slept this long—it was almost seven thirty. He sat up and yawned before looking across the small, drab room to the bed where Hannah and Michael lay sleeping.

It had been a rough night for everyone. The high they had from finding the money was soon forgotten as Hannah had to deal with another of Michael's seizures. Neither Hannah nor Adam had wanted to continue driving until he was stable, and they decided to stay in Windmere overnight to let Michael recover. With a population just slightly under one thousand, their options were limited. The only hotel in town was permanently booked out by a mining company, and they were forced to stay in a rundown six-room motel several minutes' drive out of the township. Adam had planned on booking two rooms, but Hannah asked Adam to share a room with her and Michael.

Adam wasn't sure whether Hannah's request was because she was nervous about having so much money in her possession or to help with Michael. She had a lot on her mind, and he couldn't blame her either way and agreed to her request. The night had been exhausting for them all as Michael had another two seizures during the early hours of the morning.

Deciding any more sleep on the lumpy couch would be impossible, he got up and began stretching his back muscles.

A voice whispered, "How did you sleep?"

Adam looked down at the bed to see Hannah looking up at him. Before he had a chance to respond, Hannah continued, "It was awful, wasn't it?"

Shrugging his shoulders, Adam replied, "I've slept on worse."

Hannah smiled and softly said, "You're a terrible liar, Adam, but I appreciate you staying with us last night."

"How is he doing?"

Hannah turned her head slightly and looked at Michael. He was sleeping soundly and peacefully and looked like any other nine-year-old boy.

"I can't remember a worse night. His seizures are getting worse and a lot more frequent."

"If you want to stay here another day to let him rest, that's okay with me."

Hannah replied, "Thank you, Adam, but I would like to get going as soon as he wakes up. He can sleep in the car if he needs to."

Adam nodded his agreement but said nothing. Hannah gently edged herself out of bed to avoid waking

Michael and then said, "I need a shower and a change of clothes."

Adam replied, "Are you hungry?"

While grabbing some fresh clothes from her small suitcase, she replied, "A little, but what I really need is a cup of coffee."

"How about I go and get us some breakfast from in town while you're in the shower? I need to ring Max and my lawyer, and there's no reception here."

"That would be fantastic, Adam, thank you."

As he headed for the door, Hannah called out, "Adam."

He turned around to see Hannah holding out the attache case full of money. "I would feel better if you take this with you. I don't want to leave it around here while I'm taking a shower and Michael is sleeping."

Adam was slightly stunned. He had barely known Hannah for more than twenty-four hours, and yet she was entrusting him with three million dollars and her son's future. As if reading his mind, she said, "I trust you, Adam. If you were going to run off with the money, you would be long gone by now, and there would be absolutely nothing I could do to stop you."

Struggling to find adequate words to respond, he replied, "I'll take good care of it." Looking down at Michael, he continued, "Can I get a burger for Michael? I'm sure he'll be hungry when he wakes up."

With half a frown, Hannah replied, "Hamburgers are not part of his normal dietary routine, particularly for breakfast. But this is kind of an adventure for him so... Sure, why not?"

After opening the door, attache case in hand, he

looked back and said, "I won't let it out of my sight, Hannah, I promise."

Hannah nodded and said, "Don't forget my coffee, white with one." With that, she turned, walked into the tiny bathroom, and shut the door.

The short drive back into Windmere gave Adam a chance to think. It had been an intense twenty-four hours. Adam looked across at the attache case on the front passenger seat of the Camaro and shook his head. Who gives you three million dollars to mind while they take a shower? He knew he was forming a strong friendship with Hannah, but the level of trust she was now showing in him was hard to comprehend. He thought about Michael and instantly felt strong emotions. He was a bright and extremely likable young boy who fully understood his condition. Hannah had not hidden anything from him, and Adam had to admire Michael's courage and sense of humor in spite of his situation.

As he drove into the small main street that boasted no more than a dozen single-story buildings on each side of the street, he was surprised by how quiet it seemed for a Saturday morning. He parked the Camaro in front of the same diner they had bought their burgers from the night before and then looked up and down the street. Apart from three parked cars and one dog scavenging scraps from a bin, he could see no signs of life, other than a few people eating breakfast in the diner.

He debated taking the attache case into the diner with him but thought that would only draw unnecessary attention. He would have a good enough view of the car while he was inside ordering their breakfast, and after stowing the case under the front seat, he decided that it would be safe enough with the car locked.

After walking into the diner and ordering their breakfast, he stepped outside again to get some fresh air while he made his phone calls. He looked up and down the small street again and still saw no one—even the dog seemed to have disappeared. Satisfied that he had privacy, he leaned on the Camaro and dialed his lawyer.

Aaron Winter answered on the second ring. "Adam, I've been trying to reach you. Where the hell are you?"

Adam was not overly surprised by his lawyer's opening question, which was typical of his controlling personality. He would be glad when this was all over and he didn't have to deal with him anymore.

"I'm in a small town called Windmere, the phone reception here isn't great."

Not wanting to answer any further questions, he said, "Do we have any progress?"

Winter ignored the question and pressed Adam, "What on earth are you doing in Windmere? That's the middle of nowhere."

Adam felt his patience wearing thin very quickly. "I'm helping a friend and don't want to talk about it. I don't plan on calling you again until Monday unless there have been any developments."

"You got more press on Friday than I expected. Lawyers for the government are monitoring the situation, and if it looks like it's going to take off as a media story, we might get an offer sooner rather than later. I've been working a couple of journalist friends over trying to get them to help. Right now, if there are no new major news stories over the weekend to steal the headlines, we may be able to build some momentum next week."

Adam thought for a moment before he responded. He hadn't been following the news and didn't know whether to believe Winter or not. It didn't sound as though much progress had been made. He had checked in with his lawyer as requested and didn't feel there was any point progressing the conversation further.

"I'll be back in Stanwyck on Monday, I'll call you then for an update."

Adam went to hang up, but Winter wanted to keep the conversation going.

"Hey, Adam, it's important that I can reach you over the weekend. I need to…"

Becoming impatient, Adam cut him off. "Aaron, I don't mean to be rude, but it doesn't sound like you've made much progress, and I need to go. I'll call you Monday. If anything urgent comes up in the meantime, ring me back, and if I'm out of range, leave me a message and I'll call you as soon as I can."

Without waiting for a reply, he disconnected and shook his head as he began dialing Max's number. Max often used to work in his garage on Saturdays, and he half expected the call to go through to his message service. The voice that greeted him was strained and croaky and barely recognizable as Max.

"I was wondering when you'd call…"

"Max, are you okay?"

There was a long pause on the phone before Max answered in a weary voice, "How soon will you be back, Adam?"

Sensing something was wrong, he replied, "I hope to

be back tomorrow. Max, what's happened, you don't sound yourself?"

"My house burned down last night, Adam. I'm lucky to be alive."

Max went on to explain what happened and how he had been lucky to escape with just a sprained ankle and some minor burns to his hands and face. While Max's description of what happened was detailed, he hadn't answered the one question that concerned Adam the most.

"Max, was it deliberate?"

There was a slight pause before Max replied, "I know who killed her, Adam. What happened last night has made me pretty jumpy. I don't want to talk about it over the phone, it can wait until you get back."

Adam wanted to press Max for all the details but understood his reluctance. "Okay, I'll be back tomorrow, you can fill me in then."

Adam was about to fill Max in on the road trip with Hannah and Michael but was interrupted by the sound of someone knocking on the glass window of the diner. Looking up, he saw the short order cook standing inside the front door of the diner, signaling that his order was ready. Adam realized he had spent far longer on the phone calls than he had planned.

"Max, I have to go, but I'll call you tonight. Where are you staying?"

"I'm going to stay at the garage. I'll sleep on the couch for a couple of nights and figure out what to do when you get back. We're both homeless as of now."

"Max, perhaps you should be staying somewhere less obvious? If someone's after you, that's the first place they'll look."

"The garage has smoke alarms and security cameras. To be honest, Adam, I feel safer there than anywhere else. Besides, I'm not leaving Stanwyck, and they'll find me sooner or later if they really want to."

Realizing Max was probably right, Adam ended the call with a promise to call Max that night to see how his day went. He replayed the conversation over in his mind and was fairly sure Max must have made a significant breakthrough on his own if someone wanted to burn his house down. He frowned as he walked back to the diner to collect his order. Whoever was behind this had a lot to lose if they were prepared to go to this much trouble to get rid of his friend.

The short drive back to the motel seemed to pass in seconds as Adam tried to take stock of everything that had happened in the last two days. He had expected life on the outside to be different to prison but nothing like what he was currently experiencing. A car trip to Bolton with a child who was extremely sick, finding three million dollars, and now his friend almost being murdered made life on the outside seem surreal.

Adam drove through the front entrance of the small motel complex and parked in front of their motel room. As he got out of the Camaro, he noticed the front door to their motel room was slightly ajar. His gut muscles tightened slightly as he looked left and right for any sign of Hannah or Michael. Seeing no one, he called out, "Hannah? Michael?"

After being greeted with silence, Adam locked the car and cautiously walked to the door of the motel room. The door moved slightly in the breeze, and Adam sensed something was wrong. He called their names again, this time with more urgency. "Hannah, Michael?"

When no one answered, he pushed the front door open and stood in the doorway, looking into the small motel room that was now empty. The bed was unmade, and Hannah's and Michael's bags were in exactly the same position as they had been twenty minutes earlier when he had left to get breakfast. The bathroom door was shut and his last hope.

He walked quickly to the door and knocked quietly. When no response came, he opened the door and stepped inside. The room was still steamy with condensation from Hannah's shower. Adam's focus was drawn to the shower curtain, which blocked his view of the shower stall. Holding his breath, Adam drew back the shower curtain. The stall was empty.

Adam had never panicked in his life, even when he had been arrested and charged with murder. After walking out of the bathroom and back into the motel room, he forced himself to breathe deeply. He hoped he was simply overreacting—surely there was a logical explanation?

After unsuccessfully searching the room for clues, Adam quickly went through the motions of checking outside of the motel before asking the manager if he had seen any sign of his companions. The stunned manager had not seen or heard anything and demanded room payment immediately. After paying in cash, Adam returned to the room and made a careful final search for anything that might help him understand what had happened. Finding nothing, he repacked Hannah's and Michael's bags while he contemplated his next move.

After stowing everything back in the Camaro, he came back into the motel room and sat on the bed. He quickly discounted the possibility that they had simply gone for a walk. After the night Michael had, he would need rest and care today—nothing strenuous. Adam let out a deep breath as he accepted the probability that they had been taken against their will. He knew this was about the money. Joseph had been right to be cautious. His thoughts returned to that moment in the cell when he said no to Joseph's request and silently made a promise to Joe that he'd do whatever it took to get them back.

He began to think about what Hannah and Michael might have been put through and how alone and frightened they must now feel. How many had come for them? Were they taken at gunpoint? Were they hurt? He briefly contemplated whether they were even still alive but quickly dismissed the thought—he needed to stay positive and focused. Realizing there was nothing more that could be accomplished here, he got up and headed for the door, determined to keep his promise.

Chapter Seventeen

After leaving the motel, Adam headed back into Windmere. He had no idea who he was up against, and with no gun and no backup, he decided that reporting it to the police was his only option.

He realized they would probably lose the money, but Hannah and Michael's safe return had to be his number one priority. Driving back into the tiny township for the second time that morning, he continued past the diner and parked in front of a small, red brick single-story building that was labeled as the local police station. He was worried about Hannah but even more worried about Michael. A major seizure brought on by stress could have drastic consequences.

Resigned to what he needed to do, Adam got out of the car and locked the door. He would leave the attache case under the front seat for now but decided he would be open and honest with the police if the subject of motive came up. As he made his way to the front glass door of the police station, he was surprised that the interior of the small building looked dark and unoccupied. Adam pushed against the front glass door, but it was locked. It was only then that he noticed some signage on a large board inside the front window adjacent to the door.

He honed in on the writing at the bottom which mentioned the station's hours of operation. It was always closed on Saturday and Sunday and only manned during the working week as an outpost of the Northwood police station in the larger adjoining town. Shaking his head in disbelief, Adam turned around and headed back to his car, wondering how they fought crime in Windmere outside of banker's hours. Adam leaned on the bonnet of the Camaro and contemplated what to do next. He decided that phoning the Northwood police was now his best option and went to pull his phone out of his pocket to make the call. He only got it halfway out before it started to ring.

Adam looked at a cell phone number he did not recognize on the screen before pressing the answer button.

"Hello."

A mature male voice answered, "I see you've left the motel."

There was no doubt in Adam's mind that he was talking to someone involved in Hannah and Michael's disappearance. Doing his best to control his breathing and remain calm, he answered, "Who is this?"

"That's not important right now. What is important is I have the woman and the boy…"

There was silence as the man waited for Adam to respond. Adam wasn't sure what to say but decided he needed to keep it simple in the hope of getting Hannah and Michael back quickly.

The Final Proposition

"And I have the money."

The man laughed softly as if he found what Adam said amusing. "I also have a gun, and right now, it's pointed at the woman's head. You need to understand I'll shoot her if I have to—the boy too."

Adam cursed silently, more at himself than the man. The last thing he should be doing was trying to start an argument he couldn't win.

"Are they okay?"

"For now. Whether they stay that way is up to you."

Adam had no way of knowing whether the man was telling the truth or not.

"Can I speak with her?"

"When I get my money, not before. Do you have it on you?"

"No."

The man continued in a more aggressive tone, "You've got one hour. When I call back, we arrange to meet and trade. You cross me, and I shoot them and then come after you. I know who you are and what you drive. And don't try calling the police. The moment I see anything resembling a cop car, I shoot them and walk away."

Adam went numb at the thought of Hannah and Michael being held at gunpoint. He didn't want to begin to think about what it was doing to Michael's health.

The man asked, "Are we clear?"

"Yes."

"Oh, and by the way...I know how much money was in the case. Anything short of two and a half million, and I shoot them."

Adam was about to ask how the man could possibly

know how much money was in the case, but the line went dead.

Adam pocketed the phone and got back into the Camaro. He was not sure exactly why he had lied to the man about not having the money on him, but he was glad it had bought him an hour to think.

He replayed the conversation over in his mind and thought about what he should do next. He decided to follow the man's instructions and not call the police. He had no idea if the man really had a gun, or if he was on his own or working as part of a team, but risking Hannah's and Michael's lives was not worth it. He would play by the rules. Adam started the engine, gently eased out of the parking lot, and began to drive slowly up the street.

It was now approaching nine a.m., and the number of cars parked in the street had increased to seven. He cruised the length of the street, keeping a watchful eye on all the shop and office fronts in the hope of catching a glimpse of someone watching him or some other clue as to Hannah and Michael's whereabouts. After drawing a blank, he decided to drive up and down the adjoining side streets in the hope of finding some sign of their whereabouts. There was more activity on the side streets, with children out playing and people walking, but no sign of Hannah and Michael.

Adam desperately wanted to stop and ask some of the locals if they had seen Hannah and Michael but resisted the urge. It would be almost impossible to ask questions about their whereabouts without raising suspicion. The last thing he needed was for a concerned resident to call the police or, worse still, for him to be spotted asking questions by the man who had called him.

After fifteen minutes, Adam had driven up and down each of the six streets that collectively made up Windmere. He had not seen anything out of the ordinary and knew it had been a long shot that he would have seen anything obvious anyway. He had passed dozens of houses that looked shut up. Any one of them could be where the man was holding Hannah and Michael hostage, and he would have no idea by simply driving by. As he cruised slowly to the end of the last street, Adam decided to stop the Camaro and go for a short walk to stretch his legs and think. He parked the Camaro at the entrance to a vacant lot opposite a small, well-maintained white cottage. He felt frustrated and incredibly helpless— far worse than at any time during his seven years in prison. He hoped the walk would clear his head and help him to think better.

After getting out of the car, he looked up the connecting gravel road that led into the neighboring tree-covered hills and farmlands. He wondered whether he would have phone reception if he walked any further out of the township and pulled his phone from his pocket to check reception. The signal was weak, and he could only manage three steps onto the gravel road before the signal disappeared altogether and he was left with no phone signal.

"Phone reception drops out as soon as you step off the tar."

Adam looked back across the street to see an elderly man standing behind a picket fence at the front of the white house. He watched as the man removed his weeding gloves and realized he hadn't noticed him working there as he drove up and parked.

"We've been trying for years to get the phone companies to expand the coverage, but they don't listen to us. Not enough people to make it worth their while, I guess."

Adam walked across the road and introduced himself. The man was small and slightly built with a kind, weather-beaten face. He still had a full head of wiry gray hair and looked fit and alert.

"Thanks for the tip. I'm waiting on an important phone call and need to stay where I get coverage. Obviously, I can't walk any further than here?"

"No, as soon as you leave the main town area, you lose reception. You just passing through?"

Adam wasn't quite sure how to respond. The man seemed harmless and willing to help.

"Yes. Stayed overnight and was due to leave this morning. My friend and her son went for a walk earlier, and I'm just trying to find them."

The man scratched his head. "Well, I haven't seen anyone, but I'll keep my eye out for you. It's hard to get lost in Windmere, you can cover the entire town inside ten minutes by car."

"I guess I'll just go back to the main street and wait."

The man let out a soft laugh and said, "They're probably already there waiting for you. It doesn't take long to figure out there's nothing here worth seeing, and if they're not back there already, you're in the best spot to take their call. Even inside the town area, the phone reception can be flaky."

Adam thought back to the lack of phone reception at the motel and replied, "You're right, you can't really rely on cell phones here."

"No, although mine got me out of a jam several months back."

Pointing to the hill in the distance, the man continued, "I was coming back late one night from Northwood when my car broke down at the top of Olive Hill. I was still ten minutes out of town and thought I'd be stuck on the side of the road all night, but the phone reception was perfect. Got a buddy to come and pick me up. We checked how long the reception held, but it disappeared before we got to the bottom of the hill."

Adam nodded but said nothing. As if sensing Adam's burden, the man gently smiled and said, "I'm sure they'll turn up. It's hard to stay lost in Windmere."

Adam looked at his watch. He still had thirty-five minutes to go until the man would call. He decided it would be worthwhile checking every street again, to kill time if nothing else. "You're right, they can't be far away."

After thanking the man for his help, Adam returned to the Camaro. He started the car but didn't leave immediately. He sat in the car with the engine idling and thought about how the kidnapper knew where to find them. He couldn't have known the location of the money, or he would have collected it a long time ago. He had to have been following them and waiting for the right moment to strike.

He thought about how Hannah and Michael had only been taken after he had left the motel and wondered if the man might be operating alone. If he was part of a group, they would have stormed the motel room during the night and simply overpowered them. On your own, even with a gun, things can go wrong.

He looked back across the road at the white cottage.

The man was on his knees again, weeding. He replayed their brief conversation over in his mind and looked up the long road that wound through Olive Hill and on to Northwood. It prompted Adam to ask the man a question he should have asked earlier.

Winding down his window, he leaned out of the Camaro and called out, "Sir."

The man looked up from his weeding. "You get a call from them yet?"

"No, but can I ask you a question?"

"Sure."

Pointing in the direction of the large hill in the distance, Adam asked, "Olive Hill, is it a village?"

"No. It used to be the largest olive tree farm in the district. It was sold some years back to a famous author. He only wanted the house at the top of the hill for the views to inspire his writing or some such nonsense. He had no use for the olive farm and sold it off in smaller lots."

Adam had hoped Olive Hill would be a village at least, somewhere reasonably close to Windmere where the man might be holding Hannah and Michael. He was disappointed that it was little more than a farm. He was just about to say thank you and move off when the man added, "The house is quite something. Eight or nine bedrooms and made out of stone mostly. I used to be an electrician before I retired and went there once to do some wiring. It's a shame it gets so little use these days."

"The owner isn't there much?"

"No—he comes for the winter only. The rest of the time, the place is shut up."

Adam allowed himself a glimmer of hope. He wondered if this could be where Hannah and Michael were being held. As he put the car into gear, he asked the man, "The house, is it close to the road?"

"No, you can't see much from the road, it's set back quite away and hidden by a lot of trees and gardens."

Adam thanked the man for his time and quickly checked his watch. He figured he had just enough time to make the drive to check for Hannah and Michael and still be back in time to take the call. Adam dropped the clutch and took off down the dirt road. He hadn't had an opportunity yet to discover how fast the Camaro could go. Shifting the car quickly through the gears, he knew that was about to change.

Chapter Eighteen

Max hobbled out of the police station and across the street to where he had parked his truck. After unlocking the vehicle, he climbed in and closed the door. He was exhausted and contemplated laying his head back on the seat and closing his eyes for a few moments to rest. He knew if he did, he might sleep for hours, a luxury he couldn't afford right now.

Admonishing himself to stay awake, he gently withdrew his phone from his overalls pocket with one of his bandaged hands. He was glad he had spoken earlier to Adam, but there was one other call he needed to make before he did anything else. He pulled Stacey Archer's business card from his top pocket and dialed her cell phone number. After six rings, it switched to voice mail.

"Hi, this is Stacey from GymFit. I can't talk right now, so please leave a message and I'll call you back as soon as I can."

Max waited for the beep and then said, "Hi, Stacey,

The Final Proposition

this is Max. Please call me as soon as you can. I'm sorry to bother you, but something's come up."

He needed to get to a doctor to get his hands treated and bandaged properly, but he also needed sleep—even if it was just a few minutes in the truck. Max closed his eyes but found it hard to think about anything other than what had happened last night as images of his burning house began to haunt him. After escaping from the fire, he had spent almost an hour putting out spot fires that threatened to burn the adjoining workshop and garage on his property. When the threat was finally over, he phoned the fire brigade and police from his truck but told them not to hurry, there was nothing to save.

The police had arrived first, followed closely by the fire brigade, and he spent the next two hours answering questions for the police while the fire brigade doused the smoldering remains of his house. When the fire brigade gave the all clear, he had followed the police back into town to make a formal statement about the vehicle he had seen leaving the small forest area shortly after the fire started.

The police immediately upgraded the investigation from arson to attempted murder, which complicated the night for Max as they grilled him about people he suspected might have a grudge against him. Max decided not to tell them about Judge Hanley. Even though the judge had retired, he was still very influential in Stanwyck, and Max was unsure who he could trust. He decided he wouldn't say anything more until he had spoken to Adam.

As he began to drift off to sleep, his phone rang. Max opened his eyes and checked the number before hitting the answer button. Trying to hide his exhaustion, he responded, "Hi, Stacy."

"Hi, Max, I hadn't expected to hear from you so soon?"

Max debated what to say next. He didn't want to alarm Stacey, but she of all people needed to know what was happening.

"Stacey, there was a fire at my house last night… I was lucky to get out alive."

With alarm in her voice, Stacey replied, "Max, are you all right?"

"A sprained ankle and a couple of burnt hands, but I'll live."

He was about to continue when Stacey interrupted, "Was it deliberate?"

Max was silent for a moment, and Stacey repeated the question, "Max, was it deliberate?"

"I saw a car pulling away on the fire trail above my house, just after I escaped."

There was a slight pause before Stacey responded, "This is connected to Adam and Justine, isn't it?"

"I think so, yes."

"Do you have any idea who did this?"

Max shifted uncomfortably in the seat. He knew he needed to give Stacey a straight answer but wanted her to stay as far away from this as possible.

"Stacey, I'm almost certain that I know who it was, but I have no proof—not yet anyway. I don't think anything will come of it for you, but I thought you should know, just in case someone saw you at the garage yesterday."

"Who, Max?"

"Stacey, I have no proof, so you can't say anything."

"I haven't discussed this with anyone other than you, and that's not about to change."

"Simpson Hanley—the retired judge. I'm positive he was the other man in the photos with Lennox. I'll explain all that later. For now, I just want you to be careful."

Stacey was silent for a moment before she responded, "I can't say I'm overly surprised."

"Stacey, you're a smart girl, so I don't need to tell you…"

"I appreciate the warning, Max. I don't have anything to do with him or anyone he socializes with, but I will be careful anyway. Thanks."

"It's the least I can do."

"Are you going to be okay? Do you need anything?"

"I need sleep more than anything right now, other than that, I'm okay."

Max struggled to keep the conversation going—the exhaustion was overwhelming, and he felt a migraine coming on. "Can I call you tomorrow? Just to check that you're okay?"

"Sure, Max."

"Stacey, just one more question. Jerry Lennox, which nursing home is he in?"

In a slightly uncertain voice, Stacey replied, "I don't think he's in a nursing home. Last I heard, he had private rooms at the Westleigh Private Hospital. Max, you need to be careful. Lennox may have had a stroke, but he's still rich and well connected."

"I'll call you tomorrow, Stacey."

Without waiting for a reply, Max disconnected. He needed sleep now, but later he would be paying a visit to Lennox. While Judge Hanley would remain his number one suspect, he wanted to see for himself how disabled Lennox was and whether he thought he was still capable of giving an order to have him murdered. His thoughts returned to Judge Hanley. He would need to be careful. The judge didn't strike him as a man who quit easily. After starting the engine and putting the truck into gear, he said softly, "It's not over, Judge, not by a long shot," and then pulled away from the curb and headed toward his garage.

Chapter Nineteen

Adam covered the distance between the edge of Windmere and the start of Olive Hill in less than five minutes. He had pushed the Camaro beyond seventy miles an hour for most of the journey, but the engine was loud at high speed, and he throttled back for the climb up the hill to avoid announcing his presence.

He began to understand why the author had purchased the house as he cruised up the winding road. The view through the orchard of olive trees on both sides of the road was picturesque and serene. He drove over the rise at the top of the hill and slowed to a crawl in the hope of getting a good look at the author's large stone house. The elderly man's explanation of the house's location had been accurate—it was set well back from the road and almost totally obscured by trees.

He decided he couldn't risk stopping anywhere too near the front driveway and continued on down the hill and around a small bend before pulling off the road and parking. Adam got out of the Camaro and looked back up the hill. The house was totally obscured from view by trees, which suited him fine. If he couldn't see the house, there was a good chance any occupants of the house couldn't see him either.

After quietly closing the door, Adam surveyed the hillside before deciding to approach the house from the rear. He cautiously headed up through the olive trees at an angle, continually circling left to move toward the rear of the property. After five minutes of careful walking, he finally caught his first glimpse of the house. He moved slowly forward, doing his best to choose a path through the trees that kept his position hidden. He moved closer, and as more of the two-story sandstone house became visible, he was surprised by its size. It was more like a mansion than a house, and he was immediately concerned by the large sandstone wall that ran around the back of the property. It was well over head height and would not be easy to get over.

Using the gnarly olive trees for cover, he crept closer to study the wall in more detail, looking for signs of security cameras and alarms that might alert someone inside to his presence. Seeing nothing obvious, he came out from the cover of trees and quickly walked the short distance to the rear wall. The wall appeared to be continuous and was too high for him to scale without a running jump. He decided scrambling up and over the wall would make too much noise and started walking around the wall in the hope of finding a gate or some other easier way of getting inside the property.

After getting to the southern rear corner of the wall, Adam cautiously peered around the corner to the eastern side. He scanned the area ahead and saw more olive trees but nothing else. Taking a deep breath, he walked up the eastern side of the property, keeping close to the wall. He could see what looked like an archway built into the wall as he approached the halfway point. After taking three more cautious steps forward, he found what he had hoped for—a gate providing access to the property.

The heavy wrought iron gate was painted black and constructed using an intricate rosette pattern in keeping with the house. Adam's eye was immediately drawn to the slide bolt on the gate, which was in the open position.

Without moving any closer, he peered through the gate, but from his current position, he could only see partway down the eastern side of the house. The paved area next to the house was bare except for a few large ornamental pots. Adam turned his focus to the Spanish style house and scanned the windows he could see on both the upper and lower levels. All the curtains were drawn, and the house appeared to be closed up. He stepped forward one more pace and stopped again. From his new position, he could now see most of the large rear patio area. All the furniture was draped with dust covers and didn't look like it had been used in months. He moved another step forward and now had a clear view of the rear section of the property.

Adam slowly scanned the area, looking for any signs of Hannah and Michael or their captor, but came up blank. His focus was drawn to a long single-story building that ran parallel to the rear wall of the property. Unlike the house, this building was constructed using glass and timber and housed a large kidney-shaped swimming pool. He studied the building in more detail, and his heart began to race as his focus shifted to a timber-framed glass door at the eastern end of the structure. While his view was slightly obscured by several shrubs, the glass sliding door didn't appear to be fully closed.

Adam checked the reception level on his phone as he switched it to silent mode. Just as the elderly man had indicated, he had full coverage. The hour would be up in less than five minutes. He would have just enough time to make a quick check for Hannah and Michael before the man called back. Wary of what might await him, he rescanned the house and garden area once more, looking for any sign that he wasn't alone. Seeing no one, he pushed gently on the gate and was relieved when it slid silently open. He took two steps inside the gate and then stopped again. He now had an almost perfect view of every part of the rear of the house and wanted to make sure he wasn't walking into an ambush.

Everything remained quiet. Cautiously, he moved forward and now had a clear view of the glass door and could clearly see it was slightly open, almost as if someone had been in a hurry and hadn't quite closed it properly. Making his way across the paved area, he looked around and back over his shoulder for any sign that he was not alone. He stopped a few paces short of the door and did his best to look inside, but the sun's reflection off the glass made it difficult to see anything more than shadows.

Now very conscious of time, he stepped forward and, after drawing a deep breath, slid the door back and took one step inside. He paused to allow his eyes to adjust to the lower light levels. His focus was drawn to the pool area first. The large kidney-shaped pool was surrounded by a wide paved area. Apart from a few poolside chairs and a large metal box, which he assumed was for the pool pump, everything appeared normal. He began wondering whether he was wasting his time here and should be focusing on the house instead.

He turned and looked back toward the other end of the building. It was separated from the pool area by a full-width timber wall. The one door that led to the other section of the building was closed. As silently as he could manage, he walked to the door, stood still, and listened. He could hear no sound coming from the other side of the wall, so he turned the knob and pushed the door open a fraction. The room was dark, and he could only vaguely make out several lounge chairs at one end of the room. Adam took a deep breath and stepped inside to search for the light switch. As he fumbled around, he heard a distinct click and then silence.

He stood still, listening intently for the source of the sound. The silence was broken a moment later by the sound of a man's voice from the far end of the room. The voice was as relaxed and controlled in person as it was on the phone.

"I have a SIG P226 pointed at your head. Move slowly into the center of the room, or you'll be dead before you hit the floor."

Chapter Twenty

Adam obeyed the man's instructions and moved in the dim light toward the center of the room. After he had taken three steps, the man told him to stop. As the lights came on, Adam turned to see Michael and Hannah huddled on the floor at the far end of the room. They were both handcuffed to a wooden pole that formed part of the support structure for the roof. With their mouths taped shut, they both looked terrified, and Adam's heart sank as he could see the desperate plea for help in their eyes.

The man continued, "Turn around slowly."

Adam turned around and looked directly into the barrel of a gun. It was just beyond his reach and pointed directly at his forehead. The man holding the gun was in his late fifties and had a balding, gray crew cut. He was about average height and had a slim build. Apart from an unshaven face and bloodshot eyes, he didn't look any different from any other middle-aged man you would pass on the street.

The Final Proposition

The gun stayed perfectly steady. "You're smarter than I thought. I expected I would need to call you to arrange a trade, but...here you are."

Adam went to respond, but the man interrupted in a tight but controlled voice, "You speak only when I want an answer."

The man motioned Adam to move toward Hannah and Michael.

"Stand next to the boy. You try anything, I'll shoot the boy and then the mother. Are we clear?"

Adam nodded and walked to Hannah and Michael before turning around. The gun was no longer pointed at Adam but directly at Michael. Adam desperately looked for ways to get Hannah and Michael free, but the situation looked hopeless. They were handcuffed to each other and to a short length of heavy chain that was wrapped around the pole. As the man walked toward them with the gun still pointed at Michael's head, he said to Adam, "Sit on the floor next to the boy."

Adam did as he was instructed. The man reached into his pocket, pulled out a key on a short chain, and tossed it to Adam. As the gun remained pointed at Michael, he said, "Unlock the boy's side of the handcuffs."

Michael looked terrified as tears streamed down his face. Adam did as he was instructed and whispered to Michael as he unlocked the handcuffs, "It's going to be okay, Champ. Just do what the man says, and you'll be okay. I promise."

After the handcuff was unlocked, the man said, "Michael, I want you to put the handcuff on Adam's right hand and lock it down tight. You do that, and I'll let you take the tape off you and your mother."

Adam whispered, "Do what the man says, Michael. Nice and tight."

Michael placed the handcuff over Adam's hand and, with some coaxing from Adam, secured the handcuff tightly around his right wrist. When he had finished, Michael looked at the man, who nodded. "Now bring me the handcuff key."

Michael took the key from Adam and then walked the few steps to the man and held out the key. The man took the key and then leaned down and tore the duct tape from Michael's mouth. The tape made a loud ripping sound as he removed it. Michael flinched but didn't make a sound. Adam was impressed by Michael's stoic determination not to react. The man let out a cold laugh and then motioned for Michael to remove the tape from Hannah's mouth.

Michael knelt by his mother and gently peeled the tape from her mouth. Hannah's whispered words of thanks to her son were drowned out as the man continued in a firm voice, "Michael."

Michael turned to look back at the man who now had the gun pointed at Adam. "Get Adam's car keys and phone and bring them to me."

Adam reached into his pocket with his free hand and quickly retrieved his keys and phone. He knew he needed to cooperate fully if they were to get out of this situation alive. He passed the keys and phone to Michael and said in an encouraging voice, "It's okay, Michael, do as the man says."

Michael walked across and handed the phone and keys to the man. The man motioned for Michael to sit at his feet, and then after pointing the gun down at Michael's head, he turned his attention to Adam.

The Final Proposition

"I'm sure you want the boy to live. Right now, that depends on you answering my questions correctly."

Hannah begged the man, "Please don't hurt him, he's just a little boy."

Adam quickly interjected to make sure the situation didn't escalate any further. "I'll answer truthfully. You don't need to harm Michael and Hannah, they've done you no harm."

The man broke into a wry smile, which quickly turned cold and calculating. "The money, did you bring it?"

Adam replied, "Yes. It's in the car."

"Right answer. Where did you park?"

"Over the crest and down the other side of the hill. It's parked behind some trees, just past the bend in the road, but it's easy enough to spot if you're looking."

The man nodded but didn't respond straight away. Instead, he held Adam's gaze and studied him for a moment. "If you're lying, I'll kill the boy."

"The money is in a slimline attache case wedged under the front seat."

The man replied, "I'm taking Michael with me, the money better be there."

Hannah begged the man, "No, please don't take him."

The man ignored Hannah's plea, grabbed Michael roughly by the collar, and asked him, "Do you want to see your mother again?"

Doing his best to hide his fear, Michael nodded.

"Then don't give me any trouble."

Without another word, the man walked out of the room with Michael. While Hannah cried softly, Adam tried to think of some meaningful words of comfort, but he soon realized no words could comfort a mother in this situation. Instead, he shuffled across and put his free arm around her.

Through her tears, Hannah looked at Adam and asked, "Why did he have to take him? He's just a little boy."

Adam's level of anxiety for Michael was extreme, and he knew for Hannah it would be far worse. Doing his best to remain calm and provide hope, he replied, "It's easier to take Michael with him than to find some way of tying him up here and risk him getting away."

Hannah closed her eyes and started breathing in and out deeply in an effort to calm herself down. In a voice barely above a whisper, she replied, "I hope you're right, Adam... He's all I've got."

Adam examined the cufflinks and chain and replied, "Our best chance is to give him what he wants."

Hannah opened her eyes and looked directly at Adam. "What about when he's got the money? He has no reason to keep us alive then?"

Adam thought for a moment and then responded, "Maybe, but he has no reason to kill us either. Killing people complicates a crime. He knows we can't say anything about the money, so maybe..."

Hannah didn't let him finish. "You don't know who he is, do you?"

Adam looked perplexed. "No, should I?"

Hannah moved slightly to lean her back against the pole and then replied, "His name is Leyland Darcy. He was the detective who arrested Joseph."

Adam recalled Joseph mentioning the name on several occasions when he had talked about his arrest. "I remember now, Joseph said he was dirty. He said something about a deal to get the charges dropped if he told him where the money was, but Joseph didn't know back then."

"We never talked about it. Joseph didn't tell me about Darcy until much later. There was so much going on with his trial, and he didn't want to worry me any further. By the time he told me, it was too late. He had been convicted, and there was nothing we could do. I couldn't bring myself to tell him I knew about the money. It was only when Michael got sick that I told him…"

Adam thought about what he had just learned and said, "He's been watching the whole time. He must have bet on Joseph telling me when he got sick, and he's been following me ever since I left prison."

Adam realized that his actions had led Darcy to follow them. "I'm sorry, Hannah. It's because of me we're in this mess right now."

Hannah wiped her eyes and did her best to compose herself. She leaned back against the pole again and said, "It's not your fault, Adam. We're in this together. I just need to get Michael away from him. He can have the money, I just want Michael back safe."

In the silence that followed, Adam began to think about what might happen next. He no longer felt confident Darcy would simply release them when he got the money. As a cop or an ex-cop, Darcy would know more than most that you never left anything behind that could incriminate you. He looked at the handcuffs and the chain. He was no Houdini and knew he couldn't pick the lock. He figured he had ten minutes to think of a way to negotiate their freedom before Darcy returned. As he began to formulate a plan, the silence in the room was broken by the sound of a gunshot in the distance.

Chapter Twenty-One

Adam watched as Hannah froze in terror. He replayed the sound he had just heard over in his mind and wondered if he had been mistaken. Could it have been some other sound that they had mistaken for a gunshot? He felt his heart racing as he went through the possibilities. Surely Darcy wouldn't have shot Michael? He was just nine years old and no threat.

His thoughts were interrupted by Hannah. "That was a gunshot, wasn't it?"

Adam tried to think of a way to downplay his reply, but he knew Hannah would see straight through it.

"I think so, but let's not jump to conclusions. There might be some other explanation."

Hannah slumped to the floor and wept softly. Reaching across, Adam placed his free hand on her back to comfort her. No words seemed appropriate, and he said a silent prayer for Michael instead. He could not recall a moment in his life where he had felt this helpless.

The Final Proposition

If Darcy had killed Michael, he realized they would be next. Somehow, that didn't matter. Adam felt his rage building as he thought about what might have happened. He hoped they had jumped to the wrong conclusion. If Darcy was going to shoot them, he could have easily shot them all before he left to get the money. Adam couldn't bring himself to think through the possibility that Darcy now had what he wanted and had killed Michael and left him on the side of the road. Closing his eyes for a moment, he breathed in deeply, determined to remain positive.

Without lifting her head, Hannah said, "He's taken my baby…"

Looking down at Hannah, Adam replied, "If he was going to kill us, I think he would have done it by now. He had no reason to keep you and Michael alive when he realized I had the money."

"I pray to God you're right, Adam."

Adam and Hannah sat quietly for the next five minutes. Neither of them felt like talking. Not knowing whether Michael was dead or alive was all consuming. While he reexamined the handcuffs for a way to break free, Adam thought he heard the sound of the sliding door to the pool enclosure open and close. Sitting up straight, he nudged Hannah and braced himself for what might be coming next. His heart began to race again as he heard footsteps approach the door. Adam was flooded with relief as the door opened and Michael raced into the room to be with his mother.

Hannah wrapped her free arm around her son to hug

him tight. Michael leaned in and whispered, "Mom, the man shot Adam's car tire."

Adam's relief was short lived as Leyland Darcy walked back into the room with the attache case. After dropping it on the floor, he walked directly to Adam and pointed the gun at his head. In the same calm voice he had used before, he said, "There's forty thousand missing. Where is it?"

Adam stared blankly for a moment before responding, "I have no idea. The money hasn't been touched. What you have is what I collected."

Darcy quickly strode the short distance that separated him from Adam and pushed the barrel of the gun hard into Adam's left temple. He expected Darcy to yell, but instead, he responded in a quieter voice, "I don't need you anymore. One last chance, where's the rest of the money?"

Hannah screamed, "He doesn't have it!"

Darcy turned to look at Hannah. Her determined, almost defiant look was back as she continued in a more moderated voice, "Tony's brother told us in a letter where he had hidden the money. The letter also said he had taken some of it to get medical help."

Darcy looked from Hannah to Adam and then back to Hannah again. Everybody knew what he decided in the next few seconds would determine whether Adam lived or died. After a silence that seemed to last minutes rather than seconds, he removed the gun from Adam's temple. With a small, wry smile and a slight shake of his head, Darcy said, "You're one ballsy lady..."

Turning back to Adam, he said, "Looks like this is your lucky day."

Without waiting for a reply, Darcy turned to Michael

and pointed to a doorway at the far end of the room. "Michael, grab your bag and go into the bedroom and wait for me."

Michael looked from Darcy back to his mother, unsure of what to do. With a horrified look on her face, Hannah said to Darcy, "What kind of deviant are you? He's just a little boy. You can't…"

Darcy didn't let her finish. "Relax. I've been awake for forty-eight hours and need a couple of hours' sleep before I continue. I'm not leaving him roaming around out here. If he behaves, he'll be okay."

Without waiting for a reply, Darcy walked over to a cabinet that contained several bottles of spirits. He opened the cabinet door and selected one before returning to address Hannah. "The bedroom has a tallboy, which I'm going to slide in front of the door. I'm then going to put this bottle on top and balance it upside down. It's too high up for the boy to reach, and if he tries to climb up, it will fall over and wake me. I need you to tell your son not to do anything stupid."

Hannah nodded and looked at Michael. Doing her best to seem relaxed and in control, she said, "Michael, do as the man says. Just sit on the floor quietly and read a book. Okay?"

In spite of being so young, Michael seemed to understand. He leaned in, gave his mother another hug, and whispered, "I love you, Mom," before quietly picking up his bag and walking into the other room.

Darcy waited until Michael had entered the room before he turned and looked at Adam and Hannah again. "If by some miracle you manage to slip those handcuffs, remember, I have the boy and I have a gun."

Without waiting for a reply, Darcy turned, walked into

the other room, and closed the door. Hannah and Adam listened as furniture was moved and Darcy mumbled a final warning to Michael before everything went quiet. They continued to listen, and both breathed a sigh of relief as they heard the sound of gentle snoring coming from the room several minutes later.

Hannah leaned her head back against the pole and let out a deep breath. "Do you think he'll let us go?"

"I think if he was going to kill us, we'd be dead by now. It doesn't make any sense keeping us alive now to kill us later."

Hannah seemed unsure. "Unless he's some kind of sick whacko."

"What do you know about him?"

"Only what Joseph told me. He's a crooked cop. Ex-cop in fact. Joseph heard he had been forced out of the police force about three years ago on some kind of corruption charge. Hardly surprising when you consider what he tried on Joseph when he was arrested."

"Did you ever see him following you or parked out front of where you lived?"

"No, but now that you ask, Michael whispered to me in the car when we were being taken away that he had seen him recently near our apartment building."

"Did he hurt you?"

"Not really. I was getting dressed in the bathroom, and Michael called out for me. I thought he was having another seizure, but when I opened the door, Darcy was in the room and had the gun pointed at Michael. I totally froze. It was such a shock, and I didn't know what to do. He asked me where the money was and threatened to shoot Michael there and then if I didn't tell him. When I said you had it, I thought he was going to explode. He started swearing his head off, and Michael started crying. When I finally convinced him I was telling the truth, he grabbed Michael and walked out to his car."

"He just left you?"

Hannah nodded.

"He knew you'd follow?"

"Yes. I grabbed Michael's bag and ran out the door. He had Michael in the front and made me sit behind Michael in the back seat. He then made me handcuff myself to Michael."

"Did you come straight here?"

"He asked me where you had gone and why. He knew what car you were driving, so he's obviously been following us for a while. When I told him you had gone back into town to get breakfast and make some phone calls, he mumbled something and drove off. We came straight here to the house, although he brought us straight around the back and broke the door to get into the pool enclosure."

"The house is probably alarmed, but this outer building isn't. He gets good phone reception here, and there are no close neighbors to worry about."

"What I don't understand, Adam, is how he found us?"

"He said he hasn't slept in forty-eight hours. He's probably been following me ever since I was released. There aren't many towns on this stretch of road. So he probably kept driving until he found us."

"You didn't see anyone following you?"

"No. But to be honest, my first taste of freedom in seven years and the funeral has all been a bit overwhelming. I haven't really been looking as much as I should have."

"I'm sorry I got you into this, Adam."

"No need to apologize, Hannah. I'm here by choice."

They were both quiet for a moment before Hannah said, "Joseph was right, wasn't he?"

This was a conversation Adam didn't want to have. He wanted Hannah to stay positive and simply replied, "Yes."

They were quiet for a while before Hannah spoke again. In a matter-of-fact voice, she said, "I'm not so confident he's going to just let us go, Adam."

When Adam didn't reply, she continued, "We know who he is. Tell me why he would keep us alive when we can so easily identify him?"

Chapter Twenty-Two

Max woke with a stiff neck, and his hands still felt as though they were on fire. He checked his watch. It was just after midday and time for more painkillers. He sat up on the couch and checked his phone, hoping Adam had called back and left a message. He had a missed call from the police saying they would be in touch later, but nothing from Adam.

After getting up from the couch, he swallowed two more painkillers without water and then stretched. He would have to find somewhere else to sleep—the couch was killing him. After rubbing the sleep from his eyes, he gritted his teeth and put on his boots. He figured he would be in pain for some weeks to come while his hands healed. Hobbling out of his office, he made his way slowly down the stairs to the workshop. The workshop looked deserted, and he could see no sign of any of his three mechanics.

Max called out to his chief mechanic, "Hey, Rusty," but no one answered. He was initially puzzled and then remembered it was Saturday. Hobbling into the small shop front, Max drained the last of the brewed coffee from the machine into a styrofoam cup. It tasted bitter, but he put up with it. Bitter was better than trying to open a sugar sachet with burned hands.

After locking up, Max walked slowly across the garage's driveway and climbed into his truck. He checked the time on the truck's dashboard clock. It ran between five and ten minutes fast, which he allowed for in his calculations. He figured he still had close to two hours to spare before the insurance assessor was due to arrive at what was left of his house to assess the damage.

He shifted uncomfortably in the seat and thought about his couch again. His back was giving him almost as much grief as his hands, and he decided he needed a proper bed to sleep on that night. He had plenty of friends who would gladly put him up for the night, but he wasn't in the mood for the inevitable polite and concerned conversation about the fire.

He didn't feel hungry and decided to head straight back out to what was left of his house. He would use the time while he waited for the assessor to search his garage for a mattress. He was fairly sure he had an old twin-bed mattress stored in the rafters. It wouldn't be ideal, but anything would be better than another full night on his lumpy, old couch.

Max started the engine and pulled out from the garage. He found driving relaxing, and as his head began to clear, his thoughts returned to Judge Hanley and their brief encounter the day before. He would need to be careful. If Hanley felt threatened enough by the photos to try and have him burned alive, there was every chance he would try again. He decided it would be wise to keep a low profile for the next few days. He would get some supplies on the way back into town and then bunker down at his garage until Adam returned and they figured out their next move.

He thought about his house again. It was going to be hard seeing the remains in daylight. A lifetime of precious memories of his wife and daughter reduced to ash and rubble. He was glad he was going out early. He knew he would be upset and emotional—better to get that out of his system before the assessor showed up, he thought.

After leaving the town limits, Max felt his gut begin to tighten as he approached the curve in the road where Simpson Hanley lived. He could feel his blood pressure begin to rise as he relived last night's nightmare, knowing if Hanley had gotten his way, he'd be dead by now. He looked over to his right as Hanley's mansion came into view and was surprised by what he saw. The house looked identical to yesterday, except for one small detail. Today, someone was sitting on the large stone bench next to the front door.

Almost involuntarily, Max braked and brought the truck to a screaming halt in the middle of the road. Making no attempt to move his truck off the road, Max sat and stared down the long driveway at the lone figure sitting in the shade of the large patio area. He was too far away to be certain, but the large figure dressed in light-colored clothing was almost certainly Hanley. Max debated what to do as the rage inside him built toward boiling point. He knew the smart thing to do was to drive on. Nothing could be gained by confronting Hanley today, but doing the "smart thing" had never been his strong point.

Max let his rage take control as he put the truck into

reverse to back up and turn into the driveway. As soon as his truck began to move off in reverse, he noticed the figure on the patio area suddenly get up and walk back inside the house. Max had no doubt it was Hanley. Even from this distance, his waddle was unmistakable.

Max stopped opposite the driveway entrance and debated what to do. He decided nothing could be gained by confronting the judge today and put the truck back into first gear to continue his trip home. Just as he was about to pull away, Hanley emerged again from the house. He appeared to be carrying a newspaper under his arm as he waddled back to his bench seat.

Max watched for a moment as Hanley settled back down again before something inside his head snapped. Gritting his teeth, Max turned into the driveway and drove down toward Hanley's mansion, keeping his eyes locked on the judge the entire time. After reaching the circular drive at the front of the house, Max drove slowly around until he was adjacent to the footpath that led up between the columns to the large front door.

Still clutching the rolled-up newspaper, Hanley deliberately ignored Max as he surveyed the picturesque view between his mansion and the main road. Max switched off the engine and wound down the truck window. In the silence that followed, broken only by the ticks of his truck engine as it cooled, Max kept staring at the judge who continued to ignore him. It was almost like a game—with the first person to react losing.

Max had never been good at games, and after another minute of silence, he broke the impasse. "I got a reasonable look at the guy in the SUV. You shouldn't pay him, he was sloppy."

The Final Proposition

The judge refused to look at Max, which made him even more determined.

"You know, Judge, the problem with a fire is there's always a chance that the intended victim will escape. And then what do you do? You've burned someone's house down, pissed them off, and let them know you're trying to kill them all at the same time. I'm just a mechanic, and even I'm smart enough to figure that out."

More silence followed before Max said, "You afraid of me, Judge? You should be."

Without looking in Max's direction, Hanley finally replied with a small laugh and then said, "I'm afraid of many things, but you're not one of them."

Undeterred, Max pressed on. "I still have the photos, Judge…and the diary. I left them in my truck, which as you can see escaped the fire."

Hanley finally turned and looked at Max. His face was devoid of expression, which didn't surprise Max given he had spent a lifetime impassively judging cases in a courtroom.

"You're trespassing. You've got exactly one minute to leave before I call the police."

Max felt his anger rising and did his best to remain calm as he replied, "Call away, Judge. I think it's about time they heard my side of the story. I've got nothing to lose. You took my daughter, burned my house, and almost had me killed. I'm prepared to roll the dice, it can't be any worse than this."

It was almost imperceptible, but Max noticed the judge's eyes widen ever so slightly for a fleeting moment before he turned back to the view in front of him.

Feeling he had struck a nerve, Max did his best to provoke a reaction and said, "You're going to have to kill me, Judge. I know you're involved, and I won't stop until I'm dead or I see justice for my daughter."

"I have no idea what you're talking about."

"The police have a good ID on the vehicle seen leaving my house last night. You think your hitman will give you up in exchange for a lighter sentence when he's caught?"

Hanley roared with laughter, but it was contrived. Max knew he had the judge out of his comfort zone.

"I'm going to visit Jerry Lennox too. I understand he's living permanently at Westleigh Hospital now. You need to pick your friends a bit better, Judge. Being photographed with him isn't going to pan out so well for you when he's charged with rape and murder. I've only been digging for two days, and I already know he raped a schoolgirl and then raped and murdered his own son's girlfriend.

"Imagine what I can find if I dedicate a month to it, Judge? I'm pretty sure I'll learn enough to have you both thrown in jail for the rest of your sorry lives."

Before Max could continue, the judge was on his feet. As Hanley discarded the newspaper he had been clutching, Max found himself staring at a gun the judge now held in his right hand. In the time it took Max to process what was happening, Hanley walked to the edge of the patio area and now had the gun pointed through the open truck window at Max's head.

In a soft but threatening voice, Hanley said, "Get out of the truck."

Chapter Twenty-Three

Adam shifted his sitting position again. They had spent over two hours on the floor handcuffed to the pole, and as cramps set in, no sitting position felt comfortable. He looked across at Hannah who continued to sit with her back resting against the pole and her eyes closed. They had spoken little since Darcy had gone into the room to sleep. In spite of hearing the occasional snore through the closed door, he knew Hannah remained very worried for Michael. He wondered how Michael was coping. He hoped he was quietly reading one of the books, but maybe that was just wishful thinking.

He had been surprised at how resilient Michael had been when Darcy had frog-marched him off to the car to get the money. Perhaps Michael did not fully appreciate the gravity of the situation they were in? Even though he was highly intelligent, how much could a nine-year-old really understand? Adam only had to think for a moment before deciding that Michael would understand everything. He was comforted by the fact that Michael did not appear unduly stressed when he returned from the trip to the Camaro with Darcy.

His thoughts returned to what would happen when Darcy woke up. At first, he had assumed Darcy would let them go now that he had the money. But the more he thought about it, the less confident he became. He had spent enough time with criminals to know the most ruthless never left "loose ends" behind. Anyone with the patience and guile needed to spend seven years tracking this much money was not about to leave anything to chance. Adam wondered why they were still alive.

He had thrown this question around for the better part of an hour before deciding that Darcy didn't want to leave their bodies here at the house. Maybe he was worried a pool cleaner or maintenance man would show up in the next day or two? Leaving them here would make the risk of early discovery much higher. Cold fear overcame him as he realized if he were in Darcy's shoes, he would take them to somewhere remote before shooting them. Darcy would want weeks or even months between now and when they were discovered to allow him to completely disappear—perhaps to even leave the country?

While he had not shared any of these fears with Hannah, he knew she was probably coming up with similar conclusions. Her eyes were still closed, and Adam wished he could think of some words of comfort to help her through this nightmare—but nothing meaningful came to mind. He thought about the heavy irony of his current situation as he looked around the sparsely furnished room. Here he was—finally a free man, locked up in handcuffs, and unlikely to still be alive at the end of the day. After another futile examination of the handcuffs and the pole for any signs of weakness, Adam decided their only hope of getting out of this alive was to negotiate with Darcy and convince him that they were no threat.

Turning to Hannah, he said in a low voice, "Hannah?"

Hannah opened her eyes and turned to look at Adam. Trying not to be distracted by the deeply pained look in her eyes, he continued, "We need a plan. I don't think he's going to let us go. Somehow, we have to convince him that we aren't a threat and that we're not going to go to the police."

Hannah kept her eyes locked on Adam, waiting for him to continue.

"We have to persuade him that he can get away safely and that we aren't coming after him."

"What do you have in mind?"

Adam rubbed his brow with his free hand as he thought. He wished he had spent more time thinking through a plan before saying anything to Hannah. "We need to cut to the chase as soon as he comes out. We level with him and tell him he doesn't have to kill us."

Adam looked up at Hannah and continued, "The hard part is convincing him we won't go to the police. If we tell him we're afraid of going to jail as well because this is all connected to drug money, maybe…"

Hannah interrupted, "I don't think that's convincing enough. He kills us, he gets a rock-solid guarantee we won't go to the police."

"But he'll be wanted for multiple homicides as well. He's been asleep in that room for two hours, so he'll have left plenty of DNA behind. Our DNA will be here as well. If the police ever suspect we were held here, they'll find enough evidence from all of us to figure out who's still alive and who isn't."

"I'm not convinced, Adam. I think he'll still kill us."

Adam was silent for a moment before he said, "You and I both know it's a long shot, but we have to convince him that killing us makes him a hunted man for the rest of his life. If we can do that and give him a way out of here, he might just let us live."

Hannah's reply was cut off as the door to the bedroom burst open. Standing in the doorway, Darcy looked across at Hannah and said, "There's something wrong with your kid. He's lying on the floor shaking and vomiting."

With panic in her voice, Hannah said, "He's got a brain tumor, and he has seizures. You need to unlock me so that I can go and take care of him. If his airways get blocked, he can choke to death."

Darcy disappeared back into the other room and then reappeared a moment later dragging Michael by the arms. Michael's head lolled back and forward and he appeared unconscious as Darcy dragged him through the room to where Hannah and Adam sat. Darcy dumped Michael roughly at Hannah's feet before disappearing into the bedroom again. Fighting back tears, Hannah pulled Michael toward her with her free hand and cradled his head in her lap. She quickly checked his airway before rolling him on his side. In a low voice meant only for Adam, she whispered, "His airway is clear, and his breathing is steady."

Just as Adam was about to respond to Hannah, Darcy

emerged from the side room again. Carrying a black canvas bag in one hand and his gun in the other, Darcy walked toward them and pointed the gun at Adam's head. In an instant, Adam decided Michael's seizure changed things slightly and he would let Darcy speak first.

Darcy stopped directly in front of Adam and dropped the keys to the handcuffs at his feet before stepping back. "Time to go, unlock the handcuffs."

"No."

Darcy looked slightly stunned. "No?"

Holding Darcy's stare, Adam repeated his reply as firmly and confidently as he could muster, "No."

Darcy snapped, "What the hell game are you playing? I said unlock the handcuffs. Now!"

"You have the money. The boy is very sick, and we won't be able to move until he recovers. Just leave us here."

A mean, wry smile spread across Darcy's face as he replied, "I have no intention of leaving you here, I…"

Adam didn't let him finish. "You intend to take us somewhere quiet where we won't be quickly discovered. And then you intend to shoot us. I've spent the last seven years day in and day out with criminals—I know how it works."

Darcy moved the gun and pointed it directly at Michael's head. With his gaze fixed on Hannah, he said, "You've got two seconds to unlock the handcuffs, otherwise I shoot the boy."

Adam watched as Hannah defiantly held Darcy's gaze for several seconds. Adam knew she was scared stiff and admired her resolve as she responded, "We all know you're not going to let us go…so do what you have to do."

Before Darcy had a chance to respond, Adam said, "You've got the money, you don't have to shoot us. You leave bodies behind, you'll have a target on your back for the rest of your life."

Darcy let out a short laugh, "I'll have a target on my back either way. My preference is the cops and not you and a personal vendetta."

Adam continued to hold Darcy's stare. "You're wrong. I just got out of prison after spending seven years inside for a crime I didn't commit. I'm not doing anything to risk going back inside again. Besides, when I get my settlement, I'll never need to work again."

Darcy kept the gun pointed at Michael's head as he looked slowly from Adam to Hannah and then back to Adam again.

Adam didn't like the silence and continued, "For God's sake, Darcy, the boy is seriously ill and has less than twelve months to live. Don't take that time away from him and his mother. If you need to shoot anyone, shoot me, but not them."

Adam held his breath as they waited for Darcy's decision. Darcy held Adam's stare for seconds before pointing the gun back at him. Adam felt Hannah reach her handcuffed hand across to hold his as they waited for Darcy to shoot.

After what seemed like an eternity, Darcy lowered the gun, turned his back on them, and walked over to a small cabinet that he had left Adam's phone on. He picked up the phone, dropped it on the floor, and stomped hard on the screen with the heel of his left boot. Darcy picked up his bag again and made his way to the door that led to the main pool area. He paused in the doorway and gazed back at Adam and Hannah as if in no hurry to leave.

After studying them for a moment, he said, "I've been watching you for seven years. Nothing changes—I'll still be watching. If you go to the police, I'll kill you all, starting with the boy first."

Adam and Hannah watched in silence as Darcy disappeared through the doorway and out of sight.

Chapter Twenty-Four

Max sat fixed to his seat as he stared back at Hanley and the gun.

Hanley repeated his demand, this time in a louder voice. "Get out of the truck, or I'll shoot you where you sit."

Max silently cursed himself for turning the truck off when he had parked. He calculated he would need at least five seconds to get his old truck started. Even someone old and not used to a gun could squeeze off three or four rounds in the time it took him to start up and pull away. He decided trying to start the truck to drive off was probably suicide and his best chance of survival was staying where he was.

Doing his best to remain calm, Max hoped he was calling Hanley's bluff as he replied, "Fire away, Judge, I'm not getting out."

In response, Hanley walked forward and stepped off the patio. With the gun still pointed at Max, he waddled

The Final Proposition

toward the truck and said, "Fine, you can bleed out in the truck rather than on my driveway."

Alarmed that he may have misjudged what Hanley would do, Max quickly replied, "I'm not the only one that knows, Judge. Killing me won't solve your problem…"

Hanley stopped walking but kept the gun pointed at Max's head. With a smug and confident look, he replied, "I don't care who you've told. Photographs prove nothing, and testimonies seven years on mean very little. Get out of the truck."

Hanley advanced again and was now so close to the truck, he could now lean in the passenger window and fire at point-blank range if he wanted to. The bullet that Max expected didn't come. Instead, Hanley changed tack.

"Throw your keys out of the truck, nice and easy."

He wants me to get out. Whatever he has planned, it doesn't include shooting me here if he can avoid it. Max was stoic in his reply, "Like I said, Judge, fire away, I'm not getting out, and you're not getting my keys."

A wry smile spread across Hanley's face as he replied, "Fine, have it your way."

Both men stared at one another for a few moments. While Max desperately wanted to start the truck and drive off, he didn't want to force Hanley's hand. He decided to wait it out and see what the judge's next move was before he did anything.

With the gun still pointed at Max's head and a smug smile seemingly now fixed permanently on his face, Hanley continued, "You know, stubbornness seems to run in your family."

Max felt his blood pressure rising rapidly. He had no doubt that the veiled reference to his family meant Justine. Realizing he couldn't respond without getting angry, Max remained silent. Hanley's smile widened as he realized he had scored a direct hit with his comment.

"I didn't kill her, but I did watch. We took her to one of my favorite fishing spots and worked her over for almost an hour before she…"

Max shoved the truck door open and leaped out of the vehicle as a rage built inside him that he would have never thought possible. His roar was not from the pain in his hands or ankle but the thought of Justine being tortured before her murder. Max went on autopilot as images of how she might have suffered flashed through his mind. No longer concerned about the gun or his own safety, he charged forward. Time seemed to slow to almost a standstill as he rounded the front of his truck to attack the judge.

The sound of the judge's gun discharging and the stinging pain of a bullet creasing the top of his left shoulder blade barely registered as he charged forward. The few steps that separated Max from the judge seemed to take forever as he continued to rush forward. The recoil from the gunshot kicked Hanley's right arm high above his shoulder, and Max could see the judge begin to panic as he fired wildly a second time.

Undeterred by the searing pain in his shoulder, Max found himself roaring again as his bandaged hands wrapped around the judge's throat. As he began to squeeze, he screamed, "Where is she? What have you done with her?"

In response, Hanley let out a muffled gasp as his eyes rolled into the back of his head. Max expected the judge to fight back and was surprised when the large man suddenly went limp and dropped the gun onto the gravel drive. Unsure of what was happening, Max relaxed his grip and watched as Hanley collapsed onto the gravel driveway. Quickly retrieving the gun, Max stepped back and pointed it at the judge as he prepared for what might happen next. He could not discount the possibility that the wily old man would fake a collapse in order to get the upper hand again.

He waited a few seconds for any sign of movement and noticed the color slowly draining from the judge's jowly cheeks. Taking a step closer to get a better look, he knew Hanley wasn't faking as the man's lips started turning blue.

Reaching forward, he lifted the judge's left wrist to check for a pulse but found it impossible to sense anything through his bandaged hands. Deciding he needed to be absolutely certain, he got down on his knees and leaned over the man's bulky frame to listen to his chest. He could hear no heartbeat or shallow breathing and assumed Hanley had suffered a heart attack. Max looked at the judge's face again. His features had relaxed, and his complexion was quickly turning gray. Max knew he should be performing some form of CPR but couldn't bring himself to do it.

Max rose to his full height as he recalled the judge's words: "I didn't kill her, but I watched."

He understood what was happening and whispered, "Now it's my turn to watch, Judge."

Max walked to the edge of the patio to sit on the front steps. He stared back at the judge and felt no sadness or remorse as he mulled over whether he should call an ambulance. He decided the judge had orchestrated his own fate and he wasn't about to interfere. Death was too good for him, but it would at least help bring closure.

While he sat thinking through what had just

happened, the pain in his shoulder began to intensify. He looked down at the shoulder of his jacket and discovered an elongated hole made by the bullet. After carefully pulling off his jacket, Max undid the top three buttons of his shirt and slid it off his shoulder. There was almost no blood, and the bullet appeared to have grazed the top of his shoulder blade only. He watched as his entire shoulder started to turn a dark purple color from the bruising and figured he had gotten lucky—very lucky.

After rebuttoning his shirt, Max picked up his coat and went and stood over the body of Judge Hanley. The milky film that had begun to form on the judge's half-open eyes gave Max the final confirmation he needed that Hanley was dead. Max took a few moments to look around. The judge's mansion sat on a sizeable acreage that afforded him lots of privacy. With no close neighbors, he was almost certain that what had unfolded here had gone unnoticed.

He didn't need long to decide what he would do, and after retrieving the gun, he walked up onto the patio to where Hanley had left the newspaper. After carefully rewrapping the gun in the newspaper, he walked up to the front door and was relieved to discover the door wasn't locked. He walked inside and quietly stood on the polished marble floor, looking around the large two-story foyer. His gaze was drawn to a solid wooden door that was slightly ajar on the right side of the foyer. Max shifted his position two steps to the left and was able to make out a bookcase and part of a large wooden desk—Hanley's office. He walked into the room and carefully placed the gun inside the folded newspaper on the mahogany desk.

Max took a moment to look around the room. Hanley's office was lined with memorabilia collected from his time as a prosecutor and judge. Every square foot of available wall space was covered with photographs, almost all of them featuring Hanley shaking hands with a celebrity or politician. The photos didn't surprise Max. Hanley was the kind of guy who liked to brag and feed his ego. Max studied the photos, and two images immediately caught his eye. They were side by side, and Max stood almost transfixed as he studied each photograph in detail. They were the only two photographs in the collection where Hanley wasn't in a suit or shaking someone's hand. In both photos, Hanley had swapped his suit for fishing clothes and posed with a rod and a large fish he had just caught.

Max wondered whether these photographs were taken at his favorite fishing spots. The first photo showed the judge holding up a large fish next to a small fishing boat at the edge of a lake. It was difficult to make out the background scenery in any detail, and Max knew it would be almost impossible to figure out which lake it was based on the photo alone.

He shifted his focus to the second picture. Like the first photo, this one also showed the judge holding up a fish. This time, the background was in focus and showed Hanley at the edge of a stream with an old wooden bridge in the background. The stream wound under the bridge before it disappeared on the left-hand side of the photo.

Max studied the bridge in more detail. He could only see the bottom third of the structure in the picture. It was mainly timber, and he estimated it had been constructed at least fifty years ago. The pylons that supported the bridge were built on ground that sloped sharply down to the river's edge and were covered in loose rocks, presumably to stop soil erosion. He spent several more minutes studying the photo but could not see anything else that would provide a clue to the bridge's location. It wasn't much to go on, but at least it was a start.

Max knew he had spent too much time here already. He would have liked to stay longer to investigate more, but he needed to get off Hanley's property before anyone noticed his truck parked out front. After taking one last look around, he walked out of the office and back through the foyer to the front door. He held up his burned hands and checked that his bandages were all still intact. Satisfied that he wouldn't leave any fingerprints, he walked out onto the patio and closed the door behind him.

Max looked up the driveway toward the road. Everything remained quiet—as if the world had chosen to ignore what had just happened here. He ignored Hanley's body and walked over to his truck. After climbing in, he checked the time on the dashboard clock as he started the engine. He figured he still had time to find the mattress before the assessor arrived. Without looking back, he put the truck into gear and drove slowly up the gravel driveway. He knew someone would eventually find Hanley's body, but if that wasn't for a few days, that was all right with him.

Chapter Twenty-Five

After watching Darcy walk out, Adam and Hannah listened to Darcy's retreating footsteps, followed by the sound of the outer sliding door opening and closing. They were silent for over a minute, listening intently for any sounds that would indicate Darcy was returning, before Hannah said, "Do you think he's really gone?"

Adam listened for a moment longer before responding. "The warning he gave us on his way out was pretty clear. I don't think he's coming back."

Hannah was still holding Adam's hand through the handcuffs. She squeezed gently and said, "You saved our lives, Adam. I know he would have shot us."

Adam shook his head and said, "I'm not taking any credit. The way you held your nerve when he pointed the gun at Michael. Most people would have folded."

"If he had unlocked us, he would have taken us somewhere and killed us just like you said. I've never been so terrified in my life, but refusing was our only hope."

Hannah started breathing in and out deeply again as

she relived the ordeal. Adam decided it was time to change the subject—dwelling on what had happened was not going to help.

Looking down at Michael, he said, "Will he be okay?"

Hannah checked Michael's breathing with her free hand as she cradled his head in her lap.

"His breathing is normal, which is a good sign."

"Do you think the stress of being in there with him brought on the seizure?"

"It's hard to say. Multiple seizures a day is considered normal for his condition."

Michael murmured softly. With a slightly relieved look, Hannah said, "He's starting to stir, which means his body has gone into recovery mode."

For the next ten minutes, Hannah worked with Michael until he was fully conscious again.

"How are you feeling, Michael?"

Michael rubbed his eyes and said, "Okay, I guess. How long was I out for?"

Hannah replied, "Not too long," as she stroked his hair. Adam could see the weight lifting off her shoulders as Michael didn't appear to have suffered any adverse effects.

After resting for a while, Michael rubbed his eyes again and looked around with a puzzled look on his face. "Where's the man?"

Adam answered, "He's gone, Michael."

Before Adam had a chance to say anything else, Michael replied with alarm in his voice, "He didn't take my bag, did he?"

Adam smiled for the first time since Hannah and Michael had been captured. He quickly glanced at

The Final Proposition

Hannah who was also smiling and obviously relieved to see her son returning to normal.

He responded, "No, Champ, he didn't take your bag, it's still in the other room."

Michael got up, walked back into the side room, and emerged a moment later carefully carrying his satchel full of books. He walked back across to Adam and Hannah before sitting cross-legged in front of his mother.

"I didn't feel like reading while the man slept. He was kind of creepy, so I sneaked over next to his bed and had a look in his black bag where he had put all the money."

In an alarmed voice, Hannah replied, "Michael, that's very dangerous. I don't even want to begin thinking about what might have happened if he had woken up."

"He was too busy snoring to hear me, Mom—honest."

Adam sensed Michael had more to say and said, "Go on, Champ, we're listening."

Michael looked at Hannah for approval. As she realized she might have overreacted, she encouraged him by saying, "It's okay, Michael. It's all been a huge shock. Tell us what happened. Did he hurt you?"

"No, he just kept sleeping. There was a bookcase in the room with lots of paperback books, like the ones you read, Mom. I pulled out a couple to look at them, and then I went and got my bag and brought it over."

Michael looked from Adam to Hannah and said, "I emptied out my bag and put all my books in the bookcase and made them look like they belonged."

Hannah was not sure where Michael was going with all this and was keen to get help to get out of the handcuffs. She had never known her son to ramble on, and as patiently as she could, she replied, "Okay, but why would you want to do that?"

Michael unzipped his bag and opened it up. As Hannah and Adam stared down at the contents of Michael's bag, he replied, "To make room for the money."

Michael looked from his mother back to Adam. They were both speechless as they stared at his bag which was neatly packed to the brim with bundles of cash.

Taking this as his cue to continue, he said, "Once I had all the money out, I filled the man's bag up with the paperbacks. I couldn't quite fit all the money in my bag, so I put the rest back in the man's bag on top of the books, just in case he checked."

Michael looked from Adam to his mother who both remained speechless. Michael said defensively, "It wasn't his money, Mom. It's for my operation, and he had no right to—"

Fighting back tears, Hannah interrupted Michael. "It's okay, Michael, you're not in trouble. What you did was very brave. I'm very proud of you."

Adam shook his head in amazement as he watched Hannah pull Michael toward her with her free arm. While mother and son embraced, Adam took stock of their situation, which he found completely surreal. His bitter disappointment with the money being stolen was now replaced by the euphoria of Michael getting it back so quickly. He had to agree with Hannah—if Darcy had woken up and caught Michael, he would now be dead.

Adam began to wonder how long it would be until Darcy discovered the money was missing. He would almost certainly recheck the money as soon as he got to his destination. If that was Hartbourne, they had time to get away, but if it was closer, Darcy could be back much sooner. Adam knew they would not be so lucky a second time, and every minute longer they stayed here made them more vulnerable. Not wanting to alarm Hannah or Michael too much, he leaned in close to Hannah and said, "We should be getting out of these cuffs as soon as we can."

Still hugging her son, Hannah said, "Darcy made sure we can't use your phone, but if you brought all our bags, my phone should be in there somewhere. I'd like to give Michael a little more time—just to make sure he's fully recovered—before we send him back to the Camaro to find it."

Adam thought for a moment and then replied, "We may not have to. When Darcy walked out of here, I thought I heard a sound like something being dropped in water. It's a long shot, but maybe he tossed the keys to the handcuffs into the pool on his way out?"

Continuing to hold Michael, Hannah turned to Adam and said, "He certainly wouldn't have any further use for them."

"It's worth a shot. If they're here and we can recover them, we won't need to call the police unless you want to?"

Hannah thought for a moment before firmly replying, "No. Michael is unharmed, and we still have the money for his operation."

Hannah held Adam's gaze without saying anything further. Her body language said it all as she let go of Michael. Calling the police would only complicate things and almost certainly lead to them losing the money.

Adam said, "Okay by me. If we can find the keys, it

makes getting out of here far less complicated. As soon as Michael is ready, he can go take a look."

Now on his feet, Michael looked at Adam and Hannah and said, "I'm feeling much better, can I go look now?"

Adam responded, "When your mom says it's okay, Champ. But before we go any further, even though we don't want you getting wet, can you swim?"

Puffing out his chest with pride, Michael replied, "Of course. I have my intermediate swimming certificate."

Looking slightly alarmed, Hannah added, "But we don't let you swim unsupervised on account of your seizures."

Adam added, "I agree with your mom. When she gives you the okay, we just want you to walk around the pool and see if you can see the keys in the water. If you find them, then we'll figure out how to get them out."

Michael looked at his mother, excited that he might be able to help. "I really am feeling much better, Mom."

In a firm but gentle voice, Hannah replied, "Okay, but don't get too close to the edge."

Adam held up his free hand to signal for Michael to wait. "The keys are small, and even though the pool water is clear, they may not be easy to spot."

Michael nodded, eager to start searching.

Adam continued, "So keep well back from the edge and just walk around the pool real slow. If you don't see them the first time, just walk around again slowly. If the keys are there, I know you'll find them."

Michael looked at his mother. "Can I go now, Mom?"

With a nervous smile of encouragement, Hannah replied, "Like Adam says, keep well back from the edge, Michael."

The Final Proposition

Hannah and Adam watched Michael walk out through the door to the pool enclosure. Adam leaned across to Hannah and whispered, "He's a sensible kid, he'll be fine."

Hannah held Adam's handcuffed hand again and said, "I'll be glad when we're all out of here."

In a loud voice, Adam called out, "Hey, Champ, how are you doing?"

They heard Michael's echoing voice reply, "I'm walking slowly and not too near the edge."

Hannah said, "Good boy, Michael."

Hannah and Adam waited patiently for almost two minutes. They had faith in Michael and decided questions would only be a distraction. Finally, a dejected Michael reappeared at the door.

"I've been around the pool twice and can't see them. I went real slow just like you said. I'm sorry."

Hannah replied in an encouraging voice, "It's all right, Michael, it just means we need to go to plan B."

Adam cocked his head in thought for a moment and then said, "Hey, Champ, when you went around the second time, did you go in the same direction as the first time?"

Michael nodded. "I went clockwise both times. You want me to try the other way?"

Adam replied, "Seeing things in water can be tricky. Light reflects off water in funny ways. You go the other way, you'll get a slightly different angle. It's worth a try."

With a determined look that he had inherited from his mother, Michael replied, "I'll go the other way this time."

Without waiting for a reply, Michael turned and walked quickly back through the door into the pool area. Adam whispered to Hannah as they watched him go,

"You're doing a great job raising him—you should be very proud."

"Thanks, Adam. I just want him to get better and grow up to lead a normal life."

Adam looked at Michael's bag and the money it contained. Hannah's dream of getting Michael his operation was still well and truly alive.

Hannah found the waiting frustrating and called out, "How are you going, Michael?"

"About halfway around, Mom. I haven't seen…"

Hannah and Adam waited a moment for Michael to finish his sentence. Hannah became alarmed at the quietness and asked, "Michael, are you all right?"

"I found them, Mom, I found the keys!"

Michael rushed back through the doorway and said, "They're down the deep end on the left side."

Both Hannah and Adam let out a cheer as Michael returned. Adam smiled at Michael, who looked ready to burst with pride. "I knew you would find them if they were there. Now, we need to figure out how to get them out without you getting wet."

Hannah asked, "Did you see any poles in there, Michael? Sometimes pool owners have poles with nets on them to scoop out leaves."

"I didn't see anything, but I'll go take a look."

After Michael disappeared, Adam said to Hannah, "We'll figure out a way to get them out."

"What do they say? So near and yet so far?"

They were quiet while they waited for Michael's return. Adam used the time to think about other possible ways Michael might be able to retrieve the keys. Going swimming for them was totally out of the question. His thoughts were interrupted as a dejected Michael returned again.

"I couldn't find anything. It looks like all the cleaning gear is locked up in a cupboard at the far end of the pool."

Adam replied in an encouraging voice, "It's okay, Champ, we'll think of something else."

They were all silent for a while before Adam spoke. "Michael, the other room, where Darcy slept. It had a bed and a chest of drawers, right?"

"And a bookcase and a wardrobe."

"You mind taking a look in the wardrobe for me? I'm hoping there might be some coat hangers in there—the wire kind you get dry cleaning back on."

Michael brightened and said, "I'll be right back."

Hannah and Adam watched as Michael sprinted into the bedroom and gave a running commentary. "The wardrobe's not locked. There are lots of ladies' clothes on wooden hangers and…"

Adam and Hannah both listened intently as Michael continued to search through the wardrobe. After letting out a triumphant "Yes," Michael emerged from the bedroom with six wire coat hangers.

After being handed the coat hangers, Adam inspected them and smiled as he said, "Champ, these are perfect. If you give me a couple of minutes, we should be able to fashion them into a long hook for you to go fishing."

Michael and Hannah watched as Adam unwound each coat hanger and straightened them into six straight lengths of wire. Hannah marveled at how quickly Adam was able to straighten the coat hangers, even with one hand shackled in handcuffs. They watched patiently for the next ten minutes as Adam deftly joined the coat hangers together, twisting the wires together until they formed one long, straight wire stick. He then gently bent the wire at one end of the stick to form a small L-shaped hook.

Satisfied with his work, he laid the hook on the ground and then spent several minutes instructing Michael on how to best carry and use the hook. When he was confident that Michael was ready, Hannah and Adam wished him good luck and watched as he headed toward the doorway.

Chapter Twenty-Six

Michael carefully dragged the long wire hook across the pavers to the edge of the pool. He was excited and nervous at the same time. Excited that he could help free his mother and Adam, but also nervous because he didn't want to let them down. He really liked Adam and the way he was trying to take care of him and his mom and was glad the man with the gun had gone and it was just the three of them again.

Replaying Adam's instructions over in his mind, Michael lay down on the pavers that surrounded the pool and edged his way forward until he was able to peer over the edge and down into the water. He could clearly see the keys on the bottom of the pool and gently moved the long wire over the side of the pool and down into the water. Michael was careful to always hold the wire with two hands. The last thing he wanted was to drop the wire and see it sink to the bottom of the pool.

It took Michael over a minute to lower the wire into position. Adam had been right; the wire did not bend much in the water, and he practiced moving it back and forth once the hook end had reached the bottom. It wasn't as easy as he had imagined as his eyes had to make adjustments for the parallax error of seeing things underwater. While he practiced turning the wire in his hands to spin the hook around, he heard his mom call out from the other room. Such was his concentration, he wasn't exactly sure what she had said and replied, "I'm okay, Mom, just practicing."

Relieved that she didn't ask another question, Michael returned his concentration to the task before him and edged the wire hook through the water toward the keys. He maneuvered the hook to line up with the small split ring that joined the two keys together and tried to thread the hook through the narrow split pin opening. Michael smiled when he thought he had the keys secured but quickly became disappointed as he raised the hook through the water and the keys stayed on the bottom. Undeterred, Michael lowered the hook again and tried a second time to hook the keys, but he was foiled again as he raised the hook slightly only to discover the keys still remained on the bottom.

Michael began to realize how difficult the task was and wondered if the keys would be easier to retrieve from the shallow end of the pool. Instead of trying to hook the keys, Michael experimented with using the long wire to gently push the keys along the side of the pool toward the other end. After several attempts, he found he was able to pull the keys along using the hook like a hockey stick. The process was slow, but after five minutes and several short, reassuring conversations with his mother, Michael had moved the keys all the way up to the shallow end.

Using the hook again as Adam had intended, he

The Final Proposition

managed to hook the keys with his first attempt. He allowed himself a brief smile as he slowly raised the wire hook through the water. Michael yelled with excitement as the end of the wire hook and the keys finally broke through the water. He quickly stood up and laid the wire down. When he had retrieved the keys, he shouted, "I've got them," and then ran back into the other room.

Hannah and Adam both cheered as he walked back into the room holding the keys out in front of him. After handing the keys to Adam, Michael blushed with pride as both Adam and Hannah praised his efforts. Doing his best to shrug it off, Michael watched as Adam unlocked the handcuffs and the two adults stood up, stretched, and rubbed their wrists.

With a look of pride, Hannah said, "I need a hug from my boy," and embraced her son. It was a huge relief for Michael to see his mother free from the handcuffs. He liked to see her happy, and he could tell by the way she held him that she was glad the nightmare was over. Michael looked across at Adam, who was standing back a little to give him and his mother some space. The more time he spent with Adam, the more he liked him and wished the trip wouldn't be ending so soon.

After letting go of her son, Hannah turned to Adam and hugged him. In a voice barely above a whisper and still full of emotion from what had happened, she said, "Thank you, Adam, I don't know how I can ever repay you."

"You don't need to. That's not what this is about. Seeing Michael get his operation is all the reward I need."

They held each other for a moment longer before Adam said, "We need to get out of here as soon as we can. When Darcy discovers he's only got a small part of the money, he'll be coming straight back."

Hannah didn't need Adam to say any more. "You're right, we need to leave here immediately." As she picked up Michael's satchel full of money, she said, "Let's go, Michael, we need to leave now before the man comes back."

Adam reached down and picked up his broken phone and the handcuffs as Michael and Hannah headed for the door. It looked like they would be able to continue their journey without needing to involve the police, and leaving behind evidence didn't seem like a smart thing to do. He quickly caught up with Hannah and Michael as they made their way out of the building and said, "Let me go first, just in case there are any surprises."

The three made their way cautiously across the garden area at the back of the house, retracing Adam's steps to the side gate. The gate was still open, and Adam cautiously peered through into the olive grove, looking for any signs that they might be walking into an ambush. Seeing nothing out of the ordinary, Adam signaled Hannah and Michael to follow, and the three made their way around to the outside fence at the rear corner of the property. When they reached the corner, Adam held up his hand to signal for them to stop again.

In a quiet voice, he said, "We'll make our way through the grove in single file. Keep a watch out for Darcy. I expect he's long gone for now, but we need to be careful—just in case. We should be back at the Camaro and on our way in less than ten minutes."

Chapter Twenty-Seven

After arriving back at the Camaro, Adam spent the next ten minutes changing the tire that Darcy had shot out. Michael shadowed Adam, asking lots of questions, while Hannah spent the time recounting the money and packing it back into the attache case.

After packing the last bundle of money into the case, she said, "Darcy only got forty-two thousand, the rest is here."

Adam still found it hard to believe that Michael had been able to make the switch while Darcy slept. After placing the tire wrench back in the trunk, he winked at Michael. "Are you ready to go?"

Michael nodded earnestly at Adam before turning to his mother and uttering words that were now becoming very familiar, "Hey, Mom, I didn't get breakfast, and I'm hungry. Can we stop and get something to eat, please?"

Adam looked at Hannah as he closed the trunk. "I'm a bit hungry myself."

After snapping the attache case shut, Hannah replied,

"Do you think it would hurt if we drove back into Windmere and got something to eat before heading on to Bolton?"

As they all piled into the car, Adam replied, "I think we'll be safe enough in a public street. We'll just grab something to go and eat in the car when we get back on the road."

They were all quiet for a few moments as Adam started the Camaro and they pulled back onto the road. When they got to the bottom of the hill, Adam breathed a sigh of relief as he realized they were leaving the nightmare behind them. He turned to Hannah and asked, "Are you okay?"

Hannah nodded and said, "I'm not sure I want us to be going anywhere near my sister's house until we get this money to a bank. We're too much of a target, and I don't want to put anyone else at risk, if that's all right with you?"

Adam thought about what Hannah said. He didn't mind extending his time with Hannah and Michael in the least.

"I think that's wise. You won't be able to deposit all the money at once of course—it will arouse too much suspicion. I suggest you open a couple of accounts, deposit small amounts to start with, and put the rest in a safety deposit box. Over time, you can move money from the box to your accounts without drawing attention to yourself—and all done safely inside a bank."

"I like it. It's a good plan except for one thing."

"And what's that?"

"Half of the money is yours—remember?"

Adam didn't want to go down this path again but also didn't want to start an argument.

"Okay, we'll sort something out when we get to Bolton."

Adam could see Hannah visibly relax with his agreement. When the time came for them to part company, he would make sure Hannah had enough not only for the operation but to set her and Michael up for life. They had been through more than enough to deserve never to struggle again.

"I'll call my sister when we get back into Windmere and let her know we won't be there for a couple of days. Once we have the money safely in a bank, I'll breathe a lot easier."

Hannah's mention of calling her sister reminded him that he would need to call Aaron Winter and tell him it was unlikely that he would be returning to Hartbourne before Tuesday. He looked in the rearview mirror at Michael who was sitting happily in the back seat watching the scenery as they drove along. Michael didn't seem too upset from his ordeal this morning which gave Adam an idea. Reaching into the top pocket of his windbreaker, Adam pulled out his mangled phone and held it up for Michael to see.

"Hey, Champ, you know much about phones?"

"A little, I guess."

"My phone's broken, but I'm hoping the SIM card isn't damaged. Do you think you can get it out for me?"

Adam watched in the mirror as Michael smiled and said, "Sure!"

After passing the broken phone to Michael, Hannah said, "I'm happy for you to use my phone, Adam, it's really not a problem."

"I don't know my lawyer's phone number, and he won't be back in the office until Monday. It's saved on the

SIM, so it will be easy to get back if the SIM still works. I would need to put it in your phone for a couple of minutes until I've called him, if that's okay?"

"I'm not planning on calling anyone other than my sister this weekend, so no problem."

"I got it, Adam!"

Adam looked in the rearview mirror to see Michael triumphantly holding up the tiny SIM card. "That was quick, Champ?"

Michael shrugged his shoulders and, doing his best to remain modest, replied, "The back cover was broken, so it was easy to get apart."

Michael handed the SIM to Hannah. She held it up, examined it for a moment, and then said, "It looks okay, Adam, there's no damage that I can see, so hopefully it will work."

After folding it in a small piece of paper, Hannah placed the SIM card in the car's ashtray and then held up her own phone to check for reception.

"We are only about a minute out of Windmere, so I'll call my sister as soon as we come in range. Then we can swap SIMs, and you can call your lawyer while we order lunch."

Adam nodded as he looked in the rearview mirror again. He had not seen anyone following but wasn't about to get too relaxed. He would breathe easier once they were out of Windmere and on their way again. All being well, there would be no more stops until Bolton.

The drive into Windmere gave Hannah just enough time to phone her sister. Hannah downplayed their situation by saying they had changed their plans and would probably now arrive on Tuesday. She finished the phone call as Adam parked the car in the same spot he had parked in earlier when he came to get breakfast. Hannah swapped the SIM cards in her phone, and they agreed it was safe enough for her and Michael to go and order everyone's lunch while Adam made his call.

Hannah turned to Adam as she was about to get out of the Camaro and asked, "What can I get you, Adam?"

"The largest black coffee they have and a burger would be great."

After saying thank you, Adam watched Michael and Hannah walk into the store before making his check-in call to Aaron Winter. Winter answered after two rings and was far from happy.

"Where have you been, Adam, I've left four messages for you."

Adam responded with a condensed version of the truth. "The phone you gave me broke this morning. I've only just now managed to put the SIM in a borrowed phone to make this call. I'm sorry about your phone, and I'll replace it next week."

"Don't worry about the phone, Adam, there's been a development. It looks like we can get an early settlement with the government in exchange for you agreeing to no damaging media stories. As long as you agree to no public interviews, I think I can swing a deal today or tomorrow. They're finalizing a draft proposal to send across right now."

Adam thought about what this might mean. He had never really intended to take his story public, but he wasn't sure he wanted to be officially silenced either.

"I don't know, Aaron. I should be getting the money because I was sent to prison for seven years for a crime I didn't commit. I'm not liking any condition that gags me from saying my piece."

"I understand, Adam, but let's see what they come up with before we decide. As soon as the proposal comes through, I'll read it and call you. That will hopefully be sometime in the next hour. How far out of Bolton are you now?"

"I'm still in Windmere. It's a long story. I'm planning on leaving in five or ten."

"The reception's flaky out there, right?"

"Not reliable at all once you get out of town."

"Okay, so how long until you hit the next town?"

"We should hit Northwood in about ninety minutes, give or take."

"Call me as soon as you get there, we should have an offer to discuss by then."

Adam didn't like being rushed and said as much to Aaron, "I don't see why we need to rush this, Aaron, and as I said, I don't want a gag clause."

"I understand, Adam. The point is they've come to the table to make a deal, so we listen to their offer and then negotiate. I promise you, we keep negotiating until you're happy."

Adam didn't see any point laboring the conversation. He would politely listen to the offer and then dig in until he got a settlement he considered fair.

"I'll call you when I get to Northwood."

Adam disconnected and wound his window down. He looked up and down the street, but there were only a few people still out on a Saturday afternoon, all of whom looked like locals and paid him no interest.

He thought about Darcy again and wondered where he was now. Hopefully, he hadn't made the discovery yet. Bolton was still about three and a half hours from here, and he would feel much safer when he was off these narrow back roads and back in a city again. Even though Bolton was only a small city, it would be much easier to disappear in a population of seven hundred and fifty thousand people. Once the money was safely in a bank, he hoped the threat from Darcy would be over. He began to wonder how Darcy would react when he discovered he no longer had the money, but his thoughts were interrupted as the passenger side door flew open and Michael climbed into the back seat.

"We've got burgers, Adam, and I'm starved."

Adam started the engine as Hannah got into the passenger seat and said, "They smell great!"

Amidst a flurry of conversation from his two passengers, Adam pulled out from their parking spot and headed down the main street toward the Northwood turnoff with one eye still on his rearview mirror. They would pass through the country townships of Northwood and Sanbury before finally reaching Bolton. He hoped they would prove to be less eventful than Windmere had been.

Chapter Twenty-Eight

Adam drained the last of his coffee before glancing in the rearview mirror as they drove on through the steep, heavily wooded countryside. The car had been quiet in the twenty minutes since they had left Windmere, with everyone concentrating on their lunch while Adam drove. Michael had devoured his burger in a few mouthfuls and then curled up on the back seat to sleep. Hannah had taken her time, and as she finished the last of her sandwich, she caught Adam checking the rearview mirror again.

"You see anyone?"

"No, it's all clear."

"Good. Let's hope the rest of the trip is quiet. We've been through more than enough."

"I figure with one stop at Northwood for a bathroom break and me to call my lawyer, we should make Bolton by nightfall. I've been thinking about where we should stay as well. I think we need to drive well into the city before we look for a hotel—somewhere that takes cash without too many questions."

Hannah replied, "And thanks to you and Michael, we still have the cash to pay for it."

They were silent for a few moments before Adam glanced at Michael in the rearview mirror. Concerned with Michael's condition, he asked, "Is he okay?"

Hannah twisted in her seat and looked at Michael as he slept on the back seat. "He's just tired. He had a rough night, and today's nightmare has been very draining on all of us."

"You both seem to be recovering. Most people would be a mess for weeks or even years after having a gun pointed at them."

"When you've been through what Michael and I have been through, you take everything one day at a time and thank God you're still standing. I'm sure I'll have trouble sleeping for a while, but with so much ahead of us, I can't afford to get bogged down with what happened today or any other day for that matter."

Hannah studied Adam for a moment and then asked, "What about you, Adam, are you okay?"

"Like you, I can't afford to dwell on what happened. I haven't told you yet, but when I went to get breakfast, I made a brief call to Max. His house burned down last night and almost took him with it."

Hannah looked stunned as Adam went on to explain the details, including it being a deliberate attempt at murder.

When he had finished, she replied, "Whatever is in that box must have some people very worried."

"Yes. Max has promised to keep a low profile until I return, and then we'll try and figure out what to do next.

Hopefully, it will help us find Justine's body and those responsible for her murder."

"I hope you find her, Adam. I can only begin to imagine how hard it must be to get closure when she's still missing."

"I've never told anyone, not even Joe, but the public apology and compensation for my jail time pale in comparison to finding Justine. I loved her more than I thought possible. I don't think I can really move on until we find her and whoever's responsible."

"What do they say—it's a chapter you need to close before you can start a new one?"

"It's like I'm in limbo. I remember lying in my hotel bed on my first night of freedom, thinking I should be on top of the world, but I wasn't. I kept thinking of Justine and how we can go about finding her."

Adam glanced across at Hannah who now looked deep in thought. He would have liked to share more but was not sure how to express himself. He checked in the rearview mirror again and noticed a white sedan now visible in the distance as they threaded their way along the winding, tree-lined road.

"What color was Darcy's car?"

Hannah immediately turned around to look out the rear window for signs of a car as she replied, "It was a dark gray four-wheel drive Toyota. Is someone following us?"

"We have a white car behind us. It's well back and probably nothing, but I'll keep an eye on it."

Adam noticed Hannah's concerned look and decided they needed to change the subject. "Assuming we make it to Bolton okay, how soon can you get Michael's operation?"

The Final Proposition

"I haven't seen the surgeon in a while, so it depends on his schedule. Provided Michael's condition hasn't deteriorated too much, it should be about six weeks."

Adam thought for a moment before asking his next question. "Forgive me if I'm intruding and don't feel you have to answer this, but what are his chances?"

"It's a fair question and you've earned the right to know. Most surgeons we visited were very pessimistic and only gave him a twenty-five percent chance of a full recovery. The tumor is very deep, and even though it's not malignant, it's growing, and every day we wait, the surgery gets more complicated and risky."

Adam took a deep breath—it wasn't the news he was hoping to hear as Hannah continued, "A lot of surgeons we saw said the surgery required couldn't be done. I persisted and eventually got an appointment with Dr. Ben Chan who works out of Bolton's research and teaching hospital. He's reportedly one of the best neurosurgeons in the country, and he was a lot more positive about the surgery, plus Michael really likes him. He rates Michael's chances of survival at fifty percent, which is way higher than everyone else. But the best is very expensive—over four hundred thousand for surgery and recovery."

Adam tried to hide his disappointment as he learned Michael's chances of getting better were still only fifty-fifty. He had hoped the odds would be much higher.

Reading his body language, Hannah said, "Yes, the odds are still not great, but they're the best we've got."

"Michael is a strong boy. If anyone can pull through, he can."

As if on cue, Michael murmured from the back seat, "I'm feeling sick, Mom."

Hannah turned in her seat again to look at Michael.

"You're very pale, Michael. Do you want to stop and get out for a minute?"

"I think so. I feel like I want to puke."

Adam looked for a place to pull over and said, "It's a pretty narrow road here, Champ, can you hang on a second? I'll see if I can find somewhere safe to stop."

Michael mumbled okay as Adam searched the road ahead for somewhere to stop. After cresting a ridge, Adam slowed the Camaro down and found a gap in the trees that allowed him to pull completely off the road. Almost before the car had stopped, Michael was urging his mother to open the door and let him out.

Adam watched as Hannah opened the door and let Michael out of the car. Michael immediately ran further into the clearing and bent over to vomit.

Adam was concerned and asked Hannah, "Is this connected to his condition?"

Hannah gave a brief, knowing smile. "I think this is just a nine-year-old who ate his lunch too quickly and is now carsick. I better go comfort him."

Adam watched Hannah walk the short distance to where Michael stood doubled over. Realizing they were going to be here for a few minutes at least, Adam got out of the car and walked back to the road. The terrain they had now entered was heavily forested and rocky. Adam figured the next part of the trip would be slow going on a road that would likely remain narrow and wind right through until Northwood. He looked back up the road toward the ridge, expecting the white car that had been following him to crest it at any moment. After waiting half a minute, Adam rubbed his chin as his gut began to tell him something was wrong.

Maybe he had been too distracted by Michael and

missed the car as it passed by? Adam turned and looked down the road. His anxiety intensified as he scanned the road ahead as it swept around a long right-hand bend and over a low-set concrete bridge that spanned a creek bed. He was positive no car traveling behind them would have been able to get across the bridge and out of sight in the time that had elapsed since he parked. Keeping his gaze fixed on the road back up to the ridge, Adam walked quickly back to the Camaro to find Hannah comforting Michael who was still bent over.

Stopping beside Hannah, he said in a quiet voice, "The white car hasn't come over the ridge yet."

Hannah immediately straightened up and said in a concerned voice, "Could we have missed it because of Michael?"

"I don't think so. I've checked the road below—there's no way a car could have got by us and out of sight in time."

"Perhaps it turned off earlier?"

Adam looked back up the road again and said, "Perhaps, but we can't afford to take any chances. I'm going to walk back up to the crest to check. This makes me nervous, and I don't want us in any more danger."

Hannah gently touched Adam's arm and said, "Please be careful, Adam."

After promising Hannah he would, Adam walked back out onto the road and began the short walk up to the crest. He had walked about halfway up before deciding he might be vulnerable if he stayed in the open and moved off the road to the cover of the trees. After another minute of walking steadily upward through the trees, he knew he was close to the top of the ridge and paused to get his bearings. A soft breeze began gently wafting over the ridge and down to his position. Adam frowned as he listened intently. Could he hear someone talking?

Closing his eyes, he turned his head slightly and concentrated on the sounds of the forest. The breeze continued to waft gently, but the noise had stopped. He wondered whether it was just his imagination. They had been through a lot, and he was clearly on edge.

Being careful not to step on anything that might signal his presence, Adam walked a few more steps and stopped to listen again. Putting his hand to his mouth, he closed his eyes again to concentrate. The silence was punctuated by several low whispers—a man talking quietly. There was no doubt in his mind that someone was close by and talking quietly. Standing perfectly still, Adam contemplated the possibilities. It didn't seem plausible that Darcy would have switched cars, and he had no reason to think that anyone else was following them. Perhaps it was all a coincidence and whoever it was had no interest in them or the money?

With a slight shake of his head, Adam realized he would need to check it out fully before he returned to Hannah and Michael. If they were still being followed, he needed to know more before they decided what to do. Being deliberately careful with every step he made, Adam slowly moved forward, thankful for the thick cover of trees. After ten more steps, he stopped behind a slightly denser thicket of trees to listen again. The voice sounded extremely close, almost within arm's reach. Adam didn't dare risk going any further for fear of exposing himself and gently bent down one of the tree branches in front of him to peer through the thicket.

His pulse began to race as he could see the legs of a man standing just a few feet from him. The man was wearing blue denim jeans. He figured it was highly unlikely to be Darcy, who had been wearing worn tan chinos just a couple of hours ago.

Adam slowly returned the branch to its normal position before he gently let it go. Taking a deep breath, Adam placed his hand on a slightly higher tree branch and very slowly bent it back toward him, hoping to get a better view of the man. As the upper part of the man's torso came into view, he could see the man with his back to him talking in a low voice on what looked like a large walkie-talkie.

Doing his best to control his breathing, Adam strained to hear the man's conversation but was only able to pick up odd words. The man looked to be several inches shorter than Adam, although it was hard to tell as he was slightly bent over as he talked in fervent whispers. While he watched the man in deep conversation, he wondered if Darcy had a partner. Whoever he was, Adam became increasingly certain that someone else was also after the money.

Deciding it was too risky to stay here any longer, Adam began to carefully release the branch back into position. At the same time, the man shifted his feet and turned slightly sideways. For a fraction of a second, Adam caught a side profile view of the man's face. After gently releasing the branch back into place, Adam stood still, totally confused by what he had just seen. He knew he needed to get back to Hannah and Michael as soon as possible but found it impossible to get his legs moving as he tried to understand why Aaron Winter was following them.

Chapter Twenty-Nine

Adam carefully backed away from the thicket of trees before pausing for a moment to listen for any sign that he may have been discovered. It was clear to him that his lawyer wasn't operating alone, and the last thing he needed right now was for Winter to be conveying his presence by two-way radio to whoever was with him.

The forest had returned to complete silence, which put Adam even more on edge. He felt exposed in his current position and decided he needed to move quickly. Trying to be as silent as possible, Adam walked at a brisk pace down through the trees, looking back regularly to see if he had been followed. When he reached the small clearing, he looked around but couldn't see any sign of Hannah and Michael.

Puzzled, Adam scanned the surrounding area for any signs of where they might have gone. He softly called out their names and thought he heard a faint sound coming from the path he had just returned on. Concerned that

Michael might be having another seizure, Adam walked over to the path to look back up through the trees and froze as he saw Aaron Winter standing just a few feet up the path.

His lawyer had replaced the two-way radio with a gun, which he pointed at Adam's chest. The gun looked unnatural in Winter's hand, but Adam was not about to take any chances and raised his hands slightly to show he was unarmed.

Even though Winter was the one holding the gun, he looked anxious and unsure of himself. Without attempting to hide his frustration, Adam asked, "What the hell are you playing at, Aaron?"

Winter quickly closed the gap between the two of them and pressed the barrel of the gun to Adam's chest. He looked highly agitated, and Adam didn't want to exacerbate the situation any further and raised his hands higher to show he was going to cooperate.

In a low voice, Winter replied, "If you want to live, shut your mouth and do exactly what I say."

Adam tried to remain calm, fearing any sudden movement might cause the gun to accidentally discharge. He looked down at the gun and quickly nodded his agreement.

"Do you remember the name Finn Prosser, Adam?"

Adam nodded again as he recalled the times Joseph had talked about the drug dealer his brother had been involved with.

In a low voice, Winter said, "Good. Because he's down on the other side of the next bridge waiting for you. He wants his money back and doesn't care how he gets it."

Winter paused but kept the gun firmly pressed against

Adam's chest as he waited for Adam to acknowledge he understood.

Holding Winter's stare, Adam replied, "Okay."

"He's not planning on letting you, or Joseph's wife or son, survive this. As soon as he gets his money, the three of you will be dead. So here's the deal, you give me the money now, and you get to live."

Winter paused a moment to let what he said sink in and then said, "I told him my batteries were running flat on the two-way and I was going back to the car to get replacements. I figure I've got two more minutes before he becomes suspicious. You need to tell me where the money is now, Adam, or we'll all be dead."

Adam hesitated for a moment. His lawyer had not only double-crossed him but was now in the process of double-crossing a drug dealer who had a track record of killing people that got in his way. He wasn't sure Winter would keep his promise to let him live, but he was not about to argue while he still had a gun stuck in his chest.

"It's in a case under the front passenger seat."

Adam breathed a sigh of relief as Winter withdrew the gun from his chest and whispered, "Smart move, Adam, now lie down on the ground."

Adam did as he was told and watched Winter back up to the Camaro with the gun still pointed at him. Reaching in through the open driver's side window, Winter removed the keys from the ignition and flung them into the forest.

"My insurance that you won't be following me anytime soon, Adam."

With his head slightly raised, Adam watched as Winter quickly walked around to the passenger side of the Camaro and opened the door. Getting down on his knees, Winter reached in under the seat to extract the case.

The Final Proposition

Winter pulled it forward, but the case wouldn't come out through the small opening. Winter swore under his breath, dropped the gun on the passenger seat, gripped the case with both hands, and pulled harder. The case still refused to move, and the lawyer, now sweating and clearly frustrated, pushed the case back further under the seat to try a different angle.

After several more unsuccessful attempts to remove the case, Winter turned to Adam and said, "How did you get it in there in the first place?"

Adam wasn't about to tell his lawyer that he had pushed the case in from the back seat area and that was the only way to get it out. Instead, he calmly replied, "It must have gone in at a different angle."

Winter grabbed his gun and stood up.

"Okay, smart guy, come and get it out."

Adam got to his feet, and as he walked toward Winter, they both heard a car start in the distance. Winter cursed as the engine roared to life and ran to the side of the road to look down toward the bridge.

The whole situation seemed surreal to Adam as he watched Winter turn and sprint out of sight back up through the trees and back toward the top of the ridge. While he did his best to process what was happening, Adam heard the sound of the car rapidly changing gears as it roared up the hill toward him.

Adam had only heard bad things about Finn Prosser from Joseph, including how he had gotten away with murdering a guard during one of his terms in jail. Knowing he only had a short time to hide, he reached in behind the front seat of the Camaro and removed the attache case. After slamming the car door, he quickly scanned the area for any sign of Hannah and Michael before heading for the cover of the trees. He headed in the direction Winter had thrown the keys and wondered where Hannah and Michael could possibly be.

The sound of the car grew quickly louder as it approached. Adam had counted five gear changes so far and figured the car must now be in top gear as it climbed the hill. Crouching low under the cover of the trees, he shifted his position slightly until he had a partial view of the road.

Adam breathed again as a dark blue car shot by, heading toward the crest at the top of the hill. It looked like Prosser was more interested in Winter than the money for the moment, and he hoped the confrontation would give him enough time to find Hannah, Michael, and the car keys. After he emerged from the cover of the trees, he called out in a louder voice, "Hannah, Michael?"

To his relief, Hannah and Michael emerged from the trees on the opposite side of the small clearing. They both appeared unharmed as they quickly made their way across to Adam.

Hannah said, "Michael had to pee and wanted to go behind a tree. We walked back into the forest and then heard someone coming. I thought it was you and nearly said something until I saw the gun. I made Michael crouch down, and we moved further back out of sight."

Not wanting to waste a second, Adam said, "We need to find those keys and get out of here before one or both of them come back."

Hannah nodded and said, "You're right, Adam."

They made their way further back into the trees to the area where Adam thought the keys had landed and began their search.

Adam put the attache case down and said to Michael,

"You and your mom look on the ground. I'm going to look in the trees just in case they got snagged on a branch."

They had only searched for about a minute before the silence was shattered by the sound of a gunshot at the top of the ridge, which was quickly followed by the sound of first one car and then a second car starting up. Adam listened for a moment to the sound of the two cars as they accelerated and rapidly changed gears. Adam had no doubt they were coming back down the hill as the sound grew louder.

He turned to Hannah and Michael and said, "I think they're chasing each other, but I can't be sure. Stay here and keep searching for the keys, while I go take a look. If it looks like they're coming after us, I'll yell for you to run. Grab the money and disappear into the forest and don't stop."

With an alarmed look, Hannah replied, "And what about you, Adam?"

"I'll make it up as I go along."

The sound of the two cars grew louder, and Adam knew they would have their answer in seconds.

Trying to remain calm, he said to Hannah, "It will be okay," before he turned and sprinted back to the road.

Adam arrived back at the road in time to see a white Ford flash by, followed closely by a dark blue Subaru WRX. Both cars were driving at crazy speeds, and it was clear to Adam that the WRX was trying to run the Ford off the road. Adam watched spellbound as both cars headed down and around the long sweeping bend toward the bridge.

Amidst the squealing tires and the pungent smell of rubber, it was clear the high-performance WRX had superior speed as it began to nudge the back of the Ford. Adam got a side view of the Ford as the two cars hit the straight approach to the bridge. It was clearly Winter behind the wheel of the Ford, desperately trying to escape.

With the distance to the bridge closing rapidly, the WRX surged forward again and shunted the right rear side of the Ford. Adam watched in shock as the Ford lurched violently forward across the road. Winter continued to wrestle with the steering wheel in a futile attempt to regain control. The two cars began to separate as the WRX braked to a controlled halt just short of the bridge, while the Ford skidded on out of control. The loud bang and shattering of glass that followed signaled the chase was over. Adam stared in disbelief as the Ford bounced off both concrete walls of the bridge like a chrome ball in a pinball machine before finally coming to a stop in the middle of the bridge.

In the silence that followed, Adam surveyed the carnage of crumpled metal and broken glass. He fixed his gaze on Aaron Winter who remained still in a slumped position in the driver's seat. It was impossible for him to tell from this distance whether Winter was dead or alive, but he guessed dead based on the damage and the driver's stillness.

Adam looked back at the WRX and watched as the man he assumed was Prosser emerged from the car holding a gun. The man was in his mid-thirties and had a short, blond crew cut. Adam debated leaving now to go back and find the car keys, but he knew that understanding what happened here could also be important.

Totally unaware that he was being watched, Prosser

walked confidently to the Ford with his gun drawn and pointed at Winter. He stopped several feet short of the vehicle and appeared to be studying the lawyer. Adam couldn't tell exactly what Prosser was doing but guessed he was trying to determine if Winter was dead or just faking it. Adam half expected Prosser to fire several rounds into Winter's body just to make sure, but the shots never came. Instead, Prosser stepped forward and attempted to open the driver's door, but it refused to budge. Prosser quickly walked around the car, testing each of the mangled doors without success to see if any of them could be opened.

Undeterred, Prosser placed his gun on the mangled roof of the Ford and then kicked in the remaining few shards of glass in the front driver's window before reaching in. Adam was too far away to see what was happening but suspected Prosser was searching Winter's body. A moment later, Prosser withdrew his arm from the car and walked around to the car's trunk. Adam had seen enough. Knowing Prosser wasn't going to find what he was looking for, he turned to quickly head back to continue the search for the keys.

He had only taken five steps before he heard Prosser's voice yelling with rage in the distance. Adam doubted Prosser would stay at the bridge much longer and began sprinting back to Hannah and Michael.

Hannah looked up as she heard Adam approach and asked, "What happened?"

"Winter lost control and crashed on the bridge. I think he's dead. The guy chasing him has just discovered he doesn't have the money. I think…"

Adam stopped talking as he heard the sound of the WRX starting up in the distance. The sound of the car was momentarily dwarfed by Michael as he yelled out, "I found them!"

Adam turned with relief to see Michael reaching up and gently pulling the keys off a small tree branch.

Adam strode over to Michael and patted him on the back as he took the keys. "Good job, Champ."

He quickly turned back to Hannah as the sound of the WRX accelerating and changing gears grew louder in the background. "Take the money and head deep into the forest with Michael. I'll take the Camaro and see if I can get him to follow me away from here."

With a worried look on her face, Hannah replied, "Adam, we…"

Adam cut her off. "We'll talk later when I get back." He turned and sprinted to the Camaro.

The sound of Prosser's car grew louder, and by the time Adam was in the Camaro with the engine started, he had already counted off four gear changes. Shifting the Camaro into first gear, Adam dropped the clutch and pulled out onto the road.

Adam gritted his teeth as he caught sight of the WRX already halfway around the sweeping bend and rapidly heading in his direction. He knew his chances of getting by both Prosser and the wreckage on the bridge were almost zero. As he accelerated and shifted into second gear, he decided his best option was a U-turn in the hope that Prosser would follow him on the road back to Windmere.

After accelerating slightly to pick up speed, he turned the steering wheel slightly to the right and held his breath as he pulled hard on the handbrake. The Camaro began to spin as the front wheels locked, and he hoped a maneuver he hadn't tried since he was seventeen would work. The turn had to get him facing in the opposite direction in one clean movement if he was to have any chance of getting away. He knew if he didn't get it right he would end up sideways across the road or stuck in the ditch and be forced to abandon the car and make a run for it.

While the Camaro spun through an almost perfect one hundred and eighty-degree turn, Adam engaged the clutch and slipped the Camaro back into first gear in one fluid movement. Pushing the accelerator to the floor, he dropped the clutch again and found hope as the Camaro's rear wheels spun and the car began to move away in the opposite direction.

Crouching low over the steering wheel, he willed the Camaro to pick up speed quickly as the distinctive pitch of the WRX's performance motor became much louder. With the motor in the Camaro now screaming, Adam began rapidly changing gears as the car accelerated and shot back over the crest in the road where Winter had been hiding. After changing into top gear, he glanced down briefly at the speedometer. Already doing over seventy miles an hour, he began to doubt the forty-year-old car had enough top-end speed to keep the WRX at bay for long.

The Camaro started to pick up speed but not quickly enough, and Adam braced as he heard a loud bang and felt the Camaro surge forward as it was rammed from behind. He wrestled with the steering wheel as the car swerved violently to the left and managed to keep the car on the road. He didn't need a rearview mirror to know that Prosser had caught him and was trying to run him off the road.

Keeping his foot flat to the floor, Adam cursed and

quickly went through his options as the two cars raced down a long straight section of road. He had no idea what the top speed of his Camaro was, but he knew it wasn't going to be enough to outrun the WRX. He needed a plan B and fast. Glancing in the rearview mirror, Adam saw the WRX surging again and braced himself for the second impact.

The bang was deafening this time and pitched Adam forward into the steering wheel, causing him to momentarily lose control of the car. Adam braked hard in the hope of causing a collision with the WRX as the Camaro swerved sharply across the road. Keeping his foot on the brake, Adam hung on tightly to the steering wheel as the Camaro spun out of control. After two and a half revolutions, the Camaro skidded off the road and slammed sideways into a small clump of trees.

Adam sat dazed and disorientated for several seconds before he realized the car had stopped moving. He had a splitting headache and rapidly blinked his eyes to bring everything back into focus. After realizing the Camaro was now facing back the way he had come, he tried to look out the driver's side window, in search of Prosser, but his view was largely obscured by trees that were pressed hard up against the car.

The ringing in his ears was drowned out by the sound of the WRX accelerating back toward him again. Instinctively, Adam slammed the car back into first gear and hit the accelerator. He quickly realized the car was stuck on tree branches as his back wheels began to spin. Glancing in the rearview mirror as he shifted into reverse, Adam saw the WRX bearing down on him again. This time, Prosser was holding what looked like a gun out his window, ready to fire at him.

The Final Proposition

Adam dropped the clutch again and prayed he would have better luck in reverse. He screamed, "Come on," at his car as the wheels spun for several seconds before gripping and catapulting the Camaro backward out of the trees and onto the road again. Running on adrenaline and with his eyes locked on the rearview mirror, he braced for impact as the Camaro reversed back into Prosser's car.

The impact of the two cars colliding gave him a mild whiplash as the Camaro shuddered, but Adam knew escape depended on keeping the car moving. Gritting his teeth, he kept a tight grip on the steering wheel and his foot planted firmly on the accelerator. This time the momentum was with the Camaro, and as his car continued to accelerate in reverse, the lighter WRX peeled away. Adam's gaze quickly shifted from the rearview mirror to the view through his front windshield. As he picked up speed in reverse, he was surprised to see Prosser stop and get out of his vehicle to begin searching on the ground.

Realizing Prosser must have dropped his gun, Adam was thankful for the few seconds' reprieve. He was disappointed that the damage to the WRX looked relatively minor. Once back in his car again, Prosser would have little trouble catching him, no matter how much of a head start he had. He continued to reverse up the road at speed until he spotted a small, overgrown track on the left-hand side of the road that led back down into the forest.

Braking hard, Adam quickly surveyed the track as he shifted the Camaro back into first gear. The track was covered with vines and weeds but looked passable—at least for a short distance. He knew this was his best chance of escape and hit the accelerator. The Camaro responded, and he pulled hard on the steering wheel to swing his car off the road and onto the track.

He had barely left the road before he heard a gunshot. Adam instinctively ducked down as the cabin of the Camaro filled with small pieces of safety glass. He had no idea how close the bullet had come to hitting him, but as he glanced in the rearview mirror to see his rear window shot out, he knew it had been close. Keeping low in the seat in the hope of presenting a smaller target, Adam tried to accelerate, but a combination of thick fallen debris and sharp twists and turns in the track made the Camaro's progress slower than he had hoped.

Still in first gear and finding it difficult to pick up pace, he hadn't gone far before he heard the WRX closing in on him again. As the Camaro crashed further into the forest, he realized he needed to abandon the car if he were to have any hope of survival. Pulling hard to the right on the steering wheel, Adam brought the car around a bend in the track and into a small clearing.

Without bothering to brake, Adam opened the door and leaped out of the Camaro to make a run for it. As his feet hit the ground, he skated across the muddy surface and tumbled forward. Adam rolled several times before his motion was abruptly stopped by a large, moss-covered boulder. Dazed by a sharp shooting pain that ran up the left-hand side of his neck, he lay still, looking up at the filtered sunlight that streamed through the thick forest canopy before everything went black.

Chapter Thirty

Max lay on the floor, staring up through the cobwebs and steel girders at the roof of the workshop. After meeting with the insurance assessor at what was left of his house, he had retrieved the mattress from the garage and driven back into town in the hope of getting a couple of hours' sleep. He had spent close to an hour tossing and turning, but sleep eluded him as Hanley's words kept ringing in his ears: "I didn't kill her, but I did watch."

He felt no remorse for Hanley's death. The corrupt judge had gotten off lightly. He would have preferred to see Hanley still alive and rotting in jail—stripped of his dignity and exposed to the world for what he was. He mulled over Hanley's last words about taking Justine to one of his favorite fishing spots to have her killed as he rolled over on the mattress to get comfortable.

He wondered if they had buried her there as well. He thought about returning to the judge's house to see if he could learn anything more about where the judge liked to fish but decided it was too risky.

Giving up on sleep, Max sat up on the mattress and thought about what to do next. He realized the judge's admission would drive him even harder to find his daughter. Someone must know where Hanley liked to fish? He wondered how he could find out discreetly without drawing attention to himself. He mentally went through a list of all the people he knew in Stanwyck that had some association with the judge and settled on the name of Jonas Small as a starting point. Jonas had worked part-time for Hanley as a handyman and gardener but had come to Max's garage several weeks ago seeking work because Hanley wasn't paying him properly.

Everyone in Stanwyck knew Jonas was simple. At the insistence of his teachers, he had spent an extra year and a half at school, but it had not helped much. Now in his mid-twenties, Jonas had drifted from job to job but had struggled to find anything permanent. In spite of his limited intellect, Jonas was handy with his hands and had become adept at fixing small engines. Max was still considering giving him a job and decided it would be worthwhile paying him a visit. It would be easy enough to work the judge into a conversation and, hopefully, find out if Jonas knew anything about where Hanley liked to fish.

With his mind made up, Max walked across the workshop and into the tiny shop front of his garage and picked up the wall phone. Cradling the phone between his neck and shoulder, he pulled out a small, homemade business card that he had wedged behind the phone and awkwardly dialed the number Jonas had left him. While he waited for the number to connect, he thought of his daughter again and promised himself he would find her, whatever it took.

Chapter Thirty-One

Adam opened his eyes, unsure how long he had been unconscious. He found himself lying in shadows and having difficulty breathing. The throbbing in his head made him feel nauseous, and as he blinked rapidly to bring his vision back into focus, he realized he wasn't alone. At first, all he saw was a gun barrel, and then he felt the steel cap of a boot press down firmly on his throat. He realized he must have blacked out for more than a few seconds as the full figure of Finn Prosser gradually came into focus.

Close up, Prosser looked no different from any other man Adam had seen inside prison—except for his eyes. Their emerald green color accentuated his narrow face and gave him a cold, almost deranged look. Releasing the pressure just slightly from Adam's throat so that he could respond, Prosser asked, "Where's my money, asshole?"

Adam had no idea how long he had been unconscious for. If it was minutes, Prosser would have already searched the Camaro and would know he didn't have the money. Adam debated telling him the money was hidden elsewhere but decided that was too risky. If Prosser overreacted and shot him, he would almost certainly head back to where Adam had left Hannah and Michael in search of the money—something Adam was desperate to avoid.

Trying to control his rising panic, Adam decided to hedge his bets and answered in as even a voice as he could muster, "It's hidden in the Camaro."

Prosser shook his head and said, "You're lying."

"It's in the trunk under the spare wheel."

Adam waited as Prosser contemplated his answer. Adam banked on Prosser keeping him alive just a little longer and did his best to remain calm as Prosser lifted the pressure from his boot just slightly.

"We can do this the easy way or the hard way. The easy way is you give me the money and I shoot you quick and clean."

Prosser paused as his sneer turned into a taunting smile before he continued, "But if you're lying—well, let's just say we're all alone in the woods and no one's going to hear you screaming. By the time I'm through with you, you'll have told me everything I need to know and you'll be begging me to finish you off."

Adam replied flatly, "I said it's in the trunk under the spare wheel."

Prosser signaled for Adam to get up as he removed his boot from Adam's throat and began to move back several paces. With the gun pointed at Adam's temple, he calmly nodded in the direction of the Camaro and said, "Hands in the air and walk slow and steady."

After raising his hands, Adam looked at the Camaro. After he had jumped out, it had rolled on a short distance

The Final Proposition

and was now partially wedged into some undergrowth at the edge of the clearing.

"I need to get the keys out of the ignition."

"Don't try anything stupid."

Adam slowly walked the few remaining steps to the Camaro and, keeping one hand in the air, reached in and pulled the keys out.

Raising both hands again, he looked back at Prosser as he walked around to the back of the car. He inserted the key in the lock to open the trunk, conscious that Prosser was moving around behind him. He wondered whether Prosser was going to shoot him there and then and decided to go on the defensive as best he could.

After opening the trunk, he turned slightly to get a better look at where Prosser was going to stand and said, "I'm going to have to remove some of the luggage. You okay with that?"

Prosser nodded once. "No sudden movements or it's the last thing you'll ever do."

Adam took this as his cue, reached in, and picked up the first of three bags. He deliberately picked the smallest one, and as he withdrew the bag, he half turned to his left before dropping it to the ground at the side of the Camaro.

Prosser yelled, "I said no sudden movements, asshole!"

Keeping his head down as he turned back to the Camaro, Adam caught a sideways view of Prosser. Prosser seemed to be comfortable standing in the one spot now. Adam repeated the same movements with the second bag and was relieved when Prosser gave no further reaction when he dropped the second bag alongside the first.

Adam did his best to hide a deep breath as he reached into the car to get the last bag. It was the biggest of the three, and he hoped it would hide what he was about to do. As he went to pick up the bag, he called out over his shoulder, "This one's got some of the money in it."

Trying his best to simulate the same motions he had used the previous two times, Adam grabbed the top handle of the bag with his left hand and reached around to grip the base of the bag with his right hand. As he reached behind the bag, he picked up the steel tire iron he had used earlier to replace the flat tire. Adam wasn't confident his sleight of hand would go unnoticed and did his best to mask what he was doing by continuing his explanation.

He picked up the bag and said in as natural a voice as he could muster, "It wouldn't all fit in the tire well…"

Using the same motion he had done twice before, Adam turned left with the bag and continued, "So you need this one…"

Prosser's eyes were momentarily drawn to the bag as Adam tossed it. He used the same motion as he had the previous two times but lobbed the bag slightly higher and further away from the Camaro. Prosser's attention shifted for a split second from Adam to the bag as it floated through the air.

While the time span was small, the distraction was long enough for Adam to raise the tire iron and fling it like a throwing knife at Prosser's chest. As the tire iron stuck, Adam lunged forward at Prosser. The thud of the steel tire iron cracking Prosser's ribs was all but drowned out by the sound of the gun discharging. Adam felt no pain beyond the impact of the collision with Prosser as they fell to the ground. If he had been shot, he didn't feel it yet.

Adam tried to push Prosser away as the two men

The Final Proposition

struggled before realizing Prosser still had the gun. Desperate to keep the gun pointed away from him, Adam grabbed Prosser's right wrist tightly with both hands. Adam felt like he was holding his own as the two men struggled until Prosser drove his knee into Adam's groin.

Adam gasped as his world momentarily turned black and a wave of nausea flooded over him. Fearing he would pass out with a repeat of the attack, Adam lifted his left knee high to protect the front of his body. Momentarily weakened, Adam struggled to hold the gun at bay as Prosser locked his left hand around the gun as well. Seizing on Adam's slightly weakened state, Prosser swung the gun toward Adam's head. Keeping his two-handed grip firm around Prosser's right wrist, Adam pushed back for all he was worth. Both men were now totally focused on the gun, which hovered like a large, deadly, metal wasp between them.

Second by second, Adam felt his grip on Prosser's wrist slipping as his hands began to sweat. Adam knew he was losing the battle as the gun barrel moved closer to his face.

Impatient for victory, Prosser tried to knee Adam in the groin again. As Prosser brought his knee up and connected with Adam's shin, Adam pushed back with all his strength. Sweating profusely now, Adam gritted his teeth as his hold on Prosser's wrist continued to slip. Sensing victory, Prosser made one last lunge with the gun, but in doing so, he left his lower body exposed. Desperate to keep out of the firing line for as long as he could, Adam brought his right knee up into Prosser's groin with full force. The surge of air coming from Prosser's mouth as his knee connected was fleeting and enveloped by the sound of the gun discharging inches from Adam's face.

Adam saw the upper right side of Prosser's head evaporate into a sea of red mist as the sound of the lethal discharge began ringing in his ears. Prosser seemed neither surprised or angry by what was unfolding. As the red mist dissipated, Prosser, now missing most of the right side of his face, fell forward across Adam before lying still.

Still holding Prosser's right wrist, Adam pushed the dead weight of Prosser's body up and off his chest and then rolled him away. Shutting his eyes, Adam breathed deeply and waited for his heart rate to return to normal. He wanted to get up and head back to Hannah and Michael immediately, but as shock and exhaustion set in, he lay still. After several minutes, he felt his energy levels beginning to return to normal and turned his head to look at the lifeless body of Finn Prosser.

Adam was drawn to Prosser's jawline which was now offset at an acute angle. Adam carefully tilted the remains of Prosser's head back slightly and found the bullet's entry wound just below his assailant's jawline. As he let go, he realized how lucky he had been. When the gun had discharged, their faces had almost been touching. The gun barrel would only have needed to be pointing a few degrees in the other direction and it would be him lying dead instead of Prosser.

After getting to his feet, Adam slowly made his way to the back of the Camaro and put the bags back in the car. Adam looked down at his shirt as he went to shut the trunk and realized he was covered in blood. Not wanting Michael or Hannah to see him like this, he peeled it off and reached into the trunk to grab a water bottle and a clean shirt from his bag. After rinsing off as best he could, he put on the fresh shirt and closed the trunk. He took a quick look back along the track and decided he had just enough room to drive around Prosser's WRX without having to move it off the road.

After starting the engine and executing a neat three-point turn, Adam slowly drove out of the clearing. For the first time that day, he didn't bother with the rearview mirror.

Chapter Thirty-Two

Despite the panel damage and the lack of a back window, the Camaro cruised along surprisingly well, and it only took Adam ten minutes to make the return trip to where he had left Hannah and Michael. After pulling up to a halt, he turned the engine off and sat in the car for a moment. The clearing was deserted which didn't surprise him. It had been over an hour since he had left Hannah and Michael, and he figured they would have taken his advice and would now be hidden deep in the forest.

While contemplating in which direction he should start his search, Adam tried to digest everything that had just happened. Two men who were alive two hours ago were now dead, and he was lucky—very lucky—he was not one of them. The day had long since turned into a nightmare, and he found it ironic that his life in jail now looked appealing by comparison.

He knew in time he would get over today and what had happened, provided he lived that long. He wondered what Joseph would make of it all if he were able to somehow see what was unfolding? He thought back about how many times a gun had been shoved in his face today and shook his head in disbelief as he opened the car door.

After stepping out of the car, he heard a familiar voice calling out to him.

"Adam?"

Adam turned and looked down one of the forest trails to see Hannah rushing forward to meet him. Before he had a chance to respond with anything more than "Hello," Hannah reached him and flung her arms tightly around him. After what he had been through, Adam found instant comfort in Hannah's embrace and held her tightly. He had so much to tell her, but he found the silence and the warmth of her embrace cathartic. No longer feeling alone, he allowed his body to relax as he began to realize Hannah was someone he could really trust.

Still embracing Adam, Hannah pulled back slightly and said, "We were so scared, Adam. When Prosser took off after you like that, I thought…"

In a reassuring voice, Adam replied, "I'm okay, Hannah."

"When I saw your car driving back, I was so happy. But you didn't get out of the car straight away, and then I wasn't sure. I thought maybe it was Prosser trying to trick us into showing ourselves. I thought we'd lost you…"

It had been a long time since Adam had been embraced by anyone other than Max. While he was enjoying the intimacy of the moment with Hannah, he still felt awkward. The barriers he had erected around himself as a defense mechanism during his time in prison were going to take time to dismantle. Feeling slightly unsure of what he should do next, he pulled away from Hannah and said, "Where's Michael?"

"He's safe. I told him to stay hidden until I gave him the okay to come back up."

Hannah turned around and called, "Michael, it's okay—Adam's back. It's safe to come out."

They both watched as Michael appeared from the same spot Hannah had been hiding in. Clutching the attache case, he ran toward them with a big grin spreading across his face. Adam was pleasantly surprised when Michael dropped the case and hugged him.

"Hey, Michael, I see you've been doing a good job looking after your mom."

Michael replied, "She's pretty easy to look after."

Adam and Hannah laughed as he replied, "I'm pleased to hear that."

Hannah turned serious again and said, "Where's Prosser?"

Letting go of Michael, Adam said, "Hey, Champ, how about you go and put the attache case back in the car and wait for us there, okay?"

Michael looked from Adam back to his mother and, in a slightly disappointed voice, said, "Okay," before picking up the attache case and making his way over to the Camaro. Adam waited until Michael began silently inspecting the damage to the Camaro before he answered Hannah's question.

"Prosser's dead."

Adam went on to explain how he had been chased for miles before their final confrontation and Prosser's death by a gunshot wound at his own hand.

Hannah put her arms around Adam again. "You

The Final Proposition

saved us, Adam. If he hadn't followed you, I'm sure he would have found and killed us."

Adam felt slightly embarrassed and downplayed what had happened. "I'm just glad it's over. He's dead, we're alive, and that's all that matters."

Adam paused to look around and then continued, "We need to get out of here. This place is starting to creep me out."

Hannah let go of Adam and asked, "Are you going to report this to the police?"

Adam briefly looked in the direction of Michael, who was still circling the Camaro inspecting all the damage, before answering. "The place where it happened is well away from the road. He could be there for weeks or even months before he's discovered. I'm thinking of just leaving this mess and moving on. I didn't leave any prints on the gun, and I think any traces of DNA I might have left behind will be gone in a day or two."

Hannah nodded. "I don't want to influence you one way or another, Adam, I know this must be hard for you."

"Prosser and Winter are both dead because of the choices they made. We're not responsible, and right now, the priority is Michael."

They both turned to look at Michael as he called out, "Adam, what happened to your car? It's banged up real bad."

Adam had not really checked the extent of the damage to his Camaro, and as he walked back to the car with Hannah, he realized his car, while drivable, was going to require major repairs.

"The man who chased after me ran me off the road, Champ. I'm lucky to be alive."

In a much quieter voice, almost as if he was afraid to ask, Michael replied, "Is he dead?"

Adam realized it was going to be impossible to keep the truth from Michael without lying, which he didn't want to do, and replied, "Yes, Michael, he is."

Michael said nothing more for a moment and then stepped forward and stretched out his hand. Moving it in and out of the gap where the rear window used to be, he exclaimed, "Your back window's gone, Adam."

Adam surveyed the extent of the damage before replying. Prosser's car had severely dented the rear of the Camaro when he had been rammed, and both sides of the vehicle were now badly dented and scratched. It was going to take thousands of dollars and weeks of work to repair his car. While Adam was disappointed, it was still just a car and could be rebuilt again. He was keen to lighten the mood and get them all out of here.

Looking back at Michael, Adam winked and said, "I don't think Max is going to be very happy when he sees the car. Do you think I'm going to be in trouble?"

Michael smiled and said, "I think Max is going to…"

Pausing mid-sentence, Michael sniffed the air and then dropped to his knees and began looking under the car. "Do you smell fumes, Adam?"

Adam had not smelled any fumes, but his focus had been elsewhere. Concerned that Michael might have discovered something, Adam got down on his knees next to Michael and began inspecting the undercarriage of the Camaro. He realized immediately that Michael had been right as he also smelled the unmistakable strong odor of gas fumes.

Turning to look up at Hannah, he asked, "Hannah, does your phone have a flashlight?"

The Final Proposition

Hannah pulled her phone from her jeans pocket and pressed a button on the side of the device to activate a small light. Adam thanked her as she passed the phone to him. He lay down next to Michael and began slowly moving the tiny phone light around underneath the car, scanning for damage to the fuel tank.

After two sweeps of the tank, Adam spotted a tiny rupture halfway up the sidewall. He suspected it had been punctured by a stick or something similar while he had been driving through the forest trying to get away from Prosser. He kept the light steady on the rupture and said to Michael, "You see that, Michael? You were right, we have a leak."

Adam had seen enough and got to his feet. Michael took this as his cue and got up as well. Turning to Hannah, Adam said, "Well, it's not as bad as having a gun shoved in your face, but it's not good either."

With a slightly alarmed look, Hannah replied, "So can we drive the car?"

"We can't drive it anywhere until we get that leak plugged. The car might catch on fire—it's too big a risk."

"Do we have anything to patch it with?"

Adam turned and looked at Michael. "You don't happen to have any chewing gum do you, Champ?"

Before Michael could reply, Hannah said, "Sorry, Adam, I don't let Michael have chewing gum. It's not good for his teeth."

Adam nodded. "Well, chewing gum or something similar would probably do to get us through to the next town. Most garages sell fuel tank patches that can get you out of trouble for a few days at least."

"Only, it's not safe to drive to a garage." Hannah waited for Adam's reply, but he was deep in thought. She waited patiently for a few moments before asking, "Adam, you're very quiet. What are you thinking?"

Adam replied, "Did you bring any soap?"

Hannah looked confused and said, "Soap?"

"I remember going on a camping trip with my dad when I was really small. I remember we had a breakdown and my dad complaining about gas. I remember he got a bar of soap and got under the truck for a few minutes and then we drove away."

"You think soap can fix a fuel leak?"

"It might just work. We rub it over the hole until it's filled in and see if it holds. The more I think about it, I'm positive that's what my father used."

"I have some in my bag in the trunk, but won't the fuel dissolve it?"

Adam got the keys from the ignition and walked around to the back of the car as he replied, "I remember doing some experiments with soap at school. First with hard and soft water and then with some other liquids. I don't remember much about it, but I do remember it behaved differently in different types of liquids."

After he opened the trunk, Hannah stepped forward and rummaged around in her bag before producing a large bar of white soap. She looked dubious as she handed it to Adam but said nothing.

Michael, who had been doing his best to let the adults talk, couldn't contain his excitement any longer and asked, "Do you think it will work, Adam?"

"Only one way to find out, Champ. If it's okay with your mom, you can hold the light for me while I work on plugging the hole."

Michael looked at his mother who nodded her agreement. While far from convinced that the soap would work, Hannah's respect for Adam continued to grow as she watched the way he naturally included Michael and made him feel important.

Lying on his back, Adam pushed forward until his head and shoulders were under the car. He didn't have to say anything to Michael, who was already by his side shining the flashlight on the exact spot on the fuel tank. Adam began to rub the bar slowly backward and forward across the fracture in the fuel tank. At first, he wasn't convinced it was going to work, but after a minute, the soap had completely filled in the fracture, and the dripping leak had stopped.

After spending another minute watching for signs that the tank was going to start leaking again, Adam said softly, "I'll be damned. I think it's going to work."

Turning to look at Michael, he said, "What do you think, Champ? Have we fixed it?"

Michael replied, "Let's tell Mom!"

Before Adam had gotten out from under the car, Michael was already on his feet and proudly announcing to his mother that they had fixed the car. Hannah waited for Adam to stand up and then asked, "You really think it's fixed?"

"It looks to be holding. I think we need to take it easy and maybe stop in ten minutes and check again. But for now, I think we're good to go. We'll fix it with a proper patch when we get to the next town."

Hannah replied, "Good, this place is creeping me out as well." Picking up the attache case, she hustled Michael into the Camaro. Adam needed no further convincing and headed for the driver's seat. He watched Hannah pass the attache case through to Michael to stow under the seat before he started the engine. He had an uneasy feeling that the quiet and peaceful life he had longed for in prison was continuing to slip further out of his reach.

Chapter Thirty-Three

Adam exited the off-road parking area and drove the Camaro slowly down the long sweeping bend toward the low-set concrete bridge. Even though Winter's car had ended up against the right-hand side barrier, he could see a lot of metal and glass debris from the accident strewn right across the bridge's road surface.

Slowing the car down to pull off the road again, he said to Hannah and Michael, "I need to go and clean all that glass and metal off the bridge before we try and cross. The last thing we need is for the Camaro to pick up a puncture."

Michael watched as Adam applied the handbrake and switched the engine off and then asked, "Can I come with you, Adam?"

Hannah knew that Adam had parked well short of the bridge to shield them from having to look at Aaron Winter's body. She turned to Michael and said, "This is a good spot for us to stop, Michael. I think Adam can manage without us, and we don't need to see what's down there for any longer than absolutely necessary. Okay?"

In a slightly disappointed voice, Michael replied, "Okay," and watched as Adam got out of the car.

Adam gave them both a brief smile to lighten the moment and said, "Be back soon," before turning to start the short walk down to the bridge.

Although he had already seen one dead body up close and personal today, Adam was still apprehensive about what he would find on the bridge. He was not looking forward to seeing his former lawyer all smashed up and mentally decided he would avoid looking in the car and just concentrate on the debris on the road that needed to be cleared away.

When he reached the bridge, he found it hard not to look at the car as his eyes were drawn to the carnage. Both front wheels had totally collapsed underneath the vehicle, and the entire front section of the car had been compressed to little more than a block of metal. Adam was thankful that the front windshield was smashed and the crazed opaque glass prevented him from seeing anything more than the silhouette of Winter's body inside.

Keeping his head down and his eyes focused on the road, Adam started slowly walking across the bridge, kicking aside metal, glass, and plastic to clear a path for them to cross over. As he approached the crushed car wreck, he took a deep breath—he would be glad when this was over and they were on their way again.

While he continued to move away the debris, he thought he heard his name whispered softly and stopped.

Turning around, he half expected to see Hannah behind him, but as he stood looking back along the bridge, he realized he was still alone. He paused for a moment and frowned, positive that he had heard his name called. Shielding his eyes from the sun, he looked back up along the road to the Camaro. As far as he could tell, Hannah and Michael were still in the car. Unable to make sense of it, he turned back to continue the cleanup task.

In a slightly louder, more urgent voice, he heard his name called again. "Adam."

Adam stopped again. The voice was weak and appeared to be coming from the direction of Winter's wrecked car. Adam walked several paces back toward the car and then stopped short of the vehicle to look in through the smashed driver's side window. He gasped in horror as Winter's eyes opened and his blood-covered head turned slowly toward him. Adam quickly walked the remaining few steps to the car and peered in through the broken window at his lawyer.

The car was crushed in on all sides, and there was almost no room for Winter to move. Winter's clothes were soaked in blood, and as he looked down, it appeared to Adam that Winter had been partially impaled by what was left of the car's steering wheel. He found it hard to believe that Winter was still conscious, let alone alive. He knew from Prosser's earlier failed attempts at opening all car doors that he would need to figure out some other way of getting Winter out.

While he tried to figure out what to do, he gently said, "Aaron, I didn't expect you to still be alive. How you survived this is a miracle."

In a shallow, raspy voice, Winter replied, "No miracle here, Adam, I'm not going to survive."

Not sure what to say in response, Adam tried to

remain positive. "I'm going to get an ambulance, I'm sure they…"

Winter cut him off, and in a weak and slightly frustrated voice, he said, "Look at me, Adam. I've got a steering wheel embedded in my gut and god knows what other internal injuries, and I'm bleeding out. I'm surprised I've hung on this long."

Adam knew Winter was probably right. He had no phone reception here and would need to drive much closer to Northwood before he had any hope of picking up phone reception again. He figured it would be well over an hour before he could get an ambulance here. Letting out a deep breath, he was unsure what to say next.

"Can I do anything to make you comfortable?"

Winter tried to laugh, but it ended badly with the lawyer wheezing and coughing up blood. After recovering, he replied, "A bullet's about the only thing that's going to make me comfortable now."

Adam responded, "How about I just stay here with you? Until it's…over?"

Winter was silent for a moment before he responded. In a voice that sounded resigned to his fate, he said, "Thank you."

In spite of his former lawyer having had a gun stuck in his face less than two hours ago, Adam felt sorry for Winter as he watched his life literally ebb away.

"Where's Prosser?"

Adam replied flatly, "Dead."

Winter started laughing but quickly stopped as he began coughing up blood again. He closed his eyes and waited until his breathing returned to normal. "He's had a hard-on for getting his money back ever since I first met him."

The Final Proposition

Even though he knew it was a cold thing to do to a man who was clearly dying, Adam decided he would use this opportunity to find out as much information as he could. They were still a long way from being safe, and any information Winter had might be vital to keeping them alive.

"And when was that?"

Winter coughed again before he responded. Adam didn't think he was imagining Winter's wheezing becoming noticeably worse and his breathing increasingly difficult.

"He contacted me through another inmate while I was defending Joseph when they were first arrested. He offered me big money if I could find out anything from Joseph about the money."

It all started to make sense for Adam. Prosser had somehow teamed up with his lawyer, and they had followed him. Before he could ask his next question, Winter continued, "I'm not proud of what I've done, Adam. No one was supposed to get hurt. I'm sorry."

"How did you know about the money?"

In a voice barely above a whisper, Winter replied, "I met with Joseph a few months back—just after he received his diagnosis. He told me about the money and wanted some legal advice on whether his wife could keep the money if it was recovered. He wouldn't tell me where it was, but I had a hunch he would tell you."

Adam nodded without saying anything. He suddenly felt less sorry for Winter as he thought about how the lawyer had taken advantage of his dying friend.

"I remembered my conversation with Prosser seven years ago and thought I could make some money on the side. I told Prosser what I knew, and Prosser insisted we team up to follow you. I didn't want any part of this, but he said no money until we got all his cash back."

"How did you track me?"

"The cell phone I lent you. I had it set up so we could track your location over the internet. I didn't expect we would wind up out here in the wilderness. We tracked you as far as Windmere last night and then lost you until late this morning. I stayed on in Windmere waiting, while Prosser went…"

Winter coughed up more blood, and Adam waited patiently as the lawyer closed his eyes again. For almost two minutes, he watched as Winter's breathing became even shallower and more irregular. Just when he thought it was all over, Winter's eyes opened slightly, and the lawyer whispered, "I'm glad he's dead…"

His lawyer attempted to continue, but Adam could not make sense of anything the lawyer said as the words were lost in a sea of blood and uncontrollable coughing. While he waited patiently for Winter to recover, Adam noticed the lawyer's raspy, labored breathing becoming increasingly shallow before stopping altogether. Adam watched in silence for a few moments before he reached in with his hand and held it in front of Winter's mouth. He could feel no breath at all, and as he studied Winter's half-open eyes that no longer focused or blinked, he knew the lawyer was gone.

Adam paused for a moment, unsure of what he should do next. He debated whether he should reach in and close Winter's eyes but decided against it. He had not touched Winter or left any fingerprints on the car that he could recall. Standing upright again, he decided there was nothing more he could do and backed away from the car.

The Final Proposition

After quickly clearing the remainder of the bridge, he looked back and was satisfied that it was now safe to cross.

He began his walk back across the bridge and paused as he got to Winter's car. He replayed the moments after the crash when Finn Prosser had walked onto the bridge to check on Winter. He couldn't recall Prosser getting Winter's gun and wondered whether it was still in the car. Adam wasn't fond of guns and considered whether it would be worthwhile having Winter's gun for extra protection if he could find it. He thought back to the three incidents where he'd had a gun pointed at him today, and the decision became easy.

Adam slowly circled the vehicle, peering in through each window, looking for any sign of the weapon. He could see no visible sign of it and wondered if Winter had it hidden in his clothing. Adam decided against reaching in and rummaging through Winter's blood-soaked clothes as he was bound to leave fingerprints. He tried to put himself in Winter's shoes when Prosser had come after him.

Closing his eyes, he pictured Winter racing back to his car as he heard the roar of Prosser's car getting closer. He was not sure who had fired the shot but pictured the lawyer getting into his car and taking off at breakneck speed. No time to stow a gun under a seat, or even put it in a glove box, he thought. He pictured Winter dropping the gun on the passenger seat as he started the car to make his escape.

Adam opened his eyes again and looked at the swirling mass of tire marks left by the car as it had spun around on the bridge at high speed. If the gun had been left on the car seat, it could be anywhere in the car by now, but he hoped it had simply slid off the seat as the car spun and ended up on the floor or perhaps jammed between the seat and the door. Adam had checked the floor of the car already and now decided he needed to check the small gaps between the seats and doors as well.

After walking around to the passenger side of the vehicle, Adam inched along the narrow gap between the car and the bridge wall until he reached the passenger door. Peering in through the window, he found it impossible to see clearly through the shattered glass. Quickly removing his shirt, he wrapped the garment tightly around his fist and then punched the remaining glass out of the door frame. Now able to see clearly, he peered into the vehicle, focusing his attention on the small gap between the passenger seat and door. Even though the light was poor, he saw what looked like the barrel of a gun protruding slightly from underneath the seat.

Satisfied he had found what he was looking for, he rewrapped the shirt around his hand like a glove and reached in to retrieve the weapon. Adam gently gripped the barrel, and after almost a minute of patiently maneuvering the weapon backward and forward, the gun finally came free.

He removed the gun from the car and carefully checked to see if he had left any fingerprints. Other than leaning on the car to reach inside, he had been careful not to touch the vehicle directly with his hands and was reasonably satisfied that he hadn't left any telltale signs of his presence behind. He backed away from the car and rewrapped the gun in his shirt as he began his walk back to the car. He wasn't sure how Hannah would react to him bringing back a weapon, but he figured this would be less confronting.

As he approached the car, Adam became concerned something was wrong as he saw Hannah sitting in the back seat with Michael. Adam broke into a run the moment he realized Michael was having another seizure. After laying the wrapped-up gun on the bonnet of the Camaro, he moved around to the passenger side and peered inside. He didn't think he would ever get used to the sight of Hannah cradling Michael in her lap. She was on the verge of tears, rocking Michael gently, and Adam was surprised at how much it affected him.

"Anything I can do, Hannah?"

Hannah responded with a quick shake of her head before returning her full attention to Michael. Adam knew this was always an anxious time for her, and as he waited patiently for Michael to recover, he realized everything they had been through today had been worth it. They still had the money, and Michael still had a chance.

When Michael began to stir again, Hannah looked up at Adam and said softly, "This was a bad one. I think today has taken its toll on him. The doctor said the seizures can be worse if he gets overtired or stressed."

"I'm sorry, Hannah, I wish there was more I could do."

Hannah held Adam's gaze and replied, "You're doing plenty, Adam. We're still alive, and we still have the money, thanks to you."

Adam thought for a moment before he responded. He recalled how Joseph had almost begged for help and wondered if his friend had somehow known this was going to be dangerous. It was almost as if Joseph had received a premonition. Any doubt about what he was doing or why he was here totally evaporated as Adam watched Hannah as she continued to care for Michael. It had never been about the money, and now it wasn't even about honoring a dying friend's last request.

He wasn't sure how to describe it, but the bond that was growing between them was changing everything. He realized he was prepared to pay any price to see Michael get a second chance. He looked on as Michael slowly started to regain consciousness and silently vowed to not only get them to Bolton but to be there to support them in any way they needed in the months ahead.

"Adam?"

Adam shook his head briefly as he responded, "Sorry, a million miles away."

"I just asked if Winter was still alive when you went down there?"

"Yes, he was."

Adam went on to explain what had happened to Winter and finished by pointing at the gun. "I hope you don't mind, but I figured after what we've been through, any additional protection we can get we should take."

"I agree entirely, Adam, but I would prefer you stowed it somewhere out of sight for the time being. Michael doesn't need to know about it just yet and hopefully not ever."

Adam replied, "Agreed," as he picked up the weapon. Hannah watched as he retrieved the weapon from the bonnet and carefully placed it in the glove compartment of the Camaro.

Hannah briefly smiled and said, "There's probably one other thing you should do, Adam."

"And what's that?"

"Michael will probably want to know where your shirt is."

The Final Proposition

Adam looked down, somewhat embarrassed that his bare chest had to be pointed out to him.

"Sorry, good point. I guess my mind has been elsewhere."

Hannah called out to him as he walked around to the trunk to get a fresh shirt, "It's no big deal, Adam. You've had a lot to think about."

After putting on a fresh shirt, Adam closed the trunk, came around to the passenger side of the Camaro, and resumed his watch position. With his eyes now open and exchanging short sentences with his mother, Michael looked to be well into recovery mode. Adam watched as Hannah, still comforting her son, asked Michael a series of questions. While they were innocent enough, Adam knew they were designed to test Michael's cognitive function. Adam could visibly see the relief on Hannah's face as Michael answered each question correctly.

After several more minutes recovering quietly, Michael said, "Hey, Mom, can I get out of the car for a minute before we get going again?"

"If you feel up to it, sweetie, but take it easy, okay?"

Michael paused in front of Adam as he got out of the car and said, "Hey, Adam, did you change your shirt?"

Michael quickly turned back to look at his mother who was now laughing softly in response to his question. With a frown on his face, Michael said, "Hey, Mom, what's so funny?"

Adam knew Hannah's laughter was as much a sense of relief that Michael had not lost his sharp observational edge as it had been about their shared joke.

Adam replied tactfully on her behalf, "Champ, I just needed a fresh shirt."

Adam turned to look at Hannah who was now smiling and continued, "Your mother seemed to think you would notice if I wasn't wearing the old one, and she was right."

Michael looked from Adam to Hannah and back again with a look that said "all adults are weird" before he started walking away from the car.

Hannah called out, "Not too far, Michael, okay?"

Michael replied, "Okay, Mom," as he bent down to pick up several small stones from the side of the road. While they watched as Michael became engrossed in a game of throwing the stones at a tree, Adam whispered to Hannah, "He looks to be recovering nicely."

"Yes, I think he is. By the way, I like the way you tactfully answered his question. He might be young, but he's sharp, and he knows when people aren't telling him the truth."

They continued to watch Michael, who was now totally absorbed in his game, before Adam shook his head slightly and said, "Michael is amazing. I've not had a whole lot to do with kids, except a couple of nieces and nephews, but he really seems out of the box."

"When he was much younger, I thought I was just a proud mother who was seeing their child through rose-colored glasses. I used to observe him doing things at his playgroup that other children of his age weren't capable of. When we had him undergo brain scans in Bolton to assess his condition, the neurosurgeon wanted as much information on Michael as he could possibly get, so they tested his IQ, and he got a result of one forty-two."

"That's genius level, if memory serves?"

"Yes. Apparently, I didn't have rose-colored glasses after all—he's just very intelligent."

Adam was impressed by Michael's skill as he

continued to watch the boy throw stone after stone accurately at the tree. Hannah observed Adam watching her son and said, "He wants to play baseball. I can't let him on account of his condition, but that's his dream. He doesn't care about being super bright, he just wants to be a boy."

"I'd like to take him to a game once you're settled in Bolton. If that's okay?"

Hannah smiled briefly and said, "He'd like that."

Adam looked up at the sky and said, "It's getting late. We need to keep going if we're going to make Northwood before dark."

Hannah watched as Adam got down on the ground to examine the fuel tank again and said, "There's no chance we can push on to Bolton tonight?"

He straightened back up and replied, "I can't smell any gas fumes, so the soap seems to be holding for the moment, but we can't risk it. If we make Northwood, we'll have done well. I can get a patch kit from a garage, but I'd prefer not to drive any further until it's had time to set properly. The last thing we need is for it to start leaking again and the car to catch on fire."

Hannah nodded, but Adam could see his answer sat uncomfortably with her. He realized she was as anxious as he was to get to Bolton.

"Hannah, if there was any way we could continue tonight, you know I would. I know we won't be safe until we reach Bolton and get the money in a bank, but we're not safe in a car that might burst into flames while we're driving either."

"You're right, Adam. I'm just freaked out by the thought of sleeping on the side of the road or in another motel room after what happened this morning."

Adam thought for a moment before he responded, "I don't think a motel is a wise idea. Even if we hide the car somewhere else, after what happened this morning, it's just too risky. And we can't just park on the side of the road either. We need to head out of town and park somewhere quiet. I can fix the tank, and then we'll give it a few hours to set while we get some sleep."

Adam could see the visible relief on Hannah's face as she listened to his strategy as he continued, "Also, we now have a gun."

Hannah thought for a moment before replying, "It's not ideal, but it's the best we can do."

Adam looked up briefly at the sky and noticed large black clouds starting to form in the south. "We'll get some food to take with us when we get to Northwood, and I'll see if I can get a tarp to cover the back window area while we sleep. The last thing we need is to be cold and wet if it starts to rain."

They both continued to watch Michael for several more minutes before Hannah called out, "Michael, it's time to go."

"I've still got two stones left, Mom, can I throw them?"

Before Hannah could reply, Adam said, "Hey, Champ, why don't you keep one? I used to collect rocks from places I visited when I was your age."

Michael seemed to like the idea and looked at his mother as if seeking permission.

Hannah nodded and said, "Just one, Michael, we don't need to be starting another collection of anything just now."

Michael nodded and pocketed the smoothest of the two stones before throwing the other one. He squealed in delight as it hit the center of the tree and began running back toward the car. As he approached, Adam said to Hannah in a low voice, "It might be best if you sit in the back with him while we cross the bridge. He doesn't need to see what's inside that car."

Chapter Thirty-Four

Max knocked on the door of the small timber frame house and stood back on the verandah to wait. Jonas's mother had answered his phone call and told him her son was out on an errand and due back in ten minutes. Rather than wait for a return phone call, Max had jumped in the truck and driven across town to where the Smalls lived.

The house was modest in size and set well back from the road in an immaculately manicured garden. The house had been recently repainted, and Max figured Jonas spent much of his spare time keeping the property in shape for his mother. He waited only a few seconds before the door opened and Jonas's huge frame filled the doorway. Max had always thought there was a lot of irony in Jonas's last name. The man was at least six foot five and anything but small. Jonas looked intimidating, but Max knew there wasn't a mean bone in the gentle giant's body.

"Hi, Jonas, did your mom tell you I'd be stopping by?"

Jonas nodded and said, "You wanna come inside?"

The Final Proposition

Max wasn't keen on having Jonas's mother listen in on their conversation and motioned for Jonas to come out and sit in one of the chairs on the verandah.

"Why don't we sit out here on the porch? I've still got my work gear on, and I don't want to mess up your furniture."

Jonas shrugged and then headed for a chair. After they were settled, Jonas looked at Max's bandaged hands and frowned. "What happened to your hands?"

Max didn't want to go into all the details now and did his best to play it down. "I had a fire at my house last night. The doctor says I'll be okay, I just need to rest."

Jonas nodded. "They look sore."

"I'll be fine. You know, Jonas, I'm not going to be much good in the garage for a couple of days, and I've been hearing that Judge Hanley knows a good fishing spot or two but won't tell anyone. I know you used to work for him and was wondering if he ever mentioned where he liked to fish?"

"I like fishing. I got a rod and reel too."

"That's good, Jonas. Did the judge ever take you fishing?"

A scowl broke out on Jonas's face. "He was mean to me. Didn't want to pay me properly. I might not be smart, but I ain't stupid. Mom said I couldn't work for him anymore if he wasn't going to pay me right."

"Your mom's right, Jonas. Everyone should be properly paid for the work they do—that's only fair. Now, back to the judge, did he ever say where he went fishing?"

Jonas's face became a picture of concentration. Max waited patiently as the huge man assembled his thoughts.

"He never really told me about fishing, on account of

he thought I was stupid. He mainly ordered me around and grumbled when I asked to be paid."

Jonas paused and frowned for a moment before he continued, "Every now and then I'd have to clean and check his four-wheel drive. He used to take trips up to Tangmere Lake and always took his fishing gear with him. So I guess he went fishing when he was there as well."

Max thought about Jonas's answer for a moment before he responded. He had camped at Tangmere Lake once during his childhood. He recalled going on a hike around the lake with his father—a trip that had taken most of the day. There would be literally hundreds of fishing spots around the lake.

"Did he ever say where he fished or where he stayed when he went up there, Jonas?"

Jonas shook his head. "No. The judge never told me anything."

"Did he ever take anyone with him?"

Jonas thought for a moment. "Can't remember anyone. He wouldn't even tell me when he was leaving or when he was coming back. I used to work four half days a week for him, but I never knew whether he'd be there or not."

Max could see Jonas was starting to get agitated as he shifted in his chair and lowered his head. It was clear the judge had taken advantage of Jonas and he was struggling to deal with it. Max didn't want the conversation being repeated to Jonas's mother, so he decided he had enough information for now. It was at least a starting point. He would journey up to the lake and ask around. Hopefully, someone would know where Hanley liked to fish.

"Jonas, you've been very helpful. Thank you."

Jonas looked gloomy but didn't say anything.

The Final Proposition

"Oh, one more thing, Jonas, are you still looking for a job?"

Jonas looked up and nodded.

"You know, Jonas, I've been giving some thought to our meeting the other day. I've got a lot going on right now, and I could really do with some help at the garage. You could repair all the lawnmowers and small engines like we discussed, and I'll get you to do some other jobs as well, like packing the ice machine and keeping the workshop clean."

A smile spread across Jonas's face. "Thanks, Max. I'm going to work real hard."

Max rose from his seat and said, "I'll see you Monday morning at eight o'clock sharp, okay?"

Jonas grinned as he got to his feet and shook Max's hand. "Eight o'clock."

"I'm going to go now, Jonas. You tell your mom about the job and get her to call me if she has any questions, okay?"

Jonas nodded. "She's going to be real happy when I tell her."

"I'm happy too, Jonas. I'll see you Monday."

Max turned and walked back to his truck. He hadn't planned on offering Jonas a job there and then, but it felt good to do what he had done. There was plenty for Jonas to do at the garage, and it would give Max more time to focus on finding Justine and dealing with his house.

After getting in his truck, he sat for a moment thinking about Tangmere Lake. It was the largest lake in the region and a popular destination for campers and anglers alike. It was also at least an hour's drive from Stanwyck, and Max wasn't overly surprised that Hanley went there to fish. He looked down at the dashboard clock before deciding it was too late to drive out there today. He would make the trip early the following morning and spend the day asking locals about Hanley and where he liked to fish.

Even though it still felt like he was searching for a needle in a haystack, he felt closer to Justine than he had at the start of the day. He started the truck and made a mental note to call Adam tonight and fill him in on everything that had happened. For now, he needed food, painkillers, and rest. Today he had seen his house burn down and a man die. As he put his truck into gear, he hoped tomorrow would be better.

Chapter Thirty-Five

Darcy looked down at the fuel gauge as he passed a sign on the outskirts of Sanbury. The sign told him the town had a population of thirty-eight thousand people and encouraged him to have a good day. He glanced at the black canvas bag on the passenger seat. Now close to three million dollars richer, he didn't need any sign to tell him to feel better.

He thought back over the day he had been waiting seven years for, as he drove past rows of small timber houses toward the center of the township. It hadn't gone totally to plan—Wells had been easy enough to follow in the beginning, but it got complicated when they had driven through the forest the previous afternoon. He hadn't been able to follow too closely for fear of being discovered and had lost them before they got to the town of Windmere.

He didn't panic as he figured they only had a five-minute head start on him. After driving into Windmere and realizing there was only one road out of town, he drove on through to the next town in the hope of catching them. His average speed for the trip was close to eighty miles an hour, and when he reached the outskirts of Northwood without sighting them, he was fairly sure they had either stopped for the night or doubled back to Stanwyck.

After spending most of the night slowly and patiently backtracking, he finally spotted the Camaro at a small, rundown motel just out of Windmere at around two a.m. He contemplated using the element of surprise and bursting in while they slept, but there was no guarantee they had the money, and he wasn't sure if Wells had a gun or not. He decided he would wait and follow them out of town the next day, looking for an opportunity where he could take them by surprise.

The moment came earlier than he imagined as Wells left in the Camaro early in the morning, presumably to get breakfast. He was disappointed that the woman didn't have the money, but taking her and the boy hostage was all he needed to make sure the money came to him. He hadn't planned on leaving them alive, but their stubborn refusal to move had surprised him.

He'd contemplated shooting all three of them there and then. It would have been easy, but it would have also left bodies in a location where they may have been quickly discovered. He didn't want to take the risk of drawing too much attention to what he was doing, yet he still felt uneasy that they were still alive. He didn't like loose ends, but he had finally gotten what he had come for and that was all that mattered.

Darcy checked his watch as he saw a Shell service station up ahead. It was after three p.m., and he had been driving for just over two hours and hadn't eaten anything

The Final Proposition

since very early that morning. He decided a break to get food and fuel would be good before he drove the final hour into the city of Bolton.

He scanned the complex as he turned left into the driveway and was pleased to see that he was the only customer. He could only see one security camera mounted at the front of the building just above the entrance to the shop, so he drove around the side of it and backed up next to the drive-through car wash. He needed a couple of minutes of privacy, and this spot was close to perfect. Confident he wouldn't be captured on camera, he grabbed the canvas bag off the passenger seat and headed around to the rear of the vehicle. After unlatching the rear cargo door, he placed the bag in the cargo area and looked around again.

He saw no one and took a Phillips-head screwdriver from a side pocket in the rear of the vehicle. With a practiced movement, he undid four concealed screws that held a panel in place at the back of the rear seat. The panel allowed him access to a special cavity behind the rear seat that he regularly used to store guns, money, and anything else that he didn't want to have to explain if he were pulled over on a routine stop by the police.

He looked up again to double-check he wasn't being watched as he unzipped the black canvas bag. Darcy pulled back the top flap and instantly knew something was wrong as he looked down at the bag. He did his best to control his breathing as he stared at the bundles of cash. He had packed them in neat rows, and now they were scattered haphazardly as if they had been hastily thrown in. He knew before he removed the top row that the bulk of the money was gone. As he lifted up two bundles of cash, he saw the paperback books and knew it was the boy.

He closed his eyes and did his best to control his rage. He had spent over thirty years in the police force and had gotten the better of the smartest and most ruthless criminal minds, yet he had allowed himself to be outsmarted by a nine-year-old.

Darcy slammed the cargo door shut and walked around to the driver's door. He stood holding the door handle, contemplating what he would do next. Leaving them alive had been a mistake and failing to recheck the bag after he had woken up had been inexcusable. He would get fuel and then head back to find them. As he opened the door to climb in, he vowed there would be no mistakes next time.

Chapter Thirty-Six

Adam slowed the Camaro to almost walking pace as they came over the small rise. As they continued scanning the road ahead through the headlights, Hannah pointed to a clearing ahead on the left-hand side of the forest and said, "What do you think, Adam?"

After briefly stopping in Northwood to buy a patch for the fuel tank, a tarp, and some takeout Chinese food, they drove out of town and back onto the road to Bolton in search of somewhere safe to stop for the night. They both felt drained, and after taking a small side road that led back into the forest, they had driven on for several minutes looking for somewhere suitable to stop.

Adam squeezed on the brakes and drew the Camaro to a halt just short of the clearing so that they could scan the area through the headlights. The grass-covered area was about the size of a tennis court and appeared to be an ideal spot to pull off the road. Surrounded by towering fir trees, he knew they would be safe here unless anyone deliberately came looking for them. "It looks perfect.

We're well away from the main road and reasonably well hidden."

Hannah cocked her head slightly to one side and replied, "And if I'm not mistaken, that's the river I can hear close by."

Michael chimed in, "Can we go look at it, Mom?"

Turning to look at Michael, Adam said, "Maybe in the morning, Champ. Right now, I was kind of hoping you could help me while I patch the fuel tank."

Michael looked expectantly at his mother, who, in turn, looked back at Adam. "Will it take long, Adam? We're all starved, and this food smells amazing."

Adam replied, "Not long," as he put the Camaro into gear and drove forward to park in the middle of the clearing.

"I'm also going to get the tarp out and put it across the rear window as well. There's been rain here earlier today, and there looks to be more on the way, and I don't want us getting wet tonight. With Michael's help, we'll have both jobs done in under ten minutes."

After parking the car, Adam was closely followed by Michael as he got out of the car to get the tarp from the trunk. With his willing young helper, he worked quickly to cover the rear windshield area of the Camaro. After getting the tarp in place and tying it off, he winked at Michael and said, "Now, let's fix that fuel tank."

Hannah watched as both Adam and Michael lay down on the ground and worked their way under the car. She smiled to herself as she heard earnest conversation coming from beneath the car as Adam patiently answered Michael's questions about what he was doing.

She reflected on the day again and how they were lucky to still be alive. Michael didn't appear to be suffering any post-traumatic stress at all, which surprised her. Not for the first time that day, she wondered whether living with a serious illness had made him somehow more resilient—perhaps it had made them both more resilient?

She waited for Adam and Michael to finish their work, and she shivered as she looked up at the tall fir trees of the forest that surrounded her. She wrapped her arms around herself to keep warm as the dull light coming from under the Camaro cast long shadows and made the whole scene feel very eerie. The prospect of spending the night out here was now not so appealing, and she wasn't sure she would be able to sleep. She was comforted by the muffled conversations coming from underneath the car and was glad she wasn't out here alone.

After several more minutes of patiently waiting, Hannah was relieved to see Michael and Adam emerge from underneath the car, with Michael proudly announcing, "We fixed it, Mom."

Hannah looked to Adam for confirmation. As he started to clean his hands with a cloth rag, Adam said, "We'll check it in the morning just to make sure, but it's setting nicely. We should make Bolton long before lunch if we leave early."

Keeping one eye on Michael as he snuck back into the car to examine the Chinese food, Hannah replied, "That's good, Adam, but we'd better go eat. If we leave Michael alone with the food for too long, there will be none left."

After settling back into the Camaro, they made small talk for the next half hour while they ate their meal. At the end, Adam let out a small belch, turned to Michael, and said, "You know, Champ, that's the best Chinese I've had in at least seven years."

They all laughed as Michael replied, "That's because it's the only Chinese you've had, Adam."

Hannah looked from Michael to Adam and said, "I wasn't sure I would be able to sleep tonight, but that Chinese has suddenly made me very sleepy."

Adam replied, "I think we should all try and get as much sleep as we can now. The patch only needs about six hours to set, so we can take off again early in the morning."

Hannah looked at Michael and said, "Michael, you do need to pee before you go to sleep."

Michael looked alarmed and said, "But where, Mom? It's dark and…"

Adam didn't let him finish. "Hey, Champ, I need to go big time. How about you and I walk over to the edge of the forest?"

Michael looked instantly relieved and turned to look at his mother, who nodded. "Go with Adam, we don't want any accidents in the car."

Hannah watched as Michael and Adam got out of the car and began their walk to the forest edge. When they reached the forest, she looked away to give them privacy. She began to relax and closed her eyes for a moment to enjoy the stillness of the evening. As best she could, she tried to shut out the image of Darcy pointing a gun at her, but the image kept returning.

Frustrated, she opened her eyes to erase the image. She knew there would be dark days ahead, but she was determined not to let Darcy or anything else that had happened that day get the better of her. She watched as Adam and Michael walked back toward the car and whispered, "You're not going to win, Darcy, I'm stronger than you."

Chapter Thirty-Seven

Adam and Hannah found sleep difficult in the cramped confines of the two front seats of the Camaro. Michael had sprawled out on the back seat and had taken only a few minutes to fall asleep after returning to the car. Adam whispered to Hannah, "Well, at least one of us is sleeping," as they listened to the peaceful sound of Michael's rhythmic breathing.

Hannah turned in the passenger seat to face Adam. Even though he couldn't see anything more than a silhouette in the darkness, he could tell by the tone of her voice that Hannah had started to relax.

"He's exhausted, so it's not surprising."

They were quiet again for a while, before Hannah asked, "You're very good with Michael, Adam. For a guy who has never had kids and has spent the last seven years in jail, you have an amazing way of connecting with him."

"I enjoy his company and he... You're both easy to talk to."

They both sat thinking for a moment, before Hannah said, "What do you think Darcy is doing right now?"

"I have no idea. Hopefully not thinking about us."

"I was thinking about him while you and Michael went to pee. I'm trying not to dwell on what happened today, but I guess it's going to be a long time before I get it out of my mind."

Adam wasn't sure how to express exactly what he wanted to say. He paused for a moment to choose his words before he replied, "You're an amazing person, Hannah. Joe said you were the strongest woman he had ever met, and I don't doubt it for one minute after what I've seen you come through. Once we get you to Bolton and you start to focus on Michael's operation, I'm sure you'll find a way to deal with it."

"I hope so, Adam."

"I struggled with Justine's death, but staying alive in prison isn't easy, and I had to remain focused. You were always on your guard, wherever you were. I saw more than one guy get badly hurt because he said the wrong thing or looked the wrong way. I grieved for sure, but having to stay focused on everything I said and did to stay alive was in many ways a welcome distraction."

"Do you still miss her?"

"I think I'll always miss her. It's hard to describe in words… She's been gone seven years, but not knowing where she is or how she died makes it harder—there's no closure."

"Hopefully the box you found will help you find her and whoever was responsible."

"Hopefully."

Adam could see Hannah's silhouette turn slightly in the seat as she faced forward to look out the front window.

The Final Proposition

"I can see stars now. I don't think we're going to get any rain here tonight."

"Good. Michael and I tied the tarp down as much as we could, but I think it still would have leaked if it rained heavily."

"Michael loved helping you tonight. You made him feel so important."

"I enjoyed it too."

"Do you want to be a father some day?"

Adam laughed softly. "I guess. I've not really given it much thought. I've got enough to worry about in the immediate future, but in the longer term—who knows?"

"I think you'd make a great father."

Adam was slightly taken aback. Compliments were almost unheard of in prison, even between Joe and him. He struggled to think of what to say in response or how to progress the conversation and settled for saying, "Thanks, Hannah."

Appearing increasingly comfortable in his presence, Hannah yawned and stretched. "I can't believe it, but I'm starting to get sleepy. I didn't think I could possibly sleep tonight, but here I am, struggling to stay awake."

Adam locked his car door and then reached across in front of Hannah and locked hers. "You try and sleep, Hannah. I think we're safe here, so there's no sense in us both being awake."

"You're not tired?"

Adam leaned across and popped the glove compartment. As he reached in to retrieve the gun, he replied, "A little. If you don't mind, I'll put the gun down on the floor at my feet. I don't expect we'll need it, but if it's within easy reach, I'll sleep better."

After he settled back in his seat, Hannah leaned across

and whispered, "I can't thank you enough for today, Adam. My baby and I are still alive because of you."

Before he had a chance to reply, Hannah reached a hand behind his head and gently drew him forward. Her soft lips met his in a full and lingering kiss, and although slightly surprised, he made no move to withdraw. When they finally separated, she said softly, "Good night, Adam."

It didn't take long for Hannah to fall sleep, and within minutes, Adam was alone with his thoughts. He smiled to himself as he listened to the regular breathing of his two sleeping passengers. After the ordeal they had been through, he was relieved they were both able to rest. After opening his window just slightly to let in some fresh air, he thought about the kiss from Hannah.

Was it just her way of saying thank you, or good night, or something else? It was more than just good night, he thought, but exactly what he didn't know—maybe Hannah didn't even know?

He decided thinking about it any further tonight was futile and he would need to wait and see what happened tomorrow. In an effort to take his mind off it, he reached down and retrieved the gun from the floor of the Camaro. He had very little experience with firing guns and hoped that wasn't about to change. Conscious of the horror stories he had heard from inmates about guns going off accidentally, he was careful to keep the gun pointed down at the floor as he unwrapped it from his T-shirt.

He began searching for the gun's safety catch, but he found it too dark to make out anything specific. Adam placed the gun back on the floor, found Hannah's phone in the center console, and switched it on for some additional light. Neither Hannah nor Michael seemed disturbed by the glowing light as Adam placed it on the dashboard to allow him to work with both hands. Retrieving the gun again, he held the weapon up toward the light and quickly located a green dot above the trigger next to what he assumed was the safety catch.

He carefully manipulated the catch and found it easily slid sideways from left to right. In the new position, the green dot was replaced by a red one, which he guessed was the firing position. Adam cautiously slid the catch back to the left and was satisfied the safety was now on as the green dot was once again displayed.

Adam went to put the gun back on the floor but hesitated. Turning the gun upside down, he found a small button at the base of the gun, which he carefully pressed. With a soft, metallic click, the gun's magazine popped out slightly from the butt of the weapon. Adam carefully withdrew the magazine and held it close to the light provided by Hannah's phone. Frowning, Adam lowered the gun to the floor and then held the magazine in both hands. He rotated the magazine several times and at different angles before switching off the phone.

As he sat in the darkness, he wondered how useful a gun with no bullets would be.

Chapter Thirty-Eight

Adam awoke with a stiff back and a mild headache. He blinked the sleep from his eyes and checked the time on the dashboard clock as he massaged his neck. It was just after six thirty, and he had slept far longer than he had planned. He rolled his head slowly from side to side for a few moments to free up his neck muscles before looking out through the dew-covered windows of the Camaro. It was hard to see anything in detail as the first shards of sunlight began penetrating the forest on the eastern side of the clearing. He looked across at Hannah who continued to sleep, curled up in an almost fetal position on the passenger seat. Her hair was a mess, and the small amount of makeup she used had smudged, leaving her with less than flattering smears under her eyes. Adam smiled to himself. Hannah never seemed to have a hair out of place, and although her hair and makeup needed a little work, she still looked stunningly beautiful. He looked forward to seeing her wake up and guessed she would be horrified when she looked in the mirror.

The Final Proposition

Twisting in his seat, he turned to look in the back. Curled up on the back seat, Michael remained asleep, seemingly without a care in the world. All in all, it had been a good night. Everyone had slept, and there had been no incidents. He decided he would leave Hannah and Michael to sleep a few minutes longer, content to just sit and watch the forest wake up.

Adam enjoyed the solitude for a few more minutes as the sunlight began to stream through the trees and erode the darkness. His seven years in a prison without windows to connect him to the outside world gave him a heightened appreciation of what he was now watching. He smiled to himself as he wound down his window and listened to the sound of birds calling to one another against the backdrop of water peacefully flowing in the river nearby. Framed by the tall, green fir trees, the clearing was now almost fully illuminated and had an almost cathedral quality. Although he was keen to enjoy the serenity for longer, Adam's bladder had other ideas. No longer able to ignore the discomfort, he carefully opened the door and looked back at Hannah and Michael as he got out of the car. Neither of them stirred, even as he gently pushed the door closed.

Satisfied that they would sleep for a while longer, Adam headed in the direction of the river and stopped just inside the edge of the forest to relieve himself. The sound of the river was distinctly louder inside the forest and sounded very close. Curious about just how close it was, Adam looked back at the Camaro. Both Hannah and Michael still looked asleep, and he decided he would risk a quick walk through the forest to take a look.

He set out at a brisk pace and only walked for a minute before the forest gave way to a rocky outcrop.

Cautiously, he stepped out of the forest, walked across a rock ledge, and looked down. The river was about twenty feet below and much wider and deeper than he had expected. The recent rain had turned the water brown, and Adam watched for a moment as the water swirled on the shifting currents. He had half contemplated bringing Michael across to see it, but there was no way down to the river's edge from here, and the rocky surface was slippery with morning dew.

He would have loved to stay longer and enjoy the chance to reconnect with nature, but he decided he needed to get back to Hannah and Michael before they awoke. Reluctantly, he turned and headed back through the forest and thought about the day ahead. He would check the fuel tank as soon as he got back, and provided it hadn't leaked, they would get back on the road within a few minutes with the aim of being in Bolton and finally safe around midmorning. When he came to the edge of the clearing, he realized he had become disorientated on his way back and had come out at the southern edge.

Just as he went to step out of the forest, his eye was drawn to movement on the opposite side of the clearing. Frowning, he remained still and watched for a moment, but he saw nothing further. Perhaps it had been a deer grazing in the clearing that had sensed his presence and retreated back into the forest? Or perhaps the stress of the last two days was getting to him and he had imagined it? He looked across to the Camaro, but from his current position, he could not see anything more than the rear of the car covered in the tarp. There was no sign of Hannah or Michael, and he assumed they were still sleeping in the car.

Adam stood for a moment, debating what to do. He

felt sure he hadn't imagined it. It was probably just some sort of animal, but he couldn't afford to be careless. Adam pursed his lips and watched for another thirty seconds. Surely no one had followed them here? Barely breathing, he concentrated on the spot where he thought he had seen movement, but the forest stayed still and silent. He was not sure whether he was disappointed or relieved, but in the moment he decided they needed to get moving again, he heard a sharp snapping sound coming from that general area. Although he couldn't see anything, he was convinced something or someone was there.

Retreating a step back into the forest, he still had a good view across the clearing and stood still, patiently watching and waiting. While he focused on the other side of the clearing, he replayed the sound over in his mind several times. He was fairly convinced that what he had heard was a large, dry twig or a small branch snapping, either as someone or something walked past it or stepped on it.

He decided to inch his way back to the original spot where he had entered the forest. If he needed to make a run for it back to the car, that would leave him exposed for the shortest possible distance. He walked a few feet to his left, never taking his eyes off the other side of the clearing, and stopped again. This time, he saw the shadows grow lighter then darker. He was positive he had seen movement again and moved behind a large fir tree at the edge of the forest to get a better look.

He peered between the branches and stood in disbelieving silence as he watched the dark shape of a man moving slowly around the edge of the clearing. Adam quickly looked from the man to the Camaro and back again. Now that he knew the man's location, it was reasonably easy to track his movements in the shadows as he slowly and cautiously moved around to the right-hand side of the clearing.

It was obvious to Adam that the man was using the cover of the forest to move to a position directly behind the Camaro. With the tarp still in place across the back of the car, unless someone was vigilantly watching the side-view mirrors, it would be possible from that position to edge across the clearing to the rear of the car without being seen. Adam had seen enough—it was time to get back to the car before whoever it was had a chance to get into position.

As he contemplated making a run for it, the shadowy figure of the man briefly appeared in dappled sunlight as he moved from the cover of one tree to the next.

The sunlight had illuminated the man's face for only a fraction of a second. Under normal circumstances, this brief glimpse wouldn't have been enough for Adam to recognize who it was. But these weren't normal circumstances, and Adam, with all his senses finely tuned for survival, recognized the face instantly. Adam cursed silently. There was no mistaking the receding, gray crewcut, the heavyset jawline, the grim, determined face, or the gun he carried in his right hand—it was Darcy.

Chapter Thirty-Nine

Max started the engine and pulled back onto the road that led to Tangmere Lake. He yawned as he looked at the clock on the dashboard of his truck. It was just after seven a.m., and he figured he would be at the lake in less than half an hour.

After his visit with Jonas and a stop to get Indian takeout, he had returned to the garage to eat and rest. He had taken painkillers and began to feel a little better as he ate his meal. His thoughts kept returning to Hanley and his taunts about Justine. The fact that the judge was now dead did little to ease the agony of not knowing how his daughter had died or where she was buried. He continued to think about the two photographs he had seen in Hanley's office of the judge fishing and wondered again whether it was at one of those locations where Justine had been murdered.

He had almost discounted being able to learn anything useful from the first photograph entirely. Even if the picture had been taken at Tangmere Lake, the blurry background made it impossible to pinpoint a location. The second photo with the old wooden bridge in the background would be easier to pinpoint. If the lake was one of Hanley's favorite fishing spots as Jonas had suggested, Max wondered if the bridge was nearby or somewhere else entirely. After finishing his meal, he climbed the stairs to his office, switched on his computer, and opened up Google Maps to learn more about the Tangmere Lake region.

There were only two ways to get to the lake from Stanwyck. Max traced the first route across the screen with his finger and counted three bridges, all of which looked modern. The second route was far less direct and wound through a number of small towns and villages. The route had nine bridges in total, some of which looked old and potentially a match for the wooden bridge in the second picture. Max decided this was the route he would take in the morning. He would check each bridge location against what he remembered from the photo—it wasn't much to go on, but at least it was a start.

He had set off at five a.m. and had just checked the seventh of the nine bridges. None of the bridges had been anything like the bridge in the photo, and he was now looking forward to coffee and a break in the next town. He glanced at a printout on the dashboard that he had taken from Google Maps. The second-to-last bridge was just ahead around a tight right-hand bend in the road. Max changed down through the gears as the road narrowed into one lane and pulled the truck to a halt after he rounded the bend. He left the engine running as he gazed up at the ancient structure—it was a much closer match to Hanley's picture than anything else he had seen so far.

The Final Proposition

The bridge was only wide enough to allow one vehicle to cross at a time and had been constructed using heavy, rough-sawn timber, large steel brackets, and heavy bolts that had long since turned brown with rust. It was constructed using a crude cantilever design, and he guessed it had been built somewhere between sixty and eighty years ago.

He looked out the side window down through the trees to the stream below. It ran at a gentle pace and didn't look particularly wide where it passed underneath the bridge. While he had driven mainly through farming country, this area was far more heavily wooded, and as he thought about the background in the second photograph, he began to see other similarities with the picture. He switched the engine off and sat still for a moment, trying to compose himself. He had no idea what he would find here, but as he opened the door, he sensed he would be here a lot longer than the ten minutes he had planned.

Chapter Forty

Adam debated how best to get back to the Camaro. His preference was to walk back casually, as if he wasn't aware of Darcy's presence, and then take off at high speed before Darcy had a chance to close in on them.

He tried to think like Darcy. Would he let him walk back to the car and wait until they were all together again? After losing the money once, he had a feeling Darcy would be after revenge as well. If the roles were reversed, he knew he would be lining up Darcy in his gun sights the moment he stepped out of the forest. He realized he had no choice but to make a run for it.

Moving silently back into the forest, he quickly made his way back to the spot where he had originally entered. Using the trees for cover again, he moved to the edge and waited, watching for any sign of Darcy's current location. The forest was still for another two minutes. Adam became increasingly concerned. He needed to know exactly where Darcy was and where the bullets might be coming from before he made his move.

The Final Proposition

He stood patiently watching and listening until the silence was interrupted by a sound Adam hadn't been expecting. Adam's blood ran cold as he saw the driver's side door of the Camaro begin to open. Bolting from the forest at full speed, he screamed, "Get back in the car, Michael—it's not safe!" as the young boy emerged from the car to yawn and stretch.

With a look of bewilderment, Michael turned to look at Adam who was halfway across the clearing when the first gunshot rang out. He screamed at Michael a second time as he continued to sprint. "Get down, Michael, get down!"

Amidst the sound of more gunshots, Adam closed the remaining distance to the car as Hannah began to scream at Michael as well. Scooping up Michael, he almost threw the boy into the car as Hannah screamed, "Adam, what's happening?"

Before he had a chance to respond, he felt an explosion of excruciating pain in his left shoulder. Afraid he would pass out, Adam collapsed into the car and willed himself to stay conscious. Unable to move his left arm, which was now covered in blood, Adam closed the door with his right hand and started the engine.

Hannah looked aghast as she realized Adam had been hit. "Adam, you've been…"

Hannah didn't get a chance to finish as the Camaro became the target for a further volley of gunfire. He yelled, "Heads down," as he put the car into gear and accelerated away. Clutching the wheel with his good hand, he yelled at Hannah, "Change gear for me."

As he screamed, "Two," and depressed the clutch, Hannah moved the gearshift down in one smooth motion.

Adam accelerated out of the clearing and further down the service road, away from the gunfire.

Adam willed the Camaro to pick up speed and screamed, "Three."

Hannah deftly shifted the gearshift upward and across at the correct diagonal angle. They continued to pick up speed, and Adam glanced in the rearview mirror as he heard the tarp rip away from the rear of the Camaro. Now back on the service road, he saw Darcy sprinting out of the clearing and back up the road toward a parked car.

Hannah shifted the gear lever down into fourth gear in response to Adam's signal and looked at the front of Adam's shirt, which was now fully covered in blood.

In an alarmed voice, she said, "Adam, you're losing a lot of blood."

Adam didn't have time to think about his condition—he was still conscious, and that's all that mattered. "I'm okay for the moment. We need to get out of here as fast as we can."

As they accelerated away from the clearing, Hannah asked, "Where do you think the road goes?"

"Hopefully out of the forest."

"It was Darcy, wasn't it?"

"Yes."

Hannah shook her head as she responded, "How on earth did he find us here?"

Adam was about to respond when they rounded a slight bend in the road. His vision ahead was limited by the tall trees that grew up to the road's edge, but his worst fear was realized as the road turned to forest a short distance ahead. Taking his foot off the accelerator, Adam slammed on the brakes, skidded the car to a stop, and said, "We've hit a dead end. Everybody out now—we've got less than thirty seconds before Darcy gets here."

After getting out of the car, Hannah watched Adam reach in under the seat with his good hand and retrieve the attache case.

"Adam, you're badly wounded."

Adam dropped the case on the bonnet and quickly opened it with his one good hand. He looked in the direction of the forest away from the river as he retrieved Winter's gun and said to Hannah, "Head back through there and keep the sun at your back. Keep going and don't stop until you hit the main road."

With tears in her eyes, she replied, "Adam, we can't go without you. You need…"

Adam cut her off. "If we stay together, we're all dead. This is the only chance for you and Michael."

Adam paused momentarily as he listened to the sound of Darcy's four-wheel drive getting louder before handing the gun to Hannah. "The gun's empty, but if worse comes to worst, you may be able to bluff with it."

Holding Hannah's gaze, he continued in a softer voice, "Go, Hannah, please? You must do this for Michael."

Hannah grabbed Michael's hand, looked at Adam with a mixture of fear and defiance, and said, "This isn't goodbye, Adam."

Adam watched for a moment as Hannah turned and disappeared into the forest. After closing the case, he leaned against the Camaro and looked down at his damaged arm which hanging limply at his side. The pain was still intense, but the bleeding seemed to have slowed. He was weak and not sure how long he would be able to distract Darcy—hopefully at least long enough for Hannah and Michael to escape. He paused just long enough for Darcy to see him as his car came into view and then turned and moved off into the forest in the direction of the river.

Chapter Forty-One

Adam had no time to develop any escape plan other than to lead Darcy as far away from Hannah and Michael as possible. He did his best to move silently through the forest and hoped he would at least get to the river before Darcy caught him. The forest was thicker here than where they had parked overnight, and it was difficult to see for more than a few feet in any one direction. Slightly disorientated by his pain and blood loss, Adam stumbled forward, using the sound of the river to keep him headed in the right direction.

After two minutes of walking, his body was racked with pain, and he was finding it increasingly hard to breathe. He slowed down to a walking pace and walked for several more minutes before he emerged from the dark shade of the forest. Holding the attache case up to shield his eyes from the sun, he stepped out onto a shale rock embankment high above the river and quickly looked left and right. He was surprised Darcy had not caught him yet and debated whether to head downstream or upstream.

Instinct told him most people would probably head downstream. Adam figured doing the opposite might give him a slim chance of evading Darcy and turned left to head upstream instead.

The narrow, unstable shale surface made his progress slow until he came to a spot where the shale gave way to clay and the riverbank widened slightly. Adam was almost exhausted and stopped for a moment to catch his breath. He bent over to get more oxygen into his lungs and examined his limp left arm. It was still bleeding, but the blood flow from the bullet wound itself had slowed considerably. Willing himself to continue, he took only three more steps before Darcy stepped from the forest just a few feet in front of him.

After losing the money once already, Adam had expected Darcy to be angry and full of rage. Instead, the man just stood with a mild look of amusement on his face and the barrel of his gun pointed at Adam's chest.

"So good of you to finally join me, Wells. Drop the case and turn around with your hands in the air."

Adam kept his grip tight on the attache case. He figured he had seconds to live regardless of whether he complied or not. He debated trying to dive into the river but figured Darcy wouldn't miss from this distance and that he would be dead before he hit the water. Turning slightly to face Darcy and with his back to the river, he began to raise his good arm while still keeping a firm grip on the case. "I've taken a bullet, Darcy. My arm's broken, so one arm in the air is all you get."

Darcy's features quickly hardened. "I said drop the case, now!"

With his arm now fully extended, Adam twisted slightly so that the attache case now hung just over the edge of the steep embankment.

With his heart in his mouth, Adam replied, "I don't think so, Darcy. I drop the case, and I'm as good as dead."

He dared a glance down the almost vertical rock riverbank to the water below before he returned his gaze to meet Darcy's stare.

"You want the case, you'll have to shoot me and then swim for it."

Darcy took two steps forward but stopped as Adam screamed, "Last chance, Darcy! One more step and I swear to God I'll drop the case. In this muddy water and current, you'll need a dive team to find it."

Adam held his breath as he waited for a response. While Darcy's granite face remained impassive, the man's steel-gray eyes radiated rage. Adam knew he had a stalemate—at least for the moment. Both men held each other's stare for almost a minute. As his arm began to grow tired, Adam wondered whether Darcy was just going to wait him out. He decided there was nothing to be gained by speaking and waited for Darcy to make the first move.

After almost another full minute of silence, Darcy finally responded with the semblance of a wry smile on his face. "Looks like we have a situation."

Adam said nothing. After another bout of silence, Darcy let out a short, vicious laugh. "You just going to stand there—forever?"

"Your time's almost up, Darcy. If you're still holding a gun when I let go of this, it goes into the river."

"And I'll shoot you dead."

"Yes, but you'll have lost the money forever."

Darcy sneered, "So how do you plan to trade your life for the money, hotshot?"

Adam didn't hold out much hope for getting off the riverbank alive, but as he thought of Hannah and Michael fleeing through the forest, he seized the opportunity to delay Darcy's departure as long as possible.

"We start by you putting the gun on the ground and backing up, and I'll do the same with the attache case."

"And then what?"

"We talk and see if we can figure out a way where we both get what we want."

Darcy stood still for a moment as if weighing his options. Finally, with his eyes still locked on Adam, he slowly bent at his knees and carefully placed the gun on the ground in front of him. Adam knew from the way he placed the gun on the ground, with the barrel still facing him, that his adversary had every intention of picking it up at the first opportunity to shoot him.

Adam waited for Darcy to back up several paces. He was still not confident this would buy Hannah and Michael much time, but every second helped. Without taking his eyes off Darcy, he lowered the case to the ground and placed it deliberately against his leg and within inches of the edge of the bank.

Darcy was less than impressed. "You need to move it away from the edge. It could topple over at any second."

"How do I know you're not carrying a second gun or you won't get some stupid idea about rushing me?"

The two men held each other's stare without moving. Adam briefly thought about an escape plan but realized the situation was hopeless while Darcy still had easy access to a gun. Darcy finally broke the silence and said, "What about I kick the gun into the river?"

The Final Proposition

"You probably have another gun under your shirt."

To Adam's surprise, Darcy peeled off his T-shirt and tossed it on the ground. "No gun."

Before Adam could respond, Darcy lifted each leg of his faded blue jeans in turn before turning out his pockets. Holding his hands out to his side to form a crucifix, he repeated, "No gun."

He lowered his arms and said, "I'm not carrying a second weapon, Wells, now give me the money."

Adam looked at Darcy for a moment as he contemplated his response. He figured Darcy was close to sixty, but he was clearly still in very good physical shape.

"You don't need a gun. I've got a bullet wound, a broken arm, and I've lost a lot of blood. A twelve-year-old with a stick could kill me."

Darcy let out a short laugh and shook his head again. To Adam's surprise, he stepped forward and kicked the gun off the bank. Both men watched the gun as it tumbled down the embankment and disappeared into the river. Darcy looked up at Adam again as he stepped back into his original position and said, "No gun."

He wasn't sure what to make of Darcy's action. The cruel and seething eyes were at odds with his facial expressions, which were trying to convey sincerity and cooperation. Adam didn't feel his odds of survival had improved and stood firm with his leg still resting against the attache case. He decided to buy as much time as he could for Hannah and Michael while he thought about what to do next.

"When did you realize you didn't have the money?"

Darcy's face hardened again. "What does it matter?"

"I just want to know."

Darcy looked across the river as if weighing whether

to respond or not. After a few seconds of silence, he responded, "I got as far as Sanbury but was running low on fuel. I pulled in to refuel and get food."

He turned back to face Adam before he continued.

"Needless to say, I found out very quickly that I had been stiffed by a nine-year-old…"

Adam decided to wait to see if Darcy offered up anything else and simply nodded in reply.

Darcy let out a stifled laugh and asked, "You put him up to it, didn't you?"

Adam was about to reply "No" but thought better of it. He didn't want to inflame Darcy's hate for Michael any further than it already was. "It was a long shot, but one we felt we had to take."

Darcy's features hardened again. Adam decided to change the subject as he attempted to subdue his rage.

"How did you find us?"

"I've been tracking people for thirty years. It wasn't hard."

"We could have been anywhere by now, how did you know to look here?"

As if he knew Adam was playing a delaying game, Darcy grinned momentarily before he responded, "Let's just say I do my research well and knew you were headed to Bolton. There are no other roads from here that you can take, so I started backtracking. I kept an eye on all the cars I passed and used my old police ID to ask questions at all the road stops along the way. Nobody had seen you, and I figured unless you had turned around and gone back toward Hartbourne, I would eventually find you."

"How did you know to track us up here? There must be fifty of these roads between here and Sanbury."

With a cold and calculating smile, he replied, "The

rain in the last twenty-four hours. It's easy to see fresh car tracks after rainfall on a dirt road. I only had to detour up four roads before I found you."

Adam nodded, angry that he hadn't thought of that when they had driven up the service road the night before.

"Question time's over, Wells, it's time to hand over the money."

"You and I both know I'm dead as soon as you have the money."

Darcy took several steps backward before stopping again. "You're making me nervous with that case so close to the edge. You do anything more than sneeze, and it'll end up in the water, and we all lose."

When Adam didn't respond, Darcy backed up several more steps and said, "Okay, there's no way I can rush you now. Move it back from the edge at least."

Adam thought about it for a moment before deciding that moving the case might buy Hannah and Michael some more time. Reaching down with his good hand, he slid the attache case across the ground until it was directly in front of him. In the split second he took his eyes off Darcy, he realized he had made a mistake as his adversary reached behind his back. With his reflexes dulled by the bullet wound and loss of blood, Adam didn't have time to react before Darcy withdrew a small handgun from the waistband at the back of his pants and brought it up to a firing position.

Adam heard two gunshots in quick succession as he leaped from the bank but felt no pain from a bullet as he plunged deep into the icy water. He did his best not to panic as he struggled against the weight of his clothes and the current with his one good arm as he attempted to reach the surface. Adam felt like he was going to pass out from lack of oxygen until he gulped in a huge lungful of air when he finally broke through.

He braced himself for another hail of bullets from Darcy's gun, but the river remained quiet. After quickly getting his bearings, Adam looked up to where he had jumped from to see Darcy reaching over the edge of the bank to retrieve the attache case which had lodged precariously on a small rock.

He let the strong current quickly pull him downriver as he fought to stay afloat. He took one final look up at Darcy as he retrieved the case before the current pulled him around a curve in the river and out of sight. He was safe from Darcy for the moment, but as he looked up at the high rock walls of the riverbanks that surrounded him, he wondered whether he had simply swapped death by a handgun for death by drowning.

The main claim to fame for the Heckler and Koch P2000 handgun was its compact size. It was the gun Darcy always favored when he needed to carry a concealed weapon. It had a reliable safety, and in his years of experience, he had never seen one discharge accidentally.

Like all small compact handguns, even in the hands of an expert marksman, the short barrel meant the gun became completely inaccurate at anything more than a few paces from its target. He was not surprised when the two rounds he fired at Wells's chest missed their target entirely. He could have kept firing blindly until he emptied the magazine, but the attache case was the real prize.

The Final Proposition

The sight of Wells leaping off the embankment didn't overly concern him. With the man up against a strong river current with no way out except by scaling one of the vertical rock walls on either side, Darcy suspected Wells would drown quickly in his severely weakened state. He wasn't sure whether Wells had intentionally kicked the case as he made his escape or not, but the sight of the case spinning over the edge just a few feet from him made his decision easy.

Now this close, he had no intention of letting the prize he had spent seven years hunting down disappear again. As instinct took over, Darcy dropped the handgun and dove forward, desperate to catch the case before it toppled off the embankment. Even with fully outstretched hands, his lunge brought him up short, and he watched in horror as the case disappeared over the edge. Scrambling forward, he expected his next move would be to dive into the river to rescue the case before it had a chance to sink. He peered over the edge and grinned to himself as he saw the case had lodged against a small, rocky outcrop directly below him.

After getting down on one knee, he lowered his arm slowly and carefully until he was able to grip the case securely in his left hand. When he was sure he had a firm grip, he carefully lifted the case back up onto the embankment. He stood back up again, popped the locks, and then slowly raised the lid.

He stared in disbelief for several seconds at the interior of the case before throwing his head back and roaring in rage. Realizing that Wells had outmaneuvered him, he hurled the empty case out into the middle of river and watched as it landed with a splash and bobbed momentarily on the surface of the water. He knew he never operated well when he was out of control and used the time while he watched the case fill with water and sink to bring his rage under control.

He debated taking off after Wells but decided he would let the river do its work and come back later to search for the body. Right now, the woman and her son only had a twenty-minute head start on him. He figured he would need less than an hour to find them. One way or another, they would lead him to the money before he killed them.

Chapter Forty-Two

Max stood at the edge of the stream and stared up at the wooden bridge. After struggling down the steep bank, he had planned on resting for a moment, but the scene before him changed everything. He didn't need to look any further—this was definitely the location in Hanley's second photo.

Feeling overwhelmed by his discovery, Max sat down on the sandbank next to the stream to ponder what he should do next. He hadn't expected to find the location this quickly and now wasn't sure what to do or where to start looking.

He listened to the gentle burbling sound of the water as it meandered around the bend in the stream and under the bridge. It was hard to imagine this peaceful setting could be where his daughter had been murdered. He closed his eyes and could see Justine as a six-year-old playing on a swing, laughing and squealing and begging him to push her harder.

Max opened his eyes and swallowed hard. He realized

searching for her was going to be far more difficult than he had imagined. He slowly got to his feet and forced himself to think like Hanley and Lennox as he looked across the stream at the steep, tree-lined bank opposite. Could they have brought Justine here? While the spot was close to the road, it was well below road level and virtually hidden by trees. Max only had to think for a moment before he realized all sorts of nightmares could have happened here while motorists passed by, totally unaware, just a few feet above.

Max looked upstream, and he began to wonder if his daughter had been buried here as well. The trees on both banks had overlapping, surface-level root structures, which would make it hard to dig a hole for a body without a lot of work. Max couldn't imagine Hanley and Lennox wanting to spend that much time or effort and turned to look downstream. It was hard to see anything beyond the bridge from his current position, and he decided it needed further investigation.

Keeping to the sandy edge of the stream, Max made his way under the old wooden bridge and stopped to look up at the aging structure. Although sturdy in construction, it was clearly handmade as the sunlight streamed through the ill-fitting heavy deck planks to illuminate the area below. Max studied the huge, wooden supporting pylons which were set deep into each bank. They were roughly cut, and the bottom section was covered up by a wall of loose rocks to prevent soil erosion when the stream flooded.

The rocks looked as though they had been there for a hundred years. He could even make out a waterline where the stream depth had at one time been deeper. The stillness of the setting was beginning to unnerve him. He felt

The Final Proposition

the hair on the back of his neck beginning to rise and decided it was time to move on. He began to cautiously make his way downstream, but something bothered him. Turning back to look at the bridge, he whispered, "What have I missed?"

He walked quickly back to the spot where he had stood a few moments earlier and stopped. He found it hard to breathe and had a strong sense of foreboding as he looked around again. The place reeked of evil. He was almost certain Justine was here. He looked across at the pylons on the opposite side of the stream, and his gaze was immediately drawn to the middle section of the retaining wall. The stones looked ill-fitting, as though they had been laid in a hurry or by someone other than the original builder. He turned his head slightly and with his eyes traced the high waterline across the rock wall. The line disappeared completely in the middle section. Max gasped as he realized the stones had at some point been removed and then roughly refitted.

He stood rigid for over a minute, staring and unable to move. He took a deep breath as tears began to slowly trickle down his face and then waded across the waist-deep stream. Still dripping wet, he used his two bandaged hands to lift the first of the refitted rocks from the wall. Even though it was large and heavy, it dislodged easily. In quick succession, he removed another four rocks from the same section of wall to expose a large area of loose, black soil.

He hadn't brought a spade or any other digging implement and began scraping tentatively at the soil with one hand. The soil wasn't heavily compacted, and he easily removed a handful. Using both hands the second time, he was able to scoop out a much larger quantity of earth. Satisfied that he had his technique right, he reached in again to dig out more soil. He pushed his hands into the earth and felt something soft against his fingertips. He paused for a moment and then pushed deeper until he had a firm grip.

Slowly and carefully, he began to withdraw the object from the soil. As it broke free, he instantly recognized what it was and let out a pained cry of anguish before collapsing to the ground. Totally numb, he thought about nothing and felt nothing for several minutes.

When the initial shock started to dissipate, he got to his feet and, without looking back, waded back across the stream to return to his truck. The scene under the bridge became quiet again, punctuated only by the gentle burbling of the stream. The five rocks remained where they had been dropped, almost like sentries on guard for the object Max had removed from the wall. The object also lay where it had been dropped—still largely covered in dirt but instantly recognizable as a woman's shoe.

Chapter Forty-Three

Adam had not been in the river for long before he heard Darcy's roar from the bank above. While he fought to stay afloat, he wondered if Darcy would come after him now that he realized he had been duped a second time. Near exhaustion, he knew he wouldn't last much longer in the freezing waters and desperately searched the riverbank for any crevice or outcrop that he could grip to keep afloat.

His teeth began to chatter, and he felt his whole body going numb. He could no longer feel the pain in his left shoulder and realized he would soon fall unconscious. He'd heard drowning was a peaceful way to die and that it felt more like floating off to sleep than anything else.

Resigned to his fate, he twisted onto his back and submitted to the control of the current as he floated further downriver. He looked up beyond riverbanks and trees to the sky above. The sun was disappearing and being replaced by dark and threatening black clouds. He wondered if this was an omen for what was to come.

He closed his eyes and was immediately back on the

riverbank again, watching the bullets from Darcy's gun punch holes in his chest. He floated through the forest, and he saw Hannah and Michael hiding close to the road where they had left the Camaro. Why hadn't they run? His troubled thoughts were interrupted by visions of him comforting Max as he wept by a graveside. Joseph grabbed his shoulder and began yelling at him to get up. In the entire time they had been in prison, Joe had never been so insistent—so why start now? He told Joe to leave him alone, he just wanted to roll over and go back to sleep. His thoughts returned to Hannah and Michael, but Joe was insistent and grabbed at his shoulder again...

Adam opened his eyes—the sky had gone, replaced by shadows and darkness. He was not holding onto anything, but his body appeared to be almost floating on the water. He was still cold and wet and quickly dismissed any thought that he had drowned and entered the afterlife. Confused, he looked up and vaguely made out a shadowy expanse of rock just a few feet above him. He turned to his right and saw what looked like a solid rock wall amongst the shadows, and to his left, his view was of flowing water in front of another backdrop of shadows and rock. As his eyes adjusted to the darkness, he realized the current had pulled him under a large, almost cave-like, rocky outcrop at a turn in the river.

While he lay still, trying to get his bearings, he felt a prodding pain in his good arm. Turning his head slightly, he looked up and saw that the shoulder of his jacket had caught on a jagged piece of rock just above the waterline. He wondered how long he had been stuck there as the eddy currents of the river continued to wash gently over his body.

Feeling his senses begin to return, Adam sniffed the

The Final Proposition

air and smelled an acrid smell of ammonia—almost like urine. He turned his head to the right, and in the dim light, he could see the scattered bones of long-deceased small animals along with feathers and animal feces on a rock ledge just above the waterline and now understood where the smell came from.

Desperately cold, he felt the muscles in his legs begin to spasm and realized he needed to get out of the water as quickly as possible. He was conscious of a small amount of natural light coming from behind him, which he presumed was the opening through which the current had drawn him into the cave. Straining his eyes, he looked forward, searching for where the water flowed back out into the river, but he could not see anything more than rock and shadows in the darkness.

He wondered how long his jacket would hold before it ripped and exposed him to the mercy of the river again. He had almost no energy and knew the cave could easily turn into a watery tomb within minutes. Adam reached up his good arm to get a grip on the rock above him and then gently forced his legs down. Without putting too much pressure on his jacket which continued to hold him afloat, he slowly forced his legs down against the current, trying to test the depth of the water. He was only able to incline his legs about forty degrees before he felt something hard beneath his left foot. Gently, he pressed down with his right foot as well and felt solid rock beneath his feet.

Relieved that the water wasn't more than waist-deep, he pushed up with his feet and gently unhooked his jacket from the rock. Adam held onto the rock for a moment to steady himself and then waded across to the rock ledge. The ledge was only inches above the waterline, but he knew it would take all of his reserves to drag himself clear of the cold river water.

Adam gripped the ledge with his good hand to steady himself and ignored the overpowering stench of bones, feathers, and urine. Even though he felt like gagging, right now he needed to get out of the water. Using his one good arm, he scrambled up onto the ledge and collapsed with exhaustion. He closed his eyes and savored the moment to rest as he lay on top of what he didn't care to think about. Within seconds, the pain from the bullet wound returned to his left arm, which he took to be a good sign as he thought about what he would do next.

He opened his eyes again and began looking around to see if there was any way out. He knew getting back in the water would be suicide, but so was lying on the ledge. He had no intention of joining the menagerie of dead animal corpses he currently lay on, at least not without a fight, and willed himself up into a sitting position. After several deep breaths to get his mind on top of the pain in his left arm, he looked up into the darkness at the rock formation above him. In the dim shadows, he noticed the rock was split in two with a distinct crack opening up directly above his head. Reaching up with his right index finger, he began to probe the crack and felt a light waft of air across his wrist.

Adam paused and then lowered his hand slightly and spread his fingers. He began moving his hand backward and forward and felt the subtle airflow now across the back of his hand. He wondered whether it was just the way the air swirled through the cave or something else.

He shifted his position on the ledge to get more comfortable and raised his hand again. He held his hand still and felt the same airflow again, only this time, it was definitely stronger. Intrigued, he shifted back across the ledge as far as he could and reached up to test the airflow again. It was definitely stronger and appeared to be flowing directly from the rock formation above his head.

Adam looked up into the darkness but couldn't see anything and began feeling across the rock surface for the source of the airflow. Finding the crack again, he began to slowly follow the widening gap above him until the texture changed from rock to something softer. At first, he thought the spongy surface was just moss growing on the rock, but as he pushed against it with a finger, the surface flexed slightly.

Puzzled, he scraped at the surface with his fingers and immediately began to dislodge chunks of dirt. He scraped again, this time a little harder, and was rewarded as a large chunk of the debris came loose and fell onto his back and shoulder. He brushed the material away and noticed it was very fine, more like silt than dirt. Encouraged, he began to dig out fistfuls of the substance and wondered if the river had flooded at some stage.

Adam kept digging and began to make a sizeable hole in the space above his head. He had no idea whether this would turn out to be a dead end or not, but as the hole he made continued to enlarge and the physical exertion warmed him up, he decided this was far better than simply lying down and waiting to die.

He continued to dig until he felt a solid object against his fingers for the first time. He feared he had struck solid rock, but after scraping more silt away, he realized the obstruction was just a large stick. He continued to move dirt away until he could wrap his hand fully around the exposed end. Tentatively, he pulled at the stick, but it didn't budge. Adam moved his sitting position slightly to get a better grip and pulled hard on the stick a second time, but it still refused to move. Undeterred, he tried pushing the stick upward and was rewarded with just the slightest hint of movement as more chunks of silt dropped onto his face.

With his head down to keep the silt from his eyes, he patiently worked the stick up and down and felt the stick loosening further with every movement. After another minute of patiently working the stick up and down, Adam twisted the stick slightly and pulled hard again. The stick finally came free, and he was immediately showered with a huge pile of silt and small rocks. When the debris finally stopped falling, Adam brushed the dirt out of his hair and off his face and then opened his eyes. Now able to see again, he stared at a pencil-thin ray of light that now illuminated his left foot.

Adam quickly rose to his knees and looked up into the hole, which was now slightly illuminated by the tiny shaft of light that shone through it. Buoyed by his breakthrough, he reached further up into the hole again and began to dig out handful after handful of silt. After another two minutes of digging, his hand wrapped around another stick. Adam lowered his head and pulled hard again. After several seconds, he heard a crackling sound as the stick began to give way. Pausing to get a fresh grip on the stick, Adam pulled down hard again and was showered this time with a mixture of larger rocks and silt as the stick came free.

After shaking the silt from his hair, he looked up and was almost mesmerized by the light that now streamed through the hole. Adam immediately put his hand into the hole again and began desperately pulling down more large chunks of the finely compacted silt. The hole was not yet anywhere near large enough for him to fit through, and he began to panic at the thought that he still might be trapped. After another minute of desperately scooping silt out of the hole, he was forced to take cover as another large dump of rocks and silt began to fall on him. The debris continued to fall for another twenty seconds before everything became quiet again.

Adam shook more silt from his hair and then looked up again. The gray sky was now clearly visible through a large, vertical split in the shale rock. On a good day, the split looked just wide enough to allow him to climb out. But this wasn't a good day. He had a bullet in one shoulder and was close to exhaustion. Despite the newly discovered escape route, freedom still looked a long way away.

Chapter Forty-Four

Hannah stiffened as she heard the two gunshots ring out through the forest. Holding her hand to her mouth, she did her best to control her breathing as she thought about what might have just happened. She refused to believe Adam was dead but found it hard to imagine him outrunning Darcy for long after being so badly wounded.

Michael whispered to her, "Mom, was that gunshots? Is Adam okay?"

From her position in the forest, she had a clear view of both the Camaro and Darcy's four-wheel drive. Without taking her eyes off the vehicles, she whispered, "We have to be quiet, Michael. If Darcy comes back, we don't want him to know we're here."

Not easily deterred, Michael whispered again, "But is he okay?"

After running a short distance into the forest with Michael, Hannah had hidden amongst the trees and watched as Darcy's four-wheel drive had driven up and stopped behind the Camaro. She had watched him get out of his car and disappear in pursuit of Adam, and she wished the gun Adam had given her wasn't empty.

She had waited several minutes until she was reasonably sure Darcy was well away from the area and had then quickly moved down out of the forest to check inside his car. She had hoped to find car keys or another gun, but he had left the car bare. She debated leaving Michael and following Darcy in the hope of being able to somehow disarm him before he got to Adam, but she quickly realized Adam had been right—they needed to get away from the area as quickly as possible.

Returning to Michael, she had picked up the backpack and prepared to move off again. She found herself wavering as she looked back at Adam's Camaro. The battered car that refused to quit was becoming a symbol of everything the three of them had been through. She knew staying any longer was putting Michael and her in grave danger, but Adam was no longer someone she could simply walk away from.

She wondered what Darcy would do when he discovered the attache case was empty. Would he shoot Adam if he had the chance or frog-march him back to the car at gunpoint, demanding to know where the money was? She thought about how Adam had picked up Michael in the clearing and had taken a bullet as he had saved her son's life. She wondered about his injury and how long he could keep going. She replayed her parting words to him over in her mind and knew she needed to stay.

She had then waited patiently in their hiding spot for almost twenty minutes until the gunshots rang out.

Hannah did her best to compose herself and held tightly onto Michael's hand as she answered his question,

"Adam's coming back, Michael, we just have to be patient."

Darcy stood on the edge of the riverbank and allowed himself a moment to get his rage under control. After watching the empty attache case sink into the river, his thoughts returned to the money. Logic dictated the woman had it, although in their rush to escape, it was possible the money had been left in Wells's car. He figured the woman and the boy would walk back through the forest to the road to call for help—a trip he could make by car in under five minutes.

After putting his shirt back on, he looked at his watch and wondered about a third option. Wells had roughly a thirty-second head start on him when he entered the forest—enough time to open a case and dump a bag of money while on the run. He did some quick calculations in his head and figured it would be a good hour before the woman and the boy reached the road. He walked the short distance back to where he had seen Wells leave the forest and paused for a moment to look back at the river. He would return later to make sure Wells was dead, but for now, the money was the priority. As he reentered the forest, he vowed he would finish it today—one way or another, he would be leaving with the money and no witnesses.

With a watchful eye, he began to slowly retrace Wells's footsteps back through the forest, looking for any sign of the woman or the money.

Chapter Forty-Five

Adam lay staring up at the gray sky as he tried to catch his breath. Although he had been an avid amateur rock climber in his early twenties, nothing could have prepared him for the thirty-foot climb up through the split in the shale rock. The gap was barely big enough for him to squeeze his body through and murder on his left shoulder. Totally exhausted when he reached the top, he had dragged himself clear and collapsed on the riverbank.

He had half expected Darcy to reappear and finish him off, but after several minutes with only the sound of the river for company, he was fairly sure Darcy had gone, at least for the moment. He was surprised that he had made it this far and willed himself into a sitting position to examine his damaged left shoulder and arm. The bullet wound had started bleeding again, and he was close to passing out from the stabbing pain. Closing his eyes for a moment, he slowed his breathing down in an attempt to block out the pain. In his weakened state, he began to hallucinate almost immediately and opened his eyes again as the previous images of being shot by Darcy returned.

While fighting off a wave of nausea, he began to plan what to do next. He knew Hannah and Michael would be the next targets. He struggled to his feet, and he wondered how far they had gotten. Probably not enough time to get all the way back to the main road, but surely enough time to be well away from the area and Darcy? Still feeling slightly unsteady on his feet, Adam walked off the bank and leaned against a tree at the edge of the forest as he willed the dizziness to subside.

He closed his eyes again, and the hallucinations returned. First being shot in the chest by Darcy and then flying through the forest past Hannah and Michael. The image of Hannah and Michael huddled close to the Camaro bothered him far more than the thought of being repeatedly shot. Surely they weren't still hiding near the car?

Adam opened his eyes and tried to put himself in Hannah's position. Her number one priority would be to protect Michael. Logic dictated she would flee through the forest as quickly as possible. He played back Hannah's last words when they had abandoned the Camaro: "This isn't goodbye, Adam."

He now wondered what she had meant. If she had stayed close, he didn't want to think about what would happen if Darcy found them. He hoped he was wrong and that they were now miles away and closing in on the main road, but the more he thought about Hannah's words, the more fearful he became. Pushing himself off the tree, he set off back to the Camaro and hoped he wasn't too late.

The Final Proposition

Darcy emerged from the forest next to the Camaro in a lather of sweat, wearing a scowl that matched his demeanor. He hadn't seen any sign of the money as he retraced Wells's steps, which left him the car and the woman. After ripping open the Camaro's driver's side door, he began searching the vehicle using a technique he had perfected over his thirty years on the force. He checked every crevice and potential hiding spot, including the roof liner, and was only satisfied the money wasn't there after he had slashed and checked inside each car seat.

After popping the locks for the trunk and bonnet, he spent another five minutes checking the rest of the vehicle. He wasn't surprised to find nothing. Rarely would someone leave that much money behind, even if they were fleeing for their life. That left the woman. Darcy moved a few feet away from the car and looked out into the forest. He debated doing a sweep of the surrounding area before heading back to the main road. Logic dictated the road would be where they were headed, but maybe she was close by, waiting for him to leave? He did a slow three hundred and sixty-degree clockwise turn, scanning the forest for any sign that he was being watched. If they were still here, they would be hiding close enough to watch. He saw nothing suspicious, but instinct told him he needed to be thorough.

He pulled the gun from his pocket and clicked off the safety. Taking one last look around, he whispered, "If you're here, I'll find you," before disappearing into the forest.

Chapter Forty-Six

Adam gently peeled back the branch of a fir tree at the edge of the forest and peered through at the Camaro. He had seen no sign of Darcy on his way back from the river, yet he still felt uneasy as he crouched out of sight at the end of the service road. He switched his focus to Darcy's Toyota, which was parked slightly further back on the road and blocking the Camaro in. The vision he'd had of being shot in the chest by Darcy was playing on his mind. Stepping out of the forest would make him an easy target, and the sight of Darcy's four-wheel drive was a clear signal the man was still somewhere close.

He debated what to do next. He hadn't heard any screaming or gunshots, which he took to be a good sign. He knew the prospect of Darcy returning to his car and driving off empty-handed was wishful thinking. Anyone who spent seven years following a money trail and was prepared to kill to get what they wanted would not be easily dissuaded.

While he continued to watch and listen, he thought

about Hannah and Michael. He hoped they were back at the main road now trying to flag down a passing motorist, but he sensed they were still close. He looked at Darcy's Toyota again. If they had stayed behind, it was only a matter of time before he found them. Adam realized he needed to keep moving. If they were here and he found them before Darcy did, there was still a small chance they could all escape.

Using the trees for cover, he figured he could complete a circular sweep of the immediate area in less than thirty minutes. He looked down at his wounded shoulder. He wasn't sure how much blood he had lost or how much longer he could keep going, but he wasn't about to let Hannah and Michael down. Rising cautiously from his crouched position, he moved off silently through the trees, hoping he wasn't too late.

The sweep of the forest took Adam longer than he expected. His injury slowed him down more than he expected, and after twenty minutes of moving in a counterclockwise direction, he had barely covered a third of the area. Stopping to rest, he closed his eyes for a moment to try and get on top of the pain. He felt like screaming in agony but instead breathed in and out deeply as he longed for the nightmare to be over. The vivid hallucinations did not return this time, for which he was thankful, but the sound of Michael whispering to Hannah was equally as unnerving.

He opened his eyes again, expecting the whispers to stop, but they continued for several seconds before fading out. Frowning, Adam turned his head left and right to pinpoint the direction of the sound. Was it his imagination, or did he really hear Michael's soft voice?

Staying down, Adam moved forward in the direction he thought he heard the sound coming from. He had only gone about ten paces when he stopped again, his eyes drawn to a small patch of red that he could see through the trees about sixty feet to his right. He moved slightly further away from the cover of a tree to get a better look and managed a half smile as he recognized Michael's red T-shirt. He moved another step through the trees and could now see both Hannah and Michael crouched under cover, slightly higher up in the forest and watching the service road below.

Adam desperately wanted to call out to them but realized that could be fatal. If he had found them, Darcy would as well. He stood still for a moment, debating what to do. If he simply walked forward, there was a good chance Michael would make some excited noise and alert Darcy to their position if he was close. He knew he needed to get closer and somehow get Hannah's attention first. As he took his first step forward, the silence of the forest was broken by a soft cracking sound.

He stopped moving immediately. Standing on a soft bed of pine needles, he knew it wasn't his footfall that had caused the sound. He watched as Hannah and Michael both went rigid, and it was immediately clear they had not made the sound either. With an alarmed look on her face, Hannah looked up and began quickly scanning the forest area behind her. She turned her head, and her eyes locked on Adam. Even though they were sixty feet apart and she was partially obscured by tree branches, he could see the relief spreading across her face as she realized he was still alive.

The Final Proposition

Quickly raising an index finger to his lips, he signaled to Hannah to remain quiet. The alarmed look returned to her face as she realized Adam wasn't the source of the sound. They both continued to listen intently for further sounds. Hannah squeezed Michael's shoulder and whispered in his ear. She then pointed in Adam's direction, and as Michael turned his head, Adam raised his index finger again to signal Michael to be quiet.

Before Michael had a chance to respond, they all heard another soft cracking sound from within the forest. The sound was definitely louder, and Adam had no doubt Darcy was now very close.

Chapter Forty-Seven

Max barely remembered climbing into his truck or any of the trip back to Stanwyck. Although Justine had been gone for seven years, the sudden realization that he had found the location where she had been murdered was overwhelming. The memory of digging up one of Justine's distinctive orange leather shoes would probably haunt him forever. He knew the nightmares would return and he would need to see his doctor again to be able to sleep.

He had little doubt he would have found her body if he had kept digging, but that was not a memory he wanted. As he approached the outskirts of Stanwyck, he planned to drive directly to the police station. He would tell them about his discovery, show them the location under the bridge, and leave it up to them to check for evidence and perform the recovery.

Max wasn't sure what evidence the police would find at a crime scene after seven years, but he hoped there would be something to connect Jerry Lennox to the murder. After what Stacey had told him and Hanley had admitted, he had no doubt Lennox was involved.

Max pulled onto the main road and changed down gears as he reached the town limits. It was only a three-minute drive from here to the police station. He knew the police would want to know how he had discovered the body in such a remote location. He had never liked lying and decided he would keep it simple. He had been searching for his daughter ever since she had disappeared and had finally found her. He would focus on the retaining wall and how the stones had been roughly relaid and then claim to have finally gotten lucky. Most of the senior police staff knew him as an upstanding, law-abiding member of the community—he hoped that would be enough.

As he approached the main street, the signs on the side of the road became more frequent. One admonished him to drive safely, another said to enjoy Stanwyck's hospitality, and yet another warned that Neighborhood Watch was active in the community.

It was the fourth sign, which indicated a left turn to the Westleigh Private Hospital ahead, that got his attention. He had seen the sign hundreds of times before but had never taken any notice of it. He thought about the last conversation he had with Stacey Archer and her warning to stay away from Lennox as he approached the turnoff. Max had never been overly good at taking advice. He swerved left at the turnoff and drove down the side road toward a large, multistory brick complex. He began to think about what he would do when he saw Lennox but decided no plan was the best plan. The rage welled inside him again as he drove through the front gates and around a large fountain set in manicured gardens. He did his best to get his emotions under control as he parked his truck in front of the main building.

Max walked into a large reception area and made his way toward an older blonde woman at the front counter. The place was fitted out with crystal chandeliers and original oil paintings; he could have been walking into any five-star hotel except for the slight smell of disinfectant. The closer he got to the counter, the more he could see the woman was repulsed by his appearance. In a pair of work overalls and with dirty, bandaged hands, he wouldn't have an easy time convincing the woman he was here for a social visit.

In a frosty voice, the woman asked, "Can I help you?"

"Good morning, my name's Max, and I'm here to see Jerry Lennox."

"I'm sorry, but visiting hours are between…"

"I'm not here to visit him, ma'am. There's been a fire…last night."

Max held up his dirty, bandaged hands as proof before continuing, "I'm on my way to the police station, and I was asked by the boss to call in here and make sure Mr. Lennox knew. I only need five minutes."

The receptionist fixed him with her best stare for several seconds, trying to decide what to do. Finally, she shook her head and picked up a telephone. Ignoring Max, she dialed a number and waited for a connection.

"Hi, Eleanor, it's Jan at the front desk. I have a man in overalls here demanding to see Mr. Lennox immediately —something about a fire at one of his properties. His name is Max."

The receptionist listened for a moment and nodded once before replying, "Okay, thanks."

After replacing the handset, she looked up at Max and

The Final Proposition

said, "This is highly irregular, but you're allowed five minutes with Mr. Lennox. He's due in his daily therapy session in fifteen minutes, so keep it short and don't upset him."

"Thank you."

The woman held out her hand and pointed to the right side of the front entrance. "Mr. Lennox is in E Wing. Go out the front door and turn right. Eleanor is expecting you and will show you to Mr. Lennox's suite."

Max thanked the receptionist a second time and then headed for the door. The walk across to E Wing took less than a minute. He hoped Eleanor wouldn't make an issue of his visit and would give him some privacy with Lennox. He wasn't sure what he was going to say or do, but as he thought about his daughter again, he knew that five minutes would be more than enough time for what he was now planning.

Max opened the door to E Wing and wasn't surprised that the layout was similar to the main building. The only noticeable difference was Eleanor, who was about twenty years younger than her colleague and didn't seem to have a superior attitude. As he walked into the foyer, Eleanor looked up from her paperwork and said with a smile, "Max?"

Max put on his best smile. "Yes, here to see Mr. Lennox, but only for a minute."

Eleanor got up from behind her desk and said, "No problem, please follow me."

Max followed Eleanor down a long corridor. The five-star hotel design was also evident in E Wing. *Lennox must still have a lot of money to bankroll this.* Eleanor stopped outside a large, closed wooden door and knocked gently before opening. She called out softly, "Excuse me, Mr.

Lennox, you have a visitor," and then turned to Max. "You can go in now—he's watching TV at present. Someone will be along in about ten minutes to take him to his therapy session."

Eleanor smiled and said, "If you need anything, I'll be back at reception."

Max thanked Eleanor and watched as she turned and walked back up the corridor. When he was confident she wasn't coming back, he walked into Lennox's suite and closed the door behind him. Max's eyes took a moment to adjust to the low ambient lighting. The room was massive by hospital standards and included a king-sized bed and a separate sitting area complete with a wall-mounted television, two leather lounge chairs, and a matching coffee table.

Lennox was currently slouched in a wheelchair next to one of the lounge chairs. Max had not seen him in years and found it difficult to recognize him as the same man who used to parade around Stanwyck as if he owned everything. His trademark wavy jet-black hair had turned completely gray, and he was now extremely gaunt. His once-olive complexion was gone, replaced by the pale, spotty skin of a ninety-year-old. Max guessed Lennox was only about sixty, but the stroke had taken a heavy toll and reduced him to just a shell of the man he once was.

Although he didn't seem to be able to sit up straight and dribbled from one side of his mouth, his eyes still looked sharp and were completely focused on Max as he walked across the plush pile carpet to where he sat. Max was only a few feet from Lennox when the crippled man's eyes widened in recognition of who had entered his room. Lennox reached out with a shaky hand for a small service buzzer on a tray next to his wheelchair. Realizing what he was doing, Max quickly reached down and grabbed the device before Lennox could signal for a nurse.

"Relax, you won't be needing that."

Lennox let out a volley of words in a voice barely above a whisper. The entire left side of the man's body seemed paralyzed, and the words emerged as a garbled, spit-laced hiss that Max didn't understand. Lennox continued to hiss for another thirty seconds until the lower half of his face was covered in his own spittle. Exhausted, he stopped to breathe.

Max took this as his cue and calmly responded, "I have no idea what you just said, Lennox, and frankly, I don't care. You don't need to do any talking today anyway —you just need to listen."

Lennox remained silent but fixed Max with a cold stare that said more about his contempt than most people could write in a book.

"You know, a lot of people feel sorry for you, Lennox. Stuck in a hospital for the rest of your life, sucking your food through a straw, needing someone to take you to the bathroom... But not me."

Max paused a moment and held Lennox's stare as he sat down in a chair beside the wheelchair. He leaned in closer to Lennox and said in a quiet voice, "You remember the schoolgirl, Stacey Archer? Sure you do. You raped her one night when she used to work for you."

Lennox's eyes widened slightly, and the cold stare remained intense, but the man didn't respond.

"I don't know her name, but what about your son's girlfriend? You not only raped her but went one better and murdered her as well."

Lennox's stare intensified, but he still said nothing.

Max paused to look around the room for a moment

and then continued in an almost conversational tone, "My uncle Walt had a stroke when I was about twelve. He used to take me fishing before it happened—he was a good man. I didn't understand it at first. He just lay in a hospital bed. I'd go and visit him occasionally, and over time, he regained some of his speech. Eventually, he was able to talk again. It was slurry, and you had to listen hard, but I realized there was nothing wrong with his mind... He was as sharp as ever but trapped in a body that no longer worked."

Max paused and tilted his head slightly so that he was now looking directly into Lennox's face. "That's you, isn't it, Lennox? I can see it in your eyes—you see and understand everything. Deep down, you're still the same arrogant, evil scumbag, only now you're trapped."

Lennox held Max's stare and slowly whispered, "I'm gonna have you taken care of."

Leaning in a little closer, Max replied, "Hanley's dead, Lennox. You're on your own now."

Lennox's eyes widened just fractionally.

Max let out a sigh and said, "I found her this morning, Lennox. My daughter. Just where you and Hanley buried her. And now I'm on my way to the police."

When Lennox didn't respond, Max asked, "Do you believe in God, Lennox?"

Handing back the service buzzer to Lennox, Max continued, "I believe in God... I also believe in justice. For seven years, I've thought about my daughter every day—who murdered her and why. Every day, I've prayed that they would eventually be caught and punished."

Max paused and looked around the room before returning his gaze to Lennox. "But it seems like God did what the police couldn't."

The Final Proposition

Max watched as the fury burned in Lennox's eyes and dribble started pouring out of the left side of his mouth. The man whispered, "Go to hell," before pressing the buzzer.

"You know, Lennox, I don't really care if the police catch you now. Whether you're here or in a prison hospital, you'll still be sucking your food through a little straw and needing someone else to take you to the bathroom. Either way, you're trapped just like a caged animal."

Max gently patted Lennox's leg and then leaned in close and whispered, "I hope you live to be a hundred."

Lennox hissed another volley of garbled words at Max as he rose and walked to the door. He didn't look back—there was nothing here he needed to remember.

Chapter Forty-Eight

Adam stood still, listening to the sounds of the forest. The sound of someone moving nearby had stopped. He wondered whether Darcy had spotted them or somehow sensed they were close. He looked across at Hannah and Michael who were both completely still and alert. He watched Hannah put her arm around Michael to comfort him, and he knew they were anxiously wondering the same thing as they watched and listened.

He debated moving his position to get a better look up through the trees to where the noise had come from. But with no weapon and badly wounded, he knew he would be no match for Darcy and needed to stay out of sight. Their only hope was that Darcy would walk through the area without noticing them. Fear within Adam gave way to frustration as the area remained quiet. The seconds ticked by, and he wondered if Darcy had moved on in a different direction.

He scanned the forest below him as much as he could. He could not see any movement between the trees, and everything remained quiet. He looked across to Hannah and shrugged his shoulders as a sign to her that he had no idea where Darcy was. Hannah nodded back and pointed up through the trees. From the deliberate way she was gesturing, he had no doubt Hannah could see Darcy from her vantage point. Feeling increasingly vulnerable, he decided to risk moving to a better position and signaled Hannah that he was about to move. Hannah nodded, but her worried look suggested she wasn't sure it was a good idea.

Keeping close to the ground, he crept out from underneath the cover of the branches and silently moved up to the cover of the next large tree which was a few feet away. He moved to conceal himself behind the branches, turned to his right, and gave Hannah and Michael a signal that he was okay. They both looked relieved that he hadn't been discovered but were still frightened by what was unfolding. He wondered how Michael was holding up. Hannah had mentioned that stress brought on his seizures—he hoped that wouldn't happen now that Darcy was so close.

Adam moved his position slightly to be able to see more through the branches and felt something solid against his left foot. He looked down and saw that he had almost stood on a broken tree branch nestled amongst the pine needles. After letting out a deep breath, he cautiously moved his foot sideways to avoid standing on it. The last thing they needed now was for him to be making clumsy sounds that would telegraph their position.

Satisfied with his new position, he cautiously pulled a branch down slightly to peer up through the trees. He began scanning the ridgeline, searching for any sign of movement, but he couldn't see anything. His view was still slightly restricted by the branches in front of him, and he decided to risk pulling the branch down further. It was a double-edged sword—he would see more, but he would also leave himself more exposed to discovery. Carefully and slowly, he pulled the branch down. His view began to expand, and his focus was drawn to the left-hand side of his peripheral vision.

Barely daring to breathe, he watched the determined figure of Leyland Darcy cautiously making his way down through the trees and then looked across to Hannah. The terrified look on her face left him in no doubt that she was watching his approach. He continued to follow Darcy as he silently moved forward a few more paces before stopping. With his gun drawn, he stood listening, almost as if he knew they were close. Darcy seemed unhurried and slowly turned his head from left to right as he scanned the forest.

Adam held his breath as Darcy's eyes momentarily settled on the tree he was hiding behind. His presence was shielded by the thick trunk of the fir tree and numerous branches, which he hoped would be enough. He let out his breath as Darcy's scan continued to the right. Hopefully, he hadn't been noticed, but only time would tell.

Darcy stood listening for a moment longer before taking another three careful steps and stopping again. His movement was steadily taking him away from Adam's current position and toward Hannah and Michael. Adam looked across at Hannah. The stunned look on her face said it all—Darcy would find them in under two minutes if he kept on his current course.

Adam looked around for something to pick up and throw to draw Darcy's attention away from Hannah and Michael's position. He scanned the area around him for rocks or small sticks but came up with nothing apart from the branch he had almost stepped on. He bent down and quickly examined it but decided it was too big to hurl with any effectiveness. He may as well announce to Darcy that he was here and get it over and done with.

He peered through the trees again to see Darcy continuing down toward their position. He figured another ten or twelve steps and Hannah and Michael would be exposed. He looked across at Hannah and Michael who were now getting ready to run. He was about to signal them to escape when he remembered the stone Michael had in his pocket.

He wondered whether he could somehow signal Michael to throw it in his direction. Although it was risky, it might get Darcy to alter his course away from them, even if just for a short time. He decided it might not buy them much time, but it was worth a shot. If it worked, it would at least give them time to hide again.

Making sure he remained hidden from Darcy's view, he stepped back and signaled to Hannah and Michael to stop. Hannah looked confused until she saw Adam signaling Michael. Using his good hand, Adam pointed to the pocket of his jeans and then pretended to pull something out. Michael instantly knew what he was referring to, pulled out the stone, and held it up. Adam then feigned a throwing action and then began searching for a spot where he wanted Michael to throw the stone to. With so many trees and high branches, there was no point in being too ambitious. He pointed to a spot close to his current position.

Michael looked up apprehensively at his mother. They both knew drawing Darcy away from them would almost certainly seal Adam's fate. Hannah looked completely distraught as she held Adam's gaze; her nod to Michael was barely perceptible as she mouthed the words "thank you" to Adam.

Adam could hear Darcy on the move again and signaled for Michael to quickly throw the stone. Adam watched as Michael lobbed the stone into the air and then reached down to pick up the broken branch. The stone broke the silence as it landed with a thud about ten feet from where Adam stood. He turned to signal to Michael that he had done a good job, but both Hannah and Michael had gone.

Not daring to give his position away, he resisted peering through the branches and stood still, listening and waiting to see what Darcy did next. Seconds seemed like minutes as he waited for Darcy to appear. He briefly wondered whether Darcy had discovered his position and was now positioning himself to finish him off with one final bullet.

As sweat started to drip from his face, he repositioned his grip on the tree branch while he waited. The short branch was almost too thick for him to grip properly and did not make a very good weapon, but it would have to do. The waiting was agony, but at least it offered Hannah and Michael a chance to escape. Every second that passed put them further away from danger.

Straining every muscle in his body, he listened patiently until he heard the soft footfall of Darcy on the move again. He guessed by the direction of the sound that Darcy was now only a few feet away. Adam tilted his head slightly until he was just able to see a small patch of ground on the other side of the tree through the branches. Doing his best to control his breathing, his wait was quickly over as the view became blocked by a faded pair of blue jeans.

Adam watched and waited, not daring to breathe for fear Darcy would hear him. Trying to plan what to do next was useless as he had no idea what Darcy's next move was. He watched patiently through the gap as Darcy moved forward several more steps before stopping again. With his back to Adam, he was about eight feet away and looking further down into the forest.

The forest was quiet again as Darcy stood still, his head cocked to one side, listening for any sign of movement. Adam watched Darcy start his now-familiar scan of the forest from left to right and instantly knew what needed to be done.

Holding the tree branch tight, he gritted his teeth and waited until Darcy had turned enough that he could see his gun hand. Bursting from the tree branches, Adam rushed forward and brought the tree branch down as hard as he could, hoping to break Darcy's right arm. Darcy caught sight of Adam in his peripheral vision as he swung the branch and swayed backward to avoid the blow. Adam's momentum gave him no chance to adjust his swing, and the branch just managed to clip and dislodge Darcy's gun on the way through its arc.

Darcy cursed and looked back at Adam, momentarily stunned by what had just happened as the branch hit the ground and shattered into several pieces. Adam expected him to reach down and pick up his gun, but instead, he stood his ground.

A cruel grin began to spread across his face. Darcy locked his steel-gray eyes on Adam and said, "I'm not going to need a gun for this."

Darcy roared as he rushed forward and tackled Adam

to the ground. Totally winded, Adam lay on the ground and groaned as the pain from his left arm and shoulder radiated through every fiber in his body. Adam did his best to push the man off with his one good arm, but he was no match in his weakened state. He tried to yell as Darcy's rough hands encircled his throat and began crushing his larynx, but no sound emerged from his mouth. Darcy's determined and cruel features began to dissolve as the man blurred into the background. In an instant, everything turned white and then faded to black.

Chapter Forty-Nine

Hannah had lost count of the number of times Adam had put his life at risk for them in the last two days, and here he was doing it again. Tears began to stream down her face as she looked across through the trees to where he was currently hiding in wait for Darcy. She mouthed the words, "Thank you," even though they seemed hopelessly inadequate.

She did her best to compose herself as she choked out the words, "Throw the stone, Michael, and then run."

She watched as her son launched the stone in the air and then whispered, "Let's go."

Hannah and Michael raced away down a trail in the forest. They had only gone about thirty steps before Hannah pulled Michael to a halt and whispered, "I'm going back to check on Adam. Keep going and don't look back, Michael."

Michael turned to his mother to protest. "But, Mom…"

"I'll be all right, Michael. Just keep going—I'll be along soon."

Hannah watched as her son reluctantly turned and disappeared deeper into the forest before she turned back. He was safe for the moment, and there was no way she could abandon Adam again. She wondered what she could do against a man with a gun as she ran back toward her previous hiding spot.

Emerging from the trail, she looked up and was shocked to see Darcy on the ground with his hands around Adam's neck. Darcy had his back to her and seemed unaware of her presence. She could see his gun on the ground a few feet from him and, in an instant, knew what needed to be done. Reaching into the backpack, she withdrew Winter's empty gun and rushed forward, screaming, "Let go of him now!"

Darcy turned around and looked up at her with anger and surprise.

Hannah pointed the weapon at Darcy's head and said, "No second chances, Darcy. After what you've done to us, I'll happily pull the trigger."

Hannah had no idea how credible she sounded. The gun had no bullets, and she needed to show no fear if she was going to pull this off. If he called her bluff and turned to get his gun, she knew both Adam and her were as good as dead.

She took a step closer and said, "Raise your hands now! From this distance, I can't miss…"

Darcy let go of Adam's throat and slowly raised his hands to shoulder height but no higher. His cold eyes started scanning the ground until they locked on the gun he had dropped. Hannah moved a further step forward and screamed, "You make one move toward that gun, and I swear I won't stop shooting until the gun's empty."

Darcy showed no emotion as he raised his hands higher. Hannah took two steps backward before barking her next instruction, "Move away from Adam and lie facedown on the ground."

Hannah watched as Darcy slowly moved forward and then lay prostrate on the ground. She desperately wanted to check on Adam but knew it was too dangerous to take her eyes off Darcy, even for a second.

Adam had not moved, and she feared he was already dead. "Adam, are you all right?"

From behind her, a voice called out, "Do you want me to check on him, Mom?"

Without taking her eyes off Darcy, she said, "Michael, I told you to stay in the forest."

"I'm sorry, Mom, but I was worried about you. Can I go check on him, please?"

Hannah was scared that Darcy might reach out and grab Michael and pointed at Darcy's gun. "Yes, but first bring me the other gun."

Michael circled wide of Darcy and reached down to pick up the gun.

Keeping the empty gun pointed at Darcy, Hannah said, "Don't put your fingers anywhere near the trigger, Michael. We don't want anyone accidentally getting shot."

Michael carefully picked up the weapon and brought it across to Hannah who took it from him with her left hand. Relieved to now have a gun with bullets in it, she thanked Michael and watched as he ran across to Adam.

"His chest is moving, Mom. He's still alive."

Hannah was about to respond when Adam coughed and opened his eyes. Hannah breathed a huge sigh of relief and whispered a prayer of thanks as Adam began to raise himself with his one good arm up into a sitting position. He had gone beyond pale and was now almost gray from his blood loss. Hannah knew they needed to get him to a hospital immediately if he had any hope of surviving.

Keeping both guns locked on Darcy, she called out, "Can you walk, Adam?"

Adam nodded once and said, "I think so," before raising his good hand to Michael. "Help me up, Champ."

Hannah watched as Michael helped Adam get to his feet. He looked slightly unsteady but appeared to be ready to move on.

"Are you able to hold a gun, Adam?"

Adam looked across and could see Hannah signaling that she wanted him to take Aaron Winter's gun. It was clear Darcy had no idea the gun was empty, and having two guns pointed at him would make the whole situation more manageable.

He nodded and said, "Yeah, all good."

Careful to keep both weapons pointed at Darcy, Hannah circled around and gave Adam the other gun. "We'll get you back to the car and then to a hospital straight away, Adam."

Adam nodded and said, "You'll need to lead the way."

Hannah called to Michael, "Michael, pick up my backpack and head back down to the car. Adam and I are going to escort the man down to his car. We won't be far behind you."

She watched as Michael picked up the bag and then

The Final Proposition

hugged his mother around the waist. "You did good, Mom, I'm proud of you."

She allowed herself the briefest of smiles as she whispered in response, "I'm proud of you too, sweetie."

Keeping the gun fixed on Darcy, Hannah whispered, "Can you do this, Adam?"

He nodded once and said, "I haven't come this far for nothing."

In a louder and more commanding voice, Hannah said to Darcy, "I want you to get on your feet. There are two guns pointed at you now, so you'll do exactly what I say. You make a run for it, and we'll shoot you and walk away. Are we clear?"

Darcy slowly got to his feet and replied, "Only cowards shoot in the back."

Hannah responded, "You get to walk down the trail backward. You take your eyes off me, let alone try and run, and I'll shoot you in the chest."

Darcy shook his head in a sign of protest but wasn't prepared to argue any further with the two guns that were now pointed at him. The three made their way slowly down the trail until they reached the road below.

Hannah quickly surveyed the service road as they stood between the Camaro and Darcy's four-wheel drive. The Toyota was blocking their exit, and the road was too narrow to go around it in the Camaro. She lowered her gun and pointed it at Darcy's knee. "I need your car keys, Darcy, and my patience is running thin. Give them to me now, or I'll blow your kneecap off."

Darcy scowled and then responded, "They're in my pants pocket."

"You've got guns pointed at your knee and chest, so

remove them slowly if you want to walk out of here in one piece."

Without taking his eyes off Hannah, Darcy lowered his left hand, reached into his pants pocket, and extracted the keys.

"Toss them gently to my feet and then get down on your knees."

Darcy did as he was instructed.

After reaching down to pick up the keys, Hannah said, "Michael, I'm going to move his car out of the way. While I do that, can you please get the keys for the Camaro from Adam and put them in the ignition?"

"Okay, Mom."

Hannah looked at Adam. His features had become ashen, and he no longer appeared to be able to stand straight. She was getting more worried about his condition by the second and asked in a soft voice, "Can you hang on for a couple more minutes, Adam?"

Adam kept the gun trained on Darcy as best he could and nodded but didn't say anything.

Hannah moved quickly back to the Toyota and used her left hand to unlock the door while keeping the gun trained on Darcy. She opened the door and wound down the driver's side window without taking her eyes off the man. She stole a brief glance at Adam who now looked like he was going to collapse at any moment. She knew time was critical and pointed the gun through the open window at Darcy again as she got into the car.

She called out to Darcy as she started the engine, "Keep your hands where we can see them."

Using one hand, she pulled down hard on the steering wheel to point the front wheels left and then gently eased out the clutch and accelerated slightly. The Toyota swung hard to its left and off the road. She managed to get it to move about ten feet into the forest before its progress was stopped as the vehicle wedged between two trees. Hannah quickly got out, rushed back to the road, and looked at Adam and Darcy. Darcy was still on his knees, and Adam still had Winter's gun pointed at his head.

She called out, "Hang on, Adam, I just have one more thing to do," before turning and pointing the gun at the left rear tire of the Toyota. She had never fired a gun in her life and had no idea if there was a safety on the gun as she pulled the trigger. The explosion made by the gun was louder than she expected and took her by surprise. When she refocused, she could see that the entire middle section of the tire had been shredded by the impact of the bullet.

Satisfied that the tire was not only flat but well beyond repair, she looked quickly back at Adam and Darcy before taking two steps sideways. Hannah brought the gun up into the firing position again, aimed at the right rear tire, and then pulled the trigger.

The tire instantly disintegrated, and she was now satisfied that Darcy would have to walk out of the forest. Turning back to Adam, she said, "It's time to go, Adam."

Instead of hearing a response, she watched with alarm as he stumbled forward and began to collapse. Before she had time to register what was happening, Darcy twisted around, grabbed the gun from Adam, and brought it up into the firing position. In quick succession, he pulled the trigger three times. Even though she knew the gun was empty, Hannah flinched with each click of the weapon.

Darcy's features changed from determined to puzzled and then to frustrated and angry with each pull of the trigger. By the time he had pulled the trigger for the third time, he realized he had let a woman half his age and size bluff him out of three million dollars with an empty gun.

Hannah could see his rage building and advanced on him with the gun aimed at his chest. "That's right, Darcy, it was empty all the time."

Hannah looked down at Adam who had collapsed to his knees. She knew minutes, even seconds, were now critical to his survival. "Hang on, Adam, and we'll get you into the car."

Adam nodded and said weakly, "Sorry, I blacked out for a moment."

Hannah looked back to Darcy. "You've got two choices—either help him into the car, or I shoot you."

Darcy stalled a moment as if weighing his options. Hannah helped him make up his mind. "Don't push me, Darcy, you're closer than the two car tires I just shot out."

In silence, Darcy walked over to Adam and stood looking down at him as if debating what to do. Hannah called out, "Michael, get well back from the car," and watched as Darcy lowered his hands and then bent down and helped Adam up. Without taking his eyes off Hannah, Darcy walked Adam to the car and helped him into the back seat.

He emerged from the car, looked at Hannah, and raised his hands again. "Now what?"

Hannah kept the gun trained on Darcy's chest and said, "Move back to where you were before and get down on your knees again. Michael, get in the car and wind down the window on the driver's side."

Hannah watched as Darcy walked back and dropped to his knees. His defiant, angry look remained, almost as if he was daring or goading her to shoot. For a moment, she was lost in time as she replayed the events of the last two days. A mixture of rage and despair built inside her, and she found herself moving forward to within three feet of Darcy before stopping again. As she stared him down, she raised the gun from his chest to his head and felt her index finger begin to tighten on the trigger.

Darcy didn't flinch as he looked into the barrel, but Hannah saw fear in his eyes for the first time. Her right index finger applied more pressure to the trigger, and she visualized his head exploding into a sea of red as he collapsed to the ground. She could end the nightmare here and now and never have to worry about him coming after them again. As she wondered how much more pressure she could apply before the gun fired, Michael called out, "Mom, I'm ready."

Hannah let out a breath and released the trigger pressure slightly as she continued to hold Darcy's stare.

They both knew she had stepped back from the precipice as she replied, "Coming, Michael."

Without taking her eyes or the gun off Darcy, she moved back to the Camaro and got in the driver's seat. With the gun still pointed at Darcy, she started the car and leaned out the window. He was about nine feet from the car and easily held her stare.

She studied the man for a moment before she spoke—the fear in his eyes had gone and only cold resignation remained. "I'm keeping your gun, Darcy—close and ready. You come near me or my family ever again, and it will be the last thing you do."

Hannah continued to hold Darcy's stare for several more seconds before she looked across at Michael and said, "I'm going to back up now, sweetie. If he gets up off his knees, you let me know, okay?"

Michael nodded and said, "Okay, Mom."

Relaxing slightly, Hannah started the car, turned briefly, and looked in the back at Adam. Slumped in the back seat with his eyes closed, it was hard to tell if he was still conscious. She put the car in reverse gear and whispered, "Hang on, Adam, we're on our way."

In a weak voice, Adam responded, "You shouldn't have come back. He could have killed you both."

A wave of emotion flooded over Hannah, and she bit down hard on her bottom lip to hold back the tears.

"I couldn't leave you there, Adam. After all you've done for us…I just couldn't."

There was silence for a moment before he replied, "You saved my life, Hannah… Thank you."

Blinking tears from her eyes, Hannah backed up along the service road a short distance until they came to a small clearing at the side of the road. She reversed the car into the tiny alcove before putting the Camaro into first gear. She heard a thud coming from behind her as she began to accelerate away and turned to see Adam slumped forward against the rear of the front seat. As she began to instinctively apply the brakes to stop the car, Michael began screaming, "Mom, the man's getting up. He's running toward us."

Looking across to Michael, Hannah said, "I need you to help Adam, okay? Climb in the back seat and see if you can get him…"

Hannah didn't finish her sentence as she watched in horror as Michael's eyes rolled into the back of his head and her son slumped against the door.

Screaming "No!", she reached across with one hand to hold Michael upright as he began convulsing. Now feeling completely overwhelmed, she looked from her son to Adam and then back again and felt totally alone for the

The Final Proposition

first time in years. Her daze was broken by the sound of Darcy's rapidly approaching footsteps. She looked up into the rearview mirror to see his sprinting figure closing to within a few feet of the rear of the car.

Pressing the accelerator to the floor, she pleaded in an almost childlike whisper, "Please, God, no more..." as the car accelerated away.

Epilogue

Six Months Later

Adam slowed the Camaro down as they approached the deserted white timber house Joseph grew up in. He looked across at the broken windows and the overgrown garden as they drove by. Apart from a few new flecks of missing paint, the house had not changed in six months, almost as if it were destined to remain a signpost to the past.

They drove on at a leisurely pace, and after cresting a small rise in the road, he slowed down as the dilapidated wire fence and rusted metal gate that signaled the end of the road came into view. Adam brought the Camaro to a gentle halt and switched off the engine. He let out a deep breath and looked at Hannah as he reached across and squeezed her hand.

"You okay?"

They sat for a few moments in a silence punctuated only by the occasional tick of the engine as it cooled before Hannah replied, "I think so. I wasn't sure how I would feel coming back here, but I'm coping better than I thought I would."

Adam nodded and looked out the front at the gate and the farmland beyond. The latch on the gate had long since rusted away and allowed the metal structure to swing backward and forward in the gentle breeze as if it were inviting him to enter. He took this as his cue and reached into the back to retrieve the new attache case. He smiled as he looked at Michael sleeping in the back seat. His hair had almost fully grown back, and he was getting noticeably stronger with each passing day.

Being careful not to wake him, Adam gently retrieved the case and said to Hannah, "This should only take a couple of minutes."

"Are you okay on your own?"

"I'll be fine. You stay here with Michael and let him sleep."

Adam got out of the Camaro and closed the door softly to avoid waking Michael up. He walked to the gate and then looked back at the Camaro, which shone like new again.

It had taken months to get it fully repaired, but it had been worth the wait. He saw Hannah smiling and pointing a finger at him through the car window and laughed softly. It was not the first time he had been caught admiring his car since he had picked it up from the repair shop two days ago. Turning on his heel, he walked through the gate and up the overgrown pathway.

After watching Adam until he disappeared out of sight, Hannah snuggled down into the seat and closed her eyes. As she made plans for the future, she drifted off to sleep only to be awoken by a gentle nudge to her shoulder.

"Mom, are you awake?"

Hannah opened her eyes and turned to see Michael wedged between the two fronts seats, staring at her with a concerned look on his face.

"Where's Adam?"

"He'll be back soon, sweetie."

Michael rubbed the sleep from his eyes and then looked out the window. Slightly confused, he said, "Mom, this looks like the place where you got the money from?"

Hannah sat up in her seat and turned slightly to face Michael. She still marveled at his recovery as she looked into his inquisitive eyes.

"Yes, Michael. Adam and I decided the right thing to do was to put the money back where we found it."

Michael looked confused. "But didn't you need it to pay for my operation?"

"We needed some of it, Michael. I've known about the money since you were a baby, but I never really wanted any part of it because it was never really our money. But when you got sick, it was the only way we could get you the operation you needed."

"So Adam's putting back the money we didn't use?"

"Not quite. He's actually putting all of it back, and later today, we're going to post a letter to the police telling them where to find it."

Hannah could see Michael still looked confused. She paused for a moment to figure out how best to explain everything. "You know how Adam got his money a few weeks back for being wrongly put in jail?"

The Final Proposition

Michael nodded.

"Well, it was a lot more than he expected. Like me, he was happy to use the money we found here to get you your operation, but now that we don't need it anymore, he wanted to put it back—all of it, including what we borrowed."

Hannah paused and watched as her son thought about what she had said. Finally, he looked at his mother and said, "My operation cost a lot of money—Doctor Chan said so."

Hannah nodded.

In a quiet voice, Michael said, "So, Adam really paid for my operation then?"

"He loves you, Michael. He wanted to do something good with the money."

Michael sat staring out the front window. It wasn't very often that Hannah saw her nine-year-old boy speechless.

Hannah continued, "Michael, there's something else we need to talk about."

She waited for Michael to turn and face her again before she said, "You know Adam loves me, don't you?"

Slightly embarrassed, Michael replied, "Mom, you tell each other every day, even when I'm right there."

Hannah smiled and said, "He's asked me to marry him, Michael."

For a moment, Michael looked slightly taken aback, but as he thought through what his mother had just told him, a smile began to spread across his face.

Hannah asked, "Is that okay with you, Michael?"

Michael nodded and said, "I really like Adam."

He thought for a moment and became serious as he asked, "Where are we going to live?"

"Well, for now, we'll live in Stanwyck in Max's new house, just while we look for somewhere for ourselves. Adam wants to start his furniture-making business again, so we'll need more than just a house. Max has been looking around Stanwyck for us, and he's going to take us to see two small farms later today."

"If we buy a farm, can I have a horse, or maybe even a motorbike?"

Hannah laughed. "One thing at a time, sweetie. Doctor Chan says you're well on the way to a full recovery, but we need to take it slow for another six months, okay?"

Michael nodded and became serious again. "Do I… call Adam 'Dad' when you get married?"

Hannah stroked her son's hair as she replied, "I think he would prefer you continue to call him Adam. He will love you as much as any father can love a son, but I know he wants you to always remember who your real dad was."

Michael nodded again as he thought about what his mother had just said. There was more Hannah wanted to say, but before she had a chance to continue, she was drowned out by Michael screaming, "Here he comes!"

She smiled as Michael jumped out of the car and rushed toward the gate. She thought about Joseph and knew he would be happy that Adam was now in Michael's life.

She watched as Adam and Michael walked back to the car, laughing and joking together. The nightmare of what they had all been through was still raw, but it was beginning to fade as they created new and happy memories. They were a family and had each other now, and that was all that mattered.

Also by Trevor Douglas

vinci-books.com/cold-comfort

A rookie detective. An elusive murderer. A race against time to catch a deadly predator.

New to the force, detective Bridgette Cash faces her first murder case when a young woman's body is found in the forest. Convinced it's the work of a serial killer, she must navigate skeptical superiors and scant evidence to uncover the truth. As the clock ticks and the pressure mounts, she scrambles to gather clues and catch the perpetrator before they strike again.

Turn the page for a free preview…

Cold Comfort: Chapter One

The rancid smell of decaying human flesh shrouded Bridgette like a mist as she opened the door of the unmarked police car. Suppressing the urge to vomit, she stared out through the windshield at the police tape that surrounded the shallow grave fifty feet in front of her. Bridgette recalled the words of several seasoned detectives from her final year lectures as she sat and tried to compose herself. Their confessions that they often needed to shower three and four times after attending a murder scene before they felt clean again was something she'd never understood. But now, as the overwhelming stench of death began to settle on her, she understood why.

As she felt bile rise in her throat, she knew nothing she had learned during her four-year degree would prepare her for this part of the job. In only her second week on the force as a rookie detective, the real learning was about to begin.

A short laugh interrupted her thoughts. She turned

and looked across at Lance Hoffman, who was already out of the car. At sixty-one years of age and three months short of retirement, the tall, slightly overweight, and balding Detective had an official reputation on the force as a competent investigator who held the record at Vancouver PD for the most murder cases solved.

With an amused look, her partner of less than two weeks leaned down and said, "You know, it's much easier to do the police work when you actually get out of the car, Detective."

Hoffman's reputation had been tempered by Bridgette's new boss, Chief Inspector Felix Delray, who had given her a slightly franker assessment of her partner when making the assignment.

"I'm putting you with Hoffman for your first three months. He's old, doesn't like change or women much, but he's one hell of an investigator, and he'll teach you a lot."

As a throwaway line at the end of their conversation, Delray had confided that if she could stick it out with Hoffman, she could probably work with anyone on the force. Bridgette had taken this as a challenge, and as she sat staring back at her partner, who clearly found her misery amusing, she silently admonished herself to hold it together.

Bridgette ignored the condescending jibe and pulled a small tube of Vicks VapoRub from her leather satchel. Determined not to appear weak or overwhelmed, she took her time spreading a liberal smear of the lotion just above her top lip.

Hoffman watched with amusement for several seconds before asking, "They teach you that in police school?"

The whiny tone in Hoffman's voice as he said, 'police

school,' was yet another subtle reference to her criminology degree. On their first day together, Hoffman had made it clear that he thought university courses were hopelessly inadequate in preparing anyone for real police work. To his surprise, Bridgette had readily agreed.

Bridgette quickly learned that her training partner was rude, overbearing, and opinionated. She was miserable for the first three days of their partnership as she tried to placate the crusty, aging Detective. On day four, she was tired of being polite and found Hoffman seemed to respect her more when she was rude back to him.

Ignoring his question, Bridgette finished applying the Vicks and asked, "Do you ever get used to it?"

The grin vanished from Hoffman's face as he looked across towards the grave. The medical examiner and two other technicians were already in position and ready to start the recovery.

In a slightly more reflective voice, Hoffman replied, "You learn to tolerate the smell, but you never get used to the violence."

Bridgette said nothing in response as she got out of the car. As they walked in silence through the sparse tree line towards the police tape, the smell intensified. Bridgette was thankful the Vicks was masking the worst of the odor, but as she fought the urge to gag, she knew she would need to remain totally focused to get through what was ahead of her. Hoffman put his hand up to stop her just short of the tape.

"You wouldn't be the first recruit to puke on me, but we can't afford to have the crime scene contaminated. So, if you're going to puke, do it now."

Hoffman studied her, waiting for a response.

Bridgette had deliberately not eaten breakfast and

now felt that had been a wise decision, as she responded, "I'm good."

Hoffman didn't look convinced and replied, "You look terrible. Right now, you're green enough to pass for an avocado."

Bridgette shook her head as she replied, "I'm alright. It's just going to take me a while to get used to the smell."

Hoffman kept his hand up and said, "As I explained in the car, the medical examiner and his techs will be doing most of the work here with the recovery. We keep out of their way and learn whatever we can from the crime scene. You let me do the talking—just watch and listen."

Hoffman looked across at the medical examiner and held up an index finger to signal he needed a moment more before returning to Bridgette again.

"If it's who I think it is, she's been missing for two weeks. You'll have learned enough from your fancy school to know decomposition will be well advanced. You think it smells bad now—it will get a whole lot worse when they move the foot of soil that's currently covering her."

Now getting slightly more used to the smell, Bridgette held Hoffman's gaze and said more confidently, "This is what I signed up for."

Hoffman nodded and said, "Remember who's in charge. You don't touch anything without my say so."

Bridgette was smart enough to realize that the three months until Hoffman's retirement would pass quickly and that picking a fight with him was pointless. Instead, she nodded and followed him as they passed under the tape.

Bridgette counted six police officials at the crime scene —two uniformed police officers who remained outside the police tape, two technicians who were supporting the medical examiner, a photographer, and the medical examiner himself. Hoffman ignored everyone except the medical examiner, who was putting on a mask and gloves.

"Good morning, Ray."

The stout medical examiner, who Bridgette guessed was in his late fifties, replied evenly, "Not much good about today, Lance."

"Ray, this is my new junior partner in training, Detective Casseldhorf."

The medical examiner nodded in Bridgette's direction and said, "Doctor Ray Warner," before asking, "Is this your first crime scene?"

Bridgette nodded.

Warner smiled, handed her his paper mask, and said, "Put this on. It has a perfume that ordinarily smells disgusting but works wonders with decomposing bodies."

Bridgette thanked Warner and put the mask on. The smell was strong and unusual, but it did significantly reduce the odor and her urge to vomit.

Warner smiled and said, "Better?"

Bridgette nodded again and said through the mask, "Much better. Thank you."

As the medical examiner retrieved another mask from a large plastic chest, Hoffman said, "I've briefed the detective on her role here today, but I'll get you to fill us both in on what you know so far, Ray."

Warner walked to the grave's edge and looked down at the eight small blue flags pegged out around the mound of earth.

"So, we know a call came in from a Vietnam veteran who was out walking his dog early this morning down along this trail."

Warner paused and pointed to a small hole near one of the middle flags before continuing.

"The dog gets excited and starts digging here, and the guy knew by the smell and his time in Vietnam that the dog had discovered a body."

Hoffman interrupted, "The man's name is Seymour. I've spoken to him on the phone and got some basic details. We'll visit him later today and take his statement, but he seems straight up—no criminal record that we know of."

Warner nodded and continued, "We've been here for about an hour. So far, we've removed and bagged the leaves that covered the grave and taken photographs of the area. This is going to take a while, but based on what we've seen so far, I'd say the victim has been here about two weeks."

Hoffman nodded and said, "It lines up with the disappearance of Monica Travers."

Warner's face turned grim. "Well, at least it will give her parents closure."

Bridgette had followed the story of Monica Travers' disappearance through the newspapers and in the Detective's room at Vancouver PD. Travers was a law student who worked part-time in a florist's shop. She had not returned home one evening after work, and her parents had notified the police immediately, saying it was totally out of character for their daughter.

The word inside the department was that she was a quiet nineteen-year-old who didn't do drugs or have a criminal record. After forty-eight hours with no leads on her whereabouts, most of the detectives within the division feared the worst.

Warner shook his head slightly and continued, "I've

got two extra lab guys on their way. The department won't like the Sunday overtime bill, but this will be a long day. We have seven large bags of leaf litter that we've removed from on top of the grave to examine, as well as all the soil we still need to excavate. The body is under close to a foot of soil, so there's a lot to get through."

Warner looked from Hoffman to Bridgette and said, "It might be hours before we find anything. If you want, you can go back into town and start your interviews? I'll call you if we find anything significant."

Hoffman shook his head.

"We'll stay for a while, Ray. I want to take a look around anyway and get an idea of the layout of the area. It looks remote enough, but you never know. If we find someone who saw something, we might break this wide open very quickly."

Warner nodded and then directed his two technicians to remove and sift soil from the grave's southern side. After fitting his mask, he made a few notes on his laptop and then joined his two technicians in their tedious endeavor.

Growing bored, Hoffman called out to Warner, "Hey, Ray, I'm going to check the surrounding area. I've got coverage on my phone here, so if you find anything significant, call me."

Warner looked up and briefly nodded as Hoffman moved away from the grave. Bridgette turned to follow. She was glad they were at least going to be doing something constructive instead of standing around and waiting. As Hoffman lifted the tape, he turned back with a surprised look.

"What are you doing, Detective?"

Confused, Bridgette lifted her mask and said, "I thought I was coming with you?"

Hoffman let out a short laugh and replied, "You've got your little mask, so you stay here and watch. You'll learn more from watching these guys than you can possibly imagine."

Without waiting for a reply, Hoffman moved under the tape and made his way up the bank back towards the road. Bridgette refitted her mask and shook her head. She was still trying to figure out whether Hoffman was simply obnoxious or had a personality flaw when Warner called out, "Detective?"

Bridgette turned around to see the medical examiner walking around the edge of the grave towards her.

"I'm sorry, I didn't catch your first name?"

"It's Bridgette."

"Okay, Bridgette. And you can call me Ray or 'Doc'."

Bridgette nodded as Warner looked up and watched Hoffman disappear over the top of the bank.

He said, "There are a few things you need to know about Lance. Apart from being the crustiest bastard I've ever worked with, he's good—very good at his job."

Warner paused as if collecting his thoughts before he continued.

"He's easily misunderstood. I don't know how much you know about him or what you've managed to figure out yet, but he's actually a decent guy. He has almost no clue about common courtesy, but he means well, and if you earn his respect, he'll never let you down or sell you out.

I'm not trying to make excuses for him, but he's actually one of the few people in Vancouver PD I really trust, even though I don't always agree with him."

Bridgette thought about what Warner had just shared with her. She would make up her own mind in her own time, but she appreciated the gesture.

"Thanks, Ray. It pans out a lot with what Chief Delray said. I don't imagine we'll ever be friends, but I plan to learn as much as possible from him over the next three months."

Warner nodded and said, "That's a good attitude."

He turned to head back to the two technicians and said, almost as an afterthought, "Feel free to ask us questions, Bridgette. Lance is right; you'll learn a lot from this."

Bridgette thought she detected a smile beneath the medical examiner's mask. Most of the people she had met since commencing her new job with Vancouver PD had been friendly. Several older male detectives had been cold and aloof, and she still hadn't worked out, whether that was because she was a rookie, a woman, or both.

She decided Doctor Warner was someone she could trust and watched in silence for the next thirty minutes as they carefully removed and sifted the soil. In that time, Warner and the two technicians made steady progress and had already removed about six inches of soil from the southern end of the grave.

Bridgette decided there was little to be gained by staying and watching until they exposed the body and said, "Hey, Ray, I think I'm going to take a walk back up to the road, just to get a better perspective of the site."

Warner looked up and nodded, "Okay, Bridgette, but stay where I can see you if you don't mind. It's not worth the grief if Lance returns, and I don't know where you are."

Bridgette promised she would as she bent down to

pass back under the police tape. She was not surprised by Warner's request but was amazed that senior people in Vancouver PD allowed Hoffman to dominate them as much as he did.

The short walk back up the bank brought her to a long, tall row of Katsura trees that flanked the left-hand side of the road. With winter fast approaching, the trees had lost most of their leaves and now looked more like a long row of gnarly wooden columns than a picturesque backdrop to the road. After zipping up her jacket to keep out the cold wind, she walked to the edge of the road and stood thinking for several minutes as she looked back at the scene below. The site of the grave was barely a stone's throw from the roadway, yet it was almost completely hidden from the passing view of motorists by the steep descent of the bank.

Bridgette looked across to the woods beyond the walking trail. The wooded area was much bigger than she had first assumed and looked like it would take several hours to walk around as it stretched out deep into the green valley below. She could not see any tracks or laneways that connected the woods to any of the surrounding farmland and wondered how much of it Lance Hoffman planned to explore on foot.

Her thoughts were interrupted by an approaching car. Bridgette moved back from the edge of the road and stood amongst the trees as the car passed by. She watched as the car's slipstream disturbed a few remaining leaves on the road, causing them to lift and flutter before they were carried over the bank and down the hill by the prevailing breeze.

As she watched the leaves float and swirl, she moved back to the embankment's edge, where her eye was immediately drawn back to the grave site below. Warner and his technicians were making good progress, and she could now see the outline of the top half of the body in the exposed earth. Deciding there was nothing more that she needed to see from the roadway, she made her way back down to the grave site and placed her mask back on as she passed under the police tape.

Warner motioned Bridgette to join him as the technicians moved away from the grave to allow the photographer better access.

With a grim look, Warner said, "It's her. I remembered reading in the missing person's report that she wore a monogram gold ring on her right hand. I homed in on clearing soil around her arm and hand, and sure enough, there's a ring on the right ring finger."

They watched silently for several minutes as the police photographer took photographs from different angles before a voice behind them broke the silence.

"You find something, Ray?"

They both looked around to see Lance Hoffman standing behind them.

Warner replied, "We have, Lance," before explaining what he had just told Bridgette.

He concluded by adding, "I brushed away enough dirt from the ring to read the engraving. Just one letter —'M'."

Hoffman nodded and said, "It's definitely her then."

They watched the photographer take a few more photographs before Hoffman said, "Ray, I'm thinking Detective Casseldhorf and I will head back to the office and start planning some interviews. I've scoured the area, and there don't appear to be any residences close by. If we leave now, we can spend all afternoon working up a list of

The Final Proposition

people who knew Monica Travers and hit the ground running when we get the formal ID."

Warner nodded and said, "No problem, Lance, I'll keep you posted on anything else we find here, and I'll email you photographs of the ring shortly."

Hoffman nodded and turned to Bridgette, "Let's go, Detective."

Bridgette removed her mask, and as she passed it back to Warner, she asked, "How long do you think the leaf litter has been on the ground, Ray?"

Warner looked up briefly at the Katsura trees and replied, "It's close to winter, so maybe four weeks?"

Bridgette nodded as she responded, "It's odd, isn't it? If this is the grave of Monica Travers, who we know has only been missing for two weeks, why would the killer pick a spot covered in leaves to bury the body?"

Hoffman replied evenly, "Murderers do strange things, Detective, many of which defy logic. Let's go."

Bridgette stood her ground and pointed to the woods beyond the walking trail.

"We're less than forty yards from the woods. It wouldn't have taken him any longer to bury the body in there where it might not have been found for months or even longer."

Hoffman snapped, "Where are we going with this, Detective?"

Unfazed, Bridgette continued, "This spot is right next to a walking trail and was discovered by someone who probably walks it regularly."

Hoffman replied, "Your point being?"

"It doesn't make sense. If the murderer wanted to keep the body's location a secret for as long as possible, surely he would have chosen the woods? If he just wanted to dump the body and get out of here as fast as he could, there would have been no burial?"

Warner asked, "I'm not sure I follow?"

Bridgette looked up the bank to the row of Katsura trees, then back at the grave again, and continued.

"It almost looks like he deliberately chose here so the body would be discovered once it began to smell. It's just a theory, but why else would you pick a spot where you have to remove a lot of leaves before you dig and then go to the trouble of replacing them afterward?"

Bridgette looked from Warner to Hoffman but didn't get a response to her question.

She continued, "It only makes sense when you're using the leaves to temporarily hide where you've buried a body?"

Warner nodded and then added, "Until it starts to smell."

Bridgette nodded, "Yes, until it starts to smell."

Hoffman asked, "Okay, so the murderer may have wanted the body discovered. So, what does that prove?"

Bridgette looked down at the grave again.

"If the spot was deliberately picked, it implies planning. That doesn't fit well with a spur-of-the-moment crime of passion and potentially opens up a much wider group of suspects beyond friends, family, and acquaintances. It may—"

Hoffman snapped, "What kind of suspects?"

Bridgette could see by Hoffman's body language that he was growing increasingly impatient, but she wasn't about to be rushed. She considered the question for a moment before she answered.

"I can think of two. Organized crime figures occasionally want their crimes discovered. I'm sure you've covered crimes where someone's death is used to send a warning message."

Warner was now intrigued, "And the second group?"

Bridgette looked from Warner to Hoffman and then replied, "The second group is serial killers."

Cold Comfort: Chapter Two

Hoffman let out a belly laugh and responded, "Well, now I've heard everything, Ray. Detective Casseldhorf has been on the case for five minutes, and we've got a serial killer on our hands."

Bridgette kept her anger in check as best she could and replied, "I didn't say it was a serial killer, Detective. I simply answered your question."

Hoffman turned serious and asked, "How old are you, Detective?"

"I'm twenty-seven, but I don't see what—"

Hoffman interrupted, "This is your first murder case. Don't you think you should be leaving this to the experts?"

Bridgette looked from Hoffman to Warner. She was the rookie and knew she should back down, but that wasn't in her nature. "Surely I'm entitled to ask questions?"

Hoffman replied, "Do you know what percentage of murders are committed by serial killers, Detective?"

"Between one and two percent."

"I retire in less than three months, and in my time as a police officer, I've solved seventy-one murder cases. Do you know how many of those have been serial killers?"

Bridgette held Hoffman's gaze but said nothing. She was not familiar with the breakdown of Hoffman's record and wasn't going to give him the satisfaction of an *'I don't know'* answer.

Hoffman continued, "Metropolitan Vancouver has a population of just over two million people—big enough to have a full cross-section of scumbags that commit murder. I've arrested everyone from crime bosses to little old ladies for murder, but never once have I arrested a serial killer."

Hoffman turned to Warner and asked, "How many serial killer cases have you been involved with, Doctor?"

Warner mumbled, "One that I know of."

Hoffman nodded and looked at Bridgette. "Detective, this is the real world here. It's not your police school or some Hollywood movie. Vancouver PD doesn't have unlimited resources, and I need a lot more than a few leaves put back on top of a grave before I go to the Chief and tell him we think it might be a serial killer."

Even though she knew Hoffman was probably right, the location for the burial bothered her. Bridgette decided now was not the time to argue. "Detective Hoffman, you're the lead on this case, not me. I simply asked a question."

Hoffman replied, "Let's go, Detective," before pausing to look at Warner again. "Ray, I'd like a close-up photo of the monogram ring and the grave-site sent to my email ASAP. I'm going to brief the Chief as soon as I get back, and the photos will help paint the picture."

Warner nodded, "No problem, Lance."

As Hoffman turned to leave, Bridgette said to Warner, "Would you mind also sending through some photos of the shovel marks around the edge of the grave?"

Hoffman turned back and said sharply, "Are you trying to tell Doctor Warner what to do as well as me, Detective? Because if you are, our meeting with the Chief will be more than just—"

Slightly irritated, Bridgette cut him off and said in a louder voice than she had planned, "Go take a look for yourself, Detective."

Hoffman looked at Warner and then walked back to the grave. As he bent down to examine the shovel marks, Bridgette watched Warner walk across to join him.

Bridgette gave them a moment and said, "You'll notice the shovel marks at the edge of the grave are only about seven inches wide, consistent with the size of a small portable shovel—like campers carry in their backpacks."

Hoffman looked closely at the edge of the grave for a few seconds. Without looking up, he said, "Okay, Detective, what am I looking at apart from shovel marks in the soil? You know as well as I do that shovel markings are measured and documented as part of standard procedure."

Bridgette walked over and stood beside Warner. She took a pen from her pocket, bent down, and pointed at more of the exposed shovel marks. "Do you see that?"

Warner adjusted his glasses and looked down but shook his head. "I don't see it, Bridgette."

Without replying, Bridgette moved the pen to the next shovel mark and pointed at a narrow, almost undetectable score in the earth. As she traced the score mark as it ran in a vertical line down into the soil, Warner replied, "Son of a bitch."

Warner gently scraped more soil away from the edge of the grave and pulled a small magnifying glass from his top pocket. As he began investigating the other marks left by the shovel, Hoffman leaned forward slightly and asked, "You find something, Ray?"

Warner looked at Bridgette. She nodded at him as if to say, *'this will be better coming from you.'*

Warner pulled his mask up and pointed at the shovel mark and responded, "The shovel used to dig the grave has what looks like a burr on it." Warner pointed to several of the other shovel marks as he continued. "You can see here that the shovel marks all show a faint vertical indentation in the soil in the same spot. It's not easy to make out, but you can definitely see a faint score in the soil where the blade has been pushed into the ground."

Warner rose to his feet and continued, "We'll get this all photographed properly for you, but based on what I'm seeing here, we have a way of identifying the shovel that was used to dig the grave." Warner looked at Bridgette and continued, "This is great work, Detective. Provided the burr hasn't been filed off, if you find the shovel, we should be able to positively match it to the crime scene."

Traffic was heavy, and the trip back into Vancouver took longer than expected. Bridgette had lived most of her life in the city and normally wouldn't have minded, but Hoffman had insisted on eating two pastrami and onion sandwiches he had made earlier that morning while he drove.

Still feeling slightly nauseated from the smell of the crime scene, she found the car trip miserable as she fought the urge to vomit. She was thankful when they pulled off the freeway and headed back through the outer suburbs toward the South Metro police complex.

After Hoffman finished the last of his sandwich and began to lick his fingers, he said, "The leaves bother me."

Bridgette wasn't sure how to respond. Hoffman hadn't said a word to her since they left the crime scene, and she wasn't sure where he was going with the statement. Playing it safe, she replied, "How so?"

"I'm not buying your serial killer angle, but the question about why the killer picked a spot where he had to move leaves before digging the grave concerns me. That takes time and exposes him to a lot more risk of being caught."

Bridgette thought about Hoffman's analysis as the unmarked police car drove across the four-lane iron bridge. It had rained heavily the previous evening and turned the river below a dirty brown color. She looked down at a ferry making its way slowly down the river and replied cautiously, "Maybe?"

Hoffman shot back, "Maybe?"

"Even though it's just outside the city limits, there are probably only a few houses within a half-mile radius, and you can't see the grave site from the road. If the murder took place in the middle of the night, the killer could have been there for hours with nobody knowing."

Bridgette turned to face Hoffman. In an effort to keep the conversation going, she said, "Let's assume for a moment that the killer wanted the body discovered. Why bury it at all? Why go to all that trouble if you want the world to know what you've done?"

The Final Proposition

Hoffman frowned for a second and then answered, "Maybe the killer wanted to get out of town, or even leave the country? Two weeks buys you more than enough time for that."

Bridgette considered Hoffman's answer but didn't respond straight away. Hoffman pulled up at a set of traffic lights and then asked, "So what are you thinking, Detective? Are we back in criminology school reviewing the latest crime theories by some professor who's never done a real day of police work in his life?"

Bridgette replied, "No. I was actually thinking about what you said."

Hoffman laughed and mockingly said, "Something I said?"

Bridgette ignored the taunt and said, "I think you're right. I think he was buying time—maybe not to leave the country, but maybe enough time to make it safe?"

Bridgette watched Hoffman for a moment before she continued. He was clearly uncomfortable when she agreed with him. She looked out the front of the vehicle at the traffic that was making the trip impossibly slow and said, "We know DNA evidence at any outdoor crime scene needs to be collected almost immediately. Even a slight breeze or a downpour of rain like we had last night can virtually destroy any chance of gathering usable evidence."

Hoffman made a right turn onto Canyon Street and started the final drive past a series of modern office blocks toward the Central Precinct building. He was quiet for a moment as he thought about Bridgette's analysis and then mumbled, "Bury the body close to where people walk and shallow enough so that the smell alone will ensure it's discovered sooner rather than later..."

Hoffman turned left at the side entrance of a large glass and concrete four-story complex. He drove down a concrete driveway past a sign that read Authorized Vehicles Only before pulling up at a boom gate. He flashed his police ID at the security guard, who nodded back as the boom gate rose.

As they drove around to the rear of the building, Hoffman continued, "We've got a few different angles to work on. We'll talk to the Chief when we get inside and start on the list of people who knew Monica Travers and interacted with her."

Hoffman pulled the car up at another boom gate at the back of the building. After swiping a plastic security card to gain access to the underground parking lot, he said, "After we talk to the Chief, I'll get you to ring someone from the City Council—a botanist or head gardener. I want an expert to tell us how long those leaves have been on the ground. We can't assume anything and need to make sure it's three or four weeks like Ray suggested; otherwise, your theory of the killer intentionally picking that spot starts to look thin."

Bridgette replied, "Okay," pleased that Hoffman wasn't dismissing her theory entirely.

Hoffman parked next to a group of identical late-model dark Ford sedans. As they headed for the elevator, he said, "When we get those pictures from Ray, I want you to scan our databases and see if there are any other crimes that mention a shovel with burr marks on the blade."

Hoffman pressed the button on the elevator and as the door opened, he continued, "It's most likely a dead end, but Monica Travers' parents deserve the most thorough investigation we can put together."

Bridgette followed Hoffman into the elevator, and they rode up to the second floor in silence. She thought about what they knew so far. In a way, she hoped she was wrong about the murder being planned. Whoever killed Monica Travers would be far easier to find if they had just snapped in a fit of rage, lust, or jealousy. She shuddered to think who they were up against if the killer had been able to orchestrate the discovery of his work for when it suited him.

Cold Comfort: Chapter Three

Hoffman knocked on the door to Chief Inspector Felix Delray's office. The door remained open most of the time, and Bridgette could see Delray sitting behind his aging wooden desk, concentrating on his computer screen. This was the first time she had seen him wearing casual clothes and figured Delray had other plans for his day off. She was quickly learning Hoffman and Delray weren't afraid to work long or irregular hours. Without looking up to see who his visitors were, Delray said, "Come on in," and kept reading.

As Hoffman and Bridgette settled into their chairs on the opposite side of his desk, Delray said in a quiet, distracted voice, "Guys, I'll be with you in a minute."

They both watched in silence as Delray continued to read his computer screen, mouthing some of the words and sentences to himself as he went. Bridgette marveled at how Delray's heavy, black-framed reading glasses remained perched almost on the end of his nose, seemingly defying gravity. She had only been in his office twice before and had quickly developed respect for the veteran detective's inclusive and practical style of leadership.

Delray finally pushed back from the screen and said, "Okay, I got the email from Ray with the photos from the crime scene. He's put together a short report on what he's found so far. It looks highly likely that it's the body of Monica Travers."

Hoffman nodded. "We need to go through a formal procedure, but I expect we'll have enough information late today to be able to advise the parents ahead of a formal identification."

Delray frowned and said, "She's been in the ground for two weeks. So whatever we do, she's not going to look pretty for an identification."

Hoffman grimaced and answered, "We may be able to spare the parents the need to formally ID the body. We already have her DNA on file, and we can clean the monogram ring up and show them that to start with."

Delray pondered Hoffman's response for a moment and said, "Good plan, Lance. They've got enough bad memories without us adding to them if we don't need to."

Bridgette was slightly surprised by Delray's empathy. Now in his early fifties and a veteran with over thirty years on the force, she had expected Delray to be more detached.

Delray sighed and then asked, "Okay, Lance, what have we got?"

Hoffman spent ten minutes providing his boss with a full summary of what they knew so far. He went into detail about Monica Travers' last known movements before she disappeared and then gave a full rundown of the crime scene. Delray nodded occasionally and scratched a couple of notes on a pad while Hoffman gave the briefing but didn't interrupt.

When Hoffman had finished, the room became quiet for a moment before Delray looked at Bridgette and asked, "Do you have anything to add, Bridgette?"

Bridgette looked across at Hoffman, who said bluntly, "Now's not the time to be shy, young lady. If you think there's substance to your theory, then share it."

Bridgette turned back to Delray, who had an *'I'm waiting'* look on his face. Hoffman hadn't gone into any real detail on the leaves on the grave or the shovel marks. She took two minutes to go through her observations before concluding with her theory that the killer deliberately chose the spot so that the body would be discovered.

Delray scratched a note on his pad and then turned to Hoffman and said, "Lance, what's your take?"

Hoffman shifted slightly in his seat. Bridgette thought, here it comes, expecting Hoffman to shoot down everything she had just said.

"I don't agree with all elements of the detective's theory, but going to the trouble of re-covering the grave with leaves bothers me as well, Chief. The more I think about it, the more I think he wanted the body discovered once decomposition had set in."

Delray thought for a moment and said, "If he planned it ahead of the actual murder, then Bridgette's right. We are potentially looking at a much wider pool of suspects."

Hoffman replied, "We plan to start with relatives and known acquaintances, and if nothing comes from those interviews, we'll widen the pool."

Delray ran his fingers through his short, curly dark hair as he stared down at his notes. Bridgette had seen him do this in a previous meeting and knew he was in deep thought.

Finally, he looked up and said, "If this is Monica Travers, as we expect, then it's going to get wide media coverage. I expect I'll be asked to give the Commissioner a briefing on this as early as tomorrow, ahead of a formal press announcement. It's going to get political, and we're going to be under a lot of pressure from the top to solve this quickly."

Delray looked at Hoffman and said, "Needless to say, Lance, if that happens, the Commissioner is going to want a team on this, which I'd like you to lead."

Hoffman nodded and said, "Okay, Chief."

Bridgette could see the reluctance on Hoffman's face. From what she had heard and observed, she knew Hoffman preferred to operate on his own, or at best with one partner he could control.

Delray said, "Work up your list of potential suspects as quickly as you can. I'd like to have something to show the top brass tomorrow morning to show we're on it. The last thing we want is one of them breathing down our necks because they don't see enough progress."

Hoffman nodded and replied, "Got it."

Delray replied, "Also, I'd like to get that monogram ring back here and cleaned up as a priority. If we can get a positive ID from the parents, it will help us hit the ground running."

Hoffman replied, "I'm on it, Chief."

Delray nodded and said, "Okay, we're done for now."

Bridgette took this as her cue and rose from her chair, but Delray motioned her to sit again.

"Detective, I'd like you to stay a minute?"

Hoffman gave Delray a nod and headed for the door.

Delray called after him, "Close the door as you leave, please, Lance."

Bridgette immediately assumed she was in trouble and wondered what she had done. She speculated whether Doc Warner had said something in his email to the Chief.

As she began to run through other possibilities, Delray opened with a question. "How are you settling in, Bridgette?"

"Fine, thanks, Chief."

Delray looked at Bridgette for a moment and said, "Relax, Bridgette, you're not in trouble. Everyone knows when I'm angry—something to do with steam and my ears, I've been told. You see any steam?"

Bridgette smiled and said, "No, Chief."

"Good."

Delray put his glasses back on the tip of his nose and opened a paper file on his desk. As he began reading the first page, he said without looking up, "So you know how this works. As a graduate, you get the option to rotate through several sections of Vancouver PD in your first twelve months. It gives you an opportunity to find out what you're really suited for."

He looked up from the file and said, "You saw the body up close today?"

Bridgette nodded, not entirely sure where he was going with the question, and answered, "Partially. The bottom half of the grave hadn't been fully excavated."

Delray nodded and asked, "Did you puke?"

Bridgette shook her head. "No, but it was close. I saw quite a few autopsies in the lab while I was studying, but nothing prepared me for what I experienced today."

Delray nodded again. "How do you feel now?"

The Final Proposition

Bridgette thought for a moment and said, "I'm not sure. Mostly, I'm thinking about the killer and how we narrow down the suspect list. And the family, of course."

Delray removed his glasses and leaned back in his chair.

"I've had people in your position who have requested transfers out of Homicide after seeing far less than what you saw today. I make it a point to check in with all new starters after their first crime scene. I can't afford to have people on my team that don't want to be here, Bridgette."

Delray let the sentence hang and watched for Bridgette's response. Bridgette understood Delray was going to rely more on her body language than what she actually said to know whether she was cut out for Homicide or not.

"I'm good, Chief. As I said to Detective Hoffman, this is what I signed up for. I might have to shower a couple of times tonight to feel clean again, but I don't plan on letting it get me down."

Delray nodded but didn't say anything right away. He studied Bridgette for a moment and said, "And how are you getting on with Detective Hoffman?"

Bridgette decided there was no point going into too many details and simply said, "He's not the easiest guy to work with, but I'm managing."

"Like I said before, Bridgette, he's never going to win any prizes for his social skills, but I think you will learn a lot from him before he retires."

Bridgette nodded.

Delray asked, "Is he still eating those pastrami and onion sandwiches?"

Bridgette tried not to roll her eyes as she said, "Mostly in the car."

Delray smiled and said, "He's been eating those things for thirty years. We were briefly partners back in the day, and we fought about his sandwiches more than anything else."

Delray turned serious again. "So, Bridgette, the door is always open. Come and talk to me anytime you feel the need. I think you have the makings of a very good detective, and I want to make sure you get every opportunity to develop. If there's anything else I can do, you let me know—okay?"

Bridgette nodded. She was about to rise from her chair to leave but decided Delray's offer was too good to pass up. She hesitated a moment and said, "Chief, there is one thing I'd like to talk to you about."

"Okay."

"My father."

Delray's face turned serious. "I don't know a lot about him, Bridgette, but what do you want to know?"

Bridgette wasn't sure where to start and now wasn't even sure she had made the right decision bringing this up when she had only been a probationary detective for two weeks.

"I know my father used to work here once. I just wondered if you ever worked with him?"

Bridgette watched as Delray got up from his chair and walked across to his window. As he stared out at the parking lot below, she knew she'd raised a subject he wasn't comfortable with.

Finally, he turned back and said, "We worked on the same team together—for a short period, before his transfer. By all reports, he was a very good detective."

Bridgette nodded. In a voice barely above a whisper, she asked, "Do you think he murdered my mother?"

Delray's complexion darkened.

Bridgette realized she had overstepped the mark and quickly added, "Sorry, Chief, that was out of line."

To her surprise, Delray shook his head and said, "No, actually it's not," before returning to his desk.

Bridgette watched as Delray sat down and then began typing on his keyboard. Without looking at her, he said, "All our old case files are in our database now—including your mother's murder case. I'm giving you read access to it. In your spare time, you can read the file for yourself and make up your own mind."

Delray made several more swift keystrokes and then pushed back from the screen again. He held Bridgette's gaze for a moment.

"It doesn't matter what I think, Bridgette. This is one you have to work out for yourself. Read the file on your own time, and when you're done, I'm happy to talk if you want to. I—"

Delray was interrupted by his telephone. He held a finger up to Bridgette to signal her to hang on a moment as he looked at the caller ID before answering the call. "I'm just finishing up a meeting, Danny, can you hang on a minute?"

Delray covered the mouthpiece, "I gotta take this, Bridgette. Come back to me when you've read the report. There are a few things you'll need to know that aren't in there."

Grab your copy...

vinci-books.com/cold-comfort

About the Author

Trevor Douglas is a multi-award winning author and the recipient of the Gold Medal for best Crime Fiction novel, and the Gold Medal for the best overall novel in the 2024 Global Book Awards.

Trevor is married with two adult sons and when he is not writing, enjoys bushwalking, watching AFL and discovering the best coffee shops in Brisbane with his wife.

After a long and successful career as an IT consultant, Trevor now writes full time and is currently working on his tenth book, *The Catalin Crossing*.

www.ingramcontent.com/pod-product-compliance
Ingram Content Group UK Ltd.
Pitfield, Milton Keynes, MK11 3LW, UK
UKHW040111130426
469799UK00005B/233